SUSAN A. JENNINGS

Heart of Sophie's War

Sophie's War - Book Two

SaRaKa InPrint

I dedicate this book, with humility and gratitude to those who fought in The Great War. And, all the men and women, military and civilian who have, throughtout history, protected us. And today, frontline workers of a different kind, who tirelessly serve and keep us safe during a global pandemic

"Never think that war, no matter how necessary, nor how justified, is not a crime."

ERNEST HEMMINGWAY - 1946

Contents

Preface

Sophie's story begins in the early 1900s in Italy, a young girl growing up on her family's silk farm. Sophie's father moves his family to Derby, England to manage the silk mill, leaving his brother to look after the silk farm in Italy.

After her mother's death, Sophie, an only child, becomes close to her father. Alberto, raises his daughter to think for herself and grooms her to run the business; an unusual situation for the Edwardian era.

However, tragedy befalls the family and Sophie is forced to take a maid's position at the prestigious Sackville Hotel in Bexhill-on-Sea, Sussex England.

Seeking more purpose in her life she leaves the hotel to train as a nurse. When, The Great War ravages London, Sophie vows to serve her country as a war nurse in war-torn Europe.

1

Western Front 1917

"At last, I am *exactly* where I am meant to be," Sophie whispered, curtailing the urge to shout and fling her arms in the air. She let out a long, satisfied sigh, ignoring her internal niggling doubts. She smiled at the soldier who reached to steady her as she jumped out of the army lorry. Standing still, she took in the vastness of the camp, rows and rows of tents and wooden structures. She had not expected it to be so big or so busy. Nurses in white aprons strode purposefully—she grinned to herself, *not running, nurses never run.* They passed along the miles of duckboard that connected wooden huts and canvas tents like a massive grid. The larger wooden and canvas buildings were marked with the distinctive and enormous red crosses.

Bandaged men gathered in groups on the patchy grass in the centre of the camp, cigarettes pressed to their lips, wisps of smoke twisting away to nothing. Animated conversations occasionally bursting into laughter. At first, the sound reached Sophie's ears as lighthearted fun and then she heard it, the haunting edge to the jovial bantering.

Many of the men were supported on crutches or sitting in bathchairs; a leg missing, a face and head bound in white, an empty sleeve hanging loose. Some were broken, staring vacantly into an abyss. That kind of stare Sophie recognized, but it was worse than the men at Bartley Hospital. Her initial feelings of elation were tempered by sorrow. She smiled to acknowledge the whistles and cheers of welcome at the sight of new nurses, a sanguine sign that seemed almost, but not quite, out of place.

Startled by a sharp retort, Sophie's attention was drawn to a tall, gaunt, middle-aged senior sister studying a clipboard. Her sour, ferocious expression reminded Sophie of a dragon about to breathe fire. Her steely grey eyes looked up. "Nurse Romano?" Sophie gave a nod. "Perhaps you would like to share your remark?"

She felt her cheeks flush. She had intended her comment to be inaudible. "I was commenting on how delighted I am to be here, Sister."

The woman scoffed with a sarcastic tut. "We'll see about that." Sophie withered into her woollen coat, too heavy for the early autumn, as it caused her to perspire as she attempted to avoid Sister's venomous glare. "Does anyone else feel the need to speak?" Her eyes swept up and down each nurse, silencing any further talk.

Sophie felt Trixie's trembling hand slip into hers and Emily quietly shuffled closer. Not daring to turn her head, Sophie felt the bond between the three of them, already a deep friendship, solidify into something much more.

"My name is Sister Drew. I'm in charge of the wards and Sister Potter is in charge of all nursing staff." She pointed to a pleasant younger woman, as unkempt as Sister was

2

immaculate. The mud splatter on the hem of her too long uniform emphasized her short, round stature. An angelic gentleness radiated from her smile, spreading throughout her chubby frame. Sophie mused at the two women. Sister Potter, a cuddly motherly type perhaps from a religious order, contrasted with the austere, majorly persona of Sister Drew. *Hardened by war*, Sophie thought, observing the medals on her uniform. *This was not her first experience of the battlefield.*

Suddenly, a giggle almost slipped out as she likened the two to the American cartoon Mutt and Jeff. Too late she realized Sister had seen her mouth curl, suppressing the giggle.

"Nurse Romano, I fail to see anything amusing." She shook her head with frustration, a tut preceding her comment. "You have barely set foot in camp and are already insubordinate."

"I'm sorry Sister Drew, I am tired and nervous." She paused, the explanation not enough. "And very happy to be here." She hoped the happy part explained the giggle. Sophie thought *it is true, I am happy to be here. But what is wrong with me? I'm behaving like a giggly probationer.*

"I do concede you have had a long journey." She hesitated, reading from the clipboard. "Honours and top of your class, I see, with a high recommendation from the Bartley. I hope you can maintain those high standards here. I will be keeping an eye you, Nurse Romano."

Sophie nodded, attempting to appear contrite, as she acknowledged Sister's comment. It seemed more like a challenge than a compliment.

"Nurse King?"

Trixie raised her hand. "Here, Sister."

"Sir Walter King is your father, I see." There was a tone of recognition as though she knew Sir Walter or was she

3

simply impressed by the title. "I hope your sensitivities don't hamper your nursing abilities. You look somewhat delicate. The comments from the Bartley are surprisingly good."

Trixie's fair complexion flushed with anger, contrasting her pale blond hair. Her jaw tightened as she prepared to respond to Sister's perceived accusation of weakness. Sister's piercing gaze silenced her.

"Nurse Finnegan?" Emily nodded. "I'm not sure what use you'll be. There isn't much need for a children's nurse on the battlefield." She hesitated, her face softening. "Although many of these boys are barely out of short trousers."

"Where is Nurse West?" Sophie almost giggled again as Sister peered expectantly into the empty lorry, as though Hillary, Sophie's closest friend, might magically appear from the flapping canvas.

"Nurse West didn't come with us," Sophie said. "She had an opportunity to go to medical school. Matron Hartford at Bartley Hospital was aware of her decision." Sophie wrinkled her brow, surprised that Hillary's name was still on the list.

"A woman in medical school, tut, what next? Let me be clear! I don't expect any grandiose ideas from nurses. Just do your job! At least you are preferable to volunteer aide detachments. Most of them belong in drawing rooms, not casualty clearing stations. I'm assuming they will send a replacement. A qualified, experienced nurse would be nice." No one answered, assuming it was a rhetorical comment. Sophie bit her tongue, taking offence at Sister's implication that they were not qualified. Emily had five years of experience, Trixie and Sophie had completed two years training and were using the field hospital experience as their practical year. She wondered if there would even be a replacement for Hillary.

As far as she knew, it would be no one from Bartley.

"Sister Potter will take you to your quarters. Change into your uniform and report to Matron's office in thirty minutes."

The three nurses, white faced with dark rings under their eyes from lack of sleep, stared at three trunks, wondering if they had the strength to lift them, let alone carry them to wherever they were billeted.

"I'll bring 'um for ya," a man said, as he appeared from the side of the lorry.

Sophie swung round to see a young orderly, not much taller than Sister and about as round. Sister smiled and nodded 'thank you' to him.

"Leave your trunks," Sister said, her soft pleasant voice a change from the dragon's growl. Smiling she added, "Meet Corporal Green, the best orderly in camp, always obliging and helpful. He will deliver your trunks to your quarters. Now, follow me."

The women walked at a brisk pace, their boots clomping on the wooden duckboard. Sister Potter's skirts billowed and Sophie wondered how she never tripped over the hem. They passed rows of hospital wards and Sophie tried to read the signs: Officer's Ward, Resuscitation, Evacuation, Place of Worship, Rest Centre and others with no sign. Eventually they turned to the right, reaching an enclosure of bell tents. Sister stopped abruptly, almost knocking Trixie over. She announced, "Nurse's Compound. All these tents are occupied by nursing staff. This is your home away from home."

She pulled back the canvas as though she was unveiling a prized monument. "A little sparse but with your own little trinkets it will soon be your sanctuary."

Trixie peered inside as she regained her balance and raised

an eyebrow towards Sophie and Emily. Sophie pulled the other side of the canvas open and nodded to Sister. "Thank you, we'll do our best."

"I have some things to attend to. I will be back in half an hour to escort you to Matron's office." Sister leaned forward and whispered, "Make sure your uniforms are perfect, your hair is tied back neatly and your caps are on straight. Neat as a new pin is the way Matron likes things." She gave a mischievous giggle. "Matron's a bit obsessive about neatness, everything in its place. Don't be fooled, she's hard on newcomers but she has a heart of gold. She is strict but pleasant and understanding, quite different to Sister Drew." Before they could say goodbye, Sister Potter, with skirts flapping, disappeared.

"Home away from home, ladies. I'm not sure what trinkets we'd need to make this into a sanctuary," Trixie said, smiling and glancing at the four cots lined up in the tent. Four rickety chairs and a wooden stand with a washbasin on top completed the furnishings. "Does this mean there are no water closets?" Trixie glanced under the bed and, as she feared, found chamber pots. "Oh no!"

"Knock, knock." Corporal Green appeared through the canvas. "Oh no! Don't sound good. Can I 'elp ya?"

Trixie blushed. "I wondered where the…hum…facilities were?"

"The ablution station for the nurses is just round the corner and a few minutes' walk past it are the latrines. Sister will show you." Trixie had found it difficult to get used to communal living at River House, the nurse's residence in London but this was worse. Seeing the disgust on Trixie's face, Sophie shot her a sympathetic glance.

"Where do 'ya want it?" Corporal Green puffed. "Cor' blimey this ain't half heavy."

"Over there," Trixie said, pointing to the nearest bed. "Anyone have a bed preference?" Sophie and Emily shook their heads.

Sophie stepped outside to help the orderly and gave a shiver as she saw the bloodstained wood on the wheelbarrow. Corporal Green saw her face and smiled as he hauled both trunks from the wagon, neither of them as big or heavy as Trixie's. He held one in each hand, grunting as he put them inside the tent.

Looking directly at Sophie he said, "It looks bad, but the carts are scrubbed down. We use these wagons to haul the dirty bandages and … other stuff." Sophie tried a weak smile, not daring to guess what 'the other stuff' might be. The significance of the bloodstained wagon gave her chills, reminding her of why she was here.

As though he had read her thoughts he said, "It's tough at first, but it gets easier." He paused. "Most of t' time." He pushed back the canvas, his face jovial again. "If you ladies want anything, just ask for Teddy. Nobody except the bosses calls me Corporal. A bit of advice, ladies, watch Sister Drew. She's a tough old bird and takes pleasure in making everyone's life miserable." He winked. "There's an 'eart inside somewhere, but no one has found it yet. Matron's all right and everyone likes Sister Potter." He let the canvas fall behind him as he left.

"Heart? I doubt that," Trixie said. "How does she know my father? She's even more terrifying than Papa! I'll show her just how delicate I am **not**!" Trixie pouted.

"I don't think pouting will work here," Emily teased, her

Irish brogue appearing more pronounced. "I do agree with you. Just because I nurse children doesn't mean I'm soft. If anything, it makes me stronger. She sure has it in for you, Sophie, just because you said something. What made you laugh?"

"It struck me as funny, tall straight Sister Drew and short rounded Sister Potter. I thought of the American Mutt and Jeff cartoon." Sophie started to giggle, feeling all the pent-up tension release. Emily and Trixie joined in, throwing themselves on the beds, laughing until tears streamed down their faces.

Hiccupping as she suppressed the laughter, Sophie said, "We h-had b-better get changed. I really don't want to cross Matron."

Sister Potter gave a smile of approval as they stood on a long verandah. It stretched the full length of the large wooden hut which housed Matron's office and several more official looking doors.

"Enter!" Matron called and Sister opened the door. Matron was not alone. A tall officer in his forties, with a head of thick, dark hair, nodded and brushed past the nurses, thanking Sister Potter as she held the door open. Sophie led the way and stood in front of Matron's desk with Trixie and Emily on either side of her. Matron was as immaculate as Sister had said. She had brown hair peppered liberally with grey, a soft face and warm brown eyes that regarded each nurse with a flicker of approval. At least she did not comment on any fault in the nurses' appearance.

Reading the files in front of her, Matron's cheeks plumped

with a smile, lighting up her face with recognition. "You all come from the Bartley, Esther Hartford's hospital. I've known Esther since we trained at St. Thomas and subsequently nursed in Africa." Matron cleared her throat. "Any nurses trained by Matron Hartford are welcome here."

St. Thomas' in London was founded by Florence Nightingale, and the best of the best for nurses' training. Sophie thought, *I'm going to like Matron. I'm relieved she is not another Sister Drew.*

Matron gave a nod towards the door. "Colonel Belingham is in command of this Casualty Clearing Station #28D. The colonel informed me there is to be a military push tonight and to expect casualties tomorrow or as early as tonight. I'm afraid you will have little time to settle. I have instructed Sister Potter to give you a quick orientation before dinner and then I suggest you rest. Nurse Finnegan," she glanced at the file. "I see you have operating room experience. You will be assigned to the pre-op ward in the surgical unit, under the command of Major Hughes. Nurse Romano, Matron notes you have experience with shell-shocked patients. That will be useful but, for now, you and Nurse King report to the medical ward, mostly up-patients. Please be warned, this is not London and you will find the facilities and equipment lacking at times. Sister Potter will explain what is expected when you hear the bugle call announcing a convoy from the front."

Sophie felt a pang of excitement at the mention of a push. But a push meant fighting and casualties and she immediately felt guilty. As if on cue, the ground trembled beneath her feet and her stomach twisted in knots as a long rumble like a thunderstorm approaching exploded. She held her breath, trying not to gasp as a flash of orange filled the small window and dragged her into an old memory. She looked at Matron, afraid she had given herself away.

"Yes, Nurse Romano, we are close enough to feel and hear the battlefield. I had hoped you would have more time to get orientated. I am depending on all of you to use your nursing skills and common sense. The surroundings maybe different but nursing is the same anywhere. Ladies, that will be all."

Sister Potter led the way to the mess and canteen, stopping for a welcome cup of tea. Sophie eagerly gulped the tea and almost spit it out. Emily and Trixie sipped it only because they were thirsty. Sister chuckled. "It's not usually this bad but the quartermaster is waiting for supplies. I recommend having some things, like tea, sent from home and to make your own."

This is the nurses' mess and canteen. Matron usually eats in the Officer's Mess. I prefer to join my nurses. The food is plain and not what you're used to, but there's plenty of it and you get used to the unique flavours. We get three meals a day and as much tea or coffee as you like. Eat up. You need your strength."

The nurses followed Sister's billowing skirts for a quick tour of the camp, finishing back at the canteen for dinner. Appetizing or not, they ate heartily. Sister talked incessantly through the meal but the nurses had ceased to absorb any more information until she mentioned ambulances and casualties.

"When a convoy of casualties arrives, you will hear the bugle. You are expected to assemble outside the Reception Room. I will meet you over there." She pointed to the road at the end of the camp, where the lorry had dropped them off. "Stay with me. The stretcher bearers take the injured into reception but you may be required to assist the walking wounded. I will show you how to check the medical cards and where to send the patients. It's not unlike the process in a civilian casualty department. You probably experienced it during the London bombings; just multiply it by hundreds. I'm afraid it is daunting but let your nursing instinct take over. I will bid you good night. With any luck, we'll get some sleep." Sister waved, hurrying along the duckboard and leaving the group somewhat bewildered and not sure what to expect.

"I thought the Irish talked too much," Emily said. "Did you get all of that?"

"No, I'm too tired." Trixie yawned. "I need sleep."

It was past dusk as the three walked towards their tent. Another rumble quivered under their feet. Sophie looked in the direction of the noise and saw the sun setting. Except it wasn't the sun. It was the orange hue of fire on the battlefield. She stiffened, hesitating, as her heart pounded in her chest.

Emily's brow creased with concern. "Sophie? Is something wrong?"

"Oh, no. It's just the sound of battle. I didn't expect to hear the guns and explosions so close. It's unsettling." Sophie couldn't explain that it wasn't the fear of being close to the front but of triggering her own terrifying memories of fire and explosions. She clung to the hope that her sessions with Dr Cuthbert had eradicated the nightmares but she hadn't expected her conscious reaction to real explosions. Could memories of so long ago threaten her nursing ambitions?

2

Mixed Emotions

Sophie listened to the rhythmic breathing from her companions, willing herself to join them in sleep. Although exhausted by the day's events, her eyes would not stay closed. The creaking cot, evidence of her restlessness, was likely to disturb Emily and Trixie, prompting her to swing her feet to the floor. Pulling on her boots, she grabbed her coat and slipped through the canvas opening. The evening air felt cool and a slight breeze brushed her cheeks. It felt good as she took a deep breath and looked around, surprised at how easily her eyes became accustomed to the pitch darkness. Soft lanterns, barely visible, glimmered from the lines of enormous canvas marques. She gave a start as she realized she was not alone, spotting the glow of a cigarette under a canopy. Someone placed a lantern on the ground, spreading an eerie shadow of a figure who appeared to be facing her. Her heart quickened as the figure moved in her direction, the light distorting the human frame. Rooted to the spot, she was not sure whether to leap back into the tent or wait to greet the figure.

"Can't sleep?" the figure asked.

"Something like that," Sophie whispered. "You too?"

"Na' I'm on duty tonight. I made some tea. Want a cuppa?" Sophie recognized Teddy's voice and, thinking of the disgusting tea from the canteen, she almost declined.

"This way." She obediently walked behind him to the shelter that was nothing more than a piece of canvas suspended on poles with a table in the middle and several upturned crates for seats. Teddy placed the lantern in the middle and poured liquid from a billycan into two tin mugs.

"What is this? A gathering place?" Sophie asked.

"The up-patients use it during the day to have a smoke, especially if it's raining."

"Up-patients?"

"Ah, patients who are mobile," he said, handing her a steaming mug.

"Thank you," she said, wrapping her hands around the hot mug. Taking a sip, she felt the warm liquid in her throat, realizing it tasted like tea. "This is lovely."

"You sound surprised."

Sophie laughed. "I had some tea in the canteen and it was awful."

"Ha ha, I know wha' you mean, cat-pi…um… or dishwater." Teddy reddened, clearing his throat. "Ha, sorry!" Sophie smiled. He had such a kind face and his recovery from using a 'bad' word gave him the look of a naughty school boy.

"I've heard it all and cat p… describes it well!"

"It ain't always that bad. If the quartermaster is waiting for supplies, cook keeps adding hot water to the brew, so by afternoon, there's not much tea left. Mi' mam sends me tea. I got this yesterday. Glad to share it. There's usually someone

13

prowling around to join me."

She smiled at him. "That's why you have two cups."

"Yep, I like company. It is very quiet tonight." Teddy looked off into the distance. "See the orange sky? The boys are fighting but som'ut don't feel right tonight." He shrugged. "Enjoy your tea. I'll leave the lantern so you can see your way to your quarters. I have to get back to the wards."

Sophie sipped her tea while staring at the orange horizon behind the silhouetted trees, making everything darker and quieter. Now she could hear muffled gunfire. In a different world it could have been Guy Fawkes Night, the warm glow of a bonfire and pretty explosions of fireworks. There was nothing warm or pretty about what was going on only a few miles from where she sat in comparative safety.

She didn't feel safe. Her heart pounded in her chest as she desperately pushed aside old memories from another fiery horizon that had licked her life away, leaving her with a deep sense of guilt and abandonment. Panic gripped tight. She had not felt this afraid for a long time. *How am I going to manage the war if the mere sight of an orange sky fills me with terror?* She tried to recall Dr Cuthbert's soothing voice that always seemed to calm her. *'Sophie, your father would be proud of you. The arsonists must bear the guilt, not you. You are a strong, courageous woman.'*

She imagined his big brown eyes staring into hers as he touched her arm with such tenderness that all her fears disappeared. How she wished she could talk to him now. It was a strange relationship, sometimes on the verge of romance, but quickly reverting to medical opinions. At first, Sophie's interest in the treatment for shell-shocked patients brought them together. Dr Cuthbert, a psychiatrist specializing in neurasthenia and shell-shocked soldiers, appreciated Sophie's interest. Battling her own demons, Sophie had confided in him, interpreting his interest as romantic, only to discover it was purely professional. But was it? She continued to get mixed messages from him. She sighed. "Really, Sophie, that is all behind you. You are here to nurse and serve."

She picked up the lantern and walked towards her tent yawning, her body ready to give in. She crawled into her cot and slept.

"Sophie wake up!" Emily shook her shoulders. "Top of the mornin' to ya' and a thousand welcomes!"

Sophie rolled over, her voice full of sleep. "What!? A thousand welcomes to where?"

"It's an expression Ma' uses to welcome something new and for us, all this is new."

"Is it morning? It's still dark. And did we miss the casualties?" Sophie asked, stretching and feeling remarkably well rested considering she'd had little sleep. "Where's Trixie?"

"She went to find some hot water. Typical. At least she didn't send the orderly. I washed in cold." Emily nodded towards the wash stand.

"Cold is fine for now. I guess a bath is out of the question." Sophie jumped out of bed and peered through the canvas. "The camp has woken up. It's already busy. Here's Trixie! It looks as though she found hot water." Sophie held the canvas open.

"That orderly Teddy gave me this and showed me where to get hot water. It's a bit of a walk but there's a big boiler near the cookhouse. That's what they call the kitchen here, as per Teddy. It's a massive lean-to filled with boilers, stoves and tables, and more cooks than I could count. Breakfast smelled good. I think there's bacon and fresh bread."

The girls washed and dressed. "Well, ladies, let's go meet our colleagues."

The mess tent was full of nurses. A cacophony of voices and laughter greeted them. The three stopped at the entrance, tense with nervous frowns and not sure what to do or where to sit.

"Where do we go?" Sophie whispered, filled with a sense of intruding. She was battling her fight or flight reflex and leaning towards the flight part when a familiar voice made her swing around.

"Good morning! Did you sleep well?" Sister Potter's cheerful voice was comforting. They nodded.

"We're a little lost, Sister," Sophie said. "Where do we sit, without intruding?"

"Nobody intrudes here. You sit wherever you please. Everyone is friendly. First you get your breakfast. Follow me." Sister's feet punched her too long skirt as she marched toward a row of tables filled with food.

Carrying plates of bacon, bread and butter and balancing a cup of tea in the other hand, they followed Sister to the end of a long table, occupied by nurses who quickly made room for the four and chorused, "Good morning Sister Potter!"

"Good morning, ladies! We have reinforcements from London. Nurse Finnegan will be joining the surgical team. Nurses King and Romano, general medical." Each nurse jumped up, reaching out to shake their hands with smiles and words of welcome, banishing any feelings of not belonging.

"Any news on the convoy, Sister?" A tall, broad shouldered nurse asked.

"Colonel Belingham is only just getting reports. Matron has been told to expect two hundred casualties. The first convoy is on its way. Eat up ladies it will be a long day."

"Already dilly-dallying, I see. Sister Potter, these nurses need to be on the wards now." Sister Drew's breath almost burnt the back of Sophie's neck. "We had better get the morning rounds done while we can. Nurse Romano, Nurse King, eat up. You're with me." She gave Sister Potter a wry grin, which was not returned and without a doubt, deliberately ignored. Instead, Sister Potter turned her attention to the nurses with a reassuring smile that travelled around the table. "Time to make our patients comfortable. Nurse Finnegan, I will escort you to the surgical tent."

Sister Drew's long legs marched along the duckboard, making Sophie and Trixie do a walking sprint. The tents, or marquees as Sister called them, were massive and all looked the same, except some had signs where others didn't. Sister stopped in front of several rows of unmarked tents.

"Start here. This is the medical ward. A variety of injuries but most are mobile." Sister pointed to the line of beds with still sleeping men. "When you're finished here, move down the line." Sister stared at them with fiery, defiant eyes.

Sophie looked around the ward for the duty desk and supplies, seeing Trixie do the same. They eyed each other, not sure what to do next.

Hands on hips, Sister Drew scowled. "Well, get on with it." The corners of her mouth twisted, reminding Sophie of the evil witch from Hansel and Gretel. That story had always scared her in the nursery. She also recognized Sister was taunting them.

"Sister, perhaps you are not aware that we have not had a full orientation. Matron indicated it would take place this morning."

"You're trained nurses, aren't you?" she flipped her head with a tut. "Useless!"

"Sister Drew, whatever is wrong?" They all turned to see Matron walking into the ward. "And what is useless? These girls are well trained from the Bartley." Matron's subtle movement implied disapproval.

"Um…nothing is wrong Matron, just making preparations." Sister's body tightened and her face flushed.

"Good! These girls are quite capable. However, a briefing on daily routines and incoming casualties is required. We don't have time for a full orientation." Matron turned to the three. "Sister Drew is quite correct. You are trained nurses, perhaps lacking in practical experience, but adequate. So do what you're trained to do, the morning routine is the same as in any hospital."

Sophie assessed Matron's words, not clear if they were a compliment or sarcasm or was it animosity between Sister and Matron? Sophie suspected the latter with a history long before the war. *Curious,* she thought, bringing her focus back to the ward. She was relieved to see Sister Potter breeze in, prepared to take over the briefing.

It lasted most of the morning. Trixie and Sophie quickly picked up the routine, noting the ward's layout. A stove stood in the middle with a small duty desk, which only appeared to be used at night, conveniently close to the stove. Young nurses, mostly volunteer aids, scrubbed all the surfaces and served breakfast while nurses took temperatures, changed dressings and straightened beds. The orderlies rolled up the canvas sides, opening the wards up to a bright morning and fresh air.

What they had not expected was the cheerfulness of both staff and patients. She heard bantering and teasing, a very different mood from the sterile, regimented atmosphere of the Bartley. The men asked questions wanting to know if they were getting a Blighty ticket to go home or if the nurses knew where their missing mates had gone, but that day she only had time to nod and say, "later, soldier, we're busy this morning."

There were no patients in the last group of tents, just rows of made beds. Sophie felt a shiver in her spine, her eyes scanning the beds and imagining the unknown.

Trixie put an arm on her shoulder. "It's kind of daunting, isn't it? I'm so glad we're together. Sister Drew is somewhat frightening!"

"Fire breathing Dragon Sister!" Sophie giggled. "I never thought I'd come across a sister worse than Sister Sin." She sighed. "So many beds."

"I wonder what happened to Sister Sin. She certainly deserved the nickname. A horrible woman, sent back to the convent and everything covered up," Trixie said, joining Sophie with a sigh.

"And her deviant ways go unpunished. At least Sister Drew is just strict and maybe vindictive. Sister Potter is so sweet, perhaps too sweet for this environment. I'd better get to the supply room. Where are you off to?"

"Sister Drew sent me to help the VADs, but there's no one there. All the beds are made in the expansion area. See you later."

Sophie opened the door of a wooden shed used as the supply room and met a young aide stacking clean linen. She jumped with surprise, a pile of pillow cases slipping out of her arms to the floor.

"Hello! Sorry, I didn't mean to startle you." Sophie stretched out her hand to the petite young woman. Her nurse's cap was perched awkwardly on shiny brown hair, twisted into perfect curls that were more suitable for tea in the drawing room. The young aide wasn't particularly beautiful but her aristocratic poise gave her an air of attractiveness, even confidence, which Sophie doubted she had.

"My name is Sophie, Nurse Romano, this is my first day."

"A pleasure to meet you." She stretched out her hand, dropping the remaining linen and glancing in the air as though looking for an explanation from above. "I'm so clumsy when I'm nervous. I only arrived last week." She took a deep breath, before adding, "It's awfully hard to keep up. It's all so terribly new to me. Oh sorry, where are my manners. Pippa Crawley. I mean aide Crawley. Call me Pippa."

"Short for Philippa?"

"Yes, how did you know?"

Sophie smiled at the obvious. "A lucky guess. It's a pleasure to meet you, Pippa." Sophie bent down to pick up the linen and helped her stack it on the shelves. It was only then that she noticed Pippa's hand trembling and her eyes moist with tears.

"Are you all right?"

At first she nodded, then she shook her head. "Not really. I'm not very good at this. I did well in training but out here it's all different. I watched a soldier die in agony yesterday." She hesitated, her eyes filling with tears, before covering her face. "It was so sad. It could have been my brother." Taking a deep breath and with great effort she continued. "Sister told me to stop snivelling. She was right."

"It is difficult at first, especially if you've never experienced anything like this before. Have you ever worked or volunteered in a hospital?" Sophie waited, knowing the answer.

"No, my father had his mind set that I should marry. When I refused, he ignored me."

"How did you get here? Did your father give his permission?"

"My brother signed up. I wanted to follow him and do something to help. My mother only cares about my debutante sister. I wasn't pretty enough." Her hand slipped to her neck and Sophie noticed a large brown birth mark just below the jawline. "I doubt my father noticed. He was not told I was leaving." There was no mistaking the malice in her tone. Perhaps realizing it, her voice softened. "Perry. He's my brother," she smiled a loving, gentle smile, "was very proud of me. I hope he's safe…" She frowned, her eyes almost pleading. "Now, I'm not sure I did the right thing. Sorry, I'm talking too much."

Sophie shook her head. "No, not at all. I've been nursing for two years and I never get used to losing patients. The rewards are worth it when patients recover though. You'll be fine. Give yourself…" Sophie stopped talking as she felt the ground move beneath her, followed by an enormous explosion that was too close to be from the battlefield. Glancing at Pippa's terrified face, she took her hand, thinking of Teddy's words 'som'ut don't feel right'. In a calm voice, which did not reflect the alarm she felt inside, she squeezed Pippa's hand. "It's all right. Hospitals are off limits but that does sound close."

21

3

Organized Chaos

Panic filled Sophie with fear as she viewed what at first looked like complete chaos. She soon realized that the nurses, doctors and orderlies were moving in a well-rehearsed pattern. She looked around for the cause of the explosion. Seeing no obvious signs of destruction, her eyes instinctively reached for the sky, listening for the drone of engines, but there was nothing.

Some of the up-patients who had gathered under the canvas where she'd had tea with Teddy, ran towards the tented wards, while others stood like statues. Quickly assessing the situation, she ran to the shelter, almost tripping over Teddy as he yelled, pointing to the stiffened men under the canvas. "Take those, I'll help the others!"

Sophie didn't need to be told what to do. Her training kicked in and she knew the explosion had triggered these men. She calmed herself and walked towards them, aware that Pippa was still at her side.

"I need your help, Pippa. Can you do this?"

Pippa stared at her, hesitating at first. "I'm not sure..."

Taking a deep breath, she shouted, "Yes I can! Tell me what to do."

"Good. These men are terrified. The explosion triggers memories of the horrors of the battlefield. We need to get them back to the ward. Follow my lead." Sophie smiled at her. "You'll be fine."

A plume of black smoke swirled in the air from behind a woodland about a mile away, close enough to smell the acrid burning of explosives, wood, earth, even flesh. It was a familiar odour from the London blitz but this was worse. *What has happened?* Frowning, she scanned the empty sky for aeroplanes. *Where did it come from?* She moved slowly towards a young private, his unblinking baby-blues eyes stared with terror.

First, she whispered, "You are safe with me here in the hospital." She touched his arm gently, indicating to Pippa to do the same with another soldier who was shaking and sobbing. "Come. Let's get you into bed." Hesitating, she glanced at Pippa for directions. "C Ward!" Pippa called.

The ward looked disorganized as patients wondered around, a cheerful nurse cajoling them into their beds. These patients, unnerved by the explosion, had more than physical injuries. Sophie had a knack of soothing patients, a technique she learned at the Bartley, but here it was different and extremely intense. After settling the blue-eyed private, she helped the nurses calm the bedridden men. Pippa's gentle nature had made it easy to soothe and guide the up-patients to sit on chairs or beds.

Completely unaware of the time and falling into what she did best, Sophie forgot to pick up the bandages from the supply room until she felt eyes piercing into her back. One of the nurses leaned into her and whispered, "I think Sister Drew needs you. I wish you could stay, you're really good with these patients. Thank you and good luck."

Sophie turned around, expecting Sister to bark at her but instead she beckoned to her. *At least she has the sense not to bark at me in here.* Sophie glanced back at the now nervous calm in the ward and waited to be reprimanded.

"I see you are well versed in the treatment of *these* patients. *Admirable.* However, you are in the wrong place. Rules, Nurse! You need to learn to obey rules. Do the job you were asked to do."

Sophie caught her sarcastic emphasis on the word *admirable* and her obvious lack of respect or understanding of *these patients.* She opened her mouth to defend and explain but decided against it.

By the time Sophie returned, Sister Potter was waving frantically for everyone to follow her as the bugle call blasted across the camp.

She shouted over the noise. "First, check their medical card. It should be attached to the upper pocket on the uniform. If they have a T on their forehead, it means there's a tourniquet so check arms and legs. M means they had a dose of morphine. Inspect the wound. The worst cases go for immediate assessment, walking wounded are seated while they wait."

"Are the injuries bad? Did they get hit or something?" Trixie asked.

Sister Potter shook her head. "We don't know what happened, but the convoy was attacked so be prepared for the worst."

It seemed that the whole hospital staff stood in a line,

waiting, chatting, as though they were queuing for a loaf of bread. An underpinning of apprehension grew as the earth vibrated and the hum of approaching engines grew louder. The convoy appeared in a cloud of dust. Sophie had never seen anything like it, first ambulances, then carts full of injured men. Stretcher bearers ran towards the vehicles. Everyone helped unload the ambulances and direct the patients to surgery or empty wards. Like a well-oiled machine, everybody knew what to do.

The ambulances drove off to fetch more injured from the dressing station and regimental aide post. Sophie looked up, the sight bringing her to tears. Injured men carrying bleeding, groaning soldiers piggy-back, four-hand human chairs carried hardly conscious men with unbandaged facial wounds. As if it couldn't get worse, men on makeshift crutches hobbled behind.

She heard Teddy from behind yelling for stretchers and two orderlies ran passed her. She followed them, grabbing a soldier as he fell onto her, bleeding she couldn't tell from where. It occurred to Sophie these men, already injured, had been hit by the explosion. Stretcher bearers eased him on to a stretcher and moved at an athletic pace towards the surgical tent. The line of walking wounded had thinned to stragglers. Sophie took the arm of a short round man, his face and hair caked in mud, his uniform ripped and flapping below his knee as he tried to stay upright, wincing with every step.

Sophie took his arm. "Here, lean on me."

"Thank you. What the bloody hell happened!?" Sophie listened, surprised at the female voice. "I was driving carefully, chatting with the lads to ease their pain when 'boom!' the ambulance in front of me flew in the air and the windshield hit my face. Then, my bus flipped on its side. Damn them all to hell." She started coughing and gasping for air. Sophie stopped, tightening her grip; the weight testing the strength in her arms.

"You need to stop talking and breathe. You can tell me later."

"The boys. It's imperative I return to get them out. Help me…" her words trailed off and Sophie feared she might pass out.

"The boys have been rescued. They are at the hospital. Stay with me. Can you walk a little further?" She didn't answer. Sophie pulled her closer, her hand felt wet and she realized the mud was mixed with blood from a gash on her head. How this woman was still walking, she had no idea.

Sophie yelled. "Orderly! Anyone? I need help!"

"Be there in a tick!" Sophie relaxed, hearing Teddy's voice. "Well, if it isn't my favourite driver. Quite an entrance, even for you, Jo! And how's Hazel? Did she fight back?" Teddy laughed as he took hold of her other arm. Sophie frowned, shocked at his greeting, which seemed inappropriate, except it brought a smile to the patient. *And who is Hazel?*

"Always the joker," Jo wheezed. "Good to see you, Teddy. I'm in need of a bit of help, not …" Her words slurring, she added, "Hazel, poor girl… fatal…" before trailing off. Teddy took most of her weight, leading the way towards Matron's office and on to an adjoining wooden hut. Matron held the door open. Confused, Sophie glanced around the hut, set up as a small ward of six unoccupied beds. *Of course, accommodation for women patients and few women were patients.*

Teddy gave Matron a sign only known to them, although Sophie would learn it was for urgent doctor's assessment

26

without alarming the patient. Sophie and Matron undressed and washed Jo as best they could. Sophie began cleaning the head wound. She stifled a gasp of horror seeing a large piece of glass wedged in Jo's skull. Her eyes met Matron's who nodded and quickly left the ward. Sophie dabbed antiseptic on the leg wound, assuming Matron had gone to inform the doctor. Jo's wounds, originally urgent, were now critical.

Jo stirred and groaned as she came round.

"Hello, Jo. How are you feeling?"

"My head hurts like hell."

"You have a nasty gash on your head." Jo lifted her arm towards her head but Sophie gently pulled it down. "No, better not to touch it. I've cleaned it for now. The doctor is on his way."

"My boys! I need to get up. I can't dally. Help me up."

"Shush." Sophie gently pushed Jo back onto the bed. "You aren't going anywhere. The boys are safe, the doctors are treating them now. It's important to stay still. You must rest."

"You're a bossy one and who are you?"

"Nurse Romano, Sophie. I arrived yesterday."

"Great welcome!" Jo tried to laugh but grimaced in pain. "Sophie. Nice name. Gosh, my head hurts. What the bloody hell happened, an air attack?"

"No one seems to know. Something exploded and, no, it wasn't from the air. Jo, you need to rest."

Matron returned with a tall, thin, cross looking man in a white coat thrown over a bloody apron. He grunted at Sophie, pushing past her and leaning over Jo.

"The leg wound is deep but superficial," he said, wafting his hand dismissively. He paled when his eyes reached Joe's head. "Good Lord!"

Jo's eyes darted from Sophie to the doctor. "That bad, Doc?"

"The fact that you can talk is positive. X-ray and prepare for surgery." He wrote something on her chart and marched out of the ward, slamming the door.

"Major Hughes, chief surgeon, somewhat lacking in..." Matron raised her eyebrow letting the sentence hang in the air. "He's a brilliant surgeon," she offered, as a form of explanation. Sophie heard a silenced *but* after the statement. *You have a strong opinion about the rude doctor.*

Matron bent down and patted Jo on the hand. "Mrs. Griffith, you have a head injury that requires surgery." Her smile was warm and comforting. "Nurse Romano will stay with you until the orderly comes to fetch you. I must return to other patients." Matron turned to Sophie, "Look after her until the orderly arrives." Sophie grinned, seeing Matron's tender side as she exited.

Jo's weak voice whispered, "A piece of glass is lodged in my head, right? Sophie, how bad is it?"

Sophie pulled up a chair, taking Jo's hand in hers. "Yes, I'm afraid so. I don't know how bad. You are awake and receptive. That is a very good sign. How did you guess?"

"I felt a thump on my head when the windshield shattered. I didn't think much about it until the doc said, 'Good Lord,' then I realized I could feel something in my head." Jo's eyes closed. "I'm very tired."

Remembering her training about head injuries, Sophie squeezed Jo's hand. "Try and stay awake, Jo. Tell me about yourself?"

"Nothing...to...tell..." Jo's face turned grey. Sophie felt her forehead, expecting it to be hot from fever but it was cold, too cold.

"Jo, wake up!" A terrible dread filled her as she felt her wrist. "Stay with me, Jo." Sophie felt a quiver in her voice and then breathed a sigh of relief as she felt a weak pulse.

"Looking for Mrs. Griffith," A young voice called and two orderlies entered the tent.

"Here!" Sophie called. "Be quick! Her pulse is very weak."

Sophie watched as Jo's still body was carried to the surgical unit.

She lost count of the number of patients she put to bed, wounds she'd dressed or lice-infected uniforms she'd discarded for disinfecting. Every bone and muscle ached as she stepped carefully along the duckboard. Aware it was dusk but unable to remember if she'd seen daylight, Sophie entered the mess, dying for a cup of tea. Trixie and Emily were deep in conversation, plates of mutton and mashed potatoes in front of them, mostly untouched.

"You both look how I feel. Exhausted. Where is everybody?" Sophie asked, noticing an awkward silence and a strange expression. "What's wrong? If I didn't know better, I'd think you were talking about me." She gave a nervous laugh.

Trixie laughed back. "No, of course not. It's nothing. Just been one heck of a day. Where did you get to? I didn't see you on the ward."

"I'm not sure. I started out with shell shock patients and assisted an injured ambulance driver with Matron's help. After that, I went from one place to another."

"Helped Matron!" Trixie echoed.

"She is so different with patients. I misjudged her. More than I can say for the surgeon, Major Hughes."

Emily brought three cups of tea to the table. "Here, you look as though you need it. Sophie, there's food over there. You should eat something. Did I hear you mention Major Hughes?"

"He came to see Jo, the injured ambulance driver. Not much bedside manner. Emily, did you work with him?"

"Only briefly with a head injury. I mostly did prep and assisted the other surgeon, Captain Evans. He's a nice man. More than I can say for high and mighty Major Hughes. He's a terrible man, shouting and cursing at everything and everyone. He has everyone on edge, including patients and several nurses close to tears. One of the nurses said no other surgeon is as successful or as fast. He might save lives with brilliant surgery but I'm not sure how many he kills with attitude." They all chuckled at this comment. "I have to admit, the surgery he performed on the ambulance driver was just short of a miracle. She had a big piece of glass stuck in her skull."

"That's Jo, the driver Matron and I treated." Sophie sipped her tea. "Oh, this is good. I'm hungry. What's the mutton like?"

"It's good but not very hot," Emily said as Sophie walked to the food table. "Sophie…we need to tell you something," She dithered, fiddling with a loose thread on her apron and took a sip of tea.

"What? Are you hiding something from me? Is it Jo? Did she make it through surgery?"

"No, nothing …I mean yes, she made it through surgery. That's why I was late, I had to settle her in recovery before I could leave for dinner." Trixie sighed. "Would you bring me one of those biscuits?"

Sophie frowned at Trixie, who glanced towards Emily. *What is it they aren't telling me?*

4

Sister Drew the Dragon

Two days had passed since the explosion, which was determined to be a rogue grenade. There was speculation as to whether it was caused by the Hun or one of their own, perhaps carried by a casualty and accidentally detonated by the jostling ambulance.

Colonel Belingham exuded an authoritative command when he expressed his sympathy for those lost and support for those recovering. His tone had a distinct edge of anger, as the investigation, although brief, indicated carelessness at the Regimental aide Post (RAP). By all accounts, a fair man with no tolerance for stupidity, he suspected one of his own unwittingly carried the grenade. Listening carefully to the tone of his voice, Sophie thought he would like nothing more than to punish the cause of the tragedy.

Matron reiterated the Major's sentiments, adding the importance of inspecting clothing for forgotten arms and the protocol to be followed if anything was discovered.

The news, although tragic, eased the tension, knowing that it had not been an enemy attack. Most of the camp, including

32

Sophie, felt edgy, wondering if the Germans had moved close to the hospital, normally, but not always, off limits to attacks.

Having finished her shift and waiting for Trixie to go for dinner, she wandered along to Line C to see the men she had settled after the explosion, an excuse to get close to the nursing she loved best. The nurse on duty recognized her.

"Hello. You're the nurse who assisted after the explosion. How can I help you?"

"I wondered how the men were doing," Sophie said. "It was my first day here. I wasn't sure I did the right thing. I recognized the symptoms from my work with shell shock patients in London."

"Quite the welcome, being your first day. You had the sense to use your loaf, and the help was welcome," the nurse said with a beaming smile as she extended her hand. "Kitty Wilkes, London, born and bred." Sophie would have guessed East End. Kitty's cockney accent was charming and explained her rhyming of *use your loaf* a cockney expression for *use your head.*

"Sophie Romano. I'm from Derby. Before going to London, I lived in Bexhill."

"That's a pretty name, sounds foreign."

"It is. My parents were Italian. I was born in Lucca, Italy."

"Gosh, it sounds posh."

"Not at all posh. It's a long story for another day." Sophie liked Kitty but she wasn't ready to pour out her life. "Is it permissible to see the patients?"

"I don't see why not. Those two beds, near the nurses' desk, it looks as though nurse is giving them their tea."

Sophie walked over to the beds and was surprised it was Pippa feeding a very young soldier as though he was a toddler.

"Hello, Pippa. I didn't realize you worked on this ward. How's he doing?"

"Nice to see you. I wasn't on this ward when we met but after watching you that day I asked to work here. Most voluntary aids are afraid. I find it rewarding."

"You're right. It is rewarding. How are they doing?"

"Not at all well. Private Connor has a Blighty ticket. There's nothing more they can do for him here. As you can see, he can't even feed himself. The other private seems to be doing all right." Pippa motioned to the next bed.

"You was the sister that helped me after the big bang," the soldier said, spooning a dish of rice pudding.

"Yes. I'm pleased to see you are much better."

His head bent forward, gripping the spoon until his knuckles turned white. "Better than poor Connor. His mam'll have a fit when she sees him but he gets to go home." He dropped the spoon, his hand, now in a tight fist, crushing the end of the blanket. "They's sending me back, as soon as my leg heals." He broke into quiet sobs and Sophie leaned forward, gently untwined the blanket from his fist and, taking his hand in hers, she waited for the sobs to subside.

"Sorry, nurse, you don't know what it's like out there. I can't go back…" He stared into nowhere.

It took a great effort not to weep with the poor boy. Sophie doubted he was eighteen, judging by the fluff on his chin. "It's early days yet. That wound needs about two weeks to heal. You are a brave soldier. It's important that you tell the doctor how you feel. He can help you." Sophie sounded far more convinced than she felt. If it had been at the Bartley, the boy had a chance but here, most military men didn't believe shell shock existed. It was something you *got over* if you were strong and made you nothing more than a coward if you were weak.

"Tell me about your family. Where do you call home?"

"Liverpool. Connor and me went to school together. Our pas work on the docks and they want us to do the same. But, that ain't for us. Adventure is what we're looking for and that's why we signed up."

"Not what you expected," Sophie said, with sympathy

He shook his head. "No and Mavis warned me. She's my girl. Her brother signed up at the beginning and 'e said it were bad. I thought he were just messing with 'er." He laughed. "Ya know how brothers are. I tease my little sister some'at rotten. I didn't believe Mavis."

"You are going to be all right. When things get bad, think of Mavis and your…" she stopped talking as Pippa nudged her arm and she saw Sister Drew marching towards her.

"Nurse Romano, I don't know what they taught you at Bartley but fraternizing with patients is strictly against the rules. I am reporting this to Matron. Now get back to your duties."

"I'm off duty, Sister. I have an interest in patients suffering …" Sophie's words were cut off.

"Are you questioning me?" Sister Drew puffed up with indignation, her dragon scales parting as she breathed fire. "Meet me at Matron's office now!" She turned and marched out of the ward.

"I have to go," Sophie said, tapping the soldiers hand.

Sophie began to run, slowing down as she remembered the rules. Nurses never run. She walked briskly to Matron's office, her stomach churning with fear to the point she thought she might be sick. Only three days in, was she about to be sent home? Reaching the wooden porch outside the office, she stopped and gulped several breaths to calm herself. *I did nothing wrong. Sister misinterpreted what she saw. Tell the truth and pray Matron understands.*

Raising her hand to knock, she heard Sister Drew's voice. "... holding his hand... it was disgusting, we can't have that kind of behaviour here." Sophie knocked, partly to drown out Sister's lies

"Enter!"

Sophie walked in, closing the door behind her and trying to think of what to say. "Matron," she said quietly and stood in front of her desk, willing her heart to stop thumping in her chest.

"Sister Drew tells me you were in C ward, off duty, interacting inappropriately with a patient." Matron's brow creased deeply. "Is that true?"

"No, Matron." She stared straight ahead. She didn't need to look at Sister Drew. She could feel her hot, angry breath on her neck.

"Lies!" Sister hissed. Matron raised her hand to stop Sister saying more.

"Please explain."

"On the day of the explosion, I helped Nurse Wilkes with some shell-shocked patients. After my shift today, I went to C ward to see how they were doing."

"And why would you do that?" Matron's hand came up again as she heard Sister take a breath to speak.

"During my training at the Bartley, I worked with Dr Cuthbert, a specialist in neurasthenia. I had an interest in shell-shocked soldiers and he taught me the complexities of the ailment and how to talk to patients."

"What has this to do with the patients on C Ward?" Matron asked.

"Tut! A crock of nonsense. Can't you see how she's twisting things?" Sister blurted out at Matron, who was not amused.

"Sister Drew," Matron said. "I think it better if you go to your quarters. Thank you for bringing this to my attention. I'll discuss it further with Nurse Romano and inform you of my decision."

Sophie stifled a grin as Sister swallowed her rage, an angry dragon ordered to her lair. Matron's stern demeanour did nothing to ease Sophie's fears. She was in trouble, justified or not.

Matron waited until the door had closed and stood up, walked to the front of her desk and pointed to two visitor chairs, sitting in one and indicating that Sophie should sit in the other.

"These are very serious accusations. Any form of inappropriate behaviour with a patient is grounds for immediate dismissal." Matron paused, looking Sophie in the eye.

"I understand. I would never do anything to jeopardize my nursing career. Matron, I did nothing wrong." Sophie's voice quivered as the threat of tears caught in her throat.

"I would like you to tell me exactly what happened and why you decided to go to C Ward." Her amiable tone, without even a touch of accusation, helped Sophie relax.

"I had finished my shift and was waiting for Trixie, um..., Nurse King and Nurse Finnegan who was held up in surgery. We go to the mess and usually eat together when we can. Our schedules don't always allow it. It occurred to me that I had a few minutes to spare and wanted to know how the boys were doing."

Matron interrupted, frowning. "You had had contact with these patients before?"

"As I mentioned earlier, I helped them after the explosion."

Matron nodded. "Yes, you did mention it."

"I decided to visit. If I'm honest, I miss nursing these troubled soldiers. When I arrived, Nurse Wilkes was at the nurses' station and a volunteer aide was feeding Private Connor. He's in a bad way. Nurse Wilkes said it was okay if I talked to the other private. I didn't get his name. He's scared but I think he'll be okay. He's just terrified of going back to the front. I was easing his anxiety, getting him to talk about home. Yes, I was holding his hand, but only to comfort him, not more or less than any nurse does when easing a patient's pain, whether it be physical or mental. I was talking to the patient when Sister came in."

They sat in silence. Sophie wasn't sure whether to say more but there was nothing more she could say. She eyed Matron, whose body language gave nothing away. Matron stood up abruptly and opened the door, giving some kind of instruction to Sister Potter who happened to be outside. She returned to her desk and pulled out a file.

"You trained at Bartley in London, under Esther Hartford? I believe I mentioned I have known Esther for a long time." She opened the file. "Now, Matron Hartford has nothing but praise for you and mentioned your aptitude for nursing not just shell shock patients but dealing with patients and relatives, not that we have relatives here. I doubt the few days here have changed you that much." A tap on the door interrupted. "Enter!"

Sophie was relieved to see Sister Potter's round, smiling face as she walked in with Kitty Wilkes on her heels who looked terrified. Sister turned to leave.

"Sister Potter, I would like you to stay. Nurse Wilkes, take a seat." Sister dutifully stood at Matron's side. "Nurse Wilkes, accusations have been made about Nurse Romano's behaviour while she was on C Ward. I believe you witnessed this."

Kitty's eyes popped wide open with surprise. "Accusations!"

Matron ignored Kitty's response and continued. "Please relate honestly what happened when Nurse Romano approached the patients."

Sophie paid attention, watching and listening to Kitty's every word. Kitty's recall was much the same as Sophie's with the added comment of how marvellous she was with the men and wished Nurse Romano could work on her ward all the time. Sophie glanced at Sister Potter, who gave her the warmest, most encouraging smile. If eyes could talk, Sister would be saying 'everything will be all right.'

"Thank you, Nurse Wilkes, you may return to your duties." Matron waited for the door to close behind her. "Nurse Romano, I am satisfied that this is a misunderstanding and nothing untoward happened. I will explain this to Sister Drew. The matter is closed. You may leave and join your colleagues for dinner."

"Oh Matron, thank you." Sophie's eyes filled with tears of relief that trickled down her cheeks before she could reach the door. Brushing off the wayward tears, she took a massive deep breath. She was thankful that Matron saw the truth but unnerved by Sister Drew's accusations and wondered *why*.

The fresh air cooled her hot cheeks as she walked to the mess tent, suddenly feeling hungry and smiling at the welcoming chatter from inside. She waved to Trixie and

Emily in their usual spot so busy talking they didn't see her at first. The conversation stopped when she reached the table and it seemed that all heads turned and stared.

Sophie looked around, her anxiety returned. "What on earth is wrong?"

"We bumped into Nurse Wilkes and she told us about Sister Drew." Trixie glanced around the room. "According to the nurses here, she gets pleasure out of making trouble and lies through her teeth. We were worried. What happened?"

Sophie related the story once again, including Matron's final words of exoneration and added, "I think Matron has Sister pegged. She was not too pleased. Be careful, ladies, Dragon Sister is evil." This last comment had all the heads in listening distance chuckling and nodding with agreement. The general chatter resumed with a heightened sense of camaraderie from everyone in the mess. And yet, Sophie still had a weird feeling that her friends were keeping something from her, especially Emily.

5

Getting to Know Emily

The noise of gunfire grew louder, the earth shuddered and the cot vibrated. Sophie tried to wake up but she couldn't move, pinned down by flames. Panic rose in her throat as she yelled with all her might, "Papa!"

Someone shook her violently. "Sophie, wake up! You're having a nightmare."

"Sorry." She felt her cot shake. "What is happening? Are we under attack?"

Emily was peering through the canvas opening. "No, the camp is quiet, except I can see the glow of a cigarette under the canvas shelter. I can hear guns in the distance. I'm scared. I had no idea we would be this close to the front."

Trixie rolled over. "Keep it down, some of us want to sleep."

"Sorry," Sophie whispered. Picking up the kerosene lantern, she motioned to Emily to grab her great coat and follow her. Hoping it was Teddy's cigarette and there might be tea, she crept out of the tent. She was right.

"Hello ladies. There's tea in the billycan. Help yourself." He stubbed his cigarette out. "I'm off duty and need to get some kip. By the sound of it, it'll be a busy day tomorrow. Leave the billycan here when you're done and I'll collect it later." Teddy yawned, raising a hand as he departed.

Grateful for the warm tea, they each sat on a crate, pulling their coats tight as the autumn night air was brisk and a drizzly rain made it feel cooler.

"Teddy is such a nice man. Most of the orderlies are kind and helpful but he's the best, a big cuddly teddy bear. His name suits him." Emily sipped her tea. "Not everyone treats him right. The surgeons are disrespectful, ordering him about; do this, do that, go here, go there, without even a thank you, especially Major Hughes. Teddy never complains. There are some exceptions though. Captain Evans, Sam, he's friendly when he has time. Major Hughes saves lives with his quick action and skilled surgeries, making him essential, but some respect would go a long way. Everyone puts up with it." Emily gave Sophie a tentative glance, as though deciding how to phrase her next comment.

"What is it?" Sophie said, concern in her tone. "You have a strange look about you."

"Sam tells me they are short two surgeons, both really good with patients, as well as with the surgeon's knife." Emily stopped abruptly, hesitating before adding, "It's nothing like London and, to be honest, much worse than I expected." She took a breath as though to speak, stared at Sophie, and then looked away.

"You are worried and upset." Sophie stared sympathetically. "It sounds awful. Would you have come if you had known you'd be assigned to surgery?"

"It is bad but even if I'd known, it wouldn't have stopped me. It's something else …"

42

There it is again, Sophie thought, *the hesitation, a secret. This is about me.*

Sophie pursed her lips with annoyance, making the words pop harshly. "What is it you and Trixie are not telling me? It's very hurtful to think my friends are talking behind my back. Emily, out with it!"

"We didn't want to upset you. When I found out, I told Trixie. We thought it better if you didn't know yet."

"Know what!" Sophie almost screamed. Suddenly aware it was late and they were outside, she whispered, "know what?"

"Remember I said there were two surgeons on leave? One of them is Carlos Wainwright. He's the one Sam says calms everyone and is so good with the patients, conscious or not."

"Oh, wow," Sophie whispered, leaning her elbows on her knees, her chin resting on her hands. "I wasn't expecting that. Carlos here? When is he due back?"

"I don't know. Are you going to be all right with this?" Emily asked, her tone full of concern.

"Oh yes, of course. Carlos and I had a summer fling some years ago. It's been over a long time. He's engaged to some debutante, probably married by now. Water under the bridge. He has an uncanny knack of appearing unexpectedly and he's rather good at disappearing, like he did from the Bartley, and that's not the first time." Sophie's thoughts took her back almost eight years to the villa and silk farm in Italy and then Derby. She suddenly felt hollow, abandoned and lonely. She didn't want those memories to surface, the death of her father, the yearning for a lost love. Aware that being so close to the battlefield had triggered her fears, she didn't need Carlos stirring anything else up. Perhaps it would have been better if the girls had not told her. It wouldn't have helped though.

She was glad of the warning.

"Sophie, what happened between you and Carlos?"

"It was a long time ago. Happy times." Sophie fixed her gaze on the dark night, a warm smile lifting her face. "My father and uncle owned a silk farm in Lucca, Italy and a silk mill in Derby, England, where Papa and I lived. My mother died shortly after we arrived in Derby. Papa thought I would take over the business." Sophie chuckled. "I was the son he never had. The fact that I was female made no difference to him. The summer I turned sixteen, Papa sent me to Lucca during my summer holidays. I stayed with my uncle and learned about silkworms and farming. Carlos worked for my father, an apprentice learning the trade at the mill and was sent to Lucca for the same reason. It was love at first sight. Our love blossomed all summer and he promised to marry me. That was the most wonderful summer, until we came back to England and Carlos disappeared and then everything went wrong."

"What happened?" Emily took a sip of the now cold tea.

"We lost everything. Papa died when the silk mill caught fire. I watched it burn to the ground with my father inside. I couldn't save him."

"Jesus Murphy. No wonder you have nightmares. And Carlos?"

"Carlos disappeared. I had no idea where I was going to live. I wrote a letter, telling him what had happened and that the solicitor would know where to find me. I delivered the letter to his mother, one of the worst social climbers I have ever known. She disapproved of me, especially since I was an orphan with no money or social standing. I didn't see or hear from Carlos until I bumped into him at the Bartley. He was betrothed. His mother had found him a debutante." Sophie sighed and coughed to clear her tight throat. "Emily, all this time and I still love him and the look in his eyes told me he loved me. I learned later that he never received the letter and his mother had lied to him about me. When he knew the truth, I thought he might break off the engagement and there was hope. But, true to form, he disappeared again. Probably easier to obey his mother. And here he is in my life again."

Emily raised an eyebrow. "The whole hospital thought you and Carlos were made for each other. To be honest, I thought you were playing hard to get. That's why we were afraid to tell you he was working here."

"Playing hard to get," Sophie repeated, forcing a laugh. *Is that what I was doing? It never occurred to me, but maybe it was.* "There were so many obstacles, it wasn't meant to be. I no longer have feelings for him."

"I'm not sure about that." Emily giggled, then frowned. "Our pasts are similar. I lost Ma and Da when I was sixteen, both died of consumption. It had taken two of my brothers the year before. It was up to me to look after my baby sister. Our only relative was an aunt in Dublin. She had her own brood, not wanting to take two more. Kathleen had just turned ten and, terrified they'd send her to an orphanage, I lied and told the authorities Aunt Bridie was going to fetch us. At first, I worked as a cleaner at the hospital to support us. I used to hover around the wards, desperately wanting to be a nurse. Matron took pity on me and let me in to the nursing class. That was ten years ago and I've never looked back. My sister is married with two little uns. We all have a past and some have secrets that influence us. Look at Trixie, from a posh home but you'd never know it."

"Trixie's home life isn't that great for all its poshness. Her father is brutal and disapproves of her nursing," Sophie said. *I wonder what Emily would say if she found out that Trixie had a bigger secret, one that could send her home.*

"At least you and I don't have to contend with parental interference. I wonder what Sister Drew's past would reveal. Something terrible must have happened to make her so beastly." Emily stifled a yawn.

"She's related to dragons and monsters," Sophie said, jokingly, grabbing the table as another explosion shook the ground. "I think Teddy is right. A busy day tomorrow."

Emily yawned again. "We should try and get some sleep."

The tent roof drummed with rain. The soft drizzle of the night before had turned into torrents of water. Sophie pulled her arm from under the covers and shivered as she checked the time and groaned, ten to five, almost time to get up. Rolling on her back, she stared at the strange shape of the tent roof, deformed in the darkness. She brushed droplets of water from her face and sat up, realizing the tent roof was sagging under the weight of water.

"Trixie, Emily, get up. Help me move my cot. The tent is leaking."

Trixie rubbed her eyes. "What's wrong? Is it morning already?"

Emily lit the lantern, revealing a massive bulge over Sophie's bed, which prompted Trixie to leap up and help move the cot from under the leaking roof.

"Are you girls all right?" Teddy called, a welcome greeting to the girls' ears.

Sophie ran to the entrance. "No, there's a big puddle of water on the tent roof."

Teddy put his head around the entrance. "Core blimey, that is big. Fear not, ladies, I'll show you what to do. Hand me that broom!"

The three watched, shivering in their night clothes, not even aware of the impropriety as Teddy carefully poked the broom against the tent roof until the water rushed onto the ground outside the tent.

"That's all you do but be careful, touch as little of the canvas as you can and poke it before it gets that big, okay? I'll get someone to tighten the guy lines."

In unison, through chattering teeth, the girls said, "Thank you."

"Here, you look frozen. Give me your jug and I'll go get you some hot water."

They eyed the rest of the tent roof, but the bulge had gone for now. Although if the rain kept up, it would be back.

Teddy called from outside. "Hot water for ya."

Sophie took the jug and they all enjoyed a hot sponge bath. Feeling warmer, they donned mackintoshes and waterproof hats, more suitable for fishing boats than a hospital. But then the rain was heavier than any ocean storm. The duckboards squished as they walked to the mess tent for breakfast.

A wet dog kind of odour filled their nostrils as they entered. The place steamed with warmth from cooking and wet clothing. Sister Potter stood at the entrance, looking like a round beacon in a yellow rain jacket and sou'wester.

"Good morning, ladies. Eat well. Colonel says a hundred or more are heading our way."

Sophie took a bowl of thick porridge and was delighted

to find both sugar and milk, although the milk tasted a bit sour and she wondered where it had come from. Reading her thoughts, Kitty Wilkes pushed against her. "Wondering where the milk came from?"

"Kitty, hello. Yes, how did you guess? It is rare to have fresh milk, although I'm not sure how fresh."

"It comes from a local farm, some of the meat too. The farmer takes pity on us but it's a small place so there's never enough. How are you managing in the rain?"

"Other than the tent leaking right over my bed and this huge pool of water on the roof, we're doing all right. Does this happen often?"

Kitty laughed as she gave Sophie an ominous glance. "Only when it rains cats and dogs and that's near every day. This be my second winter 'ere and this is nothing. Wait until we get frost and sleet, which is sometimes a blessing as it freezes the mud."

"How do you manage? I'm cold now."

"You get used to it. Get your family to send a blanket. Layer your clothes; wear two sets of drawers, two pairs of stockings under your uniform and keep your boots in bed at night so they don't freeze or ya feet will be cold all day."

Sophie raised an eyebrow at having her dirty boots in her bed and as far as getting an extra blanket, she had no family member to write to. Perhaps she could buy one, but from where? The nearest town was where they got off the train and that was miles away. She wondered if Kitty was pulling her leg. Could it really be that bad? But, already feeling her feet cold in her boots, she believed Kitty was serious.

6

Letters

The day passed without incident; in fact, the hospital had an eerie quietness about it. Perhaps it was the calm before the storm, knowing casualties were expected but so far no word from the Field Ambulance. Sophie finished dressing wounds, feeding patients and was pleased she would get a break, tired from her late night session with Emily. She vowed to be more diligent with sleep. Pulling her raincoat over her shoulders, she stepped onto the squishy duckboards, thankful they protected her boots from the mud.

A very wet yellow beacon was hurrying towards her. "Sister Potter, what is it?" Sophie said, concerned by her gasping breaths.

Patting her chest and shaking the wet from the hem of her uniform, she took a breath before speaking, "Matron wants to see you in her office."

"Me! Why!?" Panic edged her words. *What have I done wrong?*

Sister shook her head. "An assignment. She'll give you details. Now, off you go."

Matron's smile eased Sophie's concern as she entered the office. Being summoned to her office was always stressful.

"Nurse Romano, it has been brought to my attention that the hospital has several soldiers with minor injuries who are not recovering. The Colonel has discussed this problem with me at length. We have concluded these men are suffering from war nerves, maybe shell shock. Colonel Belingham is a medical man but not a psychiatrist. He sympathizes with neurasthenia patients but he does not have time to treat them. You are the only person here who has experience with mental injuries. The colonel requested a specialist doctor but the War Department is reluctant to grant his request. I'm sure you are aware it is often considered a weakness. I am assigning you to care for the men with shell shock symptoms. Nurse Wilkes, on C Ward, has most of the anxious patients."

Although pleased to be working with the war nerve patients, Sophie felt apprehensive. Matron seemed to think she was experienced, which she certainly was not. She had studied the condition and worked with psychiatrist, Dr Cuthbert, mostly for her own benefit in order to rid her of her demons. Had Matron Hartford said something? At one point, she had thought her breakdown at the Bartley might stop her coming but Matron and Dr Cuthbert had assured her she was fine. But the orange sky she witnessed on her first night had triggered a reaction, even nightmares, and that was worrying.

"Nurse Romano?" Matron asked curtly, with a concerned frown.

"My apologies. Of course, I will do whatever I can. It's just that," Sophie hesitated, "I don't think I'm as experienced as you have been led to believe."

Matron smiled. "I admire your modesty. You don't do

yourself justice. You, my dear, are the best we have at the moment. Colonel Belingham will help when he can. Unlike many senior officers, he is not averse to helping on the wards. The colonel is convinced that shell shock is a genuine affliction caused by the monstrosities of the battlefield and God knows they are horrific." Paleness seeped into her cheeks as she stared into the distance, remembering. Sophie felt a connection, realizing Matron had her own demons. "I also have some concerns about Mrs. Griffith, the ambulance driver."

"How is she?"

"She is recovering from the head wound but rather slower than expected. She asked after you, a friendly visit perhaps, when you have time."

"Of course."

"Colonel Belingham has informed me we have a hundred or more casualties on the way. When they arrive, report to reception and when you're finished, join Nurse Wilkes."

Sophie acknowledged Matron with a nod, opening the door to leave.

"One more thing, my dear. If you need to talk, don't hesitate to come to me."

"Thank you, Matron." She closed the door behind her. The unusual endearment of 'my dear' had not escaped Sophie. Had Matron at Bartley said something or was Matron revealing her kind compassionate side, usually covered with the strict, organized discipline needed to run an army hospital?

A noisy supply lorry drove past her with goods for the quartermaster's store, cookhouse supplies. A loud horn blasted, making her jump, as the postal lorry followed with long awaited letters.

Jovial chatter reached her ears before she arrived at the mess tent and there was quite a crowd heading in that direction. Thankfully the rain had eased and raincoats had been discarded. Trixie, already seated, waved frantically, flapping an envelope in the air as Sophie entered and took the seat next to her. "Look, a letter from Chris." Trixie pressed the unopened letter to her chest. "I want to feel him and know he's still alive and I am not a widow. I wonder what he's been doing?" She sighed dreamily.

"You need to open it and read the letter to find out." Sophie chuckled at her friend and leaning over, whispered. "Be careful or you'll give your secret away."

"I know. It slipped out. Here, this is for you." Trixie handed Sophie an envelope. "And Emily has hers from her sister. She went to fetch us tea."

Surprised, Sophie stared at the letter, her face brightening as she recognized the handwriting. "It's from Hillary. I never expected to get mail." Sophie tore open the envelope as Emily placed tea on the table.

River House Nurse's Residence

Dearest Sophie,

How I miss you and the others, but mostly you. It is so quiet at River House. A few new probationers, but most of the nurses are somewhere at war. Yes, I'm still living here. Matron said I could stay as long as I paid for my board. It is much cheaper and nicer than finding new digs and my father is happier that I'm with nurses,

*rather than medical students. It amuses me as he seems
to think they may lead me astray. Dear Papa.*

*I help out at the hospital when I don't have classes
and even take the occasional night shift. With so many
away at the front, the Bartley is short staffed. Father is
generous but the extra pay does help. Medical school is
expensive.*

*There are three female medical students, much to the
chagrin of both the lecturers and the male students. I
am grateful for the female company as the men seem to
think it is fun playing pranks on us or they treat us as
delicate females. The latter causes us great amusement
as we are all experienced nurses and there isn't much
we haven't seen before. It is the tough gentlemen who
go pale and green at the sight of blood or carving up
a cadaver. It is quite funny as we pull smelling salts
from our reticules to bring these tough men to their
embarrassed senses. There is one poor fellow who faints
so often they provide him with a chair as soon as we
enter the laboratory. I doubt he will last long.*

*How are things in Passchendaele? The news here at
home is mixed but the reports of loss are frightening. I
worry about your safety. How are Trixie and Emily? I
hope you are all keeping well.*

*I must close as I have studying to complete and it
is already eleven. The good thing about university is
lectures start at nine. At first it felt quite luxurious,
lying in bed and listening to the nurses' bustle about at
5 a.m. Cook refuses to save my breakfast past seven
and, if you remember, I like a good breakfast so I get up
at 6:30 and spend the remaining time studying.*

Do write when you can.
Your affectionate friend,
Hillary

She missed Hillary, her best friend and confidante, she missed their walks to the hospital. Hillary, a fully qualified and experienced nurse, always had good advice for Sophie. Their humble beginnings, Hillary the daughter of a clergyman, Sophie an orphan brought them together as did their mutual interest in medicine and their lack of interest in frivolous things cemented the friendship. Sophie admired Hillary for her courage and determination to become a doctor, an uphill battle against prejudice and a woman's ability to learn a profession and contribute to life beyond nursing children and managing households.

Sophie folded the letter and placed it back in the envelope, noticing the change in atmosphere. The chatter lessened and clinking cutlery had ceased as the meal finished. Only whispered, disappointed conversations could be heard from those who had not received letters. The others read every word of news from home, love from a sweetheart, even news from the rat-infested trenches. Sophie glanced at Trixie and Emily, smiles lifting their cheeks. Not wanting to interrupt, she stayed silent and then, as if an unseen task master considered time was up, a loud bugle sounded, announcing the approach of casualties.

The rain had ceased but the dampness made the air chilly as a watery sun slipped towards the horizon and darkness loomed. All available staff, doctors, nurses and stretcher bearers stood prepared and waiting. The earth rumbled, followed by grating gears, and the first ambulance appeared, churning mud from its labouring wheels. Suddenly the scene altered. As busy and purposeful as a colony of ants, no instructions were necessary as each person knew what to do.

Darkness enveloped the camp with bursts of light as the full moon periodically escaped the clouds, revealing broken men covered in mud and temporary dressings soaked in blood. Some screamed, some groaned, while others wept or joked awkwardly. The ambulances kept coming. Sophie thought it would never end. By the early morning hours, the final convoy pulled up and the cries of pain turned to banter and lighthearted joking from the less seriously injured. She waved the driver on as she supported the last two patients, both able to walk. She delivered them to a still crowded reception.

"What a night," Teddy said, lighting a cigarette and offering Sophie the package.

"No thanks." They sauntered over to a now empty bench outside the tent. "What's next?" Sophie asked.

"Surgery will go on all night, or," Teddy looked up at the lightening dawn sky, "all morning. We do our best to make the men comfortable and prepare for a busy day tomorrow or should I say today. You should get some rest. The night staff will handle things from here."

"Sister told us to go to bed. Emily and Trixie have gone. I won't sleep so I might as well help." She shifted her gaze, pointing down the mud track. "Look! Am I seeing ghosts or is that an ambulance?" Sophie let her eyes adjust and an ambulance, barely moving, emerged from a cloud of white smoke.

Teddy butted out his fag and the two ran to the ambulance.

The driver slumped over the steering wheel muttered, "I can't go any further. In the back…" her words lost as she passed out.

Sophie eased the driver from her seat. "Can you hear me? Are you hurt?"

"I don't think so. It's my head won't stop spinning."

Teddy checked the back of the ambulance, calling for stretcher bearers. "I'll see to this. You take her to Sergeant Harcourt." Teddy rushed off to help the stretcher bearers, leaving Sophie to figure out who Sergeant Harcourt was as she supported the ambulance driver. She was in a full faint so there was no point asking her.

Sophie wrapped her arm around the slight woman and took her weight, dragging her to Matron's office, not knowing what else to do. She knocked on the door, not sure if she was awake. Matron's quarters were at the back of her office. The door opened immediately and, still in uniform, Matron helped Sophie.

"I asked her if she was injured before she passed out. She said no. I think she's exhausted. Corporal Green said to find Sergeant Harcourt. I'm sorry but I don't know who she is."

"Bring her in. Sergeant Harcourt is in charge of the ambulance drivers but you did the right thing." Matron took the patient's other arm and they carried her to the women's tent.

Jo sat up, obviously not sleeping. "Gertrude, Gerty! What happened?"

"Hush, Mrs. Griffith. We'll talk later. We need to get the patient to bed and you need to sleep." Matron's voice was firm and gentle.

Matron took her vital signs. Convinced she was not in any

danger, she returned and reported the incident to Sergeant Harcourt.

Sophie fetched hot water and bathed Gertrude. Finding no evidence of injury, she placed a cold cloth on her forehead. As she expected, the cold brought her around.

"What happened? Where am I?" Gertrude's eyes darted around the ward and settled on Sophie.

"You where transporting casualties and passed out in your ambulance. Are you sure you are not hurt?"

Gertrude nodded. "Now I remember. I was on my way back to the advanced dressing station when the engine kept overheating. I knew I was late because I passed the fleet returning and I wasn't even there yet." She coughed, "Could I have some water?" Sophie poured a glass and waited for her drink. "Oh, that's better, thank you. The lads at the dressing station, were pleased to see me as they had three late arrivals, all in a bad way. I wasn't feeling well. My head kept spinning. An orderly gave me a cup of tea. After filling the rad, I headed back down the track. One of the men in the back was groaning and crying out with pain. I'm trying my best to miss the craters but it was pitch black and kind of spooky being on my own. I've always travelled in a convoy." Gertrude stopped again, turning white.

"Gertrude, when did you last eat?" Sophie asked, her fingers on her wrist taking her pulse.

"I don't know. My head…" Gertrude fainted again.

"Stay here. I'll be back." Sophie smiled at herself as Gertrude was obviously not going anywhere. She ran to the mess, thankful it wasn't closed but then realized it never closed. It was morning, so breakfast was being prepared which meant that the tea was fresh. She poured two cups of tea, laced one with sugar and picked up biscuits.

Relieved to see Gertrude's eyes open, Sophie sat on the bed, "Gertrude, can you sit up? I want you to drink this tea and have a biscuit." Sophie took her elbow and helped her sit upright. She took a sip of tea and dunked the hard biscuit in the hot liquid.

"How do you feel?" Sophie asked.

"Better. My head has stopped spinning. I'm not sure what's wrong with me but this happened earlier. Driving in the dark, I hit a mudhole and it took me forever to get the ambulance going again. I had a dizzy spell. I shook it off and continued but the damned rad overheated. When I opened the hood to cool the engine off, I got dizzy again. After two more stops, I got here but I don't remember how. Are the lads okay? I'm so sorry I jostled the ambulance so much."

"You are exhausted. I suspect you haven't eaten. A nice rest and you'll be as good as new. Teddy, our best orderly, is looking after the men. I'm sure they are grateful to be here. Now, finish your tea and get some sleep."

"Nurse?" Jo called. "I'm parched. Any chance of a cuppa?" Sophie spun around in surprise, forgetting there was another patient in the ward.

"I'm sorry. Here, have this one. It's just plain."

"Good. Straight up, same as I like my Scotch." Jo laughed and then winced, her hand going up to her head as she tried to sit up.

"Let me help you. Is your head hurting?" Sophie asked, pushing a pillow against her head before handing her the mug. "How's that?"

"Better, thank you. What happened to Gertrude? She's a good driver."

"Exhaustion, bringing in the last of the injured last night. We'll know more after the doctor checks her out but I think you'll have company for a few days. How are you?"

"Champion, if my bloody head would stop aching. I recognize you. You and Teddy brought me in and you sat with me. You realized I had a chuck of glass in my head and held my hand so I wouldn't touch it. I kept thinking, although I wasn't thinking straight at the time, this is weird, why is she holding my hand? I didn't know about the glass until after the surgeon took it out. Thank you."

"Just doing my job. Drink your tea. They'll be doing rounds soon. I'll come back later and talk if you'd like." Sophie stifled a yawn, remembering Matron's request, but she was too tired. She needed a cup of tea, breakfast and rest or she'd be taking up one of the beds, joining Gertrude and Jo.

7

Doing the Right Thing

I t had started raining again by the time Sophie left Gertrude and Jo. She tried to hurry but her feet, heavy with exhaustion, slowed her down. The smell of baking wafted in her nostrils, spurring her on. She picked up a bowl of porridge, two thick slices of grey bread and a mug of hot tea. The mess tent was unusually quiet and she was grateful to be alone at the table, assuming Trixie was still sleeping and hopefully Emily too although she doubted Emily had slept as surgery was still going on. She picked up the soft grey bread, savouring the flavour. Sliding her hand in her pocket for her handkerchief, her fingers caught Hillary's letter. She pulled it out to re-read it but tiredness made the letters fuzzy and she returned it to her pocket. Elbows on the table, she clasped her hands, resting her chin on her fists and closed her eyes.

She was startled by an angry voice. "Elbows on the table, sleeping!" She opened her eyes to see Sister Drew standing over her. *Where in the world had she come from?* Sophie thought her vision cloudy. The women looked like an aberration and, for a second, she wondered if it was a nightmare.

"Sister, sorry. I've been up all night and must have dozed off."

"You had better get to work. Matron tells me you are to work on C Ward. There is work to be done on other wards before you go to C." Sophie could not believe her ears. She had hoped to get an hour's rest. "Go on, get an early start."

Her boots had grown heavier during breakfast, making her feet plod on the duckboard, the rain having once again loosened the mud underneath. She didn't have time to get her mackintosh. Aware that she was getting soaked, she didn't care. The rain felt cool and she lifted her face, appreciating the refreshing cold droplets falling on her cheeks.

Reaching A Ward, she was astonished at how many beds were crammed under the canvas tent. Nurses squeezed between beds, dressing wounds and calming new patients. Sister Drew was right. They needed help. Sophie scanned the scene and steered a dressing trolley to the end of the ward, spotting Trixie holding a thermometer.

"Good morning," Sophie said. "Were you up all night?"

"Not quite. A few hours maybe. The noise woke me so I came to help." Trixie whispered, "You didn't come to bed last night. What happened?"

Sophie began cleaning an angry wound on the soldier's leg. She whispered, "After I left you, another ambulance arrived and the next thing I knew, it was morning. This is infected."

Trixie nodded, holding the thermometer. "He has a fever. I'll let the doctor know. I thought you were on C Ward. Did you get any rest at all?"

"No. Dragon Sister caught me resting my head in the mess and sent me to help finish up here. I'm all right. I had some breakfast and I feel better."

Trixie gave her a sideways glance. "That woman has no heart, she should have sent you to rest. Does matron know?"

"She knows I was up all night because she helped me with an exhausted ambulance driver. Nobody had much sleep. I thought it would never stop."

"It's the worst we've seen. I just spoke with Emily, getting a cup of tea and on her way back to the surgical tent. They're still doing surgeries. She's dead on her feet. I was lucky. I managed to slip away after the last ambulance. I was dying to read Chris' letter," Trixie said with a tone of apology adding, "At least I thought it was the last. I would have stayed if I'd known."

"There was nothing you could do. At least one of us got some sleep. How is Chris?"

"His squadron has been moved but he can't say where. He sounded cheerful, even excited, about the new orders. Who was your letter from?"

"Hillary. I'll tell you later." Sophie turned as the soldier groaned, his cheeks flushed and a frown creasing his forehead. She smiled at him as she fastened the dressing. "How are you feeling?"

"My leg hurts like the devil, nurse. I don't feel good." His forehead was beading with sweat and his closing eyes looked glassy.

Sophie gently stroked his shoulder. "The doctor will give you something to ease the pain. Easy now, you're going to be all right. Shush…" Her words unconvincing, the patient unconscious.

"Trixie, hand me that cloth and cold water." Sophie soaked the towel in cold water and began sponging the soldier, burning with fever. This was the infection that killed. "Fetch

Sist…" She halted, surprised to see Major Hughes, not Trixie, standing at her side, his eyes fixed on the soldier's chart. "Good morning, Major. I'm afraid the patient has developed a fever from the wound."

"The wound," the major repeated, not raising his eyes. His fingers fidgeted at his chin, the heavy stubble making a rasping sound. "Is it deep?"

"No, sir. It is a large wound but it is on the surface and no shrapnel. But there are signs of infection. I just finished changing the dressing. I could show you but I'd rather not disturb the patient."

Placing the chart at the end of the bed, the major took a breath. Sophie waited for the bark, the reprimand, but he just stared at the patient. The major's pale face was etched with deep despair and fear. He grasped the unconscious soldier's hand and placed the other on his cheek, whispering, "Fight, Son, fight for your life."

Sophie stepped back to give them some privacy, busying herself tidying the dressing trolley until the major stepped back from the bed.

"Morphine for the pain. It's on the chart. I'll do it. Hand me the syringe."

"Yes, Sir."

"Stay with him and notify me of any change." The stiff words belied the tear he brushed from his cheek, as he added, "He's my son. Save him." Losing his composure, the Major slipped out of the tent.

Sophie picked up the chart and, sure enough, the name was Captain Benjamin Hughes. The major has a heart, Sophie thought. Wringing out the cold cloth, she placed it on the captain's forehead. She began sponging and cooling his body, whispering to him, "You need to fight. Your father needs you. He was just here and he'll be back. You are at his hospital. How lucky is that?"

The captain stirred and his eyelids flickered. Sophie squeezed his hand. The morphine was easing the pain and she hoped he would come around. "How are you feeling?" she asked, not sure if she would get an answer.

"A little easier, Nurse. Was my father here or was I dreaming?"

"No dream. He was here."

She expected to see relief, knowing his father was close, but his face tightened with something like anger. He closed his eyes. "I am so tired."

Sophie frowned. *Had she imagined the expression?* More likely the fever, she thought, as he sank into restless sleep. She took his temperature, 104.8. Trying not to panic, she beckoned to Trixie. "I need help. We're losing him." Captain Hughes was shaking his head from side to side and his arms began flailing, trying to catch something in his hallucination. Sophie clasped one arm and soothed his torso with cold water. "Captain, Benjamin or do they call you Ben? You are having a dream, a hallucination caused by the fever. You are safe now. We'll take care of you." Sophie brushed the back of her hand across her forehead, exhaustion catching up to her. She shook it off. Having lost track of time, she had no idea how long she'd been there but the longer the fever lasted, the less likely a recovery. She stared intently for signs of improvement but there were none. Trixie stayed with her and they worked for what seemed like hours until eventually he stilled, muttering to the unseen horror of his dream. His temperature had dropped; still dangerous, but going in the right direction.

"Can you manage?" Trixie asked. "I need to get to other patients."

"Thank you, I'll be fine. Oh, Lord, look who's here."

"Bye!" Trixie waved, moving quickly to another patients.

"You again!" Exasperation squeezed Sister Drew's taught face. The light caught thick white facial hairs sticking out of her chin. 'Dragon Sister' suited her so well and Sophie found herself struggling not to laugh. "Nurse Romano, are you incapable of following direction? I told you to finish up, not dally with patients. You should be on C Ward now." Sister glanced down at Sophie's hand resting on Captain Hughes's arm. She instinctively pulled away and placed the cloth in the cold water, annoyed by her reaction and angered by Sister's implication.

"The patient has a high fever. He won't survive unless we get his temperature down. He is Major ..." Before she could finish the sentence, a hand was held in her face.

"Stop your nonsense. This is not the officers' ward. I'm instructing you to report to Nurse Wilkes, now!"

"With respect, Sister, I can't do that. I have to stay with this patient." Sophie could hear her heart thumping in her ears. She realized everyone on the ward, patients and staff, were holding their breath. Nobody ever contradicted Sister Drew, even if she was wrong which she was most of the time. Her reprimands were severe.

Here it comes Sophie thought *the dragon is breathing fire and I'm going to be sent to Matron.* Strictly speaking, she had not been told by her superiors to treat Captain Hughes. She had taken it upon herself, based on the Major's request, and defying an order from a superior was grounds for dismissal.

"Are you defying my orders?!"

Captain Hughes stirred and began punching the air, crying out at what could be considered either an appropriate or inappropriate moment. "Bastard!"

"Shush. It's a nightmare. You are safe here." Sophie's gentle words sounded almost angelic against Sister's violent outburst. She carefully took his arms, placing them at his side, before removing the cloth from the cold water and gently cooling his body. Sophie could feel Sister's hot, sour breath on her neck. She actually feared that the woman might hit her. Determined to stand her ground, she continued to care for the captain, afraid to speak for fear of losing her temper.

Suddenly the regular bustle of the ward continued with a low questioning chatter between patients and nurses. And then she heard someone say, "Good morning Matron!" Terrified, Sophie looked up to see Matron heading in her direction. Sister Drew jumped forward to block her path and began talking, glancing at Sophie as she spoke.

Her patient moaned and opened his eyes. The glassiness had gone. She felt his forehead, still hot, but she dared to hope the fever had broken. "How are you feeling?"

"Better, I think. A bit woozy."

"That'll be the morphine and it's normal. How is the pain?"

"Not too bad." He frowned, "Nurse, did I hear you say my father was here?

"Major Hughes was here. I'll fetch him for you. He'll be relieved you are feeling better."

"Could we wait on that? I'm not ready to see him yet."

"Of course," Sophie said hesitantly. "I will have to tell him soon."

"I understand. I need some time," he said, with a pleading

look in his eyes.

"I shall fetch the tea first and I might even find you a biscuit." Sophie smiled at him. "Welcome back, Captain." Sophie had momentarily forgotten that Matron was only a few feet from the patient's bed but when she looked up neither Matron nor Sister were anywhere to be seen.

She caught the attention of a young volunteer nurse. "Where did Matron go?"

"Matron was furious and marched Sister Drew out, ordering her to wait in her office. Then she left. I'm sorry, she didn't say where she was going. You are brave. I have so much admiration for you, standing up to Sister like that."

"Thank you. It might come back to haunt me but patients come first. It was rather intense." Sophie gave a wry smile. "Nurse, would you fetch Captain Hughes a cup of tea and see if you can find some plain biscuits, not too hard, fresh if possible."

"Captain Hughes?" the nurse repeated with emphasis on 'captain.' "Shouldn't he be in the Officers Ward? He's related to…?"

"Yes to both questions and I don't know why he's here. Tea, please?" The aide hurried off and Sophie tended to her patient. Although better, she knew he was not out of the woods yet. Infections hit hard and fast and could easily return.

"Captain, I'm going to take a look at your wound."

"I prefer it when you call me Ben."

"You heard me?" she whispered. "I'm not supposed to but sometimes unconscious patients respond to Christian names. And I made a guess it was Ben rather than Benjamin."

"I only remember you calling my name. Ouch!"

"Almost finished. Here comes your tea. Ah, it looks as

though you have a visitor." She winced. "I'm sorry, Matron must have told your father." Sophie secured the dressing and helped him sit up. "I'll leave you to it."

"Matron, Major," Sophie nodded respectfully and began to move away, hesitating and wondering if she was expected to report on the patient's progress or was she to be reprimanded. Knowing how Sister Drew lied, she wondered what accusations she had made to Matron or perhaps it was Sister Drew who was reprimanded? *Not a chance,* she thought, glancing towards Matron and hoping her expression might give her a warning.

It was the Major who spoke. "Nurse Romano, I am grateful for your attentiveness towards my son. I believe your diligent nursing and fast reaction saved his life. Thank you."

"Thank you, sir! Just doing my job. Your son is a fighter."

The major gave a shrug, not the response she expected. "How are you?" The major's words were clipped and cold. What had happened to the emotional man that stood beside his son's bed only a few hours ago? He added, "I'm in the middle of surgeries, we'll talk later."

"Nurse, come with me. We have work to do." Matron led Sophie out of the ward. "Well done, Nurse Romano. Your quick action of recognizing the infection saved that boy's life. The major will be forever grateful."

"Matron, did I do something wrong, break the rules? If so, it was unintentional."

"Absolutely not! You used your common sense. I wish all my nurses were as sensible."

"I'm sorry I defied Sister Drew but the patient could not be left. She was quite angry with me."

"Sister Drew was out of line." A statement that left Sophie

feeling that she had more to say. Perhaps she had under-estimated Matron, a shrewd woman who would no doubt be aware of Sister's deceitful ways. Matron frowned as she scanned Sophie's face. "You look very pale. How long have you been on duty?"

"Since …yesterday, I think, I don't know, Matron."

"I'm ordering you off duty. You need rest or you'll be a patient."

Matron hurried on ahead, leaving Sophie struggling to put one foot in front of the other. The thought of a hot drink and maybe something to eat spurred her on. As she passed the wooden huts that housed Matron's, the Colonel's and other offices, she heard a door slam, followed by raised voices. She slowed her pace, hesitating and straining her ears.

"This is the last time you lie to me, concocting stories. Picking on innocent nurses is one thing, endangering patients' lives is going too far."

"She was out of line. I ordered her to leave and she defied me."

"Leave a dying patient and the major's son?"

"What!? I didn't know. Why wasn't he in the officers' ward?"

"That is irrelevant. The officers' ward was full and our patients are nursed no matter their rank. These are young soldiers who need our care, not to listen to an old witch berate the nurses they depend on."

"That's not fair. He should have been in the officer's…"

"Stop right there. I've had enough. I'm sending you on extended personal leave. You can make up whatever story you like. I have applied for a replacement."

"I won't go. You can't do that."

"Oh yes I can or, if you prefer, I can dismiss you for

insubordination. You forget that, as Major, I outrank you."

Silence resumed. Stunned, Sophie made her feet move quickly, not wanting to be caught eavesdropping. She was not a minute too soon. Sister Potter came running up behind her as she reached the canteen.

"May I join you? I hear you are the hero of the hour."

"Sister Potter, of course. I'd enjoy some company," Sophie lied, as she really wanted to be alone to digest what she'd heard and maybe catch a few winks. But Sister Potter was such a ray of sunshine and she could do with some brightness.

8

Just Desserts

Sophie's stomach gave an audible rumble and was perhaps what had woken her. Stupefied with sleep, she lay on her back, trying to get her brain to work. Was it morning? Was she in her cot? It was dark but she could hear the camp coming to life and a voice yell, "Wakie-wakie, my favourite darlins's. 'Ot wowter's 'ere." She smiled at the odd accent. Buster, the new orderly, had taken it upon himself to deliver much appreciated hot water every morning. Often referred to as soldier-servants, orderlies were just that, servants expected to clean everything from floors to linen. It also surprised her that all officers were assigned a personal soldier-servant to fetch and carry, clean their quarters and uniforms. The hierarchy had surprised Sophie.

"Thank you!" Emily yelled to the 'wowter' call as she lit the lamp.

"Good morning!" Trixie gave an enormous yawn. "I'm tired. I think I could sleep around the clock, given the chance. What a terribly awful day yesterday."

Sophie nodded in agreement, swinging her legs to the

ground. "I can't believe I slept for eight hours."

"Same here. We finally finished surgeries sometime after five. I'll be glad when the other surgeons are back from leave. Sam, that's Captain Evans, the junior surgeon…"

Trixie interrupted. "Aah, Christian names already. Is he handsome?"

"It's not like that," Emily retorted. "He's not at all handsome, a bit on the chubby side, heavy looking, but a gentle man, easy going and good at reassuring the patients. He's a GP from Wales, pushed into surgery because of some early surgical experience."

"You seem to know a lot about him," Trixie said, giving her a wink.

"Would you stop the teasing?! He helped me prep some of the more agitated patients when he wasn't in surgery and we started talking, nothing more." Emily blushed slightly. "Everyone is less formal in the surgical hut. It isn't unusual to address people by their Christian name. Colonel doesn't mind but Matron doesn't approve."

"It is a bit strange. Major Hughes strikes me as a formal person. Surgeons are usually very precise," Sophie said, trying to ease Emily's embarrassment and guessing she was taken with the young surgeon.

"He is formal about everything. Sam says Major Hughes' skill in the operating theatre is unconventional at times and he is brilliant. There are soldiers walking today who would otherwise have lost a leg. But his high and mighty, God-like attitude doesn't help the patients recover. Sam says, Captain…" Emily hesitated. "The other surgeon is just as clever, with a kind and gentle manner towards both patients and staff."

Sophie tried to ignore yet another reference to the *other* surgeon, knowing Emily was being diplomatic and referring to Carlos. She didn't want to deal with her feelings for Carlos and knowing he was expected at the casualty clearing station added to her discomfort. She tried to brush it off. *Why should I care? He's engaged to a beautiful debutante and probably married by now. Maybe that was the reason for his leave.*

"I'm hungry. Did I have dinner last night?" Sophie asked, changing the subject in her head.

"I doubt it. You were already sleeping, when I came in. I hadn't eaten all day so I had dinner. I could eat some bacon."

"Two days in a row, unlikely. I think that pig is long gone." Sophie added wistfully. "I miss real milk in my tea. That powdered stuff tastes awful."

"Something we have to get used to, along with hard, teeth-breaking biscuits." Trixie twisted her mouth comically.

"How's Captain Hughes?" Sophie asked.

"Don't you mean 'major'?" Emily commented with a frown. "Is he ill?"

"Oh, you didn't hear? The major's son came in with the convoy yesterday. And Sophie was the hero of the day, in spite of Sister Drew's interference." Trixie related the events of the day before.

"Matron always seems so composed. She must have been angry," Emily said.

"She was but she quietly took Sister's arm and led her out of the ward," Trixie answered, adding, "Captain Hughes is much better, although the wound is still showing signs of infection and he doesn't rest easy. I detect friction between him and his father."

Sophie took her turn at the washstand, letting the face cloth linger on her neck and face, feeling the warmth from the hot water and soaking up the scent of lavender soap, kindly shared by Trixie. The soap in the camp, usually Lifebuoy, or even worse, homemade lye soap, irritated the skin, leaving a strong carbolic smell. The wards constantly smelled of carbolic, used for cleaning everything from hands to linen. So the hint of lavender first thing was always welcome.

Suddenly, Sophie spun around. "I almost forgot. As I was passing Matron's office, I heard Matron yelling, not at all composed. She was telling Dragon Sister that she was to take leave or else. She said she'd requested a replacement. I didn't hear it all but I think she's sending her home permanently. What a relief that will be."

"Let's hope we get someone like Sister Potter, although perhaps not so clumsy. I really like her. Her appearance belies her efficiency." Trixie giggled. "How she avoids tripping over her skirt, I'll never know." All three laughed and straightened their uniforms, ready for a new day.

C Ward was like all the wards, literally wall-to-wall beds and makeshift cots. Many had been added since she had gone off duty the day before. The unusual noise alarmed Sophie. It sounded like a fist fight at the end of a squished row of beds. Kitty was waving at her as she restrained a young soldier.

"Can you give me a hand?" Kitty's voice trembled. "He's had a bad nightmare. I just calmed him when someone dropped something that triggered him."

"What's his name?"

"Private Daniel Winters."

Sophie grabbed his arm as Kitty released it, stopping him

from punching. A black eye wouldn't help any of them. "Private, my name is Nurse Romano. What is your name?" He continued to struggle. "Private, what does your mam call you? Dan? Danny?" Sophie felt the muscles in his arm ease slightly. "Danny, you're safe in hospital. You're having a nightmare. Can you hear me?" Sophie held his now limp arm and waited. He moved his head, opened his tearful eyes and sobbed. She stayed silent, clutching his hand until he took a deep breath.

"You're going to be all right. The dreams will lessen over time."

"Me mam calls me Danny, except when she's mad. Then it's Daniel. She'd be mad with me for blubbering." Danny looked past Sophie, seeing something no one else did.

"You're not blubbering, you are suffering from shell shock. I bet your mam soothed your nightmares when you were a little boy. She wouldn't be mad at all." Sophie took the towel, dabbed his forehead, and wiped his tears away. He was no more than a boy. Her heart ached for him.

He managed a smile. "Aye, she did. Thank you, Nurse."

"My pleasure, soldier. Now let's get you cleaned up and ready for doctor's rounds. Where's home? I'm guessing Liverpool."

"Aye, it is. Down by the docks. How did you know?"

"Nurses have a way of knowing things, just like mothers do," she said, teasing.

"Nurse, mi mam's a worry wart and I'd like to tell her I'm okay. Can I write to her?"

"Of course. I'll find you some paper. Do you have a pen?" She hesitated, wondering if he could read and write. If he was a docker's son he had probably been pulled out of school to work.

As if he knew what she was thinking he said, "I can read and write. Mam insisted I stay in school. Pa wasn't too pleased. He said I should be earning me keep."

"Your mother is a wise woman. Now rest. I'll see what I can find."

Moving on to the next patient, Sophie was pleased with Danny's recovery. It always surprised her how patients could appear quite normal and a minute later act like a madman. Some soldiers managed to get over it while others got worse. She was aware that something small like the noise from scissors dropped in a metal dish could trigger an episode of terror. Would Danny be one of the lucky ones? It was possible his night terrors would pass with rest and quiet.

It was already mid-morning and there were still dressings to be changed. She'd finished the bed baths, thank goodness. Sophie found herself wishing for the ease and routine of Bartley Hospital, not that she'd thought it easy at the time. But, in comparison, it looked like a walk in the park. She sighed, thinking of autumn leaves fluttering in Hyde Park. Here she had double the patients, with injuries and illnesses even she had never seen before. There were times she wondered if she had a sixth sense as she'd hardly finished her thought before Pippa came to help her.

"I'm delighted to see you on this ward. I have never experienced it so awfully busy. I hope we don't get any more chaps," Pippa said.

"What happens if there's another push? We're full up now."

"I asked Nurse Wilkes the same question. The casualties are redirected to a different clearing station. We transfer those patients who can travel to Base Hospital and some are patched up and sent to the hospital ships to go home. If they are too ill to travel or hopeless, they stay until they either get better or—you know." Pippa gave Sophie a knowing look. "Then we attend the funeral. The rest go back to the front. As soon as we have free beds, we start all over again."

"It all sounds depressing and yet the men are mostly cheerful. I've never heard so many jokes and such bantering. Except for patients like this young man." Sophie unwound a bandage on the soldier's head, his eyes quite vacant. She cleaned the wound and put a fresh dressing on it. He had lovely blond hair, but the hole in his head had taken his life. It would never heal and was only a matter of time. She laid him on his pillow and tucked him in comfortably, pulling the meagre curtains separating some of the beds to give him a little privacy.

"So, Nurse Crawley, who's the new nurse?" a voice said as they moved down the ward. "As soon as I can walk, I'm taking you dancing."

"Corporal, always the joker. Meet Nurse Romano from London."

"Fancy name. Maybe I can take her too. We can all go to the Palais de Dance."

"Not a chance, Soldier. Now let's look at your…" Sophie looked at the chart. "Knife wound. That's unusual."The soldier went quiet for a minute and Sophie wasn't sure what had upset him. "Is something the matter?"

"It was from a bayonet. The bugger missed, or almost. I got him first but got a nasty gash in my side. My mate wasn't so lucky."

"Sorry about your mate." Sophie touched his shoulder reassuringly. "Can you roll over on your good side? Nurse Crawley will help you." Sophie eased off the dressing and had to bite her tongue not to gasp. The wound was so big. It wasn't infected, yet anyway. It would heal in time but she was amazed it had not hit any vital organs.

"It's healing well. You were lucky, Corporal. But no dancing for a while. You'll have to be content with shuffling to the canteen."

Grateful the work was finished, at least until after lunch, Kitty and Sophie walked together. The rain finally eased off. Although the ground was wet and muddy, they picked their way to the shelter that Sophie had nicknamed 'Teddy's Place.' Ignoring the cat-calls and whistles from up-patients, they smiled at the exuberance of youth, perched on upturned crates, enjoying the fresh air.

"This is nice," Kitty said, leaning against the table. "Even when it's cold, I like coming out here, particularly when I'm on nights. It is especially peaceful. On a clear night, I can gaze at the stars. Don't see nuthin' like that in London."

Sophie looked skyward, feeling the damp chill. "Is it true it gets very cold?"

"Sometimes, mostly when it snows. The worst is the rain, constant drizzle, and then it pours cats and dogs, soaking everything. At least a heavy frost freezes the mud for a while. It looks as though we have company." Kitty pointed her mug to a harassed looking Sister Potter, her skirts billowing at her ankles, tea splashing out of a mug she carried at arm's length.

"She is so lovely but, honestly, I can't help myself from wanting to giggle."

Kitty nodded, her hand obscuring her grinning face. "Sister Potter, come join us and take a rest."

"I don't mind if I do. With Sister Drew gone, so many new patients and Matron preparing for a new doctor, it's all too much. I keep telling myself the Lord never gives us more than we can handle but sometimes I question His motives." Sister reeled off the sentence or several sentences in one breath, crossed herself and plonked into the only chair.

"Oh my goodness, Sister, take a breath." Kitty moved the rickety table closer so she could put down the now half empty mug of tea. "Where has Sister Drew gone?"

Where indeed, Sophie thought, *had she been banished so quickly and in the middle of a crisis with the hospital overflowing with patients? I wonder if there is more to this. Were her previous indiscretions so bad that she had been warned or maybe threatened with dismissal before? She recalled eavesdropping and hearing Matron say 'and now you've endangered a patient's life'. That certainly might be grounds for dismissal.*

"She, hum, has taken… err… gone on leave, extended leave. She may not be back. Matron is waiting for a replacement."

"What happened? Is she ill? A family emergency?" Kitty quizzed.

Sister shifted uncomfortably on the chair, taking time to think. Sophie and Kitty remained silent, waiting for an answer and knowing it was not in her nature to lie. She cleared her throat. "It seems that …" She seemed hesitant to continue. "There was a problem. I'm not at liberty say. Matron will inform you at the appropriate time."

Sensing that Kitty was about to ask more questions, and had probably figured out that it had something to do with the incident with Major Hughes' son, Sophie shook her head slightly and mouthed 'No more questions.'

"No wonder you are so tired. You're doing the work of two or more," Sophie said, wanting to change the subject. She would tell Kitty what she had overheard later. Right now she wanted to ease Sister's anxiety. "Relax and enjoy your tea. Look, the sun is trying to shine. I want to freshen up before returning to the ward. Take it easy, Sister."

Kitty jumped up. "I'll join you."

Once out of Sister Potter's hearing range, Sophie told Kitty what she'd overheard, passing Matron's office.

"Cor blimey." Kitty put her hand to her mouth. "Oops, sorry." Shrugging her shoulders she added, "mark my words, there's a bit of malarky going on there."

Sophie couldn't help smiling at Kitty's colourful Cockney expressions, which she kept under control most of the time. Sophie hoped it indicated friendship. She liked Kitty.

"I agree, but I doubt we will ever know the truth. I am looking forward to a friendlier sister or, with our luck, she could be worse."

Kitty laughed. "Don't be daft. Nothing could be worse than the Dragon Sister."

Sophie nodded in agreement, happy not to be on the receiving end of Sister's sarcastic comments or constant scolding. She wondered why she was always the target. Although efficient and strict, at least Matron was kind and compassionate. It occurred to her how much more relaxed she felt, knowing that Dragon Sister was not lurking around the corner.

9

Old Memories, Old Photographs

Illary's letter had stayed in her pocket, waiting for a suitable time to reply, which turned out to be two days later. Sophie took an envelope and writing paper from her trunk and sat carefully on the rickety chair. Her fountain pen, a gift from her father for her sixteenth birthday, was carefully retrieved from a small wooden box she kept for her special trinkets: a locket with faded images of her grandparents, a tarnished silver necklace, a pendant belonging to her mother and photographs. One was of her mother sitting in front of the villa in Lucca, beautiful and young. She would never grow old, like the soldiers lost on the battlefield. It gave her a sense of what a mother or wife might think when she stared at a photograph of a son or young husband; forever young. She picked up the photo of her father, looking important and proud the day he opened Derby Silk Mill.

Her father, a practical man, had insisted she use dry ink pellets for her pen, perhaps because the wet ink had a habit of leaking from even the finest of pens. "Dear Papa, if you only knew how practical my pen is here in Passchendaele. I remember arguing that a barrel safety pen would not leak ink and be so much easier to use than dry ink. As always, Papa, you were right." Thoughts of her father always filled her heart with tears, both of joy and sadness. "How I wish I was writing to you at home in Derby. So much has happened since that awful fire and it seems so long ago. I love you and miss you, Papa."

She added a little water to the pen and as she did so, she heard, "I love you too, my brave Sophie." Her heart filled with love. Reassured, she smiled, knowing her papa would always be there. She began to write.

Dearest Hillary,

How delighted I was to receive your letter with news of River House. I'm happy that you were able to stay, even if the nurses have changed. There are days when I wish I was still there, chatting around the dining room table. I did laugh at Cook. I see she hasn't changed her ways. Mrs. Wilderby was the best housekeeper in the world and spoilt us all, making it difficult for Cook to step in her shoes. I still think about her.

Please don't worry about me. Although closer to action than I expected, we are a few miles away. It surprised me that the ground shakes from the guns and, during battles, the sky glows orange, even at such a distance. We are quite safe at the hospital.

The losses are heavy and the injuries are like nothing I've seen before. Your gentlemen colleagues would be prostrate on the ground, and no amount of smelling salts would revive them. I found your description quite amusing. I'm quite sure nurses have stronger stomachs than most doctors. We see people at their most vulnerable.

Emily and Trixie are well and I'm happy to say we are billeted in our own tent with a spare bed, which was yours. The news that you would not be coming did not reach Matron so your name was on the list when we arrived. Everyone here is friendly. Matron is very nice, not unlike Matron at Bartley and, by coincidence, they know each other. There is one mean Sister...

Sophie stopped writing, remembering that Matron read the letters, and decided not to add 'Dragon Sister,' although she knew Hillary would chuckle.

... but for the most part it is pleasant here.

I am told it gets very cold in the winter, which I can believe as even now the nights are already chilly from the rain. It rains almost all the time.

I do hope this is not an imposition but could I ask you to send me a warm blanket and perhaps some tea? The tea is weak and the biscuits as hard as bullets, but, strangely, when the biscuits are dunked in the tea, it improves the flavour of both. However, I still long for a decent cup of tea. That is if you have time. I imagine your studies take up most of it.

Trixie and Emily send their best wishes. Please write

soon. Our regards to Cook and Matron if you see her.

Your affectionate friend,
   Sophie

She re-read the letter, making sure the content was vague enough to pass Matron's scrutiny, who made sure locations or secrets were not unknowingly imparted to loved ones. Heaven forbid the enemy should open a love letter. But then, messages were passed on in the strangest of ways, far beyond Sophie's comprehension. She folded the pages, slipping them into the already addressed envelope. Placing her pen back in the box, she glanced at the photographs one more time. The corner of another photograph caught her eye, one she had forgotten about and it stabbed her heart. It was taken at the silk farm in Lucca. She looked so young and happy, her head nestled in Carlos' shoulder and his head bent down, looking into her eyes. Both were smiling and so much in love. She slammed the box shut, catching her finger and cursing as she placed it back in her trunk. Sucking on her hurt finger, she took a deep breath to calm herself and remove the memory.

Wrapping her woollen shawl around her shoulders against the cool evening air, she walked to the postbox outside Matron's office and popped the letter inside.

Disturbed by the photographs, even though they reflected happy times, she found the losses and memories painful. She needed company, something to distract her. Stopping at the canteen, she picked up three cups of tea, having decided to visit Gertrude and Jo in the Women's Ward. Matron had asked her to speak with Jo, suspecting the loss of her ambulance and patients had unnerved her, maybe even given her a touch of shell shock. Sophie felt guilty because she hadn't made the time.

"Well, aren't you a sight. Is that hot tea?" Jo sat on the side of her bed, with one leg on the floor, the other stretched out on a pillow. A large, angry looking scar marred the front of her naked leg. She patted the chair in front of her, her head still bandaged. "Sit. This is a jolly surprise. I'm lonely. Gerty went back on duty today."

Sophie handed her a mug, placing the other two on the crate used as a side table. "Extra tea. I brought one for Gerty."

"This is terribly kind of you. We shall celebrate with biscuits," Jo said. "If you wouldn't mind passing me that bag?" She pointed to a carpet bag at the end of the bed. "Gwen, my late husband's sister, sends me shortbread biscuits." Jo pulled out a tin and offered it to Sophie.

"Thank you," Sophie said, nibbling the corner of the biscuit. The taste of butter tickled her taste buds. "Oh, this is so good."

"A jolly nice change from the dog biscuits we get here." Laughing at her own joke, she added, "I feed my dogs better biscuits."

"You have dogs? I love dogs."

"I did on the estate. Great companions. Always do as they are told and never answer back." She laughed again, moving her leg with a grimace.

"Is your leg painful? I've been remiss, not asking how you're feeling," Sophie said between sips of tea.

Jo hesitated, taking a bite of shortbread. She looked tired. Her eyes were dull and the laughter had gone. "Ah, it's nothing. The leg is sore, but healing. I have the devil of a headache. Sitting around doesn't suit me. I want to get back to work."

"That might take a while. Head injuries are finicky, each different. It seems you were lucky and the glass didn't go deep enough to cause permanent damage but you still have to be careful and stay quiet. I know it's tough but quiet is the only cure for head injuries."

"It bothers the heck out of me that I was lucky and those poor chaps, who depend on me, were not. I can't believe I flipped bloody Hazel."

"Hazel?" Sophie laughed. "Of course. I forgot your ambulance has a name. It wasn't your fault. It was your quick action, steering out of the path of the explosion, that saved lives."

"I am a bloody good driver. I've led convoys over some atrocious tracks called roads." Jo grinned at the memories. "Even on the estate, I drove faster than my brother. Incorrigible, my father called me. Same with riding. I rode my horses hard, often off the trails and only ever got lost once. That's when I met Dickie." Silence ensued and her eyes, although dry, filled with profound grief that brought tears to Sophie's.

"Your husband?" Sophie asked.

She nodded. "Lost him in 1915. Admiralty. Part of Churchill's Dardanelles' Campaign." Bitterness twisted her face but it was gone in a flash. "Can't dwell on these things, can we?"

"No, of course not," Sophie said.

"Caused a ruckus in both families," Jo announced, changing the subject and making Sophie pay attention to figure out what she was talking about. "Refused to have a society wedding. We were married in the Registry Office by a Justice of the Peace." Jo laughed loudly, a forced effort at joviality. "In 1912, the only reason couples ran off to the Registry of Office was if the bride was in the family way, which was definitely not the case for us. Our families disowned us except for my brother who gave me away and Dickie's brother and wife, Gwen." Jo held up a shortbread biscuit. "Compliments of Gwen." Sadness passed over her again. "My father has never spoken to me since."

"And your mother?"

"Never got along with Mother, a delicate society lady and I, a rebellious tomboy. She left me with nannies and governesses, plural. They never stayed long. Then she told Papa to deal with me. Raising children was woman's work. He treated me like an adult and, together with our common love of horses, we got along well. Until I shamed him."

Sophie frowned. "You didn't shame him. Choosing not to have a society wedding is nothing to be ashamed of. It's your father who should be ashamed of treating you like that." Sophie stopped talking, wondering if she was being too opinionated.

"You are right but I did feel ashamed at the time. My brother tells me that Father regrets not giving me his blessing but not enough to apologize. I suspect he wouldn't dare defy Mother."

Having had a close relationship with her own father, Sophie recognized the bond between father and daughter that few experienced and empathized with her loss.

"Listen to me, jabbering on like a scolded scullery maid. This is what happens when I have too much time on my hands."

"It's important we talk about these things. Losing your father and your husband takes its toll…" Sophie stopped talking as Jo interrupted, her face scarlet with anger.

"And what would you know about it? A young snippet with

a name like Romano, no doubt coddled by a doting Italian mama and an indulgent father." Jo spit out the words with such venom that Sophie pushed back, almost tipping her chair over.

Recoiling from Jo's sudden mood swing, she stiffened with annoyance at the assumptions about her past. About to meet Jo's anger with her own, Sophie realized she had triggered vulnerabilities in Jo with the suggestion she talk about her feelings, something aristocrats never did. Sophie was sure Jo was short for Josephine and perhaps Lady Josephine. Matron was right to be concerned. The ambulance wreck had triggered feelings from the loss of the two people in her life she had loved and trusted. It was more than she could handle. The sad thing was that people like Jo considered showing emotion a weakness and were accustomed to covering up feelings with distractions, work, and in Jo's case, an overly loud sense of humour.

"Jo, or should I say Lady Josephine, our pasts are not so different."

"Who told you? I don't use my title. If I could get rid of it, I would." Her words were curt but the anger had dissipated.

"No one. I guessed. The way you spoke of your horses and the estate and your mother, a society lady. It makes no difference to me. A close friend comes from a society family. Her mother is not unlike yours but she is a wonderful friend and an excellent nurse."

"I was inexcusably rude. I can't explain it," Jo said her tone more confused than apologetic as she added, "I can't imagine having a *normal* family life." Her tone had switched to envy.

"My life has been far from normal. You are right in thinking I am of Italian birth. My mother was loving but suffered ill health and died when I was young. Oh, we were not aristocrats but Papa was a wealthy businessman with a certain standing in the community. Just like your father, Papa treated me like an adult, grooming me to take over his business. I adored my father."

"I wasn't so wrong in my assessment. An indulgent father?"

"Indeed. My father indulged me but not as a giddy female, as an equal. He died in a fire, his wealth destroyed with him. Like your father, he abandoned me. Being penniless meant I lost the man I loved, due to his high society mother condemning me as unsuitable." *And, Sophie thought, he haunts me to this day.* "Please do not presume to judge me." Sophie waited for Jo to respond. She didn't.

However, Sophie took the contrite expression, as she offered the tin of shortbread, as an apology. "Here, take this and share it with your friends. Gwen will send me some more."

Sophie hesitated, wanting to refuse, but quickly realized the gesture was sincere. "Thank you. Trixie and Emily will enjoy this with a cup of tea."

"Which one is the society lady?"

"Trixie, Beatrix Elizabeth Ashford King. Her father is Sir Walter King, her mother the daughter of an earl."

"And Emily?"

"Emily supported and raised her young sister after her parents and brothers died of consumption." Sophie sighed. "You see, none of us have had *normal* lives."

"Sophie Romano, you are a wise woman and I can't help but envy you. I wish I had friends. My dearest friend is Gwen but, here, I seem to frighten everyone away.

"I hope you would consider me a friend. As soon as you are

well enough to walk about, will you come and have tea with us one evening?"

"I would like that."

"I'm afraid I must leave. You need to rest and I need to sleep."

Suddenly the earth shook. Both Jo and Sophie gasped. Tapping Jo's hand, she said, "It's all right, another battle at the front. Any kind of blast will trigger memories of the ambulance explosion. You will learn to accept it, given time." She opened the door, her heart thumping in her chest as imaginary flames flickered in front of her. *I need to heed my own advice,* she thought, patting her chest to calm herself. Turning to wave goodbye, the expression on Jo's face told her she saw her fear.

Jo waved back. "Be careful. I see why you understand."

10

A New Doctor

Accustomed to the night rumblings of the battlefield developing into a busy day, Sophie braced for more casualties. Although the injured were fewer than the last big push, the hospital overflowed with newly assessed soldiers and recovering patients waiting for transfer to other locations. Keeping abreast of who was going where presented some problems. Sergeant Harcourt, in charge of this Field Ambulance unit, was a harsh woman with sergeant major qualities who took out her frustration on the ambulance crew. The noisy arguing was having an adverse effect on the patients, causing Colonel Belingham to intervene. Sophie suspected it was on Matron's request, as she had no jurisdiction over the Field Ambulance unit. The Colonel quickly turned it into a military operation, directing the patients to appropriate ambulances while Sergeant Harcourt checked the vehicles for cleanliness and roadworthiness. The latter being relative, as most of the ambulances were old and in desperate need of repair.

Finally, the camp quieted down with only a dribble of

incoming casualties, mostly minor injuries and a few cases of trench foot.

Sister Potter beckoned Sophie from her duties to once again report to Matron. It was something she was getting accustomed to but it raised eyebrows with her colleagues and created mutterings of 'teacher's pet,' which upset Sophie.

When she arrived, Matron, Colonel Belingham and Sergeant Harcourt were all in Matron's office. She hesitated, sensing discord, and wondered if she had misunderstood Sister Potter.

"Come in, Nurse Romano," Matron said. "The sergeant is leaving for the train station with a convoy of casualties headed for the hospital ship. She will return with reinforcements, Sister Drew's replacement and a new physician who specializes in war nerves. I have witnessed how you care for your patients. The colonel would like you to extend your duties to assist."

"Yes, Matron, Colonel." Sophie wasn't sure what to think. This was highly irregular and who was this new doctor? Could it be Carlos? But from what Emily had said, he wasn't new, just on leave and definitely surgical.

"Sergeant Harcourt tells us one of her best ambulance drivers will soon be back on duty because of your care," Colonel Belingham said with a warm smile.

"Mrs. Griffith's dedication to her work, while commendable, is detrimental to her health and recovery. Sometimes talking to patients allows them to relax, easing the guilt and anxiety associated with the horrors they've witnessed." The words had come out of Sophie's mouth without thought, surprising herself and, judging by the disconcerted glances in the room, everyone else. She wasn't sure why she felt defensive, even protective towards Jo. Was it Harcourt's apparent harshness or her expectations? She hardly knew the woman, who was, in fact, complimenting her. However, in her opinion, which as a nurse didn't count for much, it would be some time before Jo could safely return to duty.

The Colonel cleared his throat. "There is much truth in what Nurse Romano has to say. War changes priorities and we face new ones…" He hesitated, leaving the sentence unfinished, as though changing this mind. He stared at Harcourt. "Order, chain of command and discipline saves lives in wartime." Although he refrained from a direct reprimand, clearly his message was for the sergeant, the colonel none too pleased with her leadership.

Harcourt remained silent. At this last remark, her demeanour altered to that of a chastised child. Sophie glanced from Colonel to Matron, totally confused by the conflicting verbal, and mostly non-verbal, messages. She could only conclude that, had the words been spoken aloud, she would be witnessing a brawl. *What is going on?* she thought, *a serious infraction by the sergeant, perhaps? Did my thoughtless outburst make matters worse?*

"Permission to leave, sir?!" Harcourt broke her silence and saluted.

"Sergeant, upon your return, please escort Captain Cuthbert to my office," commanded the colonel.

Sophie felt her stomach tighten and her heart twist in her chest. What was Andrew doing there? A rhetorical question as Andrew, Dr or Captain Cuthbert, was obviously there to assist the colonel.

Matron frowned, bowed her head to acknowledge the colonel's departure, and glanced fleetingly at Sophie, who surmised the frown was for her, not the colonel. Did she know Sophie had worked and studied with Dr Cuthbert at the Bartley? Had Matron Hartford revealed Sophie's secret, that her own demons had warranted a course of treatment from Dr Cuthbert? She patted her chest, out of breath from all her own demanding questions.

Matron motioned to the chair in front of her desk as she sat down behind it. "Esther, Matron Hartford, tells me you have worked with Dr Cuthbert at the Bartley, which is the reason I am assigning you to assist the new doctor when needed. It's an unusual area of nursing for a young nurse to explore."

Sophie held her breath, waiting for the caveat, a question as to why, only silence ensued and Matron expected a reply. "Nurse Romano?"

"I found myself curious as to why some patients, both soldiers and civilians, coped and others didn't. Dr Cuthbert was kind enough to explain the symptoms, and possible treatments, for shell shock. It is a subject that intrigues me. The suffering is acute and debilitating and, all too frequently, it is wrongly diagnosed or not diagnosed at all."

"Colonel Belingham is of the same opinion. That is why he requested a specialist. It took months to get it approved. It is something the War Department, and even some members of Royal Army Medical Corps, have not acknowledged until recently. Perhaps the war has continued long enough for some officers or their sons to have witnessed war nerves first-hand. However, it is still an uphill battle."

"I am aware that not everyone understands," Sophie said.

"I'm afraid you will be expected to maintain your normal nursing duties, as well as respond to patients experiencing war nerves. I will also expect you to take the lead, enlighten your colleagues, even educate them on the proper nursing response." Matron studied Sophie before asking, "Are you up to the task?"

Sophie nodded, affirming her commitment, while her thoughts contemplated the enormity of the request. "I shall do my best. Nurse Wilkes and aide Crawley already have a willingness to learn how to treat war nerves."

"Excellent. You may approach me with questions if necessary. If I'm not available, Sister Potter is my second in command and a good resource. She will help when needed."

Sophie smiled at the mention of Sister Potter. "She is a lovely person, so kind with both patients and nurses."

Matron refrained from commenting on Sophie's remark but her smile confirmed she agreed. "Colonel Belingham will give Captain Cuthbert a tour. I would like you to be on the ward and introduce him to patients. I will send a message when I know more. That will be all."

Literally concentrating on putting one foot in front of the other, Sophie tried to stop her head spinning and her stomach doing flip flops as she headed back to the ward. What Matron was asking of her was a challenge but she didn't mind because this was exactly what she wanted to do. However, working with Andrew Cuthbert was another story. She respected, even admired, his knowledge and expertise, but he knew too much about her secrets. There was a time when she had thought he was romantically interested in her but now she blushed at the memory. It had been clinical, although she wasn't convinced that the day at the café was entirely professional. Andrew was a doctor and a gentleman. He had talked her through a difficult time after yet another tragedy in her life and that was definitely professional, with not even a hint of romance.

So why would she assume he would like it to be more? Was it, or did *she* want more? She shook her head and whispered, "He's a kind gentle man, a doctor doing his job, nothing…"

"Who's a kind gentleman?" Pippa asked, coming out of the ward and lighting a cigarette. "He sounds perfect."

Sophie laughed a little too hard. "Oh, I was talking to myself."

"Don't tell me you found a beau in this place?"

"What?" Sophie quickly gathered her thoughts as she realized how odd she must seem. "Matron just informed me a new doctor is arriving today. I know him. I worked with him in London. He is a kind, gentle doctor who treats shell shock."

"Is he terribly handsome too?"

"No, not particularly. But he's such a nice man that people like him." Sophie coughed as Pippa's smoke drifted by her. "That's a dreadful habit, you know."

"Everybody smokes. It's the fashion," Pippa said, posing and holding her cigarette in the air. "I prefer to use a cigarette holder but it hardly matches our surroundings."

Sophie rolled her eyes, grinning at Pippa's youthful rationale for smoking. She had never liked the smell and, worse, the taste of cigarettes. Because it was fashionable seemed like a ridiculous reason. She had noted how smoking often calmed the soldiers, and they had so few pleasures it seemed acceptable, except for the coughing. But who was she to judge?

"I must get to work. Anything happen while I was gone?"

Pippa finished her cigarette, stubbing it out on the grass. "I'll come with you. The head injury, Private Small, isn't doing well, a matter of hours, maybe less."

"A blessing. Even if he lived, he'd never be any better. Is someone with him?" Sophie felt a squeeze in her throat. Would she ever get used to such tragic deaths? She hoped not.

"I think so."

The young blond private lay in his bed, motionless, the white bandage on his head making his already vivid blue eyes brighter as he stared up. Sophie lifted his wrist, his pulse faint and slow. Holding his cold hand, she gave it a squeeze, enclosing it in both of hers for some warmth. Surprised, she felt his fingers move as though to cling on to her. She glanced at the chart for his name: William Small (Billy). "Billy, you are a brave soldier. Your mum would be proud of you. I bet you have a pretty sweetheart waiting for you at home." She felt his fingers again. "You can hold onto me for as long as you like." It wasn't long before his fingers relaxed, his breathing changed and he slipped away. "Rest in peace, Billy."

She motioned for the orderly to take care of things, completed the chart, adding a note that she would write to his mother. A ritual Sister Potter encouraged, unless the soldier's commanding officer chose to write. Sophie walked outside to compose herself. Brushing away a tear, she thought of the bright future this handsome young man might have had. *No, I will never get accustomed to such senseless loss.*

She felt a hand on her shoulder. "It is never easy. Was it Private Small?" She looked into Sister Potter's kind face and nodded. "Why don't you take a few minutes, get freshened up before Dr Cuthbert arrives?"

"Thank you." Taking a breath, Sophie said, "Sister, why does it hurt more sometimes than others? Nursing these men is my vocation but watching them die is hard."

"It is all part of our calling. I will grant, at times, the balance is tipped the wrong way. Take comfort in knowing that not just your nursing but your kind words, gentle touch and caring eases these soldiers to either recovery and back to their families or to heaven in the arms of the Lord. This is what nursing is all about, caring and feeling for others although it often causes painful distress within us." Sister Potter took her hand. "You, my dear, are an excellent nurse. Now, run along."

Sophie hurried to the canteen, a blue sky lifting her spirits, a welcome change from the recent grey and constant rain. Sister's words encouraged her, keeping her going and accepting her role; although she wasn't sure about 'arms of the Lord.' It was difficult to understand how a loving God would allow such wars. Sister Potter had great faith, and never questioned it. Sophie assumed she came from a religious Catholic background and wondered if she had been a nun at one time. But not all nuns were devoted, as she had experienced firsthand. Some used their faith to hide terrible flaws.

"Nurse Romano!" Sophie almost jumped out of her chair, spilling her tea at the familiar voice.

"Dr Cuthbert." She glanced at him. "You are alone?" Blushing from her toes to her cheeks, she realized how silly the question was.

He grinned, spinning around, over exaggerating the gesture. "Yes, I am quite alone."

She laughed, realizing he was teasing her. "I am not sure why I said that. You took me by surprise. I was expecting to meet you on the ward. I'm taking a break. A patient, a nice young man, just died, one of many I'm afraid. Matron was to let me know when you arrived. I have the honour of introducing you to the patients. I'm not sure why. I haven't been here very long." She stopped talking, aware that she was rambling.

"You are a breath of fresh air, Sophie." He hesitated, looking a little embarrassed. "I am alone. Sergeant Harcourt delivered me to Colonel Belingham's office but disappeared. She wasn't very friendly. The conversation from the train station was perfunctory at best."

"Do I hear a diagnosis coming?"

"No. I'm sure it was nothing more than a bad day. Although I must admit I did wonder if my presence here was as welcome as I had anticipated. The Colonel informed me he had urgent business requiring his immediate attention and he would meet me later in the officer's mess, suggesting I talk to Matron first. But her office was empty so I went a walk-about, as our Aussie friends would say, and here I am."

"Oh dear, that does not sound like the colonel. Something must be afoot," Sophie said, frowning.

"No matter. I am delighted to find a familiar face." He bent his head to one side and, with hesitation, pointed to the chair. "May I?"

"Where are my manners? Of course, please. Would you like a cup of tea? Nothing stronger, I'm afraid. You'd have to go to the officer's mess for that."

"Tea is fine. I'll pretend we are at the café in London."

Sophie giggled. "You remember. I can assure you the tea here is quite different." She stood up. *Is he flirting with me already? Be careful. He fooled you once before.*

Placing tea and biscuits on the table, Sophie resumed the conversation, choosing to keep to safe subjects. "I thought you wanted to remain in London. How did you get here?"

"I didn't have much choice. I was drafted by the war office and told my services were needed more at the Western Front than in London, which is an enormous change in attitude by the powers above. I am based here but expected to travel to other units in the area. The colonel will fill me in later."

"It's very different from the Bartley, heartbreaking at times. Some soldiers mange the horror. Others are terrified and everything in between. I've only been here a couple of months and have just recently been assigned to C Ward, where some of the more difficult patients reside."

"I respect your judgement and when Matron at the Bartley told me you were here, I was delighted I would be working with you." His gaze made Sophie uncomfortable. *Did he request to be assigned to this location because he knew I was here?* She shook her head. *No, things didn't work that way. It was pure coincidence, or was it?*

"Sophie, are you all right?"

"Oh yes, of course. Miles away, thinking." She quickly gathered her thoughts. "One patient concerns me. I'm not sure he will recover but the others are doing all right. There's also an ambulance driver in the Women's Ward who is struggling, but won't admit it. I could introduce you but I am assuming protocol dictates an introduction by Colonel Belingham or Matron."

"I'm afraid you are correct, the Colonel actually. Following orders is not my strong suit, especially where patient care is concerned. I have learned to follow the simple rules and bend those that pertain to treatment, which seems to be less threatening to my superiors."

"What a strange thing to say."

"Perhaps. I didn't take kindly to being ordered around. I learned very quickly, while in basic training, that the army requires implicit acceptance, no matter what the order." He laughed. "Not something my questioning mind accepted easily until I separated military operations from medical care."

"And now, as an officer, you give the orders." Sophie smiled, seeing a side of him she hadn't noticed before. "You'll find orders are followed automatically here but I was surprised at the familiarity in the medical corps, with the exception of Colonel Belingham. It's acceptable to use Christian names. However, Matron is not so liberal with the nurses and there is one miserable surgeon, Major Hughes, head of the surgical unit, who considers himself above all others. There are more surgeons I don't know except …" Sophie hesitated, clearing her throat. "Mr. Carlos Wainwright, who is currently on leave, is one of them."

"Carlos is here. Splendid! Nice fellow, Carlos. I haven't spoken to him since he was called up. Is there anyone else here from London?"

"Trixie King and Emily Finnegan from the Bartley. We came together."

"Your friends from River House. And Hillary?"

"Hillary was accepted into medical school. A lifelong dream for her. She writes and is doing well."

"She'll go far. I am pleased Carlos is here. He's a great surgeon. Do you know when he returns?"

Sophie shook her head, suddenly feeling stifled at the mention of Carlos. He always took her breath away, but then, she thought, *so does Andrew.* "Forgive me, I need to resume my duties, Captain." She discovered that using his military title put some distance between them.

"I'm still getting used to the title of Captain." He frowned. "Is something wrong?"

"No, I need to get back to the ward."

"I've taken up far too much of your time and I had better go to the officers mess and wait for the colonel." He gave her a second, worried glance, which annoyed Sophie. It felt invasive. Was he analyzing her? She was coping and didn't want to open any wounds.

11

Wake up Calls

Looking forward to the solitude, Sophie secured the tent entrance and slipped into her nightgown. Her roommates had opted to spend the evening in the mess playing cards, Sophie declined. Pulling the makeshift chair out from under the desk, she smiled at the resourcefulness enforced by war. The original chair had long since lost its legs but they had found a packing case about the right size and stuffed a pillow case with anything soft to avoid splinters in the behind, a danger when wearing night attire. The desk, an actual table possibly rescued from a rubbish dump, wobbled. Three legs stood firm but the fourth leg, a tree branch nailed into the top, didn't quite equalize the height.

The light had long since gone so she placed the lantern on the desk, shivering not at the cold, as the place was toasty warm, but at the feel of November with a hint of frost outside.

Smoothing her writing paper, she took her pen from her treasure box, secured inside her trunk, and began writing a letter to Hillary. She needed to tell someone about Andrew

Cuthbert and the pending arrival of Carlos. As she wrote, it occurred to her that Carlos' leave was exceptionally long, too long unless it was medical, which to the best of her knowledge it was not. Personal leave amounted to days, or occasionally a couple of weeks. Perhaps Emily was mistaken and he wasn't coming back after all. She tapped her pen against her lips, shocked as she remembered his kiss. She quickly pointed the nib back on the paper and reminded herself that he was engaged to Lady Rosamond and was most likely on leave for his nuptials, which might explain the extended period.

She began scribbling again, asking Hillary if she'd seen the wedding announcement in *The Telegraph*. Society weddings were always big news and Lady Rosamond, the only daughter of the Earl of Summers, was big news indeed. There was no doubt in her mind that Carlos' social climbing mother would flaunt her son's most suitable marriage.

Sophie stared at the light flickering on the chimney pipe, the memory of the woman's words burning in her eyes. *'Your summer romance was nothing more than a schoolgirl's crush. My son had his fling. Your family is in ruins. Mr. Wainwright and I could not possibly allow such a marriage.'* The words were spoken so long ago but she recalled them as precisely as if they had been said the day before. Taking a long deep breath, she slowly released it. "Sophie, dragging up old memories of things that happened eight years ago is silly. Put it behind you. Carlos belongs to another." She stood up and almost stamped her foot. "Now Andrew Cuthbert…?" She let out an exasperated sigh adding, "Sophie Romano, take charge of your sensibilities!"

She turned the lantern down low and crawled into bed, closing her eyes and pretending to be asleep as she heard giggles and footsteps approaching. Emily and Trixie tip-toed into the tent, whispering as they undressed and then they too crawled into bed.

"Wakie, wakie, me darlin's 'ot wowter's just for you." Sophie woke with a giggle, hearing Buster's 'wowter-call,' as they had nicknamed his cheerful wake-up. She stretched, surprised at how well she had slept, especially given her unsettling thoughts of the night before. The cheery wake-up call fit her mood. Andrew Cuthbert's arrival had reminded her of how much she liked him. As confusing as he was on the personal side, she enjoyed working with him and admired and respected his expertise. It was gratifying to know that, in his own way, he respected her nursing abilities. Andrew had reminded her why she was there—to serve and heal broken men. He'd also prompted the hopelessness of her long-ago love for Carlos. Or maybe it was the reminder of his betrayal? If she was to accomplish her purpose, she must relinquish all thoughts of Carlos Wainwright.

"Good morning, Sophie. Why so thoughtful first thing? And a smile on your face. Dreaming of fairies, are you?" Emily's Irish accent always seemed stronger in the morning and Sophie loved it.

"Buster's wowter-call always makes me laugh. Any idea where such an accent comes from?" Sophie leaned out to grab the jug of water, the steam filling the tent with warmth as she poured it into the bowl.

"No, I can't place it. I think he might have a speech impediment too," Trixie added. "Hey, how come you get the first wash?"

105

"I want to be early for breakfast so I can pop by and see Jo before I start. Andrew is giving her a check-up today."

"Ooh! It's Andrew now, is it?" Trixie teased.

"No, no nothing like that." Sophie laughed, annoyed that 'Andrew' had slipped out. "Dr Cuthbert, or Captain Cuthbert," she corrected, "is seeing Jo today. She is stubborn and it's going to take some convincing that Dr … Captain Cuthbert can help her."

Dressed and wrapped in their warm trench-coats, the three linked arms. Everyone wanting an early start, they walked to the canteen. First in the canteen often meant something special like bacon but other than fresh milk, a rare treat from the powdered stuff, and newly baked bread, breakfast was boring, lumpy porridge. The three had long realized, lumpy or not, they must eat to keep their strength up. The milk helped and was especially appreciated in tea, usually at its best first thing.

"I'm off. See you later." Sophie emptied her cup and hurried to the Women's Ward. Jo was up, sitting at the centre table with another patient. "Jo, it is good to see you up and about."

"I most certainly am up. Need to get this leg working again." She tapped a set of crutches propped at the side of table. "Doc said he'd take the bandage off my head today. I'll be back in the ambulance in a few days."

"Don't rush things, Jo. You need time to heal." Sophie glanced at the other patient, a pale, wispy nurse. "Has Jo been giving you a hard time?"

"No. I like the company but I'm feeling unwell. If you'll excuse me, I need to lay down."

"Of course." Sophie took her arm and guided her to her bed, frowning as she felt her forehead burning with fever. The nurse on duty came in and Sophie whispered her discovery to her.

"Thank you." The nurse nodded, picking up the thermometer from the tray and shaking it. "Can you take Mrs. Griffith's vitals?"

"Certainly. I need to talk to her about Dr Cuthbert's visit."

The nurse raised an eyebrow. "Good luck," she whispered with a knowing smile. "I met him yesterday. He's very good but I'm not sure Mrs. Griffith will accept his treatment."

Sophie smiled and returned to Jo. "Come back to your bed. I need to check your vitals."

"I can assure you I am alive and kicking! You can't keep me down for long." Jo hopped on one leg and slipped the crutches under her arms. Sophie steadied her as she paled, from what, Sophie wasn't sure.

"Is the leg hurting?"

"Not much," Jo answered, her pallor as white as the bed sheets. "A bit of a rush when I stood up, but okay now." With sheer determination, she forced the crutches in front of her and eased her body forward to her bed. Sitting down hard, she leaned heavily against the pillows.

Writing the results of her vitals on her medical card, Sophie said, "you need to rest. I see you are having nightmares."

"That's what they tell me. Poppycock. Just a bit restless, that's all."

"I'm not so sure. You had a nasty shock when your ambulance tipped over. It might help to talk." Sophie took a deep breath and quickly moved on. "A new doctor has arrived from the Bartley, where I trained. He specializes in trauma and is coming to see you. He'll help with the nightmares."

"What nonsense! I need to mount the horse. Best advice

Father ever gave me; get back in the saddle. I might not have a horse but getting behind the wheel is all I need."

"You could be right, but having a chat with Dr Cuthbert won't hurt." Sophie gave her a stern glare.

"Do I have a choice? I can be stubborn."

"No, you don't have a choice and I agree you can be stubborn. Would you do it for me?" Jo didn't answer but her face softened and Sophie took that as a 'yes.' "I have to go. I'll see you later."

The wooden walkway between tents was crowded with staff coming and going as the dayshift took over from the nightshift. Sophie hurried by, nodding morning greetings and bumping into Matron as she entered the ward. Was she late? Since Sister Drew's untimely departure, Matron was often on the wards, overseeing the daily routines.

"Good morning," Matron said, her smile reassuring Sophie. "Captain Cuthbert is with a distressed soldier. He requires your assistance. I have to leave to greet some new volunteer arrivals. We need the help but I do hope they left the drawing room behind." She sighed tentatively. "And, finally, a replacement for Sister Drew. I hope she's up to the task. Sister Potter will join you. Would you make sure the captain has everything he needs?"

"Yes, Matron."

Sophie was surprised at Matron's candor. It was unusual for her to make personal comments about her staff. And, she also noticed the unflappable Matron appeared anxious, most likely from overwork. The ward sisters did a good job at managing the wards but overseeing all the wards was a mammoth task. The prospect of another sister to ease the burden should be welcome.

Stsanding at a discreet distance from Andrew as he talked with the soldier. She recognized the soldier and leaned towards Kitty who was tending to the patient in the next bed. "Isn't that Private Connor? When did he arrive?" she whispered.

Kitty moved away from the patient before answering. "No, Carter. He came in late last night. He had a breakdown in the trenches. Night nurse said Captain Cuthbert was called to settle him down when he woke with terrible nightmares. He's been with him ever since."

"I thought he had a Blighty ticket?"

"You're mixed up. Connor got the Blighty ticket. This is his mate, Private Carter, who was declared fit for service and sent back to the front."

"Oh, poor fellow. He was so cheerful, teasing his friend..."

"Nurse Romano." Andrew's voice interrupted. "Good morning." He picked up the medical card and made some notes.

Sophie moved closer to the bed before replying. "Dr ..um... Captain Cuthbert, you're bright and early."

He smiled at her correction. "Duty calls. Are you on this ward today?"

Sophie nodded. "All day."

"When he," Cuthbert turned his head towards the bed, "wakes, would you sit with him?"

"Of course. Captain, were you aware this young man was here in September, physical injuries with signs of shell shock? He was being brave for his friend who was in a bad way and sent home. He was sent back..." Sophie paused. "If he'd been treated then..." She stopped.

"Let's just treat him now." Andrew looked into her eyes,

understanding. "He will get a Blighty ticket this time. Please excuse me, it's been a long night or early morning. I'm going to get some breakfast."

Sophie checked the sleeping patient and moved on to the early morning routine of temperatures, bed making, medicine, changing dressings and finally, ablutions and shaves for those that couldn't. The up-patients took care of themselves and congregated outside, having a smoke while waiting for the call from the cookhouse.

The dawn sky brightened as rain clouds parted, making room for the rare appearance of the sun. Orderlies cleaned out the stoves and washed the wooden floors while nurse volunteers scooped up soiled dressings and laundry. The whole place was a hive of bees, each worker doing his or her job. As the chores were completed, the sides of the tent were rolled up, allowing air and light into the ward. Sophie stared out at the early morning, her favourite time of day. The rising sun painted a hue of pink on the clouds and the air was still for a few seconds, until the thump of marching feet and the sergeant's calls of, 'Left wheel…eyes right, lef, lef …' rang out. Morning drills.

The final chore before doctors' rounds was feeding those who either weren't able to or wouldn't feed themselves. Sophie joined Pippa trying to persuade a determined soldier he needed to eat. He was insisting he could manage on his own. Sophie smiled, raising an eyebrow as the poor man had both arms in a sling. He looked older than most of the boys, probably used to being in charge.

"Can I help?" Sophie asked.

Pippa nodded frantically, filling a spoon with porridge and aiming it towards the side of his turned head. Sophie had the urge to giggle. The behaviour was similar to a toddler but she knew this was quite different.

She gently laid her hand on Pippa's and motioned to her to put the dish down. "Sir, how annoying to have both arms injured."

"I refuse to be fed like a child." His accent had a slight drawl. He certainly wasn't from Liverpool, or even the north of England, as most of the men had been in the last while.

"Can I see your hands, please?"

He nodded, embarrassment flushing his cheeks. "Sorry, Nurse, I'm not used to being so incapacitated."

"I cannot imagine what it's like to have both arms restrained. We'll sort something out for you but you will have to let us help you. Can you do that?"

He answered Sophie with a rich, warm grin, a shock of dark curls framing a healthy plump face, not gaunt and thin like most of the soldiers. She inspected one sling that held his arm firmly to his torso, a shoulder injury, dislocation from the look of it. She looked at his other sling which although looser, covered his arm in a splint. His fingers were free on his left hand.

"Can you raise this hand without hurting?" He bent his head forward and managed to meet his hand. "Good. Now, can you put your fingers around this cup?" He slowly gripped the handle and moved the cup to his mouth, taking a sip of tea.

"Thank you, Nurse." He grinned from ear to ear.

"Where are you from? I hear an accent but I can't place it."

"Almonte, Canada. A tiny little place west of Ottawa. My dad owns a dairy farm. I've only been here a few weeks." He lifted his hand. "Already out of commission and not exactly a heroic war act either. We, Doug and I, he's from Canada too, had a disagreement with a trench wall. We tried to stop it falling in." He laughed. "A bit stupid really. It was soft from the rain and it collapsed anyway. Doug jumped out in time but I got trapped. I felt this arm snap as one of the beams hit me. That mud is like nothing I've ever seen before and I've seen thick mud in the spring thaw on the farm." He shook his head, his jaw tensed and moisture glazing his eyes. "I thought I was a gonna. The mud just kept sucking me in. Thank God for Doug who raised the alarm. The shoulder dislocated when they pulled me out." He hesitated with a contrite expression. "I am truly sorry about the eating thing."

"Apology accepted. Fear does strange things to people but there is nothing to be afraid of here and your injuries will heal. We have our ways of getting patients to eat," Sophie teased with a smile. "Perhaps it's not up to your mother's farmhouse standard, but you must eat to regain your strength." Sophie turned to Pippa. "Nurse Crawley, he won't manage porridge. Let's try some toast and beef tea in a cup? I think this soldier will manage that on his own. What do you say, Sergeant?" He screwed his nose up at the mention of beef tea. "I know it's not the best but it will help heal those bones. Can you do that for me?"

"If it will give me the strength to get back to fight, consider it done."

Sophie gave his sling a gentle friendly tap. "Oh, and don't overdo it with your left arm or you'll finish up in surgery and I'll get into trouble for telling you to use it." She gave him a reassuring smile and looked up to see Kitty beckoning her from Private Carter's bed.

Carter's demeanour shocked her. Although used to shell-shocked soldiers, she had never seen anything like this fellow. His terrified face stared at an unknown horror. He didn't even move or blink, seeming more like a stone statue. Sophie lifted his cold hand, squeezing it gently in hers and brushing thick, brown hair away from his cold forehead with the other. She whispered reassurances that he was safe but his features did not change. His unblinking eyes were wide open but she felt a slight squeeze from his fingers and, very slowly, his eyelids closed and he returned to sleep.

"Kitty, the best thing is to let him sleep. Call me if he has another attack. I need some air."

It hadn't rained all day. The late afternoon sun shone from a clear blue sky, a rare occurrence and somewhat foreboding. She could hear the gunfire in the distance, battles that continued daily, some more intense than others. She was ashamed to think she had gotten used to the sounds that had horrified her only a few weeks earlier. She had a prickly feeling; something seemed different. She shook it off, relishing the warm sun on her face. The thought of a hot drink hurried her along the duckboard.

Tea in hand, she decided to sit outside and enjoy the simple pleasure at 'Teddy's Place.' Pulling a chair from under the canvas, she closed her eyes, shutting everything out and letting her thoughts wander. Relaxed and dreaming, she heard a beautiful, loving and reassuring voice, one she recognized. As she dreamed, the voice became clearer.

"Dearest Sophie, the only person in the world who can find and embrace the small things in life." The voice hesitated, adding in an almost, but not quite inaudible whisper, "How I've missed you." Her heart fluttered. Could it be?

A bunch of soldiers laughed in the distance, confirming it

was not a dream. Someone was standing next to her. Her heart pounded, making her ears feel like a beating drum, as her head spun a thousand times. She froze in the chair, afraid to open her eyes.

12

Emotions in War

She sat motionless far too long, and in a strange way, she understood Private Carter. She didn't want to open her eyes, to start the turmoil and confusion she knew would happen when she saw *him*. His presence changed her. If she stayed statue-like, perhaps he would go away and things could stay the same.

It was Andrew Cuthbert who broke the silence. It should have been a relief but only complicated her intense feelings.

"Well, how the bloody hell are you, Carlos!? It is a treat to see you here. Sophie mentioned you were on leave."

"Andrew, I'm surprised to see you. When did you leave the Bartley?" He stretched out his arm and the men shook hands.

"A couple of months ago. Basic training and here I am." Andrew flung his arms out.

"I've been here eight months now and just managed a week's leave before they sent me to a Regimental aide Post. It's pretty awful that close to the front." He shook his head briefly and continued. "And to my great surprise, the first person I see upon my return is the lovely Sophie Romano." He bent down to greet Sophie and for a moment, she thought he was going to kiss her. "You must have arrived after I left."

"Carlos, Andrew. Gentlemen, I am equally surprised to see both of you." She grinned, "At the same time, in the same place, right here." Sophie stopped talking, aware she was blushing and making no sense. She rose from the chair, straightened her uniform and tried to stand tall. "Gentlemen, it is a pleasure to see you. I'll take my leave and allow you two to catch up. I have to get back on duty."

Her feet pounded on the duckboard as she restrained herself from running, praying she wouldn't faint and ignoring Andrew's calls of "I need to talk to you about…" The end of the sentence blew away in the breeze.

By the time she reached C Ward, her sides hurt and she bent forward, supporting herself with hands on her knees until her breathing slowed. She didn't see Sister Potter until her skirt swooshed in front of her face. Sophie straightened her back. "Sister?"

"Nurse Romano, you look…shall we say, dishevelled?"

Words like 'dishevelled' coming from Sister Potter, who always looked that way, were alarming. She genuinely had no explanation for her appearance, other than *I just met an old boyfriend who…* She stopped her thoughts. *What exactly did Carlos do to send me in such a tizzy?* She stood, speechless, as verbalizing the real reason was out of the question.

Sister Potter leaned her head to one side, frowning. "This is not like you. Are you feeling unwell? You do look flushed."

Instead of confirming Sister Potter's observation and embracing the excuse, Sophie patted her hair, attempted to straighten her nurse's cap and smooth her skirt, sensing she was hot and clammy to the touch. "Thank you, Sister. I am quite well. A little rushed for duty. If you'll excuse me?"

Sister reluctantly stepped to one side. Once on the ward Sophie sat down at the nurses' desk, to compose herself, grateful it was quiet. Shuffling some papers to look busy, Sophie read a note from Captain Cuthbert requesting assistance from Nurse Romano for Private Carter, but the note had no specifics.

Aware that her recent behaviour had been rude, she felt a pang of guilt for having walked away from what she now realized were Andrew's instructions about the patient's treatment.

Glancing around the ward at the sleeping men with nurses busy with non-patient activities, she had no choice but to return to Teddy's place and ask Andrew for instructions. She hoped Carlos might have moved on to the surgical unit but he and Andrew were in deep conversation exactly where she had left them. Sophie hesitated, seeing the two men together, and palpitations quickened in her chest. Her body felt uncomfortably hot, aroused and confused. Remembering her propensity to faint in Andrew's arms, she quickly pulled herself together at the horrifying thought of swooning at the feet of both gentlemen. She grabbed a tent pole that supported the canvas shelter and took in two long, deep breaths, listening for an appropriate time to interrupt.

Carlos laughed at something Andrew said and replied "There was one such sister on the train, lording over several VADs, putting the fear of God in the poor creatures. Sour expression and her nose so high in the air it stuck to the carriage roof." They both laughed again. "I recognized her from the Bartley and, if I'm not mistaken, there was some kind of scandal, all hush-hush of course. Whatever it was angered Sophie, at least the way it was handled."

"Scandal? It must have been before I started. Do you remember her name?" Andrew asked

"I remember a nickname, Sister Sin … something," Carlos replied and turned, alerted by a gasp from Sophie. He frowned, "Is something wrong, Sophie?"

"Sister Singleton is here, at this hospital?" She blurted out, pressing her hand to her mouth. "How could this happen? Sister Drew was awful but Sister Sin…" She scowled. "She is so much worse." Sophie's thoughts went back to the day Trixie ran to her, scratched and bruised after an attack from the depraved sister. She had been so angry over Matron's excuse that Sister was overworked and, instead of punishment, had sequestered her to the convent to reflect on her behaviour, thus avoiding a scandal. Who would send a woman like that to a war zone?

Both men stared at her, wide eyed. Her face flushed with anger and beads of sweat peppered her forehead. She was wringing her hands and her breath was short and loud. Rage seeped into her face. This on top of all the other feelings inside her. She thought she might snap like a twig.

Glancing at Carlos, then Andrew, she ran back towards the ward, calling over her shoulder, "I must go!" She ran between the tents and found Pippa smoking. Grabbing Pippa's cigarette, she took a puff and immediately started coughing, grimaced and returned the cigarette. "I needed that." The foul tasting cigarette and the coughing had brought Sophie to her senses.

"What happened? Sophie, you've been strange all day. Not to mention taking a drag of my ciggy."

"My past is haunting me and the final straw is the new sister.

I know her from the Bartley. She's worse than Sister Drew. She arrived here today."

"How bad can she be?"

"Bad! Pippa, stay away from her. She hurts young nurses. I had better get back to work." Sophie swallowed, trying to rid the taste of the cigarette as she returned to the ward.

"Private Carter, it is good to see you awake." Sophie straightened his sheets and plumped his pillow. She observed his colour; a little pinker and his eyes were blinking, although he was still staring. She took his hand in hers. "How are you feeling? You are looking a little better this afternoon." He didn't answer. She squeezed his hand. "Take your time."

He turned his head to face her. "Could I have a cup'a tea? Nurse…" He frowned. "I think I know you."

Smiling, Sophie motioned to Pippa to fetch some tea. "You do. I nursed you last time you were here with your mate, Connor. He went home."

"Aye and they sent me back to that hellhole." Tears filled his eyes and he gripped Sophie's hand until it hurt. "I can't do this no more," he sobbed, tears streaming down his face.

"You won't be going back. We'll get you well and then send you home. I bet you have a sweetheart waiting for you?"

"'Ow can I go back to Mam and Gracie like this? Cryin' and carrying on like a baby. I can't even see Gracie's face. All I see is that monster comin' for me." Fear widened his eyes. Sophie feared he was sliding back into the horror when Pippa arrived with the tea. She was relieved to see him blink as he forced his knuckles into his eye sockets to stop the tears.

"Here's your tea. One step at a time, Soldier. We'll do our best. Now drink up while it's hot."

Sophie sat with him. Although he was silent most of the

119

time, knowing someone was there seemed to comfort him. He ate some dinner and Sophie was about to leave for her own tea when Andrew arrived.

Seeing her get up he said, "Running away again, Nurse Romano? I'm beginning to deduce that I offend your sensibilities." She heard his best drawing room tone. Although not a reprimand, that wasn't Andrew's style, it was formal enough to inform Sophie of his concern.

"Not at all Dr...Captain Cuthbert." She faltered. "Um... Captain Wainwright took me by surprise. I thought I was intruding and it was best to leave you two to talk."

"Why did Sister Sin upset you so much?"

"Oh, nothing. Just two surprises in one day."

"I see. You know Carlos well?" His tone was quizzical. As many sessions as she had had with Andrew in London about the trauma of her past, she had never told him Carlos was the man who jilted her. Judging by the enquiring psychological stare, he was seeing something she preferred he didn't.

"You are aware of my connection to Carlos. We talked about it at some length," Sophie said.

"That is true but I've always had the sense you were holding back. No matter, I'm here to treat Carter. How is he doing?"

Sophie calmed the urge to sigh with relief at the change of subject. "Much better. He talked a little and asked for a cup of tea and has eaten some beef stew. I noticed you left a note at the nurse's station with my name on it. Was that what you wanted to talk to me about, when I..." Sophie smiled. "Ran off?"

"You did hear me. And I thought my words were lost in the wind." He grinned.

She smiled, comfortable with the knowledge he was teasing

her. "Some did go into the breeze but I confess I heard the first part."

"Actually, it's about another matter. My message regarding this patient was for the ward sister. We'll discuss it after I've spoken with Private Carter."

"I'll wait at the nurses' station." Sophie eased the flimsy curtain to give the illusion of privacy.

The night nurses arrived and the day shift left for tea. It had surprised Sophie that the nurse's routine was not dissimilar to the Bartley. Once off shift, the nurses had the evening to themselves, except if there was a convoy due and then it was all hands on deck. Kitty came up to the desk and handed the nurse the charts.

She frowned at Sophie. "Are you staying?"

"Captain Cuthbert wants to talk to me about a patient. As I already ran off, leaving him in mid-sentence, I had better stay. I'll meet you in the canteen."

"Now I'm curious. Here he comes. I'll see you later." Kitty waved as she left the ward.

Andrew stopped to speak with the night nurse and joined Sophie. "He's a little better but whatever he saw is lurking in the background. I'll see him again tomorrow. Do you mind if we walk? I need to get some fresh air."

"Not at all. I brought my coat this morning. It was quite chilly. Kitty, Nurse Wilkes, has been here over a year and reports November is wet and cold, then the frost comes and sometimes snow." Sophie gave a shudder.

They walked in silence past the veterinary stables. The smell of disinfectant hung in the air from the Eusol tanks used to clean the horses. Sophie couldn't bear the thought of injured horses and rarely walked in that direction. They wandered past the woodland that surrounded the camp, passing chicken coups that provided fresh eggs and sometimes a roast. Sophie felt comfortable with Andrew.

"I wanted to talk to you about Mrs. Griffith," Andrew said. She sensed he was choosing his words carefully. "I've only had one session with her, but I have concerns. Major Hughes tells me her leg has healed and the gash in her head, although deep, did not damage her brain. She'll be fit for duty in a week. She has made it clear, to all and sundry, she's ready." He grinned.

"She's quite the character but she is far from ready for service. Her mind has not healed. The bravado is show. In my opinion, the trauma of the incident has triggered more than war nerves. I've seen this a few times recently. The patient displays mild nervousness or, in the case of soldiers or people at war, shell shock. But there is an underlying debility that is dormant until triggered when the brain is exposed to what it sees as a threat, a fear stronger than the first trauma."

"You mean like Private Carter? The first time, he seemed to recover, but the signs were there and this time he isn't likely to recover."

"Exactly! It can also trigger old trauma that has nothing to do with the war. Unfortunately, it is not a black and white subject. I can't write hard facts in a report and the army doesn't operate on unproven diagnoses."

"And you think Jo is displaying similar signs?"

He nodded, pausing before he spoke. "There's something else. Convincing the army that men are suffering from shell shock is hard enough. Even with evidence that supports the condition, the army may dismiss it as cowardly or weak. Convincing a superior, Colonel Belingham may be an exception, that a woman could be diagnosed with shell shock will be interpreted as nerves, merely a weakness, a woman's sensibilities." He hesitated, taking several breaths before continuing. "I saw it at the asylum. Women who defy their husbands or try to show independence are falsely diagnosed, even shut away for their own good."

Sophie raised an eyebrow. "Even today?"

"Not as often, but men in general consider women weak and fanciful. Here is my dilemma. They will declare Mrs. Griffith fit for duty based on Hughes' assessment and ignore mine. If I make a case strong enough to keep her under treatment, it could save her sanity but it would ruin her life, labelling her a delicate woman with fainting spells." He burst out laughing and Sophie joined him.

"Oh my goodness, Andrew, that is so funny. Not in my wildest dreams would I ever consider Jo to be a *delicate* woman prone to fainting spells." Sophie stopped laughing as she realized she had called him 'Andrew.' "I'm sorry, Captain, that just slipped out."

"I prefer Andrew when we're alone." His eyes seemed to say more.

Sophie cleared her throat, not sure how to respond. "So, Captain, how can I help? Have you spoken to Sergeant Harcourt? She's in charge of this field ambulance unit."

"Sergeant Harcourt wants Mrs. Griffith on duty in an ambulance. Her words were 'She's the best I've got, nothing wrong with her. End of discussion, Captain.'" He laughed, shaking his head. "That woman scares me!"

"She scares everyone but she too has her weak spots and Jo is probably stronger than her. Sergeant Harcourt is head of this Field Ambulance unit and, in the absence of a commanding officer, she reports to Colonel Belingham. Surely he would support you?"

"I haven't spoken to him yet. I respect your opinion and wondered if you had any suggestions. Could you persuade Mrs. Griffith to delay her return to duty?"

"I can talk to her but I doubt it will make a difference. I know it's less than ideal. This isn't London and she will cope."

"Perhaps you are right. Even in the short time I've been here I've seen and heard of things that I would never have thought the human mind could tolerate, but somehow some do." He lowered his voice, speaking his thought aloud. "It is a challenge to understand why some people cope and others don't. I pride myself on seeing the signs but war is so different."

Sophie didn't answer, assuming it was a rhetorical question and she'd said too much already. *Andrew was the doctor, a leading authority on neurasthenia, but he seemed vulnerable, a side of him she hadn't seen before. Could he be having difficulty coping so close to the front line?* She shook off such a ridiculous thought. He was an experienced psychiatrist, having seen the worst of humankind in the asylums.

"I'm sorry I wasn't more help. I will speak with Jo. That's about all I can do. If you'll excuse me, I must talk with Trixie about our new sister."

"You've been a great help. I need to get acquainted with military protocol. As you say, this isn't London. I don't have the luxury of time. Thank you, Sophie. Nurse Romano."

Sophie watched his laboured steps as he headed for the officer's mess. She surmised he was digesting the reality of circumstances in Passchendaele and accepting how those circumstances would impede his ability to do his job properly.

But, she thought, *I expect the tenacious and resourceful Dr Cuthbert will adapt. I'm not sure I will. Sister Sin's appearance is shocking and I must let the others know.*

13

Sinful News

Sophie walked into the canteen to find Trixie engrossed in a letter. She looked up, sadness in her eyes. "I could do with company. Try the beef stew. It's quite good." She waved the letter. "From Chris."

"So why so sad?"

"He has leave and wants to meet me in Paris."

"That sounds exciting, not sad," Sophie said as she went to get her dinner.

"They'll never give me leave. I haven't been here long enough, and Paris? How would I get there?" Trixie stared at her empty plate. "Bring me some rice pudding, please Sophie."

Sophie returned. "Could you try compassionate leave?"

Trixie leaned into Sophie and whispered, "They don't know I'm married. Remember? I doubt they'd give me leave to visit a boyfriend and if I confess, they'll send me home. I do miss him."

"Why don't we find out when we're entitled to leave and plan ahead? Maybe Chris could coordinate his leave."

"Let's try that, but how would I get to Paris?"

126

"By train I imagine. Did he say where he was? He must be in France."

"He's not allowed to say, same as us here." Trixie waved, beckoning to Sister Potter. Sophie grabbed her arm, pulling it to her side, afraid Sister Potter would mention the new arrival before she broke the news.

Trixie frowned. "What are you doing? Here comes Sister. She'll know about leave."

Sophie whispered, "I have something to tell you."

"What?" Trixie answered with a hint of annoyance but nothing more was said.

Sister Potter arrived in a flurry, skirts flapping, tea spilling from her cup and, as always, her face lit up with a smile. "Oh, it's good to sit down," she said as she plonked on the chair. "I will be glad with another pair of hands. Managing all the wards is more than I can handle."

Sophie nodded, not wanting to ask but rather curious as to why Sister Singleton was not making herself known. Sister's last comment had not raised Trixie's interest she was too focused on Chris and possible leave.

"Sister, can I ask you about leave?" Without waiting for an answer. Trixie continued. "My boyfriend has some leave coming and he wants to meet me in Paris."

"Leave! Paris! Nurse King, you've hardly settled in. I'm afraid it will be some time before you get any leave. A day off is about the sum of it until possibly the spring. Except in an emergency of course." Her forehead creased with a questioning frown. "Paris is some distance from here, requiring a lengthy train journey and accommodation." She was alerted at the word 'accommodation.' "Paris is not appropriate for sweethearts without chaperones." She gave a wistful smile. "But, when all this is over, it might be a nice place for a honeymoon. Your beau will have to wait."

Trixie blushed, understanding the implications. She glanced at Sophie who realized how much Trixie wanted to say 'but we are married.' She also made a note that when they did get leave, it might be better to omit the boyfriend. Sophie finished her rice pudding and once again started to tell Trixie about Sister Singleton, this time interrupted by the bugle as a convoy arrived.

The reception area was crammed with injured men. A queue, longer than any bread line she'd seen in London, snaked around the wards, inside and out. Men waiting for a life line, not for bread, but surgery. The very worst yet were a chain of blinded soldiers, marching, if you could call it marching, in single file, arms outstretched, holding the shoulder in front of them. At first they were silent, then there was the sound of heaving and coughing from gas poisoning.

These soldiers were ushered into a separate tent to avoid exposing others to the residue that clung to their clothes. The nurses worked to dispose of uniforms and clean mud and lice from the men before treatment could start. Some things Sophie would never get used to, lice being one of them.

Sophie paid little attention to the animals, tucked away in the veterinary unit at the far end of the camp. It must have been a brutal battle as the scream of injured horses and the howl of dogs rang in her ears. Veterinarian surgeons worked to save injured animals, horses that pulled gun carriages, dogs that sniffed out explosives and injured soldiers. They were all part of the war.

Matron sent several nurses, including Sophie and Trixie, to get an hour's rest before going back on duty. The two plodded along the duckboard. Sophie looked up at the dawn sky with a diminishing pink hue on the edge of dark, rain laden clouds. She found it matched her feelings, a little pink hope being engulfed in dark hopelessness. She gave her head a shake. Such morose thoughts were brought on by the night's events, exhaustion and the prospect of facing Sister Singleton. She turned to Trixie, ready to tell her the news before something else interrupted them.

"I have something to tell you. Matron has a replacement for Dragon Sister and you will never guess who it is." Sophie grimaced. "How she managed to get here, and in a position of authority, I will never know." Sophie sensed a movement by the surgical unit. Thinking it might be Emily, she stopped but only saw a lone surgeon, propped against the surgical unit wall, crumpled with exhaustion. She inhaled sharply, recognizing Carlos, his eyes focused into the distance. She had the urge to wave, even comfort him, but, for many reasons, that couldn't happen. She doubted he had seen her anyway.

"Are you going to tell me? Who is it?" Trixie said, irritated at Sophie's distraction.

"Oh yes, sorry. I thought that was Emily over there and she could hear it too. I'm so sorry. It's Sister Sin."

"What! How did she get here? I thought she'd been relegated to the convent? Who told you? Maybe it's a mistake."

"It was Carlos. He was on the same train coming here. But now you mention it, perhaps he was wrong. He told me yesterday and I haven't seen her. Peculiar as we had a convoy

129

last night and that's all hands-on deck. One would expect her to assist. Matron hasn't said anything and, as yet, no introductions."

"I can't face the woman. She's disgusting and cruel." Tears rimmed Trixie's eyes and anxiety knit her brow.

"I am sorry. Perhaps she's changed. How else would she get here?" Sophie suggested with little conviction. Sister Sin's type didn't change and, in her role, third in command, she was likely to cause all kinds of trouble. "Try not to worry. Tell me more about your letter from Chris."

"Not much to say. He can't say where he is or talk about his missions. But he misses me. I wish I could meet him in Paris."

Sophie woke to someone shaking her shoulders. "Wake up. Sister Potter is looking for you."

"Emily, what time is it? Have you only just finished?"

"Almost nine o'clock. Surgery is still going on but Captain Evans insisted I get some rest." Emily blushed slightly. "He's such a thoughtful gentleman, not like the major."

"Oh gosh, we are late. Matron said an hour and it's more than two. Was Sister Potter mad? Not that she ever gets upset."

"No. She needs you on the C Ward. Kitty is by herself."

Sophie splashed cold water on her face and slipped her uniform on, having slept in her undergarments. "You'd better wake Trixie too. Have a nice sleep. I must go. Oh, I almost forgot, be kind to Trixie, she's really upset. Guess who Dragon Sister's replacement is?" Sophie paused for effect. "Sister Singleton!"

"I don't believe you. Are you teasing?"

"No. She arrived on the same train as Carlos but I haven't seen her. Sorry, I have to run."

Sister Potter, Kitty and Matron were tending to the patients when Sophie arrived. "My apologies, Matron. I fell asleep."

Matron smiled. "You needed some rest. It's going to be a busy day. Sister Potter will help you settle these patients. More are coming. The orderlies are bringing more cots and bedding. The volunteer aids will make up the beds when they've finished on A Ward."

Sophie looked at the cramped ward, wondering how it was possible to fit in any more beds. She nodded obediently at Matron.

"Sister Potter and I will be busy orienting the new sister, Sister Singleton."

So, it was true. Sophie hesitated, unsure of what to say, until the words just came out. "Sister Singleton was at the Bartley."

Matron halted her face taught as she turned to Sophie. "The Bartley? I was under the impression she came from the convent. You know her?"

"I do. There was …an incident." Sophie deliberately hesitated. "She is very religious and left the Bartley for the convent to pray and reflect."

"Yes, I had noticed. She spent some time in the chapel last night." Matron smiled but the smile did not reach her eyes. "It will be nice for her to be welcomed by someone she knows."

Sophie raised an eyebrow and thought, *not a chance*, but said nothing. Matron had a puzzled expression as she left the ward.

Kitty nudged her elbow. "Private Carter has relapsed

from all the chaos of last night. Captain Cuthbert gave him morphine and he's sleeping. He was asking for you and someone called Gracie."

"Gracie is his sweetheart. I'll help you with the dressings. He's all right for now. Where is everyone?"

"Still receiving casualties in reception. Whatever happened last night, it was big. One of the patients said it was a surprise attack and they weren't prepared. Some didn't have their gas masks on." Kitty hesitated, "That's lethal. I've seen a lot but gas injuries are the worst."

Teddy called from the entrance. "Mornin', Nurses. Where would you like these cots?" He pointed to a cart loaded with bed frames and temporary cots.

Sophie shook her head, "I don't know where to start."

"'Ere let me give you an 'and. I've done this a few times. See those beds at the bottom? We can move 'em a bit closer together and get a cot on each side. The rest we can put in the centre. It don't leave much room to get around but it's only temporary. Most will be moved on to Base Hospital." He grinned. "See, always a solution."

Sophie appreciated Teddy's cheerful attitude and returned his reassuring grin. "Teddy to the rescue. Thank you."

"Follow me." Teddy led the way to the bottom of the ward and stood between two beds. "Mornin', lads. We's doing a bit of moving house today. Some of your mates are joining ya. Nurse here will help you up and then I'm gonna move your beds." Teddy put on a serious but animated face. "Now I don't want to sound like your mam, Private, but make sure you pack all your stuff." For a few seconds the soldier stared at Teddy, and Sophie frowned until she realized Teddy was teasing and smiled as he continued. "I reckon ya mam's a tough one for being tidy."

Both soldiers laughed and played along with Teddy's teasing. "Aye, she is that. She'd be whipping my behind. Not much to pack."

"That's good. I hope you like sardines 'cause you gonna be packed like 'em. But these nurses'll take care of ya."

"Enough with the jokes," Sophie said, grinning from ear to ear. "I need to help these men get out of bed."

Sophie and Kitty worked all day, comforting new patients and rearranging the ward. Teddy and Buster hammered beds together while the young aids put clean white sheets on the new mattresses, hardly having time to fold the neat hospital corners before the stretchers arrived, some from post-surgery, others from reception.

Finally, Kitty and Sophie stepped back, waiting for the next shift of nurses to relieve them, when they had company. Sister Potter and Sister Singleton walked on to the ward. Sweet Sister Potter was looking harassed and even more unkempt than usual. Sister Singleton stood statue-like as though a rod had been pushed down her back and a puppeteer's strings held her chin and nose up to the sky.

"Sister, C Ward is known to care for shell-shocked patients as well as physical injuries." Sister Potter's voice was as cheery as always, but Sophie sensed some of it was forced. "Nurse Wilkes has been with us for nearly two years. Nurse Romano arrived in September but has some expertise with shell-shocked patients."

Sophie's name had prompted surprise and possibly anxiety from the statue-like sister. Her eyes pierced right into Sophie and as she opened her mouth to speak. Sophie felt the hatred. "Well, what a surprise to see you, Nurse Romano. One of my difficult probationers, not nurse quality at all. But then in times of war, one cannot be choosy."

"What a small world we live in, Sister. And a long way from the Bartley. Welcome to our casualty clearing station," Sophie said, the last phrase almost choking her.

"How strange. Nurse Romano is one of our most accomplished nurses and especially skilled in shell shock." Sister Potter's voice had a sarcastic tone, rarely heard.

"We'll see about that. Shell shock is nothing more than an excuse for sinful behaviour. I see I have my work cut out here."

Sophie rolled her eyes with a reassuring smile to Sister Potter. "If you'll excuse me, I have a patient to attend to."

Sophie sat by Carter's bed with one eye on Sister Sin as she strode around the ward. Sister Potter, looking flushed and exhausted, seeming to shrink at her side even though, in the order of command, she outranked Sister Sin. A knot of apprehension gripped her. Sister Singleton had already made her unpleasant mark on this hospital.

Carter groaned, opening his eyes. The fear had gone. He even smiled, although he was groggy, making his eyelids droop. Captain Cuthbert had kept him sedated all day. She held his hand until he slipped into a fitful sleep. Too tired to stay, Sophie joined Kitty and Trixie in the mess. She was grateful to see soup at the food table. That was all her tired body could take. Trixie was pale and anxious. She had told Kitty about Sister Sin's attack on her and how she lured young nurses into unseemly and abusive relationships.

Sophie kept thinking she had forgotten something in all the chaos of the last twenty-four hours. The normal routine had been abandoned for crisis care. What had she forgotten?

Then she remembered Jo. She'd promised Andrew she would talk to her. Willing her legs to support her, she excused herself, grabbed two cups of tea and headed to the Women's Ward.

14

Nightmares

Jo had company. Several ambulance drivers were suffering from gas poisoning, mostly transferred from the soldier's uniforms. It was not as bad as the soldiers but enough to take them out of commission. Sophie sighed. This was not good news as Sergeant Harcourt, short of drivers, would be wanting Jo back on the road and Jo would be only too willing to oblige.

Sophie took a very deep breath, putting energy into her tired legs and marched to Jo's bed. "Hello, Jo. How are you feeling today?" She almost dropped the tea as a barrage of curses assaulted her ears. "Jo, what's wrong?"

"You ask me that. Bloody hell. I thought you were a friend, not a gossip, spreading rumours and implying I can't do my job. Despicable, Nurse Romano." She smirked, wiping spittle from her chin. "I've come across snivelling meddlers like you before."

"Jo, I don't know what you are talking about. Here, have some tea and tell me what's wrong."

Jo huffed. "That's a good one. I've dealt with people like

you all my life but I thought we were chums. A friend I could trusted and confided in." Her face filled with rage.

"Calm down, please! Tell me what happened?" Sophie handed her the mug, "Here, have some tea while it's hot."

"Calm down!" she mimicked, grabbing the mug. "I don't want any bloody tea," she said as she threw the mug across the room, narrowly missing Sophie's head.

The duty nurse rushed over, instructing an aide to call the orderly. "Mrs. Griffith, that is quite enough. We can talk about this like sensible people."

"Talk. Do you have the slightest idea what this woman has done to me?"

"No, Mrs. Griffith. That is precisely my point. Please explain your dilemma. Nurse Romano is right, you need to calm down."

Jo took a breath, her face paled as the purple rage lessened to deep pink of anger. Her jaw tight and lips pursed, she stopped shouting. Sophie detected shame in her moist eyes, something Sophie never expected to see in Jo. Was that causing her anger?

"Jo…"

Before Sophie could continue, Jo mumbled another barrage of curses mostly under her breath and all she heard was "Mrs. Griffith to you."

"Mrs. Griffith, I can't help unless I understand the problem."

Tears streamed down Jo's face as she began screaming and cursing again, words Sophie had never heard and others she'd rather not hear.

The last outburst seemed to lose ferocity as though her words were all spent. But something inside snapped and she suddenly lashed out, punching Sophie in the chest, then in the face and raising her arm to land another punch just as Teddy appeared and pulled her arms behind her back.

Jo stared beyond Sophie to the other patients watching with eager anticipation. *For what,* Sophie thought, *a fight?* No one spoke for several minutes, relieving the tension but not for long. The break having energized Jo, she screamed towards the onlookers, "And you lot can gawk somewhere else. This isn't a Barnum & Bailey Circus show and you, you bastard..." Jo swung around as Andrew entered the ward. "And you, you can go fuck off." The crowd gasped at such a word.

The nurse hustled the patients back to their beds and Andrew went to find Major Hughes, leaving Sophie to cope with Jo. With a lack of sleep and a hectic night and day, Sophie was near collapse herself. Her face throbbed and warm blood trickled down her cheek. Hurt by Jo's outburst, she felt confused, having no idea what she had done to cause it. Jo did not seem herself. Beyond the anger, Sophie wondered if the outburst was a symptom of war nerves. She was certainly a colourful character but her behaviour was excessive, even for Jo. Having finally calmed down, she allowed Teddy to guide her to her bed. She lay down, holding her head.

"Do you have a headache?" Sophie asked tentatively, not sure what kind of an answer might come.

"Bloody pounding." Jo squeezed her eyes and a tear lingered in the corner before rolling down the side of her face. She was in great pain, most likely from the rage. Sophie was not fooling herself. Whatever had triggered Jo's anger had not gone away, only been displaced by the pain in her head. Sophie rinsed out a cloth, placing it on Jo's forehead. Sensing no resistance, she gently held her wrist and felt her racing pulse. She was about to call for the doctor when Sister Potter led Captain Cuthbert and Major Hughes through the ward.

Andrew glanced at Sophie with concern and then at the patient, waiting for Sophie to explain. "Mrs. Griffith has calmed down but is complaining of a severe headache and her pulse is very fast."

Jo opened her eyes, a grimace on her face she looked past Andrew to Major Hughes and in a whisper said, "I want to see Major Hughes. The rest of you can leave."

Major Hughes peered at her head wound, no longer bandaged, gave a sort of grunt and said, "Sister, stay." He wafted his hand to dismiss Andrew and Sophie.

Andrew hesitated but Sophie gave him a surreptitious push, whispering, "it's best if we leave."

"What happened to your face? Let's get that attended to. What was going on? Nurse said Mrs. Griffith was having a fit, yelling and throwing things at you." Andrew sat Sophie down and called the nurse to tend to her injury, a small, superficial cut, and a bruise already forming.

"I'm not sure. She thinks I betrayed her in some way. But why? The pain in her head could be serious and possibly related."

"I should be there. It sounds as though she's suffering from mental fatigue."

"Perhaps, but she flew into such a rage I was afraid it might happen again if we didn't leave. Surely Major Hughes will call you if needed?"

"Doubtful, I'm afraid. The illustrious surgeon has made it very clear he doesn't believe in psychiatrists. *Twaddle* was the term he used, in front of Colonel Belingham who was not impressed. Fortunately, I have an ally in the Colonel."

"And Matron," Sophie added, brushing the back of her hand

across her forehead and rubbing her eyes. She was so tired it was an effort to concentrate.

Andrew nodded. "I do believe Mrs. Griffith is suffering from some form of neurosis, but the sudden and extreme headache is more likely to be the head injury. I'm assuming you were visiting at my request."

"I was, and it wasn't the reception I expected…" Sophie felt herself sway. Her legs wouldn't move and her head was spinning. Suddenly she felt her stomach lurched and she turned away, afraid she would vomit. But her heaves just made her head spin even faster. The last thing she remembered was Andrew calling her name and his strong arms catching her as she collapsed.

Coming back into the world, Sophie kept her eyes closed, mortified she had fainted again in Andrew's arms. Something she had done several times at the Bartley, all by coincidence, but it was still embarrassing. *Where was she?* It felt familiar and she heard Trixie talking and Emily's soothing voice as she sponged her forehead. It felt nice and cool. She listened harder for more voices but heard only her friends.

"She's coming around. Sophie, can you hear me?"

"Emily, what happened? I'm in my own bed?"

Emily nodded. "You collapsed in Captain Cuthbert's arms. Under other circumstances I'd say *how romantic* except you have been out cold for some time."

"How did I get here? The last thing I remember was leaving the Women's Ward and suddenly feeling dizzy. I thought I was going to be sick." She stopped talking, pink flushing her very pale cheeks. "Oh, please tell me I didn't vomit all over him." She swallowed hard, feeling queasy, but there was no unpleasant taste in her mouth.

"He looked fine, when he carried you in here," Emily said, with a giggle. "He said something about a *fight* resulting in the cut and bruise on your face and that you had fainted from exhaustion. He asked us to take care of you, and if you didn't come around in the next few minutes to call Matron."

"Probably didn't want to be caught in nurses' quarters." Trixie laughed.

Sophie eased up on her elbows and sank back into her pillow as her head began spinning. "Did he really carry me here?"

"He did! Quite the hero, carrying a damsel in distress. An excellent story for a Penny Dreadful." Emily gave a wry grin. "What happened tonight? I thought you were going to visit Jo Griffith."

"It is a long story. The events of tonight will explain why Andrew, um…Captain Cuthbert brought me here."

"Perhaps it should wait until morning." Emily tapped her hand, concern creasing her forehead.

"I'm so tired and, to be honest, I have no idea what caused Jo's outburst." Sophie yawned. Exhaustion taking over, she pulled the covers up to her chin and fell into a deep sleep.

An eerie mist swirled around a solitary figure standing in a mud sodden field. Leafless trees rattled like skeletons, the earth groaned, heaving up and down in tune with lingering howls in the distance. What was that? Where was she and where was everyone? Her words only echoed, returning to her in silence. A shape emerged on the horizon, a horse and rider galloping at speed, the light catching the blade of a sword as it moved closer, the rider yelling muted curses. In the distance two shadows wearing white coats rose above the ground. Relieved, she screamed for help, but the shadows faded into the mist. Silence. All she heard was the pounding of her heart.

Too late, a voice in her head called, 'Run! Run!' She couldn't move. The quagmire was sucking her deeper into the groaning earth. The horse's thumping hooves drew closer, so close she could see its nostrils open like caverns, its hot breath hitting her face and its cry of anguish assaulting her ears. The rider lunged with the sword and Jo's wild face leered at her. She screamed, "No!"

Her scream jolted her from sleep. Catching her breath, her eyes sprang open. Emily was beside her, a cool cloth on her forehead. Trixie's hand held hers.

"Sophie, wake up. You're having a nightmare."

"I was right there, in no-man's land, being sucked into the quagmire. It was horrible." She was shaking. Gripped with fear and grateful for her friends, she gave a guilty grin. "I was screaming, wasn't I? I woke you."

"You've been tossing and turning and talking in your sleep most of the night." Emily took the flannel off her head and felt it. "You may have a fever, but you don't feel hot."

"I'm all right. Overtired and Jo's attack really upset me. The nightmare was Jo coming for me on a horse with a sword. She wanted to kill me." Sophie gave a nervous laugh. "I know she was angry, but angry enough to kill me? I still can't figure out what I've done." Sophie sat up, taking a sip of water she glanced at her friends. "You don't know about Jo."

"Captain Cuthbert gave us a brief account when he brought you here, mostly to explain why it was unwise to take you to the Women's Ward," Trixie said. "But I don't understand. You've been kind to her."

"I don't either. She says I spread rumours about her. It does not make sense." Sophie yawned, followed by both Trixie and Emily. "I think we need to get some sleep before we hear our wowter call."

"Are you sure you're all right?" Emily asked.

"I'm fine. Now get some sleep." Sophie yawned again and slipped under the covers.

She listened, as she so often did, to her companions' rhythmic breath as they slept. Her eyes fluttered and closed but no-man's land spilled into her mind and fear tugged at her chest, making it hard to breathe. She forced her eyes to stay open and stared at the roof of the tent, listening to the soothing pitter-patter of rain on the canvas and trying to make sense of Jo's outburst and her strange nightmare.

Jo was a strong woman, someone she admired. She wasn't some frivolous maiden prone to delicate nerves, drawing room swoons or fits of hysteria. Sophie was aware that the latter was frequently labeled by fathers and husbands as insanity or female neurosis in an attempt to control what they considered as wayward wives or daughters doing nothing more than voicing opinions. She gave a wry grin. *Even in war time, with women working alongside men, some could not comprehend that a female mind was as intelligent as the male. I was so lucky to have a father who treated me as his equal. How I miss you, Papa!*

Her mind wandered to other men in her life. The two white coats in her dream. Could they be Carlos and Andrew? *Carlos treated me with respect and yet he married one of those frivolous damsels. His mother's strong influence.* She stifled a laugh. *Mama's little boy. Andrew has always treated me as an equal in a professional sense, discussing patients' treatments. However, his opinion of me, the woman, might lean towards damsel in distress as I do faint in his arms, rather too frequently.* She felt her cheeks grow warm, hoping he hadn't remembered the other times at the Bartley. *Perhaps I am as weak as a drawing*

143

room damsel. Aware her last thought was laughable, she heard her father say, *You are the son we never had, my Sophie. Strong as any man. Was it significant that neither of the men in my dream, came to my rescue? But I cannot deny the trauma of my early life and certain things here on the Western front triggered those memories, leaving me feeling helpless. Was that Jo's problem too? She's certainly not a damsel in distress, but she is troubled.* Sophie's eyelids began closing, so tired she slipped into a restful sleep.

15

Foreboding Clouds

"Wakie, wakie, my beautiful nurses, 'ot wowter is here!" Buster called out, waking all three with a start. Having slept hard as a result of last night's events. Sophie couldn't open her eyes, her body felt heavy, her head woozy, definitely not well rested. She was worried how she was going to get through the day, afraid she might collapse again. As if her words had been heard, Sister Potter appeared at their tent.

"Sister Potter!" Trixie called. "Come in. Is something wrong?"

"No, no, nothing is wrong. Matron sent me to talk to Nurse Romano."

Sophie stayed under the covers, guilt gripping her stomach. What had she done now? She was too tired to deal with anything else, even sweet Sister Potter. She wanted everyone to go away and leave her alone.

Emily whispered, "She's still sleeping. She had bad nightmares last night. The incident with Mrs. Griffith really upset her."

"That's why I'm here. Now you girls run off and get your breakfast. There is much to do today."

Sophie stretched and sat up, swinging her legs to the floor. "I'm up, I'll join you in the canteen. Sister Potter, I'm sorry about yesterday. I honestly don't know what I did to upset Mrs. Griffith."

Sister pulled up a chair and sat beside the bed. "Mrs. Griffith had surgery last night to relieve some pressure on her head. She's doing fine but Major Hughes attributes the outburst to the head injury. Matron thought it might help if you understood the patient's condition. Also, she is concerned about your health. How is the bruise?"

Sophie lifted her hand to her cheek, which felt swollen and sore to the touch. Then she froze. Did they think she had neurasthenia? Had Matron at the Bartley told them of her problems or worse, had Andrew?

"Captain Cuthbert spoke with Matron this morning and told her about your collapse." Sister hesitated as Sophie took an audible gasp of breath. "In light of the events, he explained to Matron he took you to your tent and not the Women's Ward, knowing Nurse King and Nurse Finnegan would take care of you." She smiled before continuing. "I suspect he needed to explain the perceived impropriety. I think he might have a fondness for you, perhaps from working with him in London."

Sophie wanted to hide, fearing she might blush. At first relieved to hear Sister's concern was for her physical health, her reference to London was troubling and Sophie wasn't sure what the conversation was really about.

"Major Hughes has left strict instructions that neither you nor Captain Cuthbert are to speak to Mrs. Griffith, which is why I am here." She fidgeted with her apron. "Major Hughes doesn't believe in, shall we say, illnesses of the mind. Not an opinion shared with either Matron or Colonel Belingham. He's a most unpleasant man." Sister hesitated, a rare hint of anger in her usually soothing blue eyes. "Enough said." Sophie had the sense that Sister would have liked to say a lot more.

"Matron would prefer you report to the Women's Ward for some rest, but that isn't possible. She asked me to assess your condition and see if you are well enough to report to duty. How are you feeling?"

"Rest assured, I will stay away from Mrs. Griffith. One tongue lashing is quite enough. I am sorry her head wound has worsened. I hope she recovers quickly." Sophie sat forward. "Sister, honestly I am fine and feel quite healthy. Tired, but then so is everyone else. I assure you I am fit for duty." Her words sounded hollow. She was to the point of exhaustion but she could not afford to collapse again, nor could she appear weak.

Sister felt Sophie's forehead and held her wrist, feeling her pulse. "No fever. Your pulse is a little fast. I see no reason why you shouldn't return to duty. Please go and have a good breakfast. Nurse Wilkes needs some help with Private Carter. And, Nurse Romano, take it easy today, please. If you collapse again, you could be sent home."

Sophie gave a nod. "Yes, Sister."

She dressed quickly and was delighted to see eggs and bacon for breakfast, a rare treat. The bread was stale and needed to soak in the tea to be chewable. She ate heartily, feeling much better as she paced along the duckboard.

"I am glad to see you but Trixie said you were unwell," Kitty

147

said, with a sigh of relief.

"Just overtired. I passed out last night in front of Captain Cuthbert so Matron was informed. Sister Potter had to make sure I was fit for duty. I'm fine this morning. Sister Potter said Private Carter needs help."

"He's not doing well. Night nurse said he had nightmares most of the night. At times he seems all right and others he's out of it. He must have quite the John Dory."

Sophie raised an eyebrow. "John Dory?"

"Oh sorry, me cockney rhyming. I sometimes forget. John Dory means his story. Could you sit with him for a while? He seems to know you."

"Story, John Dory. I like the rhyming. Anything you need me to do before I sit with him?"

"We've got a full staff today. Some patients have been moved to Base Hospital and there are a few with Blighty tickets due to leave soon. Still a bit crowded, but we can manage."

"That's good news for some. Has Captain Cuthbert been in this morning?"

"He was here earlier. Why?"

"I just thought he might have some instructions."

"If there are any, they'll be on his medical card." Kitty frowned, puzzled by Sophie's question.

Sophie picked up the card and scanned its contents. The only note was the time of last injection. "Good morning, Private! How are you feeling today?"

"Better, now I'm awake. Nurse, when will the nightmares stop?" Sophie touched his hand, encouraging him to release the sheet he was twisting and holding as if it was a life line.

"As time goes by, they will lessen. It helps to think about nice things. Remember the last time you saw Gracie. What did she say to you?"

He nodded a reply, his lips trembling. He pulled his hand away and scrubbed at his eyes. "I'm afraid I'll never see her again." He grabbed the sheet again to stop his hands trembling and Sophie patted the top of his hand.

"Tell me about home. Do you ever hear from Connor? If my memory is correct, you two are old school friends?"

"We's go back a long way. Our dads work at the docks, our mams gossip together." He leaned back, relaxing, and managed a grin at the memory. "Connor don't write much. I receive letters from Gracie regular. She says he's getting better, except I dunna believe her. Mam says Mrs. Connor worries about 'im. And now it's me. I want to go home but how can I like this?"

"You will get better and your mam will be happy to have you home."

"Do you know if I'll get a Blighty ticket? I just canna go back to that hell."

"I don't know. That's the doctor's decision but Captain Cuthbert is a good man. Have you written to your mother?"

"I dunno what to say."

"We'll do it together. Your mam will be worried, so let's write her a letter." Sophie found a pen and a sheet of paper, somewhat crumpled but it would do.

As soon as he started writing, he scribbled the whole page and asked Sophie for more paper to write to Gracie. She glanced up and saw Captain Cuthbert heading her way. Trying not to blush, she greeted him with an overly cheery, "Good morning!"

"Good morning, Nurse Romano! How are you feeling today?" Sophie caught an emphasis on the *how are you* part and she suddenly felt hot and clammy. "I'm surprised to see you on duty."

"I am quite well, thank you, Doctor. And Private Carter is much improved today."

"I see that. Writing home, Private?"

"Yes, Sir! Nurse is helping me."

"Nurse Wilkes tells me you had some bad nightmares last night."

Sophie went outside to give them privacy, glad of the cool air and rain on her hot face. She ran to 'Teddy's Place' for shelter and joined Pippa who was smoking.

"You have such a gentle way with crazy patients. That poor man was writhing in agony when I came on duty this morning, screaming and fighting imaginary aggressors," Pippa said, adding, "I dropped a pair of forceps on the floor and the noise triggered him."

"I like working with nervous patients, and have some experience from London. Pippa, try not use words like crazy. These men are as ill as those with crushed limbs or fevers. You have a talent. I've watched you talk to these soldiers. Sometimes all they need is someone to listen."

"I'll try." Suddenly the clouds released torrents of rain without warning. "Oh my goodness, look at that rain. Come on!" Pippa called and the two ran giggling, back to the ward, bumping into Captain Cuthbert.

"Captain, it's raining!" Sophie blurted out.

Andrew ginned. "I can see that, Nurse Romano. Actually, I wanted to speak with you."

"Oh, of course. But it's raining,"

Andrew made no attempt to hide his amusement, his grin now laughter. "I am quite aware of the rain."

Sophie wanted the earth to swallow her up. *What is wrong with me? Obsessed by rain?* "I was just thinking it's too wet to go outside." A loud clap of thunder drowned her words.

"Sorry I didn't hear that," Andrew yelled over the thunder.

"Nothing," Sophie called as the rumble subsided.

"Right here will be fine," he said with smiling eyes. "I am pleased with the private's progress but it is early days. I don't believe he is as well as he seems but his progress makes it difficult to justify a Blighty ticket. I'm listing him as 'under observation.'"

"He's not well. The slightest thing will trigger an episode."

"I agree. So we wait." He stared at Sophie, making her feel uncomfortable. "I was surprised to see you. I suggested to Matron that you take a day off. You collapsed last night and this is not the first time. You are exhausted."

"I slept and feel quite well today," Sophie lied, embarrassed. Of course, he remembered the fainting episodes at the Bartley. "If there is nothing more, I must get back to work, Captain."

His grin had turned into a frown of concern, his eyes fixed on Sophie. "It is important you look after yourself so that you can nurse the patients." He looked away and sighed at the rain. "I shall make a run for it. We'll talk later."

Sophie knew he was right and she wondered why she was being so stubborn. It was too late so she'd have to pace herself throughout the day. She returned to Private Carter.

"The captain is pleased you are recovering well but he's keeping you for a while longer."

"Does that mean I have to go back to the front?"

"Not necessarily. You need to be well enough to travel, no matter where you are going, and that won't be for some while."

151

"He's a nice doctor, the captain, good to talk to." Carter smiled. "He's sweet on you, ya know. I sees the way he looks at you."

"We're colleagues, that's all. It's nice to see you smile and I remember how you teased Connor. Now get some rest. I'll come by later." Sophie had to shout to be heard over the rain that pummelled on the tent roof. Volunteer aids were running around, placing buckets where the tent leaked. Without warning there was a clap of thunder, followed by a flash of lightning. The ward erupted in fear. One patient curled up in the fetal position, crying. Another jumped out of bed, fighting for his life. Orderlies and nurses attempted to restrain him.

Sophie ran back to Carter, who was shaking violently, punching the imaginary enemies and narrowly missing Sophie's head. She reached for his hands to restrain him and called for help but he flung himself free. In less than a second he grabbed Sophie's neck. She heard a guttural sound come from her throat as he squeezed the life out of her. Kitty and Teddy ran over to release Carter's grip, just as Captain Cuthbert arrived with a syringe. Sophie fell on the floor, choking and gasping, Kitty took her arm and helped her to a chair. Feeling the dizziness, she bent her head over her knees and willed herself not to faint. *Please no, not again.*

The patient crumpled as the effects of the sedative took hold and Kitty tucked him back into bed. Captain Cuthbert glanced over at Sophie, who sat up straight, straining to focus as her head spun. She rubbed her neck, a bruise beginning to form on one side.

"Are you all right? Let me see." He examined her neck. "You'll have a nasty bruise. Does your throat hurt?"

"A little. I was taken by surprise," she croaked.

"The thunder triggered shell shock. He will sleep for a while. You need to take a break. It's quiet now. The storm has passed through." He beckoned to Sister Potter. "Sister, please insist Nurse Romano take a break. She's had a nasty shock."

"Sweet tea for you, Nurse. After me." Sophie obediently followed Sister's billowing, and now sodden wet, skirt. The rain had eased off to a steady drizzle. She was surprised to find them going to her tent. "You are to rest. I will be back with tea."

16

Solving Problems

The last thing she remembered was Sister Potter handing her a cup of hot, and very sweet, tea with orders to get into bed. She rubbed her neck. It felt stiff and sore. Private Carter's attack came back to her. She had been so frightened. His grip had been so strong and the poor man so delusional that only brute force from Teddy had stopped him from strangling her.

Moonlight lit up the tent as she awoke, rested from several hours sleep. She slipped out of bed, pulling on her greatcoat and boots. She saw a small circle of orange light. Someone was smoking under Teddy's shelter and she hoped it was Teddy himself. The moon disappeared behind the thick black clouds. It was almost pitch black as she walked towards the cigarette light, picking her way carefully to the shelter.

"Hello," she said, realizing it wasn't Teddy. The person was familiar but it was too dark to see features.

"Sophie, what are you doing up at this time of night?" Carlos took a long drag on his cigarette, lighting up his face.

"Carlos." Sophie felt her heart miss a beat. She had not

expected to see him. "I thought you were Teddy. He often has tea if he's working the night shift."

"I was on call. I just finished an emergency surgery and needed a break. It's too late, or early, to go back to bed. Teddy's not around tonight. Sorry, no tea. You are obviously not on duty so why up so early?"

She pulled her coat tighter around her, aware she was in her nightdress. "It's a long story. I almost slept around the clock and don't need any more sleep."

"I heard a patient attacked you. Two patients, I believe. Are you all right?"

"News travels fast around here. I'll be fine. My pride was hurt with one and a close call with the other."

"The pride one would be the ambulance driver."

"Yes, how did you know?"

"The esteemed, and very annoying, Major Hughes made a scene about you and Andrew interfering with his patient. I tried to put him straight but he's as narrow-minded as a fish."

Sophie chuckled. "A fish?"

He laughed. "The best I could think of. He's an extremely clever surgeon with no personality. A cold, wet fish comes to mind." He laughed again. "And the biggest and worst ego I've ever come across."

"Emily can't stand him either."

"Emily?" Carlos asked.

"Nurse King. She was on the children's ward in London. You might not have met her as she didn't live at River House."

"Ah, the Irish girl. She did seem familiar. Now I remember. One of the nicest, kindest nurses, especially with the young soldiers. More than I can say for the miserable Major Hughes. He should have returned to London. He was only here to

155

cover my leave but then I was sent to the Regimental aide Post and I hate to say it, but we need him right now."

"I wondered why your leave was so long." Sophie hesitated, part of her wanting to ask about his wedding. The other part she didn't want to know.

"Fancy us both being here. I was so surprised to see you, and then Andrew. Lots of Bartley people."

"Quite a coincidence, but then Matron Ross is a good friend of Matron at the Bartley so I think that's why the nurses are here. It may have been Matron's influence on Colonel Belingham that brought Andrew here as well."

"A small world." Carlos gave a sarcastic chortle. "And what about that pious sister? How did she get here? I thought she'd been sent back to the convent?"

Sophie shook her head. "I can't imagine Matron Hartford sending her here, but maybe she's repented."

"Unlikely. She uses her religion to cover up her cruelty and homosexuality." Carlos stared into the pre-dawn sky.

Sophie tried to hide the shock at his coarseness. As worldly as she was, his blatant language had offended her.

"She is a cruel, abusive woman. That has nothing to do with her sexuality." Carlos stated in a matter-of-fact manner.

"I agree with you." Sophie tried not to be embarrassed, discussing such things with a man. Even if it was Carlos, it was not appropriate. "How do you explain her cruel and abusive behaviour towards young women?"

"I can't except that cruel and abusive people have often suffered themselves. I think Andrew would know more about this subject."

"She scares me at times with her threats. She certainly doesn't like me. I'm afraid for the young nurses. Some of those volunteers see the world through the politeness of the drawing room." He didn't answer and she followed his gaze. The bright stars twinkled in a dark sky, the night reluctant to give way to morning. She realized there were no muffled gun shots, just a calm, peaceful scene that relaxed her. Or was it Carlos' presence?

"Matron and the colonel are good leaders. She won't fool them."

"I hope you're right," Sophie replied, her words full of doubt. "I'd better get back. Nice talking to you."

"Maybe we could have tea sometime?" Carlos called after her.

Sophie waved as she walked away, thinking it highly unlikely. After all, he was a married man. It was strange he never mentioned the wedding or Rosamond.

Although it was only 4:30 a.m., Sophie was wide awake, having slept for twelve hours, and felt better. She lit the lantern, turning it down low, and washed in cold water, flinching as the flannel caught the bruise on her face. She dressed quietly so as not to disturb Emily and Trixie. Her stomach growled loudly in the quiet and she couldn't remember the last time she ate. She was starving.

Cook was stirring a vat of porridge when she got to the canteen. He smiled. "You're up early, Miss. It'll be a few minutes yet. Tea's fresh and bread not too bad. Got jam today."

"Thank you." Sophie spread a thick layer of jam on top of the bread, feeling guilty at such extravagance. It tasted divine and the tea was hot and fresh. She giggled to herself, acknowledging how war had made her appreciate some of the simple things in life. She loved mornings and decided to take a walk, appreciating the lack of distant guns. She headed towards the woods. First there was a tweet from one bird, then two, then more until the morning chorus danced in her head. A slight breeze brushed her bruised cheek, the air fresh but not too cold. A cockerel crowed. *It must crow every morning*, she thought, and yet she couldn't remember hearing it. She walked by the chicken coup, a cacophony of clucking hens laying eggs. How could this be in the middle of a war zone?

Then the smell of disinfectant hit her nostrils and a horse whinnied. She was near the stables. She jumped when a dog barked. Dispensable animals to save human life. She wondered if they were cared for properly. Even in peace time people often treated animals as things. Annoyed with herself for spoiling her pleasant mood and quiet morning walk, she thought about peace time.

She'd never ridden a horse or owned a pet of any kind. She couldn't quite imagine herself clutching a small Pekinese dog, the kind found with neurotic ladies in stuffy drawing rooms. The closest to live animals she had experienced were the silkworms on the farm when she was a little girl. Now she thought about it, her father and uncle always cared for the tiny creatures. But silkworms were a far cry from horses and dogs.

She recalled the conversation with Jo, admiring her love and respect of horses and the gentle way she spoke of her dogs. Sophie could relate to the affection and love for something that was shared with her father. It must be invigorating to ride a horse across an open meadow.

Sophie stopped walking, the answer striking her like a bolt of lightning. "That's it. Horses and neurotic ladies!" She shouted to the trees. "Why didn't I think of that sooner?! Now I know why Jo was so upset with me. It makes so much sense."

She hurried back to the camp, needing to talk to Jo, but remembered Major Hughes' orders. For a brief second, she considered disobeying. Not a good idea. It was a military hospital and the punishment for disobeying orders was rather excessive. If it was anyone else other than Major Hughes, she might have taken the risk.

"Andrew. I need to find Andrew. He will know what to do."

Having dallied in the woods, Sophie was almost late for duty and had no time to search for Andrew. She hoped she could speak with him when he did his morning rounds.

Sister Potter greeted her on the ward. "There you are. We've been worried about you."

"Worried? Why?"

Sister's head went to one side with a derisive look, unusual for the easy-going Sister. "Yesterday you were quite ill and distraught and this morning you are nowhere to be found. I only discovered by accident that you were up and quite well, according to the breakfast cook."

"Oh Sister, I am very sorry. I woke up at 4 a.m. well rested after twelve hours of sleep. I got up, had an early breakfast, and went for a walk in the woods. As you can see, I am quite well." She put her hand to her face. "The bruise is tender and my neck a little sore but nothing more. I am quite recovered."

"No harm done but, in future, maybe leave a note for your roommates."

Sophie gave a compliant nod and moved into the ward to start the morning routine of dressing wounds, taking temperatures and making beds.

Currently the men were all up-patients. Other than assistance with jackets or trousers, they could wash, dress and attend the canteen for meals.

Private Carter still confined to his bed, needed help. Sophie intended to get him out of bed though. The night's attack had unnerved her but she needed to get back in the saddle, as Jo would say. Aware that the thunderstorm had triggered the episode, it was unlikely to happen again.

Leaving Kitty and Pippa to finish the dressings, Sophie went to Carter. He was trying to drink his tea but his hands shook so badly the tea spilled before it got to his mouth. He put it down, leaning his head back in frustration.

"Let's try that again," Sophie said.

He sat up, waiting for Sophie to bring the mug to his mouth but she didn't. Instead, she poured half the tea into an empty cup and handed him his mug. "Try this." He frowned, held the mug handle and took a sip of tea. Smiling he took a bigger sip. Not one drop spilled.

"Thank you, Nurse."

"How about some bread and jam? You can lift with your fingers." Sophie asked Pippa to fetch him some bread and jam and half a mug of beef broth. "You need to keep your strength up. Remember, if I'm not here, ask the nurse to only half fill your mug with liquid and stick with finger food. Just for now."

Sophie was happy to see him eat more and he seemed brighter. He rubbed his chin and she heard the raspy stubble. He had a thick beard for a young man. "Nurse, can I get a shave?"

Pleased he was showing an interest, she said, "That's a great idea but I'm not sure your hands are steady enough just yet.

How about I ask Teddy to give you a shave?"

"Okay." He grinned. "No offence, Nurse, but I'm not too keen on a woman shaving me. Teddy's all right."

"No offence taken, Soldier. Although, if I had to I could. Finish your tea and I'll find Teddy."

Stepping out of the ward to look for Teddy, she bumped into Andrew and almost fell over. Andrew grabbed her arm. "We really do have to stop meeting like this, Nurse Romano," he finished with a chuckle.

"Andr …I mean Captain Cuthbert. I'm so sorry. I didn't see you there. I was going to find Teddy to give a patient a shave. He doesn't really want a woman shaving him but I'm glad to see he's taking an interest. I need to talk to you about something else though. I had this great idea." Sophie stopped talking, aware she was babbling and probably sounding incoherent.

"Slow down. First, how are you feeling? That was quite an ordeal yesterday." He kept his hand on her arm, leading her away from the entrance.

"I am fully recovered. A good sleep was all I needed. I'm back on duty with no after effects, except a couple of bruises that will heal in time."

"Good. How do you feel about treating Private Carter?"

"I'm fine. He doesn't remember attacking me and he's doing much better this morning. He ate breakfast. We had to adapt things because of his tumbling hands but he asked for a shave. I was looking for an orderly when I collided with you."

"Excellent! I believe you said you wanted to discuss something else, unrelated to Carter?"

"It's about Mrs. Griffith. I've found a solution and maybe an explanation."

161

"You know we've been ordered to stay away," Andrew said tentatively.

"I wouldn't dream of crossing Major Hughes, but hear my thoughts and then we can see what we can do." Sophie gave a shiver. "Do you mind if we talk at the nurses' station? It's cold out here."

Andrew picked up a chart and they sat at the nurses' desk, as though discussing the chart. "I think Jo, Mrs. Griffith, was angry with me because she interprets treatment of trauma and/or shell shock as a weakness. We actually alluded to it earlier. I didn't associate it as a cause. Jo thinks we are treating her like a delicate drawing room lady prone to fainting and hysterics which, as we know, is laughable, as Jo is the last person to do that. She wants to be tough, like her male counterparts and like her father. Jo thinks I betrayed her, which I did not. But the fact that you went to talk to her made her think I had repeated what she had told me in confidence. I impugned who she is, who she believes is the true 'Jo Griffith.'"

"You might be right. A dainty, hysterical lady she is not and she would be furious with the implication. I see it all the time. Young capable women who bow to men's wishes afraid of being accused of neurosis or hysteria."

"I'm not finished yet. Given her head injury, it is unlikely she will be able to return to the ambulance corps. This will be devastating for her. She needs to get well, both physically and mentally, even if she disagrees with the latter. In one of our conversations, she told me how she and her father loved horses and she rode every day in peace time. What if we found her a position in the stables working with the veterinarians? I'm sure they could use the help. Jo would fill a void and be useful."

"Sophie," he said, lowering his voice. "You are brilliant."

"It sounds good in theory, but how do we get around Major Hughes?"

"I'll work something out. Maybe I'll see if Carlos can help us. She's recovering from surgery so we have some time before she's ready. I'll talk to the senior veterinarian. He's a nice chap. We met in the mess a few times. If it looks possible, I can speak with Colonel Belingham. Now we'd better get back to work."

17

Caring in War

The latest storm and deluge of rain had stirred the earth into thick, sticky glue that clung to everything. Grunts, groans and curses emanated above all other sounds as ambulances, lorries and any wheeled vehicle, even wheelbarrows and handcarts, were pushed and coerced into reluctant forward movement. The rain had stopped but it would be a while before the roads could support motor vehicles. Horses were the alternative.

Sergeant Harcourt bellowed orders to the ambulance drivers as they pulled up to reception. Not her usual crew, only those who could handle reins. The horses snorted, lips parted, nostrils flared, as if sneering at Sergeant Harcourt, aware of her discomfort around animals. An orderly stable boy held the reins and stroked its neck. The driver climbed down and patted the horse's flank. "Good job, old girl!" There were no walking wounded. Those casualties unable to walk with feet wrapped in trench slippers were either stretchered or piggy-backed into the reception. Jokes about horses and piggyback were rampant. One young Canadian fellow, being carried on an orderly's back, lifted his arm as though spinning a lasso and called 'giddy-up,' which set his mates, the nurses and orderlies into fits of laughter.

Sophie, on duty at reception, couldn't help herself and began laughing. The bravery of the young men astounded her at times. Even in pain and crisis, jokes and bantering kept coming.

It didn't take long to admit the first casualties. Thankfully the rain seemed to have subdued the fighting and battle injuries were few. She suspected a couple of the trench feet would require surgery. Others had hopefully been caught in good time. Trench foot was the result of wet feet clamped in boots, often for days at a time. The soldiers were instructed to remove their boots and socks and dry their feet every day, but they either forgot or didn't think it important. The army had initiated a buddy system to encourage the habit, which helped somewhat, but it was still a massive problem. Sophie pulled back the tent flap to get some air and remove the lingering smell.

Sergeant Harcourt yelled more orders as ambulances moved away, making room for the next wagon. She glanced towards Sophie who gave a smile, which was returned with a flash of anger as she jumped out of the way of two massive Clydesdales pulling a large wagon up to the quartermaster's store. Sophie wondered if the anger was directed at her or the horses. A bit of both she thought. If the sergeant was aware of Jo's experience with horses, she would be annoyed that Jo was not back on duty and would undoubtedly blame Sophie. It wasn't rational, as Jo's deteriorated condition had nothing to do with Sophie, but Sergeant Harcourt wouldn't see it that way.

What had started as a quiet day turned out to be long and tiring. Mud-caked men arrived constantly throughout the day. The reception area usually cleared quickly as patients were assessed, washed, had dressings changed and moved to a ward or the surgical unit. But that day the reception area was full, nurses and orderlies exasperated with the time it took to clean off the mud splattered soldiers. Even the dressings had to be soaked in peroxide before the bandages would come off.

A loud authoritarian voice boomed into the tent. "What the hell is going on here? My team is waiting! Captain Evans and Nurse Finnegan will collect those that need surgery." Major Hughes' presence filled the entrance. He wasn't a particularly big man but his self-righteous attitude formed a thick black cloud around him that pushed people away. Emily was standing behind him, next to a larger man bending down to whisper something to her. She gave a brief smile and glanced up at him. Obviously tired of waiting, the surgical team had come to claim their patients.

Sister Singleton, who had been as busy as all the nurses, stepped forward. "Major Hughes, collecting patients is highly irregular and quite unnecessary. The condition of these *mud-caked* patients…" Sophie noticed the emphasis on *mud-caked*. "…has taken more time than usual. None are in danger. These young men need to be cared for properly, not at the whim of an impatient sur…" She hesitated, hastily correcting her comment. "Impatient team." A wise move, Sophie thought, as directly criticizing a surgeon, particularly this one, would be grounds for reprimand. Sophie suppressed a grin. Major Hughes had met his match. *I think this will be very interesting. Perhaps the major would divert Sister's anger from the nurses.*

166

"You will find two patients have been delivered to the surgical unit and are waiting for you, just as impatiently." Sister gave a snort, returning to duty and eliminating any chance of a retort. The major visibly caught his breath, his face red with anger, or was it embarrassment? Sophie wasn't sure. Emily gave Sophie a shoulder shrug, a commiserating grin and mouthed 'Good luck.' Knowing that men like Major Hughes needed someone to blame and that would most likely be Emily, she noticed the other doctor had rested his hand protectively on Emily's back as they hurried to keep pace with Major Hughes.

She whispered under her breath. "Emily Finnegan, are you keeping secrets from us?" Sophie smiled. Emily deserved some love in her life, having given up so much to raise her sister and accepting that being close to her sister's family life was all she expected. Perhaps that could change.

"Nurse Romano, concentrate on your work. There's another ambulance coming. It looks like the last one for today." Sister Singleton pointed to a motorized ambulance. "The roads are drying out and passable."

Sister Sin's apparent change in attitude unnerved Sophie as she had braced herself for constant reprimand. *Could Sister Sin have repented after all?* She shook her head. *Not likely, but she had not used the words 'sinful' or 'God' all day, even in the altercation with the major.*

Sophie jumped as Sister Sin shouted. "Nurse Romano, how many times do I have to tell you?! Back to work. Your sinful ways are intolerable!"

Oh my goodness, here it comes, I spoke too soon, Sophie thought, unable to speak. Suppressing a giggle, she moved quickly towards the approaching ambulance. Mud up to its axles, it was hard to imagine how it had moved at all. The driver jumped out, also covered in mud. Glancing at Sophie she said, "Got stuck a few times. The boys have been in here a long time. Never complained."

"We'll soon have them cleaned up and comfortable." Sophie eyed the driver. "How are you? You look exhausted. Why don't you grab a cup of tea in the canteen? We'll see to these men."

"Thanks, but I'll stick around. I need to clean the bus. Sergeant is in a bad mood, judging by that frown." She motioned towards the sergeant who was backing away from a horse.

"You'd be right. She's not too keen on horse-drawn ambulances and you're the first motorized one we've had all day."

"I envied the horses as they passed me. We got stuck six times. I'm so glad to be here at last."

"I'll cover for you. See that shelter?" Sophie pointed to 'Teddy's Place.' "I see Teddy is there and he always has tea. It's almost dark and she won't see you. I'll keep my eye open and call you when we're done."

"Thanks. I'd like that."

Teddy gave Sophie a wave, lifting his mug. She waved back, wishing she could join him. Tea would be welcome but the patients came first. She glanced at her watch. Only an hour before they would be off for the night. Just four patients to assess and clean up.

"Nurse Romano!" The voice was familiar but she couldn't place it, nor could she see where it came from. Then a whisper. "Is that really you or am I dreaming?" She looked around, wondering if she was hearing things. She scanned the row of latest casualties, all looking much the same, skinny young men covered in mud. Then she saw a hand lift and a smile cracked the muddy face. "It's me! Stan. Stanley Maggs." His weak voice sounded forced to be heard. "I'd recognize my angel anywhere."

"Stanley?" Sophie asked.

"Fancy meeting you 'ere." He grimaced as he moved. Sophie glanced at the trench slippers and, judging by the odour, it was bad. Noting that in that stage it should be numb, she wondered why he was in pain.

"I could say the same thing. It's good to see you but you don't look too good, Stanley."

"Not at my best. A bit of shrapnel grazed me." He pointed to a tear in his uniform shoulder. "It stings a bit but is naut really. Me feet look as if the rats got 'um, but they don't hurt." He gave a sheepish grin. "I smell bad. Can you clean me up?"

"That's what I'm here for." Sophie brushed her hand across his forehead, surprised at how hot he felt. His coherency didn't indicate a high fever but his condition did. She gently removed his uniform and opened his shirt. The gash was not big but it appeared deep, red and oozing with infection. "Did they treat this at the aide post?"

"Na, it's just a graze, I didn't tell 'em about it."

"Private Maggs, you should have reported this injury. The wound is infected."

"Are you mad with me? Why did ya call me 'Private'?"

"Because the ward sister is coming. We are not allowed to use first names. And no, I'm not mad but, in future, you must report even the smallest wound." Sophie smiled to hide her concern, aware that even a minor infection could be lethal and, together with his infected feet, Stanley was in danger. "First we get you cleaned up and in clean pyjamas. The doctor will determine treatment. Tell me about your son, little Charlie, and your sister? How are they doing?"

"Charlie's growing up a treat. He's walking now and…" He winced as he put his arm into the sleeve of the pyjama top.

Sophie put clean dressings on his feet. "All done. The doctor will see you soon."

"Sooner than you think." Carlos' deep voice sent shivers down her spine. She stifled a gasp, annoyed at her reaction.

"Captain Wainwright!"

"That is me." He gave her a cheeky grin, mirroring her tone. "Nurse Romano!"

After examining Stanley's shoulder wound and feet, Carlos sighed, worry frowning across his forehead. He had seen the same as Sophie. That's what she liked about him. He didn't just stitch soldiers up, he cared about them.

"Private, the wound on your shoulder needs debridement. It's a fancy word for deep cleaning and is a surgical procedure. It's the only way to get all the infection. I think you know your feet are bad. There's no gangrene yet so we'll see if we can get them better without surgery." Carlos patted his leg, seeing his face blanch, most likely at the word gangrene, which soldiers perceived as meaning amputation. "You're going to be all right. You have the best nurse in the hospital."

"I know that, sir. She took care of my Millie before she died and found me sister to take care of my baby son, Charlie, when she were in London. She's a real angel."

Carlos looked at Sophie with a warm smile. "So, you know she's the best. It's a small world, Private. Now get some rest. Nurse, walk with me."

Carlos leaned in and whispered. "Sophie, I want to warn

170

you, things don't look good for Private Maggs. I might be able to save his feet. I'll get him into surgery right away for the shrapnel wound. The infection is deep. We'll treat the feet with salves and dry air and see if we can get the lesions to heal." He sighed. "Only time will tell."

Sophie lowered her voice. "Don't call me 'Sophie' here. I have Sister Singleton on my back. She will have a fit." Taking a breath, she raised her voice to a normal level. "Do your best. He's been through a lot."

"I'll do everything I can. Always the gentle, caring Sophie. I miss you."

"Shhh!" Sophie glared at him for ignoring her request. *Was he flirting? What did he mean 'I miss you'?*

"Nurse Romano, please have Private Maggs sent to surgical unit." Carlos' amused expression, teasing her with his formality, annoyed Sophie. *What was he playing at?*

"He likes you." Stanley winked.

"What? Oh no, nothing like that." In spite of herself, Sophie felt her cheeks warm. "I have known Captain Wainwright a long time, that's all. We're acquaintances. He worked at the Bartley. I have to leave now, but the orderly will take you to surgery. You'll find another face you know. Nurse Finnegan works in the surgical unit."

Stanley's face brightened. "I got the jackpot. Two of the best nurses. I'll be better in a jiffy."

"That's the spirit. I'll come and see you later."

Sophie wished she had as much confidence. Infections killed, probably more than guns. She had seen worse that had healed, although some had not. The wound looked nasty but his fever was manageable and Stanley was a strong man. She remembered how strong he'd been for Millie, and then for

Charlie. He had a lot to live for.

Glad the shift was over and Stanley in good hands, she hurried to the canteen for something to eat.

Mail bags, waiting for sorting, lined the outside of Matron and Colonel's offices, part of the morning Clydesdale's cargo. The mail from home lifted spirits. Sophie could feel people's mood change as they walked by. Not having any family, mail was not as important to her as it was to others. She did look forward to news from Hillary though. She knew Trixie was eager to hear from her secret husband, Chris, and letters from Emily's sister describing the antics of her niece and nephew always entertained them. Everyone needed that connection to loved ones.

"Nurse Romano!" Sophie stopped and sighed. *What now? All I want is to rest my legs and have a cup of tea.* She turned to see Matron standing outside her office. "A moment, please."

Matron held her office door open and motioned for Sophie to take a seat. She sat next to her, not behind her desk. Sophie felt nervous.

"My apologies. I'm sure you are tired after your shift but this can't wait. I had a request from Mrs. Griffith that she would like to see you."

Sophie's eyes widened in surprise. "Major Hughes forbade me and Captain Cuthbert from going near her. Mrs. Griffith herself made it abundantly clear that she did not want to see me." She instinctively touched her cheek. *I'm not about to be attacked again.*

"I have no explanation for her change of heart other than she said you had been a good friend to her." Seeing Sophie's hesitation, Matron added, "It's quite possible the head injury had something to do with her behaviour. Major Hughes relieved some of the pressure and she is quite calm now. Her recovery is slow and I suspect the trauma of the accident to be the problem. However, without a professional opinion, I'm merely guessing based on my experience…"

Sophie finished the sentence. "But she refuses to see Captain Cuthbert? What about Major Hughes' orders?"

"Colonel Belingham had…" Matron wavered. "Shall we say he had a chat with the surgeon?"

That sounds interesting, Sophie thought. *I'd like to have witnessed that chat.* She almost grinned but remembered where she was and replied. "I am happy to talk to her but I would like someone with me, at least at first."

Matron nodded. "I understand. Report to the Women's Ward at 7:30 a.m. tomorrow morning. I will make sure I am on the ward at that time."

"Thank you." Sophie hesitated waiting to be dismissed, her mouth dry from the anxiety and long day.

"I believe you mentioned you are acquainted with Sister Singleton. Is that correct?"

Sophie nodded her head. "She was in charge of training when I was a probationer at the Bartley."

"Really!" Matron reached over to her desk and picked up some papers. "Her papers indicate she was recruited from a convent in Warwickshire. The Bartley isn't mentioned. How long was she at the Bartley?"

"I don't know. She was there when I arrived and departed for the convent during my training. A very religious woman." Sophie hesitated.

"Is there something you are not disclosing?" Matron's expression gave nothing away. Sophie wasn't sure if the question was related to her own behaviour or Sister's.

"Sister didn't like me. I asked too many questions." She reflected on what to say next. "But there was an unpleasant incident that involved Nurse King. I am not comfortable saying more. Perhaps you could ask Matron Hartford at the Bartley?"

"Sister Potter had the impression there was some animosity between you. Your discretion is appreciated. I will write to Esther."

"Thank you." Sophie appreciated Matron's diplomacy and felt a warmness towards Sister Potter, always looking out for her nurses.

"That will be all. You look tired. Get some rest and I'll see you in the morning."

Sophie brushed her apron as she left Matron's office and realized she was splattered with mud. Feeling grubby from all the dirt and filthy uniforms infested with lice, she didn't want to be sociable. She grabbed a bowl of stew and headed to her quarters, stopping to ask Buster if he'd bring her some hot water for a wash.

18

Relationships

Buster arrived with two massive jugs of hot water and poured it into the tin tub where Sophie had already poured a jug of cold water in the bottom.

"Here, I'll stoke the stove for ya before I go. Get the place nice and warm for me dwarlings."

Sophie almost chuckled at his 'dwarlings.' Instead, she thanked him, securing the tent flap, after he left. She looked at the two inches of water in the small tub and wished she was at the Sackville Hotel. Before the war, even the servants could fill the bathtub with as much hot water as they wanted. Sophie liked it up to her chin. That was a long time ago and her thoughts turned to recent times. A bath at River House was two inches, but that was at least a full-size bathtub. A tin bath was better than nothing and she really needed to wash the dirt off. Her hair felt itchy, something that made her wonder if some wildlife had taken a leap from a patient. She pulled the pins out of her hair and let it fall over her shoulders. Nothing was moving but, just in case, she decided to wash it, which was always a challenge in a small space.

The stove roared as she stepped out of the bath. Thankful for the heat, she dried off, wrapped the towel around her wet hair and slipped into her nightgown.

"It's just me!" Emily called from the tent flap.

Sophie laughed. Emily must have realized she was in the tub. "Come in. I'm decent."

"What a day. I was so surprised to see Private Maggs. I'm glad it was Captain Wainwright who did his surgery. I would hate for him to deal with the miserable major who shall be nameless. Is that water still warm?" Emily swished the bath water with her hand. "Not bad. I'm going to jump in."

"How is Private Maggs? Did the surgery go well?" Sophie asked.

"I think so. There were no special instructions but it was a long one and he was still in recovery when I left." Emily grinned. "He made such a fuss when he came in, chatting away about seeing his two favourite nurses and telling jokes. Thank heavens Major Hughes was busy. It's so much nicer when he's not around and today was the worst I've seen him. He was in a rage and none of us knew why. Nothing had happened in the unit."

"Oh, I know. Matron hinted that Colonel Belingham had spoken to him regarding Captain Cuthbert and Jo Griffith."

"Tell me more," Emily said, lowering herself into the tub.

"Matron called me to her office as I was coming off duty. Apparently, Jo has asked to see me, something of a surprise. I was worried about the orders to stay away. She diplomatically said it would not be a problem as Colonel Belingham had spoken with the major."

"No wonder he was in such a rage. He can't abide anyone telling him he's wrong. I would have liked to have seen that encounter."

"Me too." Both women giggled at the image.

"What's so funny?" Trixie asked as she pulled the tent flap open and quickly closed it. "Oh, sorry, Emily. That bath looks good but I have some reading to do." She wafted a letter in the air and handed one to Emily and a parcel to Sophie. "Sister Potter just handed the mail out."

"A parcel for me!" Sophie looked at the label. "It's from Hillary."

She pulled at the string to release the knot and as the brown paper slipped off, she felt something soft. A multi coloured fabric appeared. "It's a blanket and there's something inside." Unfolding the blanket carefully, first she took out a letter, then a tin of biscuits and next to it, a tin of Tetley Tea. Sophie handed the tin to Trixie. "Let's make some proper tea, ladies."

Hot, steaming mugs in hand, they each settled to read their letters. Emily sat at the desk while Trixie sat cross legged on her bed with a shawl wrapped around her shoulders. Sophie preferred to curl up on her bed, her legs covered with her new blanket. The only noise was the occasional cough from the fumes that inevitably escaped the stove pipe and the rustle of paper as they read.

River House Nurse's Residence

Dearest Sophie,

I hope this letter and parcel finds you well. I enjoyed your last letter and have tried to accommodate your requests. I wish I could send more but rationing makes it difficult. I don't have a spare blanket and the store bought were expensive so I asked for Cook's advice. She introduced me to her friend who unravels old sweaters and knits blankets with the wool. You'll notice the different colours. She does a great job of making a pattern out of it. I am in awe of such talent. She gave me the blanket for you and refused payment. It is a gift from Mrs. Gibbs (Cook's friend). She said she was grateful for the work nurses do at the front. Her husband was injured in France. He's home now but he said it was the nurses who saved his life so she is forever grateful. The tea is a gift from me. I can't imagine not having a good cuppa. In case you are wondering about the biscuits, I'm sure, knowing my domestic abilities, you realize I did not bake them. When I told Cook I wanted to send you some treats, she insisted on baking her special biscuits. I was allowed to taste them before she packed them in this fancy tin. They are delicious. Cook said she would like the tin back. I understand that might not be practical but in Cook's mind, good biscuit tins are hard to come by these days.

My studies are going well. My fellow lady students and I have learned a few tricks to counteract the constant harassment from our male counterparts. To our surprise, the professor is showing us respect and actually complimented me on a paper I submitted. It might have something to do with the mid-term examinations. Three of the four of us were in the top ten and I was top of the class. I find this preliminary work easy, not unlike our nursing training. I expect once the classes get harder I will slip off the top spot.

It's disappointing that the gentlemen think we cheated, or worse, the professor favoured us. It is laughable. These fellows cannot get their heads around the fact that women are intelligent. Perhaps they are afraid we will challenge their manhood? It doesn't help that I am taller than all but one. Do I intimidate them? I am being bold but you will understand. Thankfully the professor is not of the same opinion. We do have to prove ourselves every day, which is taxing but so worth it. I am extremely happy with my choice and, at times, I allow myself to envision wearing a white coat, discussing medical issues with male colleagues.

The bombing in London is getting worse. A bomb dropped right next to the university and blew out a section of the library. It was a miracle no one was hurt. Students study there late into the night but there was enough warning that the place was empty.

I must close as I have much studying to do. Cook said she would take the parcel to the post office. She asks after you and Trixie all the time. The new bunch of probationers are a bit staid and not much fun. With her self-important attitude, you would think Cook would like the newcomers but, deep down, she misses our crazy group. Although she is different from dear Mrs. Wilderby, she has a good heart. Write soon. I miss you terribly.

Your affectionate friend,
  Hillary

"Time to open the biscuit tin," Sophie announced, jumping off the bed.

"I agree," Emily said, a broad grin on her face. "Listen to this. Sean, that's my nephew, has taken to playing marbles with his friends. Maggie, she's my niece, teases him and hides his favourite marbles, which of course always finishes up with squabbles and tears. But this time the tears said something was wrong. Emily read the letter aloud, "*Emily, you'll never believe this, but Maggie put Sean's favourite marble in her nose; an attempt to hide it. Try as I may, I could not get the slippery thing out. I panicked and called DrCooper who removed it with a little suction cup. He even laughed and said it happens quite often. I'm not ready to laugh yet but I am smiling at the incident. We now have strict rules about marbles...*"

"I'm glad Maggie wasn't hurt. You must admit it is funny. They sound like such great kids," Sophie said, pouring more tea.

"Kathleen wouldn't think so at the time. It's hard on her, raising them alone. Paddy was sent to Egypt. That is such a long way away and with me here, she has no one." Emily's voice faded into thought.

"Trixie, can you drag yourself from Chris' letter? Is he still planning on meeting you in Paris?" Sophie frowned, seeing tears in Trixie's eyes. "Is something wrong?"

"All leave has been cancelled. The squadron has been told they are on a highly classified mission. Chris says this will be the last letter for some time. He'll write when he can. Under the circumstances, he told his friend the truth about us." Trixie gave Sophie a knowing stare. "And there's more. He wrote to his father."

"Did he say why?"

"No. Do you think he told him about us?"

"I doubt it. Don't worry, he'll be fine. Chris has been on classified missions before." Sophie tried to be reassuring but, in truth, classified missions for pilots meant few returned.

"The tone of his letter is different. Why would he tell his friend? Unless he's afraid he won't come home?" Tears flowed as Trixie uttered the last words.

"You can't think that way. Chris will come home. For both your sakes, you have to believe that." Sophie embraced her.

"We need cheering up." Emily opened the tin of biscuits, placed it in the middle of her bed, and patted the cover, inviting Sophie and Trixie to join her. "And perhaps you'll tell me what I obviously do not know? You two have a secret." Emily pretended to pout, which made them laugh as it was Trixie who was the pouter in the group and Emily looked comical.

"Oh, these are good." Trixie sighed, her tears fading. "I'm sorry, Emily, but the only person privy to this secret is Sophie." She hesitated, taking another bite of biscuit and looked at Sophie, who guessed Trixie wanted to reveal it. Sophie smiled and nodded her support, prompting Trixie to continue. "I would like to explain *the secret* but you have to promise not to breathe a word."

"Good heavens, this is serious. Of course, I promise." Emily's sincere tone was so like her. In spite of her Irish cheerfulness, being the eldest in the group she was often the most responsible.

Trixie took a deep breath and lowered her voice. Canvas walls were thin. "Chris and I are married. We eloped. Our families wanted us to wait until after the war. His mother was hoping the war would part us as she doesn't like me much.

181

Do you remember when he went missing? His squadron was shot down over the English Channel."

"I do." Emily nodded her head. "That was awful and nobody would tell you anything."

"Exactly! His mother wouldn't even answer the phone. It was the butler who let things slip. Nobody really knew what had happened until Chris appeared unhurt and joking about the whole thing, which upset me even more. Chris felt bad, never wanting that to happen again. The War Office will only keep next of kin informed and that would be Chris' parents. Aware that his mother would not give me any information, the only thing to do was make me his next of kin."

"Wow. How did you get away without anyone finding out?"

"Sophie covered for me. I was over twenty-one so I did not need my father's permission. Chris made all the arrangements. He informed his commanding officer he was married, showed him the marriage certificate, and my name went on as next of kin. It's wartime so people don't ask as many questions."

"If they find out here, you'll be sent home," Emily said.

"Exactly. That's why only Sophie and Chris' commanding officer are aware of our marriage. And now you. And it seems Chris' friend, whoever he might be."

"It's time they eased the rules regarding married women," Emily stated with some conviction.

"Change comes slowly and this war has made people think twice about women's roles. Not all of us want to be owned by a man and have babies." Sophie visibly trembled at the thought. She couldn't quite reconcile her thoughts about Carlos and Andrew. If she didn't want marriage, what did she want?

Trixie yawned and rubbed her eyes, still pink from crying, "I'm ready for sleep."

"Me too," the others chorused and within minutes all three were fast asleep.

At first, Sophie kept her eyes closed. The new blanket made her feel cozy, although her cold cheeks told her the stove was out and it was a cold morning. She pulled the blanket up to her nose. It smelled of lavender. She thought of Mrs. Gibbs and Cook's kindness and how excited she was for Hillary following her dream. She questioned her own dream though. Was she following her path? She thought so. She loved nursing, although at times she found it challenging. Not only the nursing part but being out there on the Western Front. She found herself confronted with intense feelings, both past and present.

Carlos and Andrew seemed to trigger something primal in her. She didn't want the complications of love and yet the more she denied it, the more she thought about it. *Sophie Romano, put such thoughts out of your mind. Carlos is married and Andrew sees you as a respected colleague, which counts for something. You are here to nurse and help shell-shocked men... and women.* Her thoughts rested on Jo. How she wanted to help Jo, whose suffering might well go untreated. There was hope. Jo had asked to see her and that was a good start.

She swung her legs out of bed and heard scurrying as she lit the lantern. One bold little field mouse sat on its haunches, nibbling biscuit crumbs. He eyed Sophie before scurrying off to join his or her friends or family. She didn't mind mice but drew the line at rats, which thankfully had not made it to their tent. She made a mental note to be more careful with food.

Buster had not arrived with the hot water so she splashed cold water on her face and brushed her damp hair, tangled from the last night's washing. Sophie's Italian features were quite beautiful and her crowning glory was her thick, long, dark hair. She did question its practicality in war conditions. Many of the nurses were wearing easy to manage bob-cuts. *I'm not quite ready for that yet,* she thought, running her fingers through the soft waves. It triggered a childhood memory of her mother's smile as she brushed her own long tresses. She sighed, rolling her hair tight and securing it with pins to fit under her nurse's cap.

"Time to wake up, ladies. No wowter call today. I have to get breakfast early as I'm meeting Matron on the Women's Ward. Wish me luck. Let's hope Jo Griffith doesn't try to attack me this time." Sophie laughed as she buttoned her boots and headed to the canteen.

After she finished her breakfast, she hovered by the tea pot, wondering whether to pick up two cups, but decided to keep her meeting with Jo professional. First of all, Matron would be there, and the memory of the mug flying past her head flashed through her mind.

19

Sage Women

A long table surrounded by occupied chairs filled the centre of the wooden hut known as the Women's Ward. Sophie entered somewhat tentatively, surprised to see Matron seated at the table in deep conversation with several women, including Jo.

"Nurse Romano, good morning. Come and join us. We were discussing the issues nurses and other medical personnel come up against but rarely speak about."

Sophie nodded, sitting in the only vacant chair, which happened to be next to Jo. She wondered if it was by design or coincidence. Matron's cheeks lifted into a subtle smile. Her eyes gave Sophie a reassuring glance as she continued talking. Sophie listened with astonishment. She had long ago determined Matron to be a sage woman and as she listened, Matron's words became wiser and wiser.

"Ladies, our role here is to take care of injured, war-damaged soldiers and nurse them back to health so they can fight some more." The last phrase was said with a hint of sarcasm. "Or we send them home to their families and far too many times, make them comfortable as they near the end of life. A job that everyone does extremely well but we also pay a price. Physically, the work is taxing. The long hours are exhausting and, although mostly rewarding, it can, on occasions, be disheartening or frightening. Wartime nursing exposes you to catastrophic injuries never seen in a civilian hospital where most of you trained. We are expected to carry on as though it was a cut needing a bandage." She gazed purposefully around the table. "Some of you have not had the advantage of nurses' training, freely giving your time as volunteers." Matron looked towards two young volunteer aids then pointedly at Jo, whose expression was sullen, bordering on hostile. This surprised Sophie who expected Jo to be welcoming, but she had made no attempt to make eye contact. Why had Matron told her Jo had requested to see her? Obviously, nothing had changed.

The door opened and Teddy entered, carrying a billycan of tea in one hand and the handles of china cups looped through his fingers in the other. He placed everything on the table and pulled a pile of saucers from his pocket. Sophie wanted to giggle. The china cups with saucers and the billycan looked out of place and, at the same time, intimate.

"Thank you, Private Green," Matron said.

"It's a pleasure, Ma'am. Oh, Cook sent you something extra." Smiling, he pulled a brown paper package from another pocket.

Matron unwrapped fresh biscuits. "Please thank Cook. This is a treat."

"Yes, Ma'am." Teddy saluted as he retreated.

Munching a biscuit, Sophie lifted her cup and restrained the urge to raise her pinky finger as she enjoyed the luxury.

Although they did have china in the nurse's mess, they mostly drank from tin mugs. Glancing at the others, she saw everyone relax. Even Jo's scowl softened. *Sage woman indeed,* Sophie thought. *I'm beginning to see where this is going. So clever and wise.*

"I am not a stranger to war. I served in the Boer War. I was a young nurse, fresh out of nursing school and arrived in Africa, keen to do my part. An attitude I'm sure all of you had on your arrival here. I was not prepared for the atrocities of war, the unimaginable injuries and men dying, calling for their mothers. Something you are all familiar with. We ignore how it makes us feel, carrying on the way we've been trained. I suffered with nightmares and more, resulting in a breakdown. If it wasn't for a kind sister recognizing my dilemma, talking to me and helping me deal with my destructive inner thoughts and vivid nightmares, I would have been sent home and never nursed again."

Matron sipped at her tea, and letting her words sink in. "War also attacks our minds. The injuries are subtle but just as real as a broken leg or a shrapnel wound. We see it in soldiers and we call it war nerves or shell shock. It is a new science. The war office has recently, and only partially, recognized these afflictions as illness, not cowardice. I'm sorry to say many traumatized soldiers are labeled as cowards and punished accordingly. As nurses, you all know war nerves are a genuine injury and nothing to be ashamed of, but it has a stigma." Matron hesitated, draining her tea cup. The rattle of the cup on the saucer broke the silence and several heads nodded in agreement. "I'm here to advise you that these same afflictions can, and do, affect us all. There is only one way to recover: talk about what you want to forget. How many of you have nightmares?"

Sophie raised her hand, followed by two more nurses and then, to her surprise, Jo raised hers.

Matron nodded her approval at the show of hands. "Colonel Belingham has been an advocate for soldiers and it was at his request that Captain Cuthbert was assigned to this hospital, not only for the soldiers, but for anyone needing his help. I invited Nurse Romano to join us because she has worked with Captain Cuthbert in a civilian hospital, treating shell shock. She is an ideal person to speak with and to learn from." Matron's eyes locked for a few seconds on each individual. "I see some skepticism. Perhaps you are associating war nerves with ladies' sensitivities, fainting, or swooning in overheated drawing rooms or corsets laced too tight. I see none of that. You are strong women. Otherwise, you would not be here. What I am talking about, and what Captain Cuthbert treats, is quite different. I hope I have made myself clear. I expect you to be responsible and talk if you need to. I promise you there is no shame and many benefits. Mrs. Griffith, I believe you asked to speak with Nurse Romano." She stood to leave, glancing at the time, and then at Sophie. "I will inform Sister that you will report for duty in thirty minutes."

"Yes, Matron." Sophie moved towards Jo's bed, expecting her to follow. Instead she felt combative eyes on her back. Without turning, she said, "Mrs. Griffith?" Jo moved slowly, like a sulking child, and sat on her bed. "Jo, did you ask to see me or did Matron insist?"

After a long sigh, Jo answered. "I did ask to see you."

"So, what is wrong? Have you changed your mind?"

"I don't apologize often but you deserve an apology from

me." She put her hand up to her head. "I'm sorry for the things I said before the surgery. Major Hughes explained the swelling caused me to react. I'm fine now."

"Apology accepted. How are you?"

"The head wound is healing with no infection but I don't feel myself. Major Hughes dismisses me."

"Not the friendliest of men but I'm told a brilliant surgeon."

"Sergeant Harcourt wants me on duty but I don't want to work for her anymore."

"Why not? I thought you respected Sergeant Harcourt. What changed?"

"I can't respect someone who doesn't treat animals well. One of the girls came by to visit and told me about the horses pulling the ambulances through the mud." She smiled. "Amazing animals. She also told me the bloody woman kicked the horse because it didn't move."

"Is that the only thing?" Sophie asked, knowing there was more. She needed Jo to voice it.

"I don't understand. Damn it, I've never been afraid of anything but the thought of getting in an ambulance puts the fear of God in me. I can't work like that. It wouldn't be fair to the chaps. They need to trust the ambulance is going to get them to safety."

"First of all, you are not well enough to return to any kind of duty. That wound has to heal. Jo, you may feel differently when you're healed." Sophie took a deep breath, preparing for outrage. "You are suffering from trauma. The explosion and the events around it shocked your system."

"Poppy-cock! Don't talk bloody rubbish." Spittle followed her outrage but not as venomous as Sophie expected. "I'm strong enough to take anything. My father saw to that. Oh,

Matron's little speech was good but not for me." She rubbed moisture from her eyes.

"The horses were amazing. One of the ambulance drivers told me she envied the horses as her ambulance was stuck in the mud. It took her all day to get the men here."

"If I wasn't stuck in this bed, I'd be driving the horses. Damn these dizzy spells."

"What dizzy spells?" Sophie asked, and at the same time realized the trauma was not the only reason Jo could not be driving. She had assumed from Andrew's comments that it was shell shock, but the dizziness undoubtedly related to the head wound. It appeared the doctors didn't expect it to improve. Sophie smiled. They didn't know Jo.

"It's nothing. Annoying, that's all. Now, if I had horses and not an engine, I'd have no problem with the ambulances. Horses are perceptive. They find their way home and they know when people like them or are afraid. They'd soon detect the animosity and fear." Jo's eyes flickered with humour. "They can be naughty and tease with such people."

Detecting a positive tone, Sophie saw her opportunity. "I'm sure Sergeant Harcourt would appreciate someone like you. She certainly did not get along with the horses." She caught her breath. "Jo you may not recover sufficiently to return to the Field Ambulance." Jo's eyes flashed with anger and Sophie stepped back.

"Relax, I'm not going to hit you. Bloody hell, what are you saying? Of course, I'll be back on duty." Sophie heard hesitation. "Eventually. What else can I do? Damn it! Are they sending me home?"

"I don't know but I have an idea. How would you like to work at the stables?" Her comment was met with silence, which surprised her. "I can't promise anything and we'd have to involve Captain Cuthbert. Is that a problem? I understand you don't want to talk to him." Sophie sat back and waited. *Why isn't she answering? Am I pushing her too much? Is she too afraid to get back to any kind of work?"*

"You are a bundle of surprises! Of course, I'd like to be with the bloody horses, but I'm not sure. The horses here are not the kind I'm used to and the conditions, the injuries…" Her words trailed off.

"Will you think about it? Perhaps talk to Captain Cuthbert?" Sophie held her breath.

"All right, I'll consider it."

Sophie checked the time. "You look tired and need some rest. I have to get on duty before Matron comes looking for me."

"Will you visit again?"

"Of course."

Sophie let out a big sigh. She was late, but happy, with her conversation with Jo and hoped to see Andrew and tell him of her progress. She was in luck. Andrew was talking to Private Carter. Not wanting to disturb them, she helped Kitty with the dressings, keeping a close eye on Andrew. She need not have worried as Andrew came to her, or perhaps it was coincidence, that he just happened to attend the same patient and Kitty moved on to another bed.

"Good morning, Nurse Romano! How are you today?"

"I am quite well, Captain. I'm almost finished dressing the sergeant's wound."

"I thought I'd missed you. I look forward to your smiling

face to brighten my day."

Somewhat mystified by his personal enquiry, she searched for an appropriate answer, unsure if the comment merely implied a nicety or if it meant more. *How does he do that? He always managed to keep me off balance.*

"I'll take that as a compliment. Brightening people's days is part of the job."

He raised an eyebrow. "And you do that well. Why so late?"

"A meeting with Matron, which actually involves you. Jo Griffith requested to see me. I received an apology and I believe I made some progress. She might agree to see you."

"That is progress. Can you speak about it after I finish rounds here? I would be grateful if you could check on Private Carter. He has a Blighty ticket but doesn't seem happy about it."

"Of course. Let me know when you're finished."

Sophie finished her rounds and went to sit with the private. He looked worried. "Hey, why so glum? I hear you have a Blighty ticket. You're on your way home."

"I am happy but what about my nightmares? Mam'll have a fit and I can't go back to Gracie. It's not fair to her."

"One step at a time, Soldier. First, your mam will be happy you're home and out of danger. She'll do what mothers do, look after you, just like she did when you fell and scraped your knee as a little boy. If Gracie loves you, she will help you. What about your friend Connor? You'll be able to see him again."

"Not sure, Nurse. Mam said he wasn't doing well."

"Perhaps you can help each other."

"I never thought of that. We were great friends and always talked to each other. Maybe I can help him."

"That's the spirit, Private. You will get better. It won't be easy and you'll have to be patient because healing takes time. Can you do this?"

He nodded. "Me mam was always good at mending me scraped knees. I was a wild kid and so was Connor so we had a lot of them. I'm not sure about Gracie. I guess I'll find out. I'm leaving this afternoon. I'll miss you, Nurse Romano."

"I'll miss all my favourite patients. I'm happy you're going home, though. Take care, Soldier."

"Fraternizing with the patients, I see." Sister Sin's harsh voice assaulted Sophie and she froze. *Here it comes.The inferences, twisting of words and even downright lies. I can't even defend myself.*

"Sister, what can I do for you? Private Carter is leaving us today. I was wishing him well."

"Is that what you call it? I call it sinful. Both you and Nurse King. I see you haven't changed your ways. Now get to work!"

"Rounds are finished, Sister. The patients have been attended to. Nurse Wilkes and I are going for lunch, unless there is something you would like us to do."

Sophie held her breath, waiting for more reprimand, for what, was a mystery. Sister was talking in riddles. Mentioning Trixie was very odd as they rarely worked together.

"Go ahead. I'm just familiarizing myself with the hospital."

Kitty frowned and beckoned Sophie to follow her to the canteen.

"What was that all about? I thought Sister Drew was bad but this one is worse, and she sure has it in for you."

"A long story…" Sophie stopped talking as they walked right into Captain Cuthbert.

"Oh, Captain, I completely forgot. We were to meet after

193

rounds."

"Actually, I was coming to tell you I've been called away." Without another word, he disappeared towards a waiting lorry.

"A morning of surprises," Kitty said with a laugh.

Sophie shrugged her shoulders. "It is. We were supposed to discuss Jo's progress and treatment."

20

Infections

The wooden duckboards glistened with a hint of frost and the air felt fresh; almost invigorating, if Sophie wasn't so tired. Wrapping her arms around her middle, she stared up at the clear sky where a few stars twinkled in the darkness. *A perfect night for a walk,* she thought, hesitating at the entrance. But the glow of warmth beckoned her inside.

Trixie had the stove lit and was already in her nightgown, sitting cross legged on her bed reading. She looked up from her book. "You look as though your day was as tough as mine."

"Yes, it started early and finished late with a visit from Sister Singleton."

"She inspected our ward too and made some unnerving comments. The woman terrifies me. How could Matron accept her?"

"I doubt she had any choice. I can tell you Matron does not know about the problems at the Bartley. She was surprised when I told her Sister Sin had worked there. With any luck, Matron will contact the Bartley and discover the truth."

"We can only hope," Trixie said, turning the page of her book.

"What are you reading?"

"Jane Eyre. It's one of my favourites."

"Romantic and brave for her time."

"Did you know the critics thought her brazen and wanton for writing a female character with opinions of her own?" Trixie grinned. "Can you imagine what they would think if they saw us today."

Sophie grinned, nodding her agreement. "Charlotte Brontë and her sisters would approve of women's progress. I'm not sure they'd approve of the changes in romance."

"Is it so different?"

"Maybe not." Sophie thought about how Carlos had romanced her in her youth and now it was innuendoes and assumptions. Like the Brontë's characters, assumptions were often incorrect. What if he wasn't married? He wasn't wearing a ring but that would be because of scrubbing up for surgeries. She shook the notion from her head and came back to the conversation. "Except women can work beside men today without it being romantic. Even if it is awkward …" Her words trailed off as ambiguous thoughts of Andrew came to mind. Emily's entrance interrupted her.

"What a day!" Emily called as she almost fell into the tent. "I am exhausted. One infection after another, all needing surgery. Even after my shift was finished, more patients came in. The wards are going to have a busy night nursing fevers."

"There must be something in the air. My day and Trixie's were just as bad."

Emily's expression suddenly went serious. "Sophie, Private Maggs isn't doing so well. Normally we keep patients in recovery longer but we needed the bed so he's back on the ward. Captain Wainwright said he'd check on him later."

"You said he was okay at lunch. Has his condition deteriorated?" Sophie asked, as she continued to get undressed.

"Surgery did go well but he has a fever. It's not unusual and maybe I'm overreacting but I find it difficult when you know someone. It's so much easier to stay detached when the patient is a stranger. I remember how good he was with little Charlie. All I can think about is that little boy. He's already lost his mother."

"Should I go and check on him before I get ready for bed?" Sophie asked, a frown creasing her forehead.

"Wait until morning. There's nothing you can do tonight," Emily said, yawning.

Sophie had never relinquished the habit of waking long before dawn. Between her hotel and nurse's training, her internal clock had a permanent 4:45 a.m. alarm setting. As usual, her companions were still fast asleep. She hadn't slept well, worried about Private Maggs, so she dressed and slipped out of the tent to check on him.

The ward was quiet and the duty nurse sat at the make-shift desk, updating charts. Sophie whispered, "Good morning."

The startled nurse looked up at Sophie. "Good morning. You're early."

"I wondered how Private Maggs was doing. He's an old patient from when I nursed in London." Sophie felt the need to explain.

"Just a minute." The nurse looked through the charts. "None of them are doing well. Most have been up all night with nightmares and hallucinations."

"I'm sorry. Have you been on your own all night?"

"No. An orderly checks in and I sent the aide for a break while it's quiet. Please don't disturb them. Maggs is down there on the left."

Sophie tiptoed along the ward, keeping her heels from clicking on the wooden floor. Private Maggs was tossing fitfully in his sleep, deep furrows on his sweaty forehead and unspoken words forming on his lips. He was burning up. Sophie squeezed the cloth over the cold water and gently sponged his head. He opened his eyes, terror reflecting in the glassiness.

"It's me, Nurse Romano. Sophie," she whispered. "Don't be afraid. Stanley, I need you to fight as hard as you can. Think of Charlie. He needs you to get well." Sophie rinsed the cloth until it was cool and wiped his arms and torso around the dressing. A nudge on her arm made her turn as Buster placed a bowl of fresh, cold water at her side. She mouthed a 'thank you.'

Suddenly a shriek came from the other side of the ward. The duty nurse ran to the patient and Buster was already restraining the poor man terrified by his nightmares.

Private Maggs shot up into a seated position, his fists up to his chest, ready for a fight. His eyes were darting from side to side. Sophie clasped his wrists. "It's all right, Stan, you are safe in hospital. Remember me? Nurse Romano. I want you to lie back." Her hand on his chest, Sophie gently pushed him towards his pillows. His heartbeat thumped from his pulse to her hand so hard she wondered how much more he could take. But gradually, she felt it slow down and he relaxed. She saw a brief smile as he closed his eyes again, which surprised her as the ward was noisy. A mixture of complaining soldiers needing more sleep and fevered patients hallucinating. Sophie patted Stan on the arm. "Rest. The nurse needs some help. I'll be back."

The ward quietened down and she returned to Stan. He lay on his back, not moving. For a brief second, she couldn't see his chest rise and fall and she panicked. Holding his wrist, she sighed with relief at a strong pulse. Private Maggs was in a restful sleep. The fever had broken and he was going to be all right.

"How's he doing?" Sophie froze. Carlos' deep voice took her by surprise and when she didn't answer, he leaned towards her and whispered, his breath catching on her neck, "Sophie, how's he doing?"

Clearing her throat, she hoped that might stop the blush. "The fever just broke so he's going to be all right."

"That's very good news." Looking puzzled, he added, "you're up early."

"I could say the same to you," Sophie responded curtly.

"Touché. I came to check on Private Maggs, which I suspect is the same reason you are here."

"He's a special kind of person." She cleared her throat adding, "He needs to stay alive for his son."

"I know. You told me. Most of these poor fellows need to stay alive for someone." His eyes lingered on Sophie's face. "I do my best. Don't get too attached. It only makes it harder." As he said the last phrase, Sophie instinctively knew he wanted to comfort her. She could almost feel his embrace. Unbidden tears welled up and filled her eyes. Were they tears for Stanley? Was he telling her Stan wasn't going to make it, or something else entirely?

Carlos' gaze moved hesitantly from Sophie to the patient. First he checked the shoulder wound and gave a satisfied grunt. Without taking his eyes off the patient, he moved to his feet, examining the sole and his toes. It was only then that Sophie noticed the discolouration and blisters on two of Private Maggs' toes. They were easily missed as both his feet were covered in bruises, lesions, broken skin and pockets of infection. Carlos' knitted brow told her the discolouration was an indication of something more sinister.

Private Maggs moved in the bed, trying to sit up. Sophie puffed up his pillows. "Welcome back, Private. How are you feeling?"

Rubbing his eyes, he looked around. "Nurse Romano, I'm feeling better. Captain Wainwright, did the surgery go well?" Maggs looked at his shoulder and gently patted the dressing.

"Surgery went well, Soldier. You'll have a scar but it should heal. You've had a high fever but I think you are on the mend."

"Thank you, Sir!" Glancing down he added, "what about me feet?"

"We'll see. You are doing well, Private. I'll be back later." Carlos nodded and left the ward.

"Nurse, som'ats wrong with my feet. Why didn't the doc say anything?" He leaned forward. "Look at them toes. I know what happens if gangrene sets in. I'll lose mi leg."

"Slow down. Your legs are fine and will be staying right where they are. You have trench foot and it takes time to heal. Captain Wainwright will be back later. He will keep a close eye on those toes and treat them accordingly. Now, I have to get to work."

"You came specially to see me?"

"I did. I was worried about you. You and Charlie are

200

special."

"I heard you." He looked knowingly at Sophie. "I heard you tell me to fight for Charlie. I'm glad you did because I was slipping away. Thank you." He coughed and his voice faltered. "Don't let them take me legs."

"Stan, nobody is taking your legs. Stop worrying and get some rest." Sophie felt confident his legs would be okay but his toes might not be. She was sure his toes were showing signs of gangrene but Stan didn't need to know that just yet.

"I like it when you call me Stanley or Stan. My Millie called me Stanley sometimes. She said it made me sound important."

"And, so you are important. Using Christian names is against the rules and I could get into a lot trouble if anyone heard me call you 'Stan or Stanley.' I'll stop by later."

Hoping she had time for breakfast before her shift, she glanced at her nurse's watch and walked straight into someone. "Oh, sorry!" Looking up, she realized it was Carlos.

"Why such a hurry?" he asked, reaching out to steady her.

"I'm on duty in fifteen minutes. Have you decided about Private Maggs' toes?"

"I'm afraid so. There are early signs of gangrene. If I amputate the toes, I can save the foot."

"I should warn you, he's terrified of losing his legs."

"His legs?" Carlos shook his head, "Whatever gave him that idea?"

"The word gangrene means lost limbs to these men. They see it too often. Infected wounds, trench foot gone very bad, and suddenly the leg is gone."

"It makes sense. However, most often a small amputation of the gangrenous tissue prevents amputation of limbs. But these chaps wouldn't see it that way. I'll have a chat with …

what's his Christian name?"

"Stanley. I must run." *No time to eat now*, she thought.

Stanley Maggs had two toes amputated that morning with his full consent. Carlos had spent time with him, explaining why the surgery was necessary and why it was vital to stop the gangrene from spreading into his foot. He even sent her a message to say the surgery was successful.

It had been a quiet day on the ward and Sophie slipped out early to visit Private Maggs. He was sitting up in bed, his foot bandaged and elevated. There was even a dab of colour in his cheeks.

"I'm pleased to see you are doing so well and both legs, I see, are still intact," she said, teasing.

"Ya. Missing a couple of toes but doc says they'll heal and I'll forget they were ever there. He explained everything. Do I have you to thank for that?"

"Maybe. Captain Wainwright is a caring doctor. I just let him know you were worried. How are you feeling?"

"All right. A bit groggy but not like yesterday. They gave me som'at for the pain. I can't feel anything."

"Rest and do as you're told. You'll be better in no time. I'm off to see a woman about a horse." They both laughed. "That's what I like to see, a smile."

"You do say some funny things. I thought I was the joker. Will you come back later?"

"Tomorrow. Now rest."

Sophie hurried to the Women's Ward, hoping Jo had followed through and agreed to talk to Andrew. The suggestion of working with horses seemed to have worked and she hoped she had not spoken out of turn. After all, she didn't even know if Andrew had spoken to the veterinarian. Her knowledge of horses and army stables was limited, except that she was aware horses were a valuable commodity. She'd certainly seen first-hand how the horses plodded through the thick mud, undoubtedly saving lives and bringing supplies. She had been horrified at the implication that a horse was more valuable than a soldier's life. Men could be replaced but the supply of healthy horses had diminished to practically nothing. Thousands of animals had met a cruel death. Was that the reason Jo hesitated? Fresh, organized stables on an elite estate with a pleasant gallop through her father's acreage was a far cry from a make-shift stable in the middle of a war zone.

"Hello," Sophie called as she walked on to the ward. Jo was playing cards with three other patients. Judging by the level of concentration, she suspected it was poker and perhaps at a critical stage. True to its name, she couldn't tell who was winning.

"Straight flush!" Jo called, placing her cards on the table and breaking the silence with a chuckle.

"Nurse Romano, have you come to see me?"

"How are you doing? Did you talk to Captain Cuthbert?"

"We had a good chat. He's not that bad a chap. I quite liked him."

Sophie raised an eyebrow. Andrew was good at his job but even she was surprised at Jo's response. "I'm delighted to hear you liked him."

"More than I can say for the other chap, Hughes." She patted her head. "I should be grateful to him for fixing this. He says another week." Jo shrugged. "Not sure what happens then."

Sophie's heart sank. There was no mention of the stables. "Have you given any thought to the horses?"

"I have. Hughes thinks I'll be fit to drive the ambulance but Captain Cuthbert says it's too early. Like a bunch of silly kids arguing. At least Cuthbert suggested it was unprofessional to talk in front of the patients. Hughes went purple with rage, calling Cuthbert a quack doctor. I could take a swipe at Hughes, the pompous ass. Cuthbert's all right. He stayed calm and walked out. It was quite entertaining." She turned to her companions. "Right, girls?"

A communal giggle went with nods and grins. Jo seemed to be the leader of the group. She certainly appeared to have recovered. Sophie wondered how much was a cover-up for deeper feelings but the fact that she respected Andrew was encouraging.

"It is rare to see doctors arguing. It's definitely not professional. You've changed your opinion of Captain Cuthbert."

Jo nodded. "He's arranging for me to talk to the veterinarian who is eager for some help. I'm meeting him in his office to discuss…" She hesitated, giving Sophie a knowing look. "…things."

"One step at a time. You aren't considering going back to the ambulance corps, are you?"

"Sergeant Harcourt wants me back. She's short-handed. But with the way she treats horses, I've lost respect for her. Captain Cuthbert suggests we explore my options."

Reading between the lines, Sophie had the sense Jo had succumbed and would take Andrew's advice but wasn't quite ready to admit it.

21

Winter

The beginning of December brought snow and unusually cold temperatures. Sophie could never remember being so cold. It was even colder than the attic bedroom at the Sackville when the gale force winds blew in from the English Channel and whistled through the eaves.

She had layers of clothes under her uniform, kept her hands tucked in her pockets and her boots pinched with the bed socks under her stockings. The orderlies tried to keep the stoves going and the canvas tents were surprisingly warm but the heat easily escaped.

A thin dusting of snow sparkled on the icy duckboards, making every step a challenge as Sophie shivered towards her tent, relieved the day was over. The cold brought yet another affliction for the men and nurses to deal with: frostbite. On top of trench foot, ears and fingers were now burnt by the cold.

A wall of warmth hit her as she entered. The stove was set as high as they dared, without using too much fuel or setting the place on fire.

The empty bed, cleared of clutter, was made ready to greet another roommate. Jo Griffith's head injury had left her lightheaded and prone to dizziness, symptoms Captain Cuthbert had predicted, and they precluded her from driving an ambulance. She was now part of the veterinarian group, a small one that had no assigned quarters, resulting in Jo being billeted with the nurses and the bed initially meant for Hillary assigned to her.

Sophie liked Jo but she was unsure how it would work out with a stranger in their midst, and a bossy one at that. Having no choice in the matter, the three made the best of it. Trixie put a small bar of her lavender soap at the side of Jo's bed and Emily found an extra mug and made tea. Sophie opened the tin of Cook's precious biscuits.

"Hello!" Jo called from the tent flap.

"Come in!" All three chorused. "Welcome to our humble abode. I'm Trixie and this is Emily."

Jo nodded, clutching a beat-up leather bag with books tucked under her arm and making no attempt to shake Trixie's extended hand.

"Thanks," she said. "You all know who I am." Pointing to the empty bed, she added, "mine I assume?" Jo dropped her bag on the floor and sat heavily on the side of the bed. A smile crossed her face briefly as she lifted the soap. "Lavender. It's been a while since I've smelt lavender. I don't go in much for frivolous things. The army issue is fine for me."

"It's a little welcome gift. My mother sends it. It feels nice on your skin." Trixie's words were clipped with hurt. Sharing her soap was a generous offer, which their guest did not appreciate.

"Oh, no offence Trixie. It's awfully kind." Jo's words were

also clipped but Sophie thought more from discomfort. She was unaccustomed to random acts of kindness.

An awkward silence ensued and Emily hovered around the table, not sure whether to serve the tea or not. She cleared her throat. "What do you think of this cold weather? I'm not sure I'll ever get used it."

"It's brisk but to be expected this time of year. We just have to get on with it," Jo replied, which did nothing to ease the tension.

"I've made some tea to warm us up. I even managed to find you a mug." Emily giggled, holding up a battered looking enamel mug. "It's not Royal Doulton but the tea is hot and Sophie has some biscuits."

Sophie patted the one chair by the table, pulled snuggly to the stove. "Come join us. It's not champagne but we wanted to welcome you and make you feel comfortable." She smiled and raised an eyebrow, sending a subtle message to Jo.

Jo glanced first at Sophie, then at Trixie and Emily, and hesitated. A contrite expression filled her face and, without saying a word, she moved to the table, accepting the only firm chair while the others perched on rickety stools that had once been chairs. Emily poured tea from a chipped ceramic teapot and Sophie passed the biscuit tin around.

"This is luxury. If I close my eyes, I might think I was at the bloody Savoy." Jo started laughing. "The ambulance girls get bunk beds squished together in a sardine tin, except it's a wooden hut not much bigger than a sardine tin." She stopped laughing and raised her mug. "Thank you for rescuing me from the sardines." Everyone burst into laughter and, finally, the tension was broken. The group chatted away until fatigue forced them to bed.

Sophie lay on her back as she often did, always the last to fall asleep. She had trouble switching her thoughts into sleep mode and that night Jo's snoring and the feel of the earth shuddering made it even more difficult. The earth tremors meant a battle's heavy casualties the next morning. She sighed. Would it ever end? She was relieved Jo was fitting in, even if it was a rocky start, and she knew there would be tension. Jo had a strong personality, which she surmised would eventually clash with someone. But, for now, things were good.

Anticipating a busy day, Sophie slipped into B Ward to see Stanley. His foot was strung up on pulleys and his face was pasty looking, but he managed a big smile when Sophie walked in.

"Good to see ya. A bit early in't it?"

"Early is normal for me and I wanted to check on you before my shift. How's the foot?" Sophie sensed he wasn't doing well.

"Foot's okay. Doc says it's healing nicely. I can't wait to get this contraption off and walk with crutches. That depends on the shoulder."

"That is excellent news. Is everything else all right?"

"I couldn't sleep last night. I kept feeling the floor tremble. It really scared me." He hesitated, shifting in the bed and trying to lean forward. "I thought I was back in the trenches, waiting for the Hun to shoot me," he whispered. "I was so scared, I daren't close me eyes." He brushed the back of his hand across his face. "Am I losing me head? There's a poor fellow in here that screams and the nurses have trouble calming him. Is that what's happening to me?" His last words, no longer a whisper, were full of angst.

"Shush, Stanley." Sophie took his hand in hers. "It's all right. The trembling earth triggered your memory of the battlefield. In some soldiers it's really bad but in others it is mild and eventually passes. Stanley Maggs, you are one of the strongest men I've known. You will get past this."

A weak smile lifted his mouth. "Your words mean so much. I keep thinkin' of little Charlie. He don't want a crazy dad but …" He looked at Sophie. "I want to go home to my little boy. Is that so bad? Does that make me a coward?" Tears trickled down his cheeks, catching in his beard stubble before dropping to his chest.

"No, never. You are a very brave soldier. Don't you ever forget that. Charlie will be proud of his soldier father, who fought for his country. We all want to go home, away from this war and it will happen soon." Sophie wondered why Stanley didn't have a Blighty ticket. His injuries certainly qualified him for going home.

Stanley's eyelids fluttered with sleep. "Stay with me. I won't dream if you're 'ere."

"I'll stay until you fall asleep."

Stanley gripped her hand and his eyes closed. His breathing relaxed and then his hand released its grip. Sophie sat with him, feeling sad for him and Charlie. She felt the same for everyone fighting this terrible war. All of a sudden, she felt a tingling sensation on the back of her neck, warning her that she was being watched. She turned towards the entrance but there was no one there. Her eyes swept the ward. Everything looked normal and all the other staff were busy with patients. She felt it again but nothing seemed unusual. *That's all I need now, paranoia.*

The bugle call announcing the arrival of casualties, although expected, startled Sophie. Stanley opened his eyes wide and she patted his hand. "Go back to sleep. I have to go help some soldiers."

Organized chaos greeted her, always a sight that filled her with awe. Everyone had a sixth sense of exactly what to do and what appeared chaotic was actually a well-trained and well-rehearsed operation. She joined the stretcher bearers and nurses waiting for the ambulances that drove in with ease. The thick sticky mud, now frozen by the cold temperatures, made the roads passable. Trixie and Jo appeared at her side.

"Jo, what are you doing here?"

"Helping, of course. I can't drive the bloody bus but I know how to get these poor buggers out of the ambulances." Jo gave Sophie a challenging stare. "Anything wrong with that?"

Sophie shrugged and moved forward, taking the arm of a soldier hobbling on one foot and guiding him into the reception area. Sister Singleton stood at the side of Major Hughes as he barked orders, which amused Sophie. Everyone got on with their jobs, completely ignoring the pompous surgeon and pious sister. The latter just stared into the chaos until Matron took her arm, rather firmly, and they left reception.

Hughes disappeared into the surgical unit with one final order to Captain Evans who was assessing an unconscious soldier bleeding from his abdomen. Emily stood at his side, trying to stop the bleeding. The expression on both faces left little doubt that the soldier's injuries were critical. A worried smile, directed towards the doctor, lifted Emily's cheeks and their eyes locked for a second. He gently touched her shoulder, a gesture of affection. The doctor beckoned an orderly to take the patient to surgery and Emily followed to prep him. Glancing over her shoulder, towards Captain Evans, she caught sight of Sophie and they exchanged complicit smiles

Whatever had happened at the front had resulted in catastrophic injuries and too many of them. Every nook and cranny had a bed in it. Colonel Belingham finally had to redirect the ambulances to another casualty clearing station. Sophie, comforting a young soldier, placed a hot water bottle on his abdomen to ease the shivering. His blond hair was glued to his baby face with dirt. One leg was shattered and the other damaged. She asked for Carlos because if anyone could save at least one leg, it would be him.

"You called for me?" Carlos' deep voice echoed in her ears.

"This soldier needs you," she whispered. "If anyone can save him, it's you." She almost frowned at his tired, exhausted face and wondered how many surgeries he had completed since the convoy arrived. How many limbs had been lost, lives saved and some not?

Carlos' examined the soldier, his expression grave. With a momentary glance at Sophie, he addressed the soldier with a smile. "There's a lot of work ahead of us, Soldier. I will operate as soon as theatre is ready."

The soldier's voice was barely audible. "Will I lose my legs?" Tears filled his eyes.

Carlos crouched by the stretcher. "Let me worry about that. I need you to be strong. I can't make any promises but I will do my best." Carlos turned to Sophie and she saw the anguish in his face. "Have an orderly move him to surgery."

The reception area finally cleared in the middle of the

afternoon. Sister Potter ordered all but one nurse to take a break. Sophie remembered she had been called away while visiting Stanley Maggs before breakfast and hunger grumbled in her tummy. Emily sat at the table with her hands wrapped around a mug. Suddenly, Sophie felt the cold, which she had been too busy to notice before. As she slowed down, her fingers throbbed and her squished toes hurt. She suspected chilblains.

"What a day!" Sophie said, sitting next to Emily.

"Some terrible injuries. There was one surgery after another."

"Reception was overflowing and the men seemed different. Usually even the injured soldiers joke and banter between themselves but today everyone was sombre, subdued. Do you know what happened?" Sophie asked.

"One soldier said they were taken by surprise. The Germans advanced and they had no warning, forcing a retreat. The poor fellow sounded resigned to defeat."

"I can feel it. The boys are losing hope. Does that mean we're losing the war?" Sophie asked, a hint of alarm in her voice.

Emily shook her head. "I don't know anymore. The severity of the injuries might explain the hopelessness. Colonel Belingham usually has encouraging words for the soldiers but today he looked wretched. He didn't talk to the men, just to Captain Evans."

"Why was the colonel in the surgical unit?"

"He often comes by to talk to the men, especially when a convoy arrives. He tells the men how brave they are and thanks them. It really boosts morale but not today. The colonel is a decent fellow, as are most of the doctors, except

Major Hughes."

"Would that include Captain Evans?" Sophie asked, teasing.

Emily blushed. "Of course. He's very good with the patients, and a gentleman."

"A gentleman and …" Sophie raised an eyebrow.

"Sophie Romano, the romantic. There's nothing. He's the junior surgeon and usually gets the less complicated cases. I like working with him. That is all." Emily took a breath. "We attended Private Maggs after the amputation. How's he doing?" Emily diverted her eyes towards the entrance. "Here comes Trixie."

"He is healing and hopes to be on crutches soon. You are changing the subject. Emily, you deserve a little romance in your life."

"There's no romance. I'm much too busy for frivolous things, to use Jo's expression." She laughed. "Speaking of Jo, she's an interesting character. I was anxious at first. She seemed so aggressive but she has a great sense of humour. I'm hoping she'll get used to us. It must be difficult."

"Hello. You must be talking about Jo," Trixie interrupted. "Quite an introduction and she is very different to us. Can I get you anything?"

"Not for me. I must return to surgery. I'll see you later," Emily said.

"I can stay for a few minutes." Sophie's feet hurt. She was tired and not looking forward to another two hours.

"What a day! You look how I feel." Trixie stretched her back before sitting down. "Even Matron was helping out."

"That's what I like about her. She's not afraid to roll her sleeves up. Not many matrons would do what she does. We are lucky to have her and Sister Potter." Sophie frowned. "I don't remember seeing Sister Singleton. Was she working with you?"

"Now you mention it, she was nowhere to be seen. With everyone in reception, she must have been watching the wards." Trixie glanced at Sophie. Hesitating, she leaned forward and whispered. "She makes me uncomfortable. I feel her eyes boring into me."

"I don't think Matron knows her history. She was surprised when I said I knew her from the Bartley." Grinning, Sophie added, "if it makes you feel any better, Sister Sin was as surprised to see us. Think about it. She must have lied her way here, thinking no one would know her secret. And then she finds herself face to face with two people who know it, her worst nightmare. Ironic, don't you think?"

"Which makes her even more dangerous. Fear does strange things to people like her."

"Try not to worry. Matron is shrewd. She'll sort it out. Let's change the subject. Have you heard any more from Chris?"

Trixie shook her head. "He can't write while he's on a mission. Sophie, I'm serious about Sister Sin. Watch your back."

"I will. I must get back to the ward for two more hours."

Little did she know it would be four before she would finish. Pippa and Kitty had cared for the ward alone all day and now the influx of casualties had filtered onto the overflowing wards. The added disarray had unsettled several of the nervous patients. Normally Captain Cuthbert would have been called. He was amazing at calming the patients but he had not returned from wherever he had gone. It was up to

Sophie to quieten and reassure the patients, allowing Pippa and Kitty to settle new ones.

By the time everything was done, Sophie's feet hurt so much she felt like ripping off her stockings and walking barefoot, cold or not. That would get her into trouble so she unbuttoned her boot to ease the pain. Too tired to join the others in the mess, she went to her quarters. First, she kicked off her boots, rubbed her feet and found some ointment for the chilblains. She slipped into her nightgown, wrapped Hillary's blanket around her and sat on the bed with Cook's biscuit tin open on her lap. With a big sigh, she relished the hot drink, munched on the biscuits and enjoyed the quiet. There were no distant battles and she wondered if there were any soldiers left in the trenches.

22

Keeping Secrets

ndrew Cuthbert jumped off the lorry, almost knocking Kitty and Sophie off their feet. "I beg your pardon ladies." He quickly grabbed Sophie's arm to prevent her from falling and cleared his throat. "Um, Nurse Romano, Nurse Wilkes, forgive me for not watching where I was going. This was the only transportation I could get from the train station this early in the morning. A rather bumpy ride, sitting on mail bags." He made a vain attempt to brush down his uniform. "May I ask if your duties include C today?"

Sophie nodded an affirmative. "We have many agitated patients. We had a convoy while you were away." She had never seen him so dishevelled. His uniform was creased and dirty and Sophie guessed he'd not slept since he left two days before.

As though reading her thoughts, he said, "Forgive my appearance." He rubbed his bristly chin. "I must wash and change."

"You look as though you could do with some sleep too." Sophie frowned. "Are you quite well? What took you away so urgently?" She blushed slightly aware it was an impertinent question.

He grinned, making his tired eyes twinkle slightly. "Classified, but thank you for your concern. Always the kind Soph … " He glanced at Kitty, making the correction. "You are always so kind, Nurse Romano. I have patients to treat and I'll be on the ward within the hour."

Curious about Andrew's condition and unwillingness to divulge the purpose of his sudden departure, Sophie wanted to ask more questions but Kitty grabbed her sleeve and hurried them on to the ward.

"You'd better not let Sister Sin hear him call you by your first name or you'll burn in hell for it." She gave a wistful laugh. "He has a glint in his eye. Is there something you're not telling me?" she asked with a giggle.

"It's nothing. The familiarity comes from when we were in London."

"If you say so," Kitty said, grinning.

Sophie caught the implication but couldn't even decide what she herself believed. Every contact with Andrew put her off balance. She could never be sure if his attention was professional respect, or if he was trifling with her affections. Perhaps the confusion lay in her own head. She appreciated the apparent respect, not often forthcoming from doctors, but did her fluttering heart deceive her?

An agitated Emily greeted them at the nurses' station. At first Sophie felt relieved, as her presence halted Kitty's prying questions, but that was quickly followed by surprise. "What are you doing here?"

"I had to see you," Emily blurted out. "I think Trixie's secret is about to be discovered."

"What? How?"

"I'm nursing a very ill patient in recovery, a pilot with an abdominal injury and burns. He asked me if I was Trixie Belingham. At first, I thought he was delusional or mistaking me for someone else. Then I thought the only Trixie I know is Trixie King, except her married name would not be King and I wondered if it was Belingham."

"It is. What did you say?"

"I said no, that my name is Nurse Finnigan. I made a joke of it and asked if Trixie was his sweetheart. He shook his head, mumbling something. I thought I heard sister and that would make sense if it was just a coincidence with the first name. But I also heard 'wife.' Unfortunately, he passed out on the morphine."

Sophie gasped. "Oh no, not Chris!"

"I thought the same and then read his chart. His name is Major Robin Belingham." She glanced over her shoulder and lowered her voice. "And that's not all. Colonel Belingham is his next of kin. When you asked me last night about the colonel being in the surgical unit, I didn't realize they were brothers."

"Could it be a coincidence? The colonel has to be 20 years older than Chris. How old is the patient?"

"Hard to say but he's not young. Forty maybe. You're right. There's too much of an age difference but that doesn't explain the name 'Trixie Belingham.' Has Trixie ever mentioned Chris' brother?"

"Not that I recall. Only his parents, Lady Belingham in particular." Sophie rolled her eyes. "Where's he from? That might give us a clue."

"I don't know, other than he's Royal Flying Corps, a

squadron commander."

"Chris is RFC but I don't know which squadron. I think we should tell Trixie."

Suddenly Sophie felt a shiver on her back, aware that someone was standing next to them. Sister Potter stood with arms folded, staring with an uncharacteristically stern expression, Sister Sin at her side. "What is going on? Why are you not on the surgical ward, Nurse Finnegan?"

"Hum ... I was sent over with a patient's belongings, err ... that had been misplaced." Emily lowered her eyes at the subterfuge.

Sister raised an eyebrow. "Are the said belongings in their rightful place now?"

"Yes, Sister." Emily fled before there were any more questions.

Sophie dared not look at either sister. A heavy weight held her motionless, waiting for a reprimand. "Nurse Romano, we have a busy morning ahead of us. Captain Cuthbert has returned and requests progress reports. Also, Matron informs me that Major General Macdonald is arriving shortly and there will be an inspection. Please prepare the patients." Sister Potter flipped her hand in a forward motion, one of her habits to hurry the nurses along. "Get on with it." Sophie breathed a sigh of relief even as she was somewhat curious about Sister Sin's silence. She felt those piercing eyes on her back as she moved down the ward and repressed the urge to turn and challenge the malice.

Captain Cuthbert scrutinized the charts and, at times, seemed exasperated and intense as he concentrated on his notes. Contrary to Sophie's earlier thoughts, rounds were professional without even a hint of flirtation.

Before being called away, Andrew had requested Blighty tickets for two patients he considered unstable, making them unfit to serve and a danger to their fellow soldiers. Sophie agreed with him. One poor fellow, a young Canadian, hadn't slept in days, terrified to close his eyes to nightmares. The other young soldier, professing to be eighteen, was curled up in the fetal position, calling for his mother at every loud noise. Sophie suspected he was barely sixteen. As terrified as they were, afraid of being labelled 'crazy,' or worse, 'cowards,' they did everything to appear normal in front of senior officers.

Colonel Belingham had received orders to cease all Blighty tickets until after the Major General's inspection of the casualty clearing station, either that day or the next. Senior officers and officials frequently visited the hospital under the guise of boosting morale and recharging the men with patriotism. However, rumour had it that this particular inspection had come about on the grounds that too many able-bodied soldiers were shirking their duties, with a not-so-subtle implication of cowardice and suspicion of a lenient command.

It was beyond Sophie's comprehension that anyone could call these brave men cowards, but hardened, career military men deemed anyone unable or unwilling to fight, a coward. Many of them had sat behind a desk so long, they'd forgotten the toll the battlefield took on soldiers.

"Nurse Romano!" A familiar voice jolted Sophie from her thoughts as they moved down the ward.

"Stanley! When did they move you here?"

"Last night. Captain Wainwright needed more beds. The

place were full to overflowing and Sister said I was to see that nice doctor you're always talking about."

"And who would that nice doctor be?" Andrew grinned, relaxing for the first time that morning.

Flustered, she replied quickly. "You both have London in common. I nursed Private Maggs' late wife and Nurse Finnegan nursed his baby son in at the Bartley. I might have mentioned it to you."

Andrew nodded as he read Stanley's medical card, his demeanour serious again. "Private Maggs, I'm sorry for the loss of your wife. In the London bombing, I presume?"

Tears welled up in Stanley's eyes. "I miss my Millie some't awful."

"How is your son?" Andrew asked.

"He's doing fine, living with me sister and her husband on the farm. Nurse Romano helped find me sister. I don't know what I'd have done if she hadn't helped. Charlie would 'ave gone to an orphanage, like me, or been adopted." Tears hovered on his eyelids. "And when I got gangrene, I thought I was a gonna and Charlie would have lost his mam and pa." He gulped, stemming the flow of tears. Sophie took his hand in hers, perturbed at Stanley's sudden breakdown, which was not like him. As heartbroken as he was after Millie died, he'd been strong for Charlie.

"It's all right, Soldier." Andrew rubbed Stanley's shoulder. "Tell me what you can. I'll see if we can get you home to your son."

"I keep havin' this nightmare that the ..." He stopped talking and glanced at Sophie. "I never told ya. I didn't want ya to worry. I keep seeing the Hun grab Charlie and stab him .... Just like they stabbed me mate, Duncan." Stanley broke down

221

in uncontrollable sobs and Sophie pulled the flimsy curtain as far as it would go, thankful that his bed, one of the few, had a curtain to give him a bit of privacy. Andrew sat on the side of the bed and said nothing until Stanley had calmed sufficiently to talk. Sophie surreptitiously moved away, leaving Andrew to start the healing. She felt guilty, her suspicions confirmed that Stanley was suffering from shell shock. She had seen the signs, albeit mild. So had Emily, as far back as London when Millie died. He seemed to cope, perhaps too well, with the grief of losing his wife and worry of finding a home for Charlie. Now she wished she'd consulted with Andrew at the time. Instead, he'd been sent back to fight. *I hope it's not too late and he can recover. At least Andrew will send him home. I don't understand why the Blighty ticket hasn't been issued. Surely the missing toes alone would qualify him.*

A large portion of boiled mutton was dolloped on Sophie's plate, followed by potatoes and a suspicious looking vegetable, probably a mixture of turnip and carrot. She glanced at the shiny layer of fat on the mutton, not sure she could eat it. As usual, hunger outweighed the visual appearance and she ate heartily with Emily and Trixie. It was a rare treat for them to be in the canteen at the same time these days and an opportunity to discuss the possible discovery of Trixie's marital state.

Unbeknownst to anyone, Trixie was aware that Chris had two much older brothers. One of them would be heir to the earldom and that was all she'd known about either of them, until she arrived at the casualty clearing station. When confronted with the name Colonel Belingham, she wrote to

Chris with amusement that the commanding officer had his name. Quite unexpectedly, Chris had replied that Colonel Belingham was indeed his brother. As Trixie was known as Nurse King, their secret was safe. But she dared not share this part of her secret with anyone, not even Sophie. The latest discovery that Chris' other brother was at the casualty clearing station, and not only knew their secret but was also his squadron commander, was more worrisome. Would he pass the news of Chris' marriage to his brother, the colonel?

Trixie pushed her half eaten dinner to one side, her face ashen. Deep frown lines creased her forehead and a touch of anger flickered in her eyes. "I'll be sent home as soon as they make the connection. Why didn't Chris warn me? He never mentioned his other brother. Are you sure it's not just a crazy coincidence?"

"I'm afraid not. Colonel Belingham's presence by the major's bedside has confirmed they are brothers, which means Chris is the younger," Sophie said with a sympathetic sigh.

Trixie ignored Sophie. "Emily, what exactly did the major say to you?"

"He was in a lot of pain from the burns and highly medicated so to be honest, it's hard to say. It was the mention of your name plus Belingham that alerted me to the coincidence. He muttered 'sister' and 'wife' but his words didn't make sense."

"When did you last hear from Chris?" Sophie asked.

"Not since he was sent on this latest classified mission."

"It would make sense that this new mission was with a different squadron. I'd say he hasn't been able to tell you. If I recall, he told you he couldn't write for a while," Sophie said.

"That's right. Whatever the mission was, it was secret and

dangerous. Now his commanding officer is gravely injured in our hospital." Trixie brushed her cheek. "So what happened to the rest of the squadron? Were they all shot down!? Oh no!" A tear trickled down her cheek and fell to the table. She glanced around the canteen afraid someone would see her grief.

"I'll see what I can find out from the major. He'll be able to talk by the morning. I'm sure Chris is fine," Emily said reassuringly. "I'm tired. Anyone joining me for fireside tea?" She smiled as she cleared away her plate and the others followed.

Sophie put her arm around Trixie's shoulder and leaned in to whisper. "I think your secret is safe with Chris' brother. If Chris didn't trust him, he wouldn't have told him. In my opinion, he was delirious and your name slipped out."

"I'd like to believe you but that's not all I'm worried about." Trixie's eyes glistened with tears. "If he was flying with the squadron, where is he? Was he shot down too?"

"He's all right. The major has been here long enough that if Chris was with him and injured, he'd be here or you would have heard any bad news."

"News doesn't travel that fast in wartime," Trixie said with resignation.

"With two high ranking officer brothers, it would travel very fast," Sophie insisted. "Try not to worry. Emily will find out more tomorrow."

23

Major General

On a normal morning, the clearing station woke up relaxed and cheerful. Buster's 'wakie-wowter' call brought smiles to everyone. But this was no ordinary morning and smiles were replaced with anxious frowns. Sophie questioned why such a high-ranking officer was visiting their particular hospital. It wasn't unusual for someone to visit, just not a major general. For some inexplicable reason, she didn't have a good feeling about it.

A palpable tension gripped the camp all morning. Gossip and rumours painted Major General Macdonald as a tough military man, a career soldier who had served in Africa, a hero and great strategist, known to be a close adviser to the war department. But what did that have to do with a casualty clearing hospital? His reputation for ordering court martials preceded him, especially his intolerance for cowardice, no matter what the reason. Sophie shuddered at the thought of any kind of court martial because of the punishments, dishonourable discharges or worse, a firing squad. It was a practice Sophie deemed barbaric and should she have the opportunity, she wasn't averse to sharing her opinion with the major general.

It surprised her when he arrived with little fanfare in the sidecar of a motorbike, a normal method of transport for officers. It just didn't seem appropriate for a major general. Sophie suppressed a nervous giggle at the cartoonish scene. Colonel Belingham, Major Hughes, Captain Cuthbert and Sister Singleton stood to attention, arms in a salute as the large man unfolded from the sidecar, his monumental presence towering over the officers. In spite of herself, she gave him full marks for the dignified and, she suspected, well-practiced extraction from the sidecar. The group disappeared into the colonel's office.

When the meeting concluded, the group escorted him to selected wards and by mid-afternoon the camp was rife with chatter as the major general boosted morale with stories of victory, praise for bravery and encouragement to get back on the battlefield. But that was not all. Along with his words of bravery came disparaging remarks of the unsoldierly condition of war nerves. He wasn't afraid to call it a weakness, with implications that those who accepted the condition were themselves weak. It was subtle but the implications went beyond individual soldiers and, to the discerning ear, may well imply a weak command.

Supporting Private Maggs as he stood up, Sophie steadied the crutches. She felt, rather than saw, the great man march onto the ward. She stiffened, as did Stanley, and motioned for him to sit on his bed.

Major Hughes and Captain Cuthbert stood a few paces

behind the Major General Macdonald and Colonel Belingham, with Sister Singleton leading the group onto the ward. Matron was nowhere to be seen. If Matron was unavailable, and Sophie couldn't think of any reason so important to take her away from the major general's visit, Sister Potter should have replaced Matron as second in command. What was *she* doing hosting the major general? From her superior and almost flighty demeanour, she was enjoying every minute. He leaned in to Sister and said something that wiped the flightiness from her face. Looking confused, she scanned the ward, fixing her stare on the two shell-shocked soldiers, patients of Sophie's, and nodded towards the beds.

The major general frowned at the young private. "How old are you, Son?" Sensing the soldier's hesitation, he barked as if he were commanding a whole battalion instead of one frightened soldier. "Your real age. Not what you told the recruiting office." As if to counter the major general's loudness, Sophie stood very still, afraid that the booming voice would trigger an episode. The poor boy's shoulders curled forward but he bravely maintained a salute.

"Just turned eighteen, sir." His voice trembled and tears brimmed but did not fall.

"I'd say not even sixteen. Soldier, I don't condone lying but your patriotism is admirable. Send him home," he said with a grunt, turning to the next bed. "What is your injury?"

"A bit of shrapnel and I can't sleep, Sir."

"Nobody sleeps in war. I see you fought at the ridge. Commendable! Are you ready to serve your country?"

"Yes, Sir!"

Sophie heard Andrew's sudden intake of breath and turned towards the approaching group. The man should be sent home, his shell shock worse than most. She cleared her throat, ready to speak. She needed to make him understand how fragile the patient was and that he would never survive. Andrew stared at her and gave a subtle shake of his head, quieting her. Worry knitted his forehead and she knew he felt as she did. Maybe voicing their thoughts would make things worse. They exchanged complicit smiles as the group moved to Private Maggs.

"Private?" Stanley made a valiant attempt to stand up, thrusting the crutches under his arms and attempting a wobbly salute.

"At ease, Soldier!" The major general stared at the crutches. "Working hard to get up and about. Excellent! What happened?"

"Lost two toes, Sir and a grazed shoulder." Private Maggs answered as though his injuries were a badge of honour.

The major general actually smiled, hearing the pride in Stanley's voice and Sophie wished he hadn't been quite so noble. "Your handiwork, Major Hughes?"

"No, Sir. Captain Wainwright, one of my surgeons from London."

"Is this man able to fight?"

"Yes, Sir!" Hughes stared directly at Andrew, a triumphant expression curling the edge of his mouth. "Once the incisions have healed, he'll be ready."

The major general nodded with approval, patting Stanley on the shoulder. "Good work, lad. Still got three toes left and ready to fight."

"Yes, Sir," Stanley said hesitantly, glancing at Sophie with confusion. Amputations were a given for Blighty tickets. Was the major general sending him back to fight? Sophie was angry at first because Hughes was undermining Andrew and secondly because Andrew had not requested the Blighty ticket sooner. Stanley was not well enough to go back into battle but now it looked as though he had no choice.

The group moved on through the ward and Sophie patted Stanley's shoulder. "Don't worry. It will be a while before you are healed and Captain Cuthbert has the last say."

Encouraging Stanley to take a few steps, she watched the entourage leave. Sister Sin had been notably quiet throughout the inspection but as they left, she turned with narrowed eyes, glaring at Sophie and triggering an involuntary shudder down her spine. Why had Matron not accompanied the major general? Did Sister Sin have an ally in Major Hughes? She brought her attention back to Stanley and the possibility he could be sent back to the front. She knew Andrew would do his best, but this was the army and Hughes outranked him.

The sound of relief from the camp mimicked the roar of the motorbike returning the major general to headquarters. He had left a trail of patriotism with the patients and increased Major Hughes' sense of self-importance. It left a big problem for Matron, Colonel Belingham and Captain Cuthbert. The Blighty list had been reduced to physical injuries, mostly amputated limbs. The only exceptions were three teenage soldiers. The latter was an odd move as the man displayed no compassion for injured soldiers, no matter how serious, barely acknowledging that a soldier without legs could not fight. But when he spotted an underage soldier, he was immediately sent home. He had dismissed Andrew's diagnoses, stating that shell shock was a coward's way of shirking his duties. He implied that Andrew encouraged such unsoldierly behaviour. He also reminded the colonel that this was a clearing station. Casualties were treated and moved on to Base Hospital for further treatment or back to their regiments. This was true at the beginning of the war. As the frontline moved, so did clearing stations. However, large casualty clearing stations became more permanent if they were in close proximity to the railway, critical for the effective evacuation of injured troops. It was something the major general chose not to take into account, leaving everyone on edge. Even the morale boost faded by the evening and a cloud of gloom settled on the camp by nighttime.

Sophie crawled into bed, a bad feeling in the pit of her stomach and her head full of questions about Sister Sin, Sister Potter and Matron's absence. Then Jo began to snore. Having her in their tent, for the most part, was fun but she snored like drunken man. While it didn't bother the others, it kept Sophie awake. She sighed loudly, tossing and turning, until Trixie stuffed her pillow over her head and whispered. "Settle down. Some of us want to sleep."

"Sorry," Sophie whispered back. Putting on her thick coat and boots she snuck out of the tent to 'Teddy's Place,' not sure whether she was hoping for Teddy and tea or Carlos and … what?

"A bloody awful day!" Teddy declared. Steam rose from the billycan as he poured, handing Sophie a mug. Sophie wrapped her hands around it, sipping the warmth.

"So much for boosting morale, if that was the real reason for his visit," Sophie said.

"Blighty!" Teddy stated.

Sophie frowned. "What do you mean, 'Blighty'?"

"We're short of men. Every Blighty ticket is one less man on the battlefield. If a bloke has two legs and two arms, even if his head is a bit wonky, he can fight. If he don't follow orders, he's for the firing squad." Teddy gazed into the blackness of the night. "It's that simple and terrifying."

Sophie felt his bleakness and couldn't find the right words to reply because she knew it was true. She'd seen the major general in action. She too was terrified for the soldiers.

"The colonel and doctor need to be cautious too." Teddy poured himself more tea. "Sometimes the most dangerous fighting happens off the battlefield."

"I don't understand." Sophie pressed her mug to her cheek, suddenly needing the warmth. "I understand the Blighty rationale, and I'm thankful the colonel is more understanding than the major general, but why do the colonel and doctor have to be careful? Do you mean all the doctors or just one?"

Teddy ground his cigarette into the ground. Immediately lighting another one, he blew smoke rings, obviously thinking of how to answer.

"I'm in charge of the orderlies. I hear a lot of gossip from my gang. We are invisible so people talk and we overhear stuff. Not eavesdropping. People just don't see us. Most of the time we ignore it but sometimes we hear important stuff."

"You heard something between the colonel and major general, right?"

He nodded. "Me and Buster were heading to the quarter-master's store just as the inspection of the wards finished. Major General Macdonald were talking to the others, more like arguing. It was a lively conversation until they got to the colonel's office and then all hell broke loose. I heard the colonel say, 'Sir, these men are not fit for duty.' And then Captain Cuthbert added, 'They are a danger to their own troops. If an episode is triggered at the front, there is no saying what they are capable of.' The major general barked at the top of his voice. 'An episode! Is that what you call it? Disobedience and cowardice that's what the army calls it and it deserves the firing squad.' Captain Cuthbert tried to argue and was cut off with 'Watch yourself, Captain. Insubordination is grounds for court martial." There was silence and the colonel said, "Sir, don't let's be too hasty." The major general's response was, 'I cannot tolerate a weak command. Colonel Belingham, get your troops in order.'

"We heard a chair slam on the floor and we hurried along. I wasn't getting caught eavesdropping." He started to chuckle. "I thought Buster would wet his pants, he was so scared. Oh, my apologies for the crude language." Teddy shrugged his shoulders. "I guess someone realized the colonel's door was open and we heard a mighty bang as it slammed shut. They were still there half an hour later when we passed with the supplies."

"So, unless the colonel and captain comply, they will be punished?" Sophie's words were stilted with fear, realizing Andrew's life's work and treatments, as well as his civilian reputation, were all at stake.

"We are at war. Obedience and discipline are paramount. Right or wrong, orders have to be obeyed. The major general is a highly respected soldier and commander." Teddy hesitated. "And he's a bully. But he has a job to do, winning this war. Desperation and fear does terrible things and the army has suffered heavy losses recently."

Sophie understood the meaning of his last statement. It didn't ease her worry over sick soldiers being sent back to the front to face certain death. She knew she shouldn't get personal but the thought of Stanley back to the front terrified her.

"I've never seen you so serious, Teddy."

"It's only temporary." He smiled. "I feel better for talking to you, Nurse Romano. I know why the blokes like you so much."

"Me! I'm just a nurse, trained to make sick people better." She frowned. "What else did you hear on the *Orderly's Telegraph*?"

His face lit up with a warm smile. "I like that. Orderly's Telegraph. We know the nurses who care and the ones who have other agendas. That new sister's agenda has nothing to do with nursing."

"That is an astute observation, Teddy. 'Sister Sin' as we nicknamed her at the Bartley, is very bad news. If you see her getting familiar with young nurses, intervene." He raised a knowing eyebrow but said nothing, waiting for Sophie to continue. "I can't say more. I was surprised to see her escorting the major general. Where were Matron or Sister Potter?"

"I didn't see Matron on the tour but she was in the colonel's office afterwards. Sister Potter, I haven't seen her all day."

"Don't you find that odd?"

Teddy shrugged but didn't answer her question. "Looks like we have company."

Sophie stared into the blackness where a tall, white figure walked towards them, stopping to light a cigarette. The flare of light revealed Carlos' tired face.

"Busy night?" Teddy asked.

"No, it's quiet. I was checking on a patient. I'm off duty and hoping to catch up on some sleep. Is there any tea in that billycan?" Carlos turned towards Sophie, a hint of surprise in his voice. "Sophie? I didn't recognize you. You look different."

She was suddenly aware of her attire. Even though her coat was securely fastened over her thin nightgown, she felt naked in Carlos' presence. Her long hair fell loose down her back and around her face and she self-consciously tucked it behind her ears.

"You look beautiful," he said in a whisper, clearing his throat.

Teddy handed him a mug. "Here. It's the dregs, I'm afraid. Um… Well, I best get back."

Hardly aware of Teddy's departure, Sophie stared into her tea, willing her heart to be quiet and convinced Carlos could hear it thumping in her chest. He placed his mug on the rickety table, his hand brushing hers. She stifled a gasp, as pleasant tingling shot up her arm. Carlos' fingers gently pulled her hair back around her face. She felt his warm breath on her cheek as he spoke. "Sophie. This is the Sophie I remember, carefree on the silk farm in Lucca. I miss those simple days. You are as lovely now as you were then. I have missed you so much." She moved closer, desperately wanting him to kiss her. His moist lips brushed hers and she ran her tongue along his parted lips. Her invitation accepted, his lips caressed hers as he wrapped his arms around her. It was gentle at first, until the passion squeezed the breath out of her but she didn't want him to stop.

She opened her eyes, peering over his shoulder, and seeing a shadow retreat towards the officers' mess.

"Carlos, someone is there." She felt panicked. "I must go." She untangled herself from his embrace and ran to her quarters, not daring to look back.

24

Sinful Trickery

Sister Potter did not look well. She was pale, quiet, and unsteady on her feet. Sophie recalled her absence from the tour the day before. Maybe she was ill. It was so unlike her that she worried. Or was it a relief to have her mind occupied with something other than Carlos? The mere thought set her heart pounding. *What was I thinking and what was he thinking? A married man!* She felt ashamed of her primal instinct, of how she had enjoyed returning his kiss without hesitation. The feel of his arms around her and, worse, the pleasant tingling of arousal as she craved more. A cocktail of conflict, confusion, desire and shame whirled in her head, tightening her chest. The most shameful was the desire for more, the desire to love Carlos as she had loved him all those years before.

Dare she believe he felt the same way? She shook her head as Rosamond, his bride, came to mind. *How can I pursue someone who is not mine?* A sense of déjà vu caught her off guard, remembering Bill Blaine from the Sackville Hotel. She had loved him too. Bill secretly yearned for her friend Anna, despite her betrothal to another. Sophie had always known but hoped her love for Bill was strong enough for them both. It was not and she had been crushed. A smile of irony passed her lips at the serendipity of the situation. *Am I doomed to love men not available to me?*

"Nurse Romano?" An irritated but weak voice shook her from her thoughts. Sister Potter was staring at her. "Patients need your… Oh dear." She staggered, grabbing for Sophie's arm. "I feel quite unwell."

Sophie held onto her and called out. "I need some help here!" Just as Sister crumpled into a faint, Buster came running and caught her before she hit the floor. Kitty arrived with the smelling salts. Sophie didn't like the look of her face. It was almost translucent and the smelling salts did not revive her. Sophie looked around for a spare cot but every bed was occupied.

"Buster." Sophie hesitated. Sister Potter was short but rather robust. "Can you carry her to Matron's office?"

"O' course. I'll get 'er to Matron. Don't you worry, luv." With very little effort, Buster gently lifted Sister into his arms, carrying her to the offices. Sophie followed.

Matron's office door was closed and she hesitated before knocking. It was Captain Cuthbert who opened the door. "I need to see Matron. It's urgent. Sister Potter is not well."

Andrew swung the door wide open, allowing Buster and his charge to enter. Matron leaped up from behind her desk, pointing to the old sofa. "Whatever happened?" Buster laid Sister on the sofa and Matron tucked a pillow under her head.

Sister, who had come around, was making a valiant but weak attempt to object. Finally, her head sank into the pillow and her eyes closed. Sophie knelt down to take her pulse and felt her forehead.

"Her pulse is fast and she feels clammy. She may have a fever." Sophie looked at Andrew who was at her side, nodding agreement.

"Can you tell me what happened?" Andrew directed his question to Sophie. Matron had dismissed Buster and was sitting on the sofa, holding Sister Potter's hand.

"She looked very pale this morning. Not her usual bustling self," Sophie said, explaining in detail what had happened.

Andrew rubbed his chin. "Matron, can you find a bed for her in the Women's Ward? I think Colonel Belingham should examine her."

Matron nodded at Andrew and returned her attention to Sister Potter. "Vi, it's me, Hetty. How are you feeling? Are you in pain?"

Sophie stepped back. Hearing Matron use their Christian names made her presence intrusive. Sister tried to open her eyes but even her lids seemed weak. She began to speak, her words barely audible. "My stomach hurts. Indigestion. I was sick yesterday morning and throughout the day and night. The vomiting stopped this morning so I thought I was all right and went about my duties." She closed her eyes briefly, taking an extra breath before continuing. "I assumed I'd eaten something that didn't agree with me. The symptoms were like food poisoning but Sister Singleton was not ill and we had breakfast together so we could discuss the major general's visit. I felt quite well until the biliousness came on about an hour later. I'm sorry, Hetty. I was too ill to escort the major general. Knowing you had been called away, I instructed Sister Singleton to take over."

"Shush, you did the right thing. Why didn't you send for

me?"

"You weren't here."

"I returned before the major general completed his tour. I'm sorry, Vi. I wasn't informed you were ill. Sister Singleton was vague when I asked where you were, being somewhat preoccupied with the major general." She glanced at Andrew. "I didn't pursue the reason for your absence. Rest assured, Sister Singleton managed surprisingly well with the captain and major's assistance." Matron's tone had a hint of sarcasm and Sophie was sure she heard her mutter, "a bit too well."

"What's your diagnosis, Captain?"

"It could be a number of things, food poisoning being one of them. I'm not aware of anyone else being ill so that is unlikely. It's possible it's appendicitis but I'd like an opinion from Colonel Belingham and Captain Wainwright."

"Nurse Romano, help me assist Sister Potter to the Women's Ward and Captain, would you ask the colonel to meet us there as soon as possible?"

Eager to hear about Sister Potter's condition, Kitty and Pippa rushed to greet Sophie as she entered the ward. Sophie relayed the events and reassured them she was in good hands after being admitted to the Women's Ward. "Matron will inform us of any news. She was worried. I never realized they were friends. It was strange hearing them use Christian names. Vi, I assume short for Vivian, and Hetty." Her thoughts drifted off, wondering what Sister Sin's Christian name might be. Chastity seemed fitting. She almost smiled but a sense that something was not right made her frown.

"You look worried. Is she going to be all right?" Kitty asked.

"I think so. It looks like some kind of digestive problem. Both Colonel Belingham and Captain Wainwright are being consulted. I'm sure she'll recover soon." Kitty leaned her head to one side, prompting Sophie to continue. "It seems peculiar that Sister Singleton…" Sophie almost cried out when Kitty jabbed her in the ribs.

"Back to work!" Sister Singleton's voice snapped. "And Nurse Romano, gossiping does not become you. *You* would do well to leave well alone." Her eyes drilled into Sophie. "Whether it be past or present." Moving closer, she lowered her voice to a whisper. "We all have secrets we'd like to keep, and that goes for your meddling friend too." Sophie cringed. Did she know about Trixie and Chris? A chill ran down her spine as she considered the consequences of Sister Sin's words. They were not just a warning, but a serious threat.

Removing her focus from Sophie, Sister addressed the ward. "Sister Potter is indisposed and will be off-duty for some time. I am in charge." The whole ward, patients and nurses, went quiet. A sense of dread quelled the men's lighthearted bantering and the staff quickly busied themselves. Calling over her shoulder she said, "I'll be back for inspection."

"Phew! I thought Dragon Sister was a tyrant but Sister Singleton is worse," Kitty said. "And what kind of inspection?"

"I warned you," Sophie said with a smile. "Come. These poor fellows need our attention. That woman puts everyone on edge. Inspection? I don't know but I can assure you she will nitpick everything and no matter what you do or don't do, she will call it sinful. The fire and brimstone kind and off to hell we will go!" They burst into peals of laughter, releasing the tension. The patients close by heard the comment and yelled "Here, here!" They laughed along with the nurses and soon the whole ward was jolly. Some were oblivious to what trigged the laughter, but that didn't matter.

Sophie attended to Private Carter. Agitated by the noise, he was pacing the floor and wringing his hands, muttering to himself. She took his hand and guided him to his bed. He sat and stared intensely into nowhere. His expression told Sophie he was reliving a horror. She felt, rather than saw, the change in his demeanour. While restraining his arms she said, "Jack, look at me. What you're seeing is not real. I want you to look at me. I'm here to help you." She let out a long breath of relief as his eyes focused on her. In as steady a voice as she could muster, she asked Nurse Wilkes fetch Captain Cuthbert.

Andrew roughly brushed past her to examine his patient. "Details, Nurse!" He commanded in a way Sophie had never heard before. She carefully relayed the events of the past ten minutes as Andrew examined Carter.

"Thank you, Nurse. I'll take it from here." His words were dismissive and he made no attempt to face her. Confused by his attitude, Sophie went about her duties.

"Why so glum?" Private Maggs asked as he maneuvered his crutches along the ward.

"It is good to see you walking," Sophie said, ignoring his question. "You have mastered the crutches well."

"Doc says I'll be good to walk without these crutches soon." Anguish creased his forehead. "Are they really going to send me back to the front?"

Sophie walked close to him. "I don't know, Stanley. I hope not." Seeing his eyes drop to the floor, she quickly continued. "Hey, chin up. You'll soon be home with Charlie. I can't say whether or not you'll go back to your battalion but it would be unusual, given your injuries. However, I do know, regardless of the decision, you will get some leave."

"Oh, that be music to me ears, Sophie … oops, I mean Nurse Romano." They both laughed.

"Good to hear you laughing, Private Maggs." Andrew pushed past Sophie again. "How are you feeling? Any more nightmares?"

"Nightmares keep me awake. It's always the same one. I'm so scared for me son. Doc, is there any way I can go home? Nurse said I might get some leave."

"I see." Andrew glanced at Sophie with displeasure. Or was it anger. *What did I do?* She shook her head. *I am so confused. Why is Andrew upset with me?* He gave her another irritated glance, possibly because he saw her shake her head.

"I have good news for you. I have discussed your condition with Captain Wainwright. He is pleased with your progress and we both agree you will heal faster on British soil. Colonel Belingham approved your Blighty ticket." Andrew held up a buff coloured ticket on a string, attaching it to his uniform. "You will be transferred to the hospital ship and then to a military hospital in Britain to convalesce and allow the amputations to heal properly. You're on your way home, Soldier."

Stanley was speechless. Taking an enormous breath, he composed himself to speak. "Thank you! Does that mean I can stay home?"

"One step at a time. The doctors in England will make the final decision. In my experience, you'll get a medical discharge." Andrew slapped him on the back. "Good luck, Soldier. Go take care of your son."

Andrew marched out of the ward, leaving Sophie stunned

and confused. Stanley frowned. "Som'ats got up his craw."

"What?" Sophie asked absent-mindedly and grinned. "That's a strange expression, but fitting. I wish I knew what I had done to upset him."

"It's an expression me dad used when his boss at the factory was out of sorts. Why do you think it's some't you've done? More like that bossy sister or the big wig major general."

Sophie had assumed she was the cause but it made more sense if it was the major general. Was he defying orders? The major general had indicated Stanley should go back to fight. Stanley was not on the Blighty list, so technically he wasn't defying orders. Was that why he had stalled on issuing Stanley his ticket? *That sounds like Andrew, protecting his patients. How will he protect Private Carter?*

"Listen up!" The corporal bellowed into the ward, making Sophie jump and Stanley wobble on his crutches. "Transport is ready to take you to the train station. I call your name, gather your things and fall in line." Holding a clipboard, he called eight names in alphabetical order. The men scrambled to push their meagre belongings into their kit bags and fell in line. Andrew rushed into the ward and showed the corporal a Blighty ticket. He copied the name to his clipboard and Andrew attached the ticket on Private Carter's uniform.

Sophie helped Stanley load his bag, that was thankfully only half full, as he tried to balance it on his shoulder, crutches under his arms. "How can I thank you, Sophie?" he whispered.

"No need. Write to me and let me know how Charlie is doing."

Stanley hobbled on his crutches, dropping his kit bag. Teddy ran over and picked it up with several others. The sound of the corporal's left, left, much slower than his normal morning drill had a lilt of hope as the group marched to the waiting lorries, their first leg towards home.

The nurses slipped out of the ward and waved the men off. Sophie felt a mixture of sadness to see two of her favourite patients leave, especially Stanley. She would miss them but she was happy they were going home. A pang of anguish gripped her insides. Andrew had defied the major general and she dreaded the consequences.

Sister Singleton's inspections during Sister Potter's absence were brutal and included berating and bullying any nurse who crossed her path. Upon discovering the unnecessary, ruthless and often vicious behaviour, Matron was furious, ordering Sister to her office. What happened behind closed doors was unknown but a contrite Sister Sin ceased her rhetoric, at least temporarily. Aware of Sister's past, Sophie knew it was only a matter of time before the woman found another outlet for her vindictive nature.

Kindly nursing, beef tea and rest, hastened Sister Potter's recovery. Quickly gaining her strength, she returned to the wards two days later. The doctors remained puzzled as to the cause of the illness. Captain Wainwright had ruled out appendicitis. No other staff member or patient showed signs of gastric illness, so food poisoning could not be the cause. Although not totally convinced, the colonel had grave concerns. Sister had ingested something unsavoury, causing her illness. But with no proof of anything sinister, the doctors finally, if somewhat tentatively, agreed that her illness was due to an unknown and mysterious digestive disruption.

25

Consequences

The mood in the camp relaxed after a week of tension. Sophie heard lively chatter among the nurses and the patients whistled tunes. Laughter and bantering had returned to the wards. The flow of casualties had lessened. Although that would not last long, it gave everyone a breather. Even Sister Singleton changed her tone to pleasant and accommodating. She cajoled the staff with encouragement and praise. She even had a pleasant word for Sophie.

Sophie and Pippa joined Trixie and Emily in the canteen for a meal of bully beef and rice pudding. Leaning back in their chairs, they relaxed, drinking tea.

"Not often I see you gals so relaxed," Jo said, placing a plate of food on the table.

"It is pleasant. The wards are quiet and no inspections from officers or Sister Sin." Sophie rolled her eyes. "Whatever Matron said to her certainly had an impact. I hope it lasts. But be warned. She's a snake in the grass."

"She's not so bad, Sophie. Aren't you being just a tiny bit harsh? She was awfully nice to me yesterday," Pippa said.

Trixie glanced at Sophie before responding. "Sophie's only trying to protect you. Sister Sin is not a nice person."

"I'm quite capable of looking after myself," Pippa replied, a defiant pout on her lips.

"Just be careful. That's all we're saying." Trixie drained her tea cup. "Anyone want a refill?"

"Not for me," Sophie said. "Jo, how are things in the stables?"

"Similar to the wards. It is relatively quiet. Some horses have been sent back to England to recover. Others …" Jo's voice faltered. "And, sadly others we can't save. I'm treating a sniffer dog at the moment. She injured her paws on shrapnel and has a cough, probably from gas. She's awfully clever at sniffing out injured men. They nicknamed her 'Nanny' because she looks after the soldier until help arrives. She follows me around and comforts the injured horses. She's a very special dog. I've got rather attached to her."

"It's amazing how animals creep into our hearts," Trixie said. "We had golden retrievers when I was growing up. When Rex, the older one, died I was heartbroken."

"I know how hard it is," Pippa said. "My father had a frightfully difficult time when a horse needed putting down."

Jo's face brightened. "Do you ride?"

"Yes, of course. I miss riding on the estate. The feeling of freedom, the green rolling hills stretching out in every direction. It's hard to believe that such lush countryside still exists. I'd guess that even this muddy wasteland was once as green as home. I miss home and my horse, Dante." Pippa laughed. "I named him Dante because he is spirited. Papa said he had the devil in him. He never once threw me but he didn't like strangers."

"How about you two? Sophie? Emily? Do you ride?" Jo

asked.

Sophie laughed. "We didn't have riding horses, just ones that pulled the wagon. It's difficult to ride a silkworm."

"Silkworm!" The group chorused with peals of laughter.

"Of course. I forgot you were raised on silk farm and you, Emily, where did you grow up?"

"Dublin. Nothing fancy like you. My pa brought us all to London for a better life." Emily gave a weak smile and glanced at Sophie.

"Emily's parents and brothers died. She was left to raise her baby sister. She's the bravest person I know," Sophie said, placing her arm around Emily's shoulder. "Giving up your youth was hard but I detect a twinkle in your eye. That might have something to do with a certain Captain Evans."

Emily grinned. "There might be some truth in that. Enough of the teasing. You're making me blush. Here comes Sister Potter and she's carrying letters."

"Emily Finnegan, you are changing the subject. Tell us more about the good doctor!" Before she could reply, Sister Potter sat down with a thump and handed out letters to everyone but Trixie.

"How are you feeling?" Sophie asked, while glancing at Trixie's worried face. No letter from Chris. Did that mean he was injured somewhere or worse? After all, his brother was lying in a hospital bed right there. In all the chaos, she had forgotten and wondered if Trixie had spoken to her brother-in-law, or if anyone else had realized the connection.

"Much better, thank you. Just a little tired. Enjoy your letters." Sister heaved herself off the bench and continued handing out letters to other nurses.

Sophie yawned. "I'm going back to the tent. Anyone joining

me?" Jo nodded and stood up to leave.

Emily slipped her letter in her pocket. "I'll read this later. Trixie, join me for a walk? It's a beautiful night. I have to collect something from the surgical unit."

Trixie hesitated, frowning at Emily. "I'm not feeling well. Another time." Emily leaned in and whispered something. "Oh, a walk would be nice. Cheer me up a bit."

"What's going on with those two?" Jo asked.

Sophie shrugged her shoulders, not wanting to answer. She had a strong suspicion that Emily was taking Trixie to see Chris' brother. This time in the evening, with only a few casualties, the surgical ward would be quiet. "I am anxious to read Hillary's news. Do you have a letter from your sister-in-law?"

"Yes. I was hoping for some more biscuits but not this time. In her last letter she said rationing was getting tighter and it was hard to get flour."

The tent was warm as an orderly had lit the stove. Sophie sat on her bed and opened Hillary's letter.

Dearest Sophie,

How are you? Is it cold like London? We had snow yesterday. That horrible, sloppy stuff that soaks into one's boots and the hems of skirts. I sat through my examination with wet stockings. I must have a hole in my boots. I hate to ask Father for new boots as I know he struggles to pay my fees. The extra money I earn from nightshifts at the Bartley usually pays my rent and personal extras. I declined four shifts in the last two weeks so I could study. Cook was obliging and willingly deferred the rent until after exams. She's so kind under that grumpy exterior and insisted I needed my rest, although I admit I studied into the wee hours of the morning.

You asked me about Carlos in your last letter. I'm not one to follow the society pages but I did scan several issues of The Telegraph. I found no reference to Lady Rosamond's marriage. I asked Lady Adele. She's from an aristocratic family, although you would never know it and I can't remember if her father is a duke or an earl. She is a nurse probationer here at River House. Adele isn't acquainted with Lady Rosamond or the family but the aristocracy knows of everyone. She did remember Lady Rosamond's engagement a long time ago and thought she was married but couldn't be certain. I wish I could be more help. Is he still flirting with you? Maybe it's time to move on. What about the handsome DrCuthbert? I believe you said he was available.

Sophie re-read the last paragraph. Was it disappointment or hope that tugged at her heart? She hoped she would have had proof of Carlos' nuptials. It still sounded vague but it was unlikely the wedding had gone unannounced or unnoticed. She was certain Carlos had married Rosamond. So why was he flirting with her? She felt her cheeks warm at the thought of the kiss. Maybe Hillary was right and she needed to move on. It didn't necessarily mean Andrew. Her life was too full to be entangled in romance.

What a relief the first term is complete and yesterday was my last examination. We have two weeks off for Christmas Holidays. I'm not sure what I will do. I wish you were here and we could walk in Hyde Park or browse Selfridges' windows down Oxford Street. They are as pretty as ever, in spite of the war.

I had planned to see Papa but Mary has invited the whole family to the estate, including me. I have declined, not wanting to be subjected to questions about my choice to be a doctor. It is no longer a secret. Father informed Mary I had been accepted to medical school. He omitted saying he used his savings to pay for it. Dot says her children are excited to be spending Christmas on a big estate. She worries that the Earl will not be welcoming. He is not a kind man and I think Mary suffers terribly at his hand. Perhaps with Papa's presence, he will mellow somewhat.

Cook is planning a celebration at River House. It won't be like the old days but it will be pleasant enough. I shall miss you very much. Will you celebrate Christmas?

Sophie stopped reading at the mention of Christmas. Her eyes prickled and homesickness almost brought her to tears. She thought of the fun they had had decorating the tree at River House, coming home on Christmas night, eating too much, exchanging little gifts and laughing as they drank a little too much wine. No one had mentioned Christmas in the camp. She returned to the letter.

Matron was hurt in a bomb blast. Sister Kay has been looking after her office with the help of Beth. There was an air raid and several houses near the hospital were bombed, including Matron's. She received burns from rescuing her neighbour. I understand she is coming back to work after Christmas. I expect to be called in over the holidays, which is good. I'll be able to pay my rent and buy new boots.

I have sent a parcel but am not sure it will arrive for Christmas. In case this is the last correspondence before the holiday, Happy Christmas, my dear Sophie. Please write soon.

Your affectionate friend,
  Hillary

Sophie lay back on her bed, staring at the ceiling as orange light danced on the tent roof and muffled explosion made her heart tighten in her chest. She tried to resist letting her mind slide into the horror of the day the silk mill had exploded in flames and her father burnt to death. Quelling the panic and the urge to scream or run, she glanced at Jo, still reading her letter. She seemed not to notice. Sophie forced herself to relax. It was just her mind playing tricks. The burning sky and muffled explosions were not new, nor was her reaction. She was over the panic so why that night? Andrew had tried to explain that often something unknown triggered the mind into seeing danger, reliving something that was no longer there. She saw it every day in the soldiers. What had triggered her? A pleasant letter from Hillary or a quiet day was unlikely, except she sensed danger. Andrew came to mind. He was annoyed with her. She relied on him to understand and protect her and she had an unrealistic feeling of abandonment. What had she done to upset him?

"Hey! Are you okay? You're as a white as a sheet." Jo had moved to the side of her bed.

"It sounds stupid but sometimes the explosions spook me. It's crazy. It comes from nowhere but takes me back to a dark place."

Jo studied her for several minutes. "That's how you knew I was in trouble. You have attacks too. I was so angry with you but now I understand."

"I do understand, and see the anguish and fear in others. I want to find a way to take away the fear, not just for me but others who suffer." She fixed a smile affectionately towards Jo. "It will go away. It always does. I'm fine really. I need to clear my head. I'm going to get some air."

Sophie took a few paces outside. Something big was happening at the front and the sky was bright enough to see Emily and Trixie walking towards her. "Wow!" Trixie said. "That is very close. Sophie, what are you doing out here?"

"I needed some air. I'm glad to see you," she whispered. "Did you see Chris' brother?"

Trixie nodded, steering Sophie away from the tents. "He's very ill, burns mostly. Emily took me to see him because he's being shipped back to England for treatment."

"Did he really ask for you by name?"

"He doesn't remember but he was hallucinating for days. Chris confided in him. He knows we are married but says his brother, the colonel, doesn't know."

"Well, that's a relief. And Chris? Where is he?"

251

"He doesn't know or is not telling me. Chris was not on the same mission. I'm not sure I believe him because he then went on to say he doesn't know how many planes returned to base. He thinks the airfield is about 100 miles from here. All the squadrons' activities are secret and classified."

"So, Chris is all right? Still on the secret missions?"

"That's what he says. He's a real gentleman and very friendly. He told me to call him Robin and not to worry. He welcomed me to the family and said his mother would come around but it might be awhile before she forgives me for not having a society wedding. He laughed when I said that will be my mother's first reaction too."

"Who is the heir, Robin or the colonel?" Sophie asked.

"Robin is the eldest brother, heir to the estate and title. He reminds me of Chris. He has the same eyes. We couldn't stay too long because he's in great pain from the burns and it was an effort for him to talk. We tried to be discreet but an off-duty nurse speaking with an officer might raise eyebrows. Emily is friendly with the night nurse and persuaded her to let us in. I don't know what she told her but she seemed all right with it. I kept looking over my shoulder, I was so nervous. At one point I heard someone lurking outside. Emily checked but there was no one there and we laughed at my imagination."

The ground shook beneath their feet and Sophie gasped as the sky filled with black smoke, in contrast to the orange. She let out a long breath, her hand on her heart. "That sounds ominous. Does anyone else smell the acrid burning? I get the feeling it's closer than usual."

"Whatever it is, we need to get some sleep." Emily looked skyward. "Lots of casualties tomorrow."

The bugle call came two hours later, only seconds to the sleeping women. Within minutes they were dressed and racing across to reception, quickly preparing for the casualties as the distant drone of ambulances grew closer.

Sophie and Jo made a good team. They stood waiting alongside the orderlies and stretcher bearers as the first ambulance crept into view through the darkness.

"It doesn't get any easier," Jo said.

"No, and judging from that sky it will be bad tonight," Sophie replied.

26

Past and Present

Sophie sat on her bed, rubbing her feet that were tired and sore from hours of standing. The chilblains throbbed. She wrapped a clean bandage around them and pulled on fresh stockings. There was still work to be done. The reception area had cleared for the tenth time but more injured were expected as casualties were retrieved from no man's land. This she dreaded, as the soldiers were close to death, full of infection and few could be saved.

She hadn't expected such terrible injuries, the burns, the blisters from gas poisoning and the hacking, retching coughs. It was the burns mostly, having to clean the scorched and melted skin. Her father's image blurred her vision. She felt helplessness, trying to ease the pain and mend the skin as each man shrivelled away, screaming. The smell caused her stomach to retch and her body swayed as she fought against passing out from exhaustion and repulsion. She kept repeating her dear Papa's words. *'You can do this, my sweet Sophie.'*

Straightening her back, she moved one foot in front of the

other back to reception. Bending to take a pulse, she shook her head and pulled the sheet over a soldier, torment gone from his face as he passed into the next world. She beamed a smile to another in agony from a bayonet wound. She hated that she would hurt him even more.

"I'm afraid this will hurt a little but I have to clean your wound." She felt a familiar presence over her shoulder.

"Nurse." The deep voice wrapped around her like a blanket. "Morphine will ease his pain." Carlos gently examined the soldier. "A little surgery will patch you up, Soldier. Nurse will give you something for the pain." Carlos smiled. "You're going to be all right."

Sophie stared at Carlos' tired face, seeing the same agony she felt. She wanted to reach out and touch him, feel his strong arms around her and hear him say she'd be all right too.

"How many?" she asked.

"I lost count. More surgeries than I've ever performed in one twenty-four-hour session and the worst losses I've experienced, mostly gas poisoning. This fellow can be saved. Send him to Nurse Finnegan. She'll prep him for surgery." Carlos lingered, his eyes on Sophie. She waited, expecting him to speak but his face was full of melancholy. Seeing his patients die took a terrible toll on him. He said nothing and she wanted to embrace him and tell him she understood. Tears filled her eyes, weeping for something that could never ever be.

"Forbidden fruit," she whispered as he left.

Finally, her shift was over and it was dark. She didn't

remember seeing any daylight, and yet, a whole night and day had passed. Several cigarettes glowed from 'Teddy's Place' and the flame from the stove lit up three silhouettes under the canvas. Sophie hesitated, wondering if Carlos was one of them. Teddy called to her. "Tea's on!" How could she refuse? As she came closer, she recognized Andrew sitting on a rickety crate. Pippa blew cigarette smoke at a young officer and giggled.

"Back to the grindstone," Pippa said.

"May I escort you, Nurse Crawley?" Sophie caught the young officer's blush in the light of the lantern and she felt sorry for him, so young, so new, and so out of his comfort zone.

Pippa tried hard not to giggle but she was obviously flattered as they retreated to the ward.

Teddy handed Sophie a mug, a broad grin on his face. "What a day to arrive here. Poor fellow. And talking posh is not going to get him far." Teddy mimicked "may I escort you."

"He's pretty taken with Nurse Crawley," Andrew said, standing and stretching. "Here Sophie, have a seat. You look dead on your feet."

Surprised, Sophie sat down. "Thank you. Is the new fellow a doctor? He doesn't look old enough," Sophie asked, trying to avoid Andrew. She still didn't know why he had been so dismissive and now considerate. She chided herself. *Andrew constantly makes me feel off balance and it's best you remember that, Sophie Romano.*

"No, he's working with the colonel. Sent from HQ," Andrew said. "I don't know much about him. Colonel Belingham had requested some assistance but wasn't expecting anyone today."

Teddy turned off the little stove and placed the billycan on the old table. "Help yourself." He waved and left.

"You look exhausted, Sophie. Everything all right?" Andrew asked.

Sophie wanted to tell him of the flash backs the burns had prompted, but she wasn't sure. She sensed hesitation in his voice, slight but there.

"Tired. I haven't slept in a day and a night. I've lost count of how many wounded and I've dealt with some of the worst injuries I've seen." She stared directly at Andrew. "Is everything all right with you?"

Andrew frowned. "What do you mean?" A guilty expression came over him.

"A couple of days ago you were abrupt and dismissive with me as though you were angry. Have I done something to upset you?" The words flew out of her mouth, surprising herself. "And today you are friendly."

There was definitely something. Andrew fidgeted and paced around the table before leaning against it and crossing his arms. "No, I was just preoccupied."

"I don't believe you."

"That is your prerogative." The hostile tone she'd heard before returned. "I might as well ask." He cleared his throat. "Is there something going on between you and Carlos?" Before she could answer he added, "of course it's none of my business."

Sophie felt guilt redden her face and hoped the yellow lamp light disguised it. "No, it isn't any of your business. Why do you ask? Carlos and I have history. You know about that," she said. *Not all of it. She had never told him the whole story.* "He flirts more than I would like," she said, adding to her thoughts.

257

Now who's lying? She remembered the kiss and wanting more. She let out a forced laugh, "Are you jealous of Carlos?"

"A little." His tone had changed to that of a bashful school boy. "I am fond of you, Sophie, and not just professionally. I do find it difficult. I have so much respect for you as a nurse, but I like *you* very much." Sophie was taken aback with his honesty and realized he too felt off balance.

"I can say the same for you, Andrew. I like you and respect your professionalism. Sometimes there is a fine line between the two, especially here in a war zone, and I am grateful to you for helping me with my demons who raise their heads all too often."

"It's how you handle your past that makes me admire you so much. I sensed a strong woman the first time we met. I would like it to be more, Sophie."

"I would like to get to know you better, too. Is wartime the best time or should we be cautious and wait until we're back in London?" Sophie asked, knowing she was stalling. She needed to forget Carlos before she could love Andrew.

He reached for her hand and squeezed it. "Always the sensible Sophie. I'm fine with that but, as your doctor, I'm ordering you to bed. You are exhausted."

Sophie opened the tent flap to find all three of her room-mates staring at her. "Is something wrong?"

"We need to know. You and Captain Cuthbert? That was a long and intense conversation," Trixie said.

"Nothing to get excited about. I thought Andrew was angry with me. I confronted him. It turns out he has feelings for me. I suggested he wait until we are all safely tucked away back in London, whenever that will be."

"You could do a lot worse," Emily said. "Or is it something

to do with the handsome Captain Wainwright who stares at you with such earnest? It's enough to make an innocent girl blush." Emily patted her hair and gave a coquettish look, making everyone giggle.

"What do you mean?" Sophie asked, rather more sharply than she intended. Guilt swept over her and the memory made her uncomfortable. Someone had seen them.

"I didn't mean anything. I'm only teasing." Emily looked puzzled.

"Sorry. I'm tired. Anyway, Carlos is married to Lady Rosamond."

"Are you sure about that? He never mentions a wife. I've never heard her name until just now. The doctors chatter all the time and in the confines of the surgical unit we nurses hear everything. They talk about their sweethearts, wives and, like us, the things they miss from home." She chuckled. "And more than I care to hear about their preferences for women. Sophie, Captain Wainwright has never mentioned a wife. In fact he is quiet compared to the other surgeons."

"I am sure he's married. Lady Rosamond was hand-picked by his overbearing mother. Anyway, I am exhausted and need sleep." Sophie thought of Hillary's letter. Could there be a chance she was wrong?

The night shift was boring and mostly consisted of calming nightmares and reassuring frightened soldiers, a welcome break from the daytime hustle and bustle. However, she had mixed feelings. The solitude allowed her to think, something she didn't want to do. The recent reappearance of her past fears made her anxious. Keeping busy stopped her from thinking and the exhaustion put her to sleep but sitting alone at the nurse's station, one lamp casting her in a spotlight, she couldn't avoid her thoughts. She could almost hear a distant voice saying, *'Time to face the music, Sophie.'* She listened for her father's gentle, supportive messages but even he had deserted her that night. She only heard the heavy breathing of slumbering men; a cacophony of snores, whimpers and groans with the occasional desperate yell or scream.

There was no artillery firing guns and for that she was grateful, aware that they triggered the resurgence of the mill fire and it scared her. If the visions became worse, would she be able to keep her demons hidden? She planned to return to the Bartley, finish her studies, and resume nursing under Matron and Sister Kay. She had never told anyone that she had aspirations of becoming a matron one day, or at least a sister. Would the scars of her past and the terrible war take that away from her? She shook her head, letting her mind shift to Andrew. He too felt off balance. How did she feel about that? Moving towards the stove and feeling its warmth she thought of the heat of Carlos' arms around her and the almost carnal desire that stirred inside her when they kissed. Standing up, she almost knocked the chair over, shaking off thoughts of Carlos.

She took the lantern and made her rounds. All but one patient slept. She pulled a chair close to the bed.

"Time for sleep, young man." She looked closer and realized that he wasn't young. His face had a haggard look of a worried father.

"I like the quiet nights, Nurse. I can think and try to make sense of this war."

"Do you have nightmares?" Sophie asked.

"No, but I worry about some of these young lads."

Sophie held the lamp over his medical card. A lieutenant with leg injuries. "It's my job to look after these boys. You need your sleep to get better so you can look after them at the front." She pulled his cover up. He seemed to understand and closed his eyes. She smiled. *So I'm not the only one who likes to think in the quiet of the night.*

"Sleep! And that's an order, Lieutenant," Sophie said, turning to see where the sobbing was coming from.

She moved down the ward to a bundle shivering and curled in the fetal position and took his hand in hers. "Hey, brave soldier. Are you in pain?" He slowly straightened out and rolled onto his back. Rubbing his eyes, he tried to smile, shaking his head. Sophie felt his forehead. There was no fever so fear caused the shivers. "Nightmares," she said simply and he nodded. He looked very young. If he'd been admitted during the major general's inspection, there's no doubt he would have been sent home. "Can you tell me about it?"

"I never thought it would be this bad. Me and me mates signed up because we thought it would be a lark." Tears filled his eyes. "If it weren't for the lieutenant, we'd all be dead."

Sophie whispered, "You are alive and so is he." She realized this young man was one of the lieutenant's and understood his fatherly attitude. Tomorrow morning she would have the orderly move the beds close to each other. It would help them both. "What is your sweetheart's name?"

"Millicent." He smiled. "Kind of a posh name. I like it but she liked to be called Millie," he said, brushing his wet cheek.

"Tell me about her. Is she pretty?"

"The prettiest girl on the block." He closed his eyes and grinned.

261

"I want you to think of Millie as you fall asleep. You're going to be all right." He didn't open his eyes but his expression told her he was dreaming of Millie. For how long, she didn't know, but even a little peace would help him heal.

She rubbed her hands together over the stove and shuffled her cold feet. Seeing a rat, she stamped her foot and watched it scurry away. She would never get used to the vermin but at least she refrained from screaming and jumping on chairs. Waking a ward of shell-shocked soldiers was not a good idea.

Sophie leaned back in her chair, trying not to yawn. Night duty played havoc with her sleep. Even in London she had difficulty sleeping during the day. She hoped one of the orderlies would come by. Hearing someone enter the ward, she grinned at the materialization of her thoughts. Expecting to see Buster or Teddy, she gulped when she saw Andrew.

"Oh, I thought you were one of the orderlies."

"No, I was checking on ..." he paused, "a patient. What are you doing here?"

"Eh, night duty." She chuckled and he gave her a knowing smile but it didn't reach his eyes. Something was wrong. "The patients are all sleeping. I just finished rounds."

"Oh, that's good," he said absentmindedly. Now she could see the worry in his face and smell brandy on his breath. Andrew rarely drank.

"Andrew, what is it? You didn't come to see patients, did you?" She lowered her voice to a whisper as patients stirred, hearing the chatter.

"No, I was strolling. More like pacing around looking for a distraction. I peered into the ward, hoping a patient needed my assistance, and saw you at the desk."

Sophie gripped his sleeve, guiding him to a screened area

used to store supplies. The two chairs indicated it was also used for breaks. "As long as we talk quietly, we won't disturb the patients here." Sophie leaned around the screen, making sure she could see the entrance and the patients. "Andrew, I've never seen you look so worried. Has something dreadful happened?"

"Remember the young lieutenant sent from HQ?" Andrew rubbed his chin, a habit he had when he was upset.

"I do. He flirted with Pippa."

"He does more than flirt and he's not the naive fool he appears. The colonel had his suspicions when he appeared unannounced and they were confirmed when he found him scouring old files, ones unrelated to his secretarial position."

"Blighty files," Sophie said, guessing what this was about.

"Exactly. Colonel Belingham made enquiries through some buddies at HQ. Major General Macdonald discovered I, with the colonel's approval, defied his orders and sent Private Carter home. He's furious and his rage was exacerbated when he heard that Private Maggs had been sent to a military hospital in England, resulting in a medical discharge. There is nothing he can do about Maggs, that was my intention." He gave her a wry smile.

"Stanley received a medical discharge. I'm so happy for him." Sophie almost clapped her hands, forgetting where she was. But seeing Andrew's hurt expression she added, "I'm sorry. This does not bode well for you or the colonel."

Andrew shook his head, misery filling his face. "Court martial and dishonourable discharge at best and disobeying a senior officer and the firing squad at worst."

Sophie flung her hand against her mouth to quieten a cry. Taking a breath to calm herself, she said, "Can they really do that? Wouldn't the court understand why you made the decision to save lives?"

"A court martial only sees disobeying an order. In the military, the reason is irrelevant. It doesn't matter which way you look at it, I disobeyed a direct order and Colonel Belingham was complicit. I feel sorry for him. He's a career soldier. Whatever the outcome, his career will be over."

"And what about you?"

"As long as they don't shoot me. Depending on how serious they consider the disobedience will determine whether the crime warrants the firing squad. I can hope for a dishonourable discharge which will impact my career but I can rebuild as a civilian doctor. However, my work with shell-shocked soldiers might be compromised." He rubbed his chin again, the stubble making a raspy noise.

Sophie leaned over and rested her hand on his forearm. "Andrew, I am so sorry. Does the colonel know if they are proceeding with a court martial? Maybe the major general will change his mind."

"We haven't had official notice. The weasel lieutenant is just snooping around, we assume gathering evidence. I'm sorry to burden you with this, Sophie. I only just found out. The colonel invited me to his quarters and plied me with brandy." He laughed. "I'm not a drinking man so I think the liquor loosened my tongue." He stared at her fondly. "I'm so glad you were here. Talking about it has helped. Thank you." She saw the affection and wondered if she felt the same or only sympathy for his plight.

"I wish I could do more. Now I must get back to work."

"While I'm here, I'll check on the new admissions. Anyone you are concerned about?"

264

"The lieutenant in the first bed feels responsible for his men and it's bothering him. There's a young, very young, private who's struggling. I talked to him for a while but I see he's back in the fetal position."

Andrew checked the lieutenant who was sleeping and moved on to sit beside the young private. Sophie was right. The poor fellow needed the psychiatrist.

27

Watching Over

Kitty arrived early, shivering and brushing snow off her coat. she called, "Good morning, Sophie! How was the night?"

"Mostly quiet. Captain Cuthbert came by to see a patient. It's all on the chart. Is that snow on your coat?"

"Yes, it's coming down fast. It's quite pretty. It looks Christmassy," Kitty said, putting her coat away.

"I was wondering about Christmas. Do we celebrate?"

Kitty nodded. "I'm surprised they haven't started decorating. The orderlies go crazy cutting down trees, the canteen has streamers and bunting strung from the rafters. Cook does his best to get a Christmas dinner together and the colonel finds wine. Last year they had a concert, which was a hoot. I'm sure they'll get started soon. Now I'd better get started. You must be tired."

"I'm hoping I'm tired enough to get some sleep today. Nights don't suit my sleeping pattern."

"Try having a light breakfast with warm milk, if there is any, instead of tea. And stuff cotton wool in your ears. It doesn't look pretty but it works for me. Oh, and make sure you're warm. Cold feet will keep me awake."

Sophie pulled her coat tight around her before venturing outside. Looking up at the snowflakes fluttering down, she agreed it did look like Christmas. She stuck her tongue out to catch the snowflakes and bumped into Jo walking Nanny the dog.

"I've heard of catching flies but snowflakes, this is a new one on me." She laughed with Sophie. "On your way to bed?"

"I am tired enough to sleep the clock round. Is this Nanny?" Sophie bent down to pat the dog and she wagged her tail in response to the attention. Sophie looked at the bandaged paws. "Is she getting better?"

"She's doing awfully well. The cuts have healed. It's amazing how animals heal so quickly. Her pads are sensitive so the vet said to keep them covered when we're walking. She's still coughing so it will be some time before she can go back in the field. I don't mind. I enjoy her company."

Sophie gave Nanny one last pat and waved, heading to the canteen. She took some toast with an egg and asked cook for warm milk, carrying her breakfast to the empty tent. Pulling her boots off, her feet throbbed as she unwound the bloodstained bandages. She washed her feet carefully. The disinfectant made the chilblains sting but she continued. The last thing she needed was an infection. Leaving her feet open to the air, she wrapped Hillary's blanket around her and reread her letter as she sipped the comforting, warm milk. She should really reply but she was too tired and slid into bed, pulling the blanket around her and slept.

She woke to something soft and wet on her face. Heavy breathing wheezed by her ear and a familiar but muffled voice commanded, "Come!" Sophie opened her eyes to see a brown furry face staring at her and Jo standing over her, mumbling. She couldn't hear until she pulled the cotton wool from her ears. "Well, that worked."

Raising on her elbows, she saw a large tongue aim for her face and pulled back, laughing. "No licking, Nanny. What are you doing here?" Sophie reached out, patting the dog.

Jo ordered Nanny to sit, which she did, with her tail thumping on the wooden floor. "Darn dog," Jo said, lightheartedly. "I'm sorry we woke you."

Sophie sat up, patted the bed, and Nanny didn't hesitate to jump up, curling up next to her. "I can't think of a better way to wake up." She glanced at the clock. "Four o'clock. It's time for me to get up anyway. I've slept for seven hours. Warm milk is a great sedative."

"Warm milk? Ha, my nanny, not this one." Jo laughed. "My childhood nanny, one of the few who stuck around when I was a kid, and the only one I liked, used to give me warm milk when I couldn't sleep."

"It's a great discovery. Kitty recommended it along with cotton wool in my ears. What are you doing here at this time of the day?"

"I spilt a bucket of water on my trousers and came to change before I froze into a damned icicle. It's bloody cold today. I must go. Come, Nanny! Be careful, it's slippery on the duckboards."

Swinging her legs out of bed, Sophie shivered. Jo was right. It was cold. She gently eased her sore feet into slippers. The chilblains had healed somewhat while she'd slept. She'd clean and bandage them after. Keeping her blanket wrapped around her, she shuffled to the wash stand. Peering into the jug, she found a film of ice cover the water. It made her shiver more but her back felt some heat. Jo had lit the stove and there was a pan of water on top. "Jo Griffith, you are an anomaly. All prickles on the outside and soft and kind on the inside." She relished the warm water, washed and quickly dressed, taking time to rub the chilblains with ointment. Opening her trunk, she took writing paper and her father's pen from her treasure box and headed to the canteen for a snack while she wrote to Hillary.

Usually a quiet time, the place buzzed with activity. Teddy hauled in a sparsely branched tree. It was definitely not a fir tree but obviously the canteen Christmas tree. Once secured in the upright position, the kitchen staff unloaded a box of ornaments. Not the usual, although there were a few coloured baubles, the majority were handmade by patients and staff over the past years. Other people stood on chairs, hanging paper garlands.

Sophie slipped her pen in her pocket and joined the tree decorating group, wanting to feel the joy of Christmas. She admired the decorations. Some were intricately carved from sticks and branches, others little snowmen made of cotton wool or dried berries threaded on string. The final touch, and much to her surprise, was an angel carefully unwrapped by the head cook. It was obviously a ritual as someone thumped a drum roll on the table and cheered as she was placed on the top of the tree. She had white feathery wings, a white satin dress, a gold halo and blond curly hair that framed an angelic porcelain face. Her arms reached out and she seemed to be saying, 'I'm watching over you and keeping you safe.'

269

The work finished, Cook came round with steaming cups of cocoa. Sophie stood next to Teddy and asked, "Where did the angel come from? She's beautiful."

"It were before my time but the story has it the mother of an injured soldier, he were on his death bed, sent the angel to him for Christmas. He were too ill to open the present so the nurse opened it and put the angel by his bed. He made a miraculous recovery. The day he left he went to the canteen to say goodbye to his mates. Seeing them decorating the tree, he climbed on a chair and put the angel on top of the tree. She's looked after Christmas ever since."

"What a lovely story and it explains why she is looked after so well, a precious gift of hope." Sophie sipped the cocoa.

Teddy nodded, his forehead creased with worry. "We might need a whopping angel's miracle this Christmas."

Sophie rarely saw anything but a smile on Teddy's face. "Why would you say that?" Was Teddy talking about the battles getting closer or was it something else?

"It's getting too close. Orderlies hear things. The colonel is anxious. There's talk of moving the whole casualty clearing station and that major general is stirring things up soma't awful."

A sense of panic grabbed her chest. Was Teddy referring to Andrew and the colonel's disobedience charge or the closeness of the Huns?

"Here, I'm sorry. I didn't mean to upset ya." Teddy's smile was back. "Christmas is a fun time. Are you girls entering the concert?"

"I don't know." She laughed at the thought. "I don't think we have any talents."

"Ah, everybody has talents. Sing or dance or tell jokes."

"I cannot see any of us telling jokes." Sophie laughed. "Although seeing us sing and dance might be a joke."

Sophie left the canteen, laughing to herself and feeling a sense of excitement. Perhaps they could do something for the concert. She put her pen away. She obviously wasn't going to write any letters and readied herself for the night shift.

As she approached the ward, she saw a tall figure hovering by the entrance and realized by the uniform that it was Sister Singleton. Even as Sophie came closer, she didn't move.

"Good evening, Sister!"

Sister Sin spun on her heels, an expression of a naughty child with her hand in the biscuit tin spread across her face. It was brief but Sophie caught it and grinned.

"I was looking for aide Crawley."

"aide Crawley?!" Knowing Sister's history, Sophie frowned. "She will be off duty in a few minutes." Sophie stared at her, wondering why she hadn't entered the ward. Was she eavesdropping?

"Oh pardon. It can wait for another time," she muttered as she straightened her tall figure, sneered at Sophie and marched away.

It wasn't the first time Sophie had seen the tall, shadowy figure. She'd seen someone the night Carlos kissed her. After Andrew's weird behaviour she had thought it was him but could it have been Sister Sin? She'd seen the same shadow hovering around the surgical unit but had brushed it off as a trick of light. Sister frequently lingered near Matron's or Colonel Belingham's offices. It was not unusual as she would have cause to consult with Matron. It was the hesitation that was odd.

Sister Sin was devious and secretive, and what did she

271

hope to gain by eavesdropping? Sophie suspected that Sister Sin had something to do with Matron's absence and Sister Potter's illness during the major general's visit. *Am I being irrational?* Snooping around and playing tricks on unsuspecting nurses was childish behaviour for a senior sister, and for what purpose? But she knew the answer. It was jealous revenge for what she saw as Sophie and Trixie's meddling that ultimately caused her dismissal from the Bartley. Maybe she was afraid Matron might discover her past?

The fact that Matron Ross appeared to be unaware of Sister Sin's past and her unhealthy interest in young nurses surprised Sophie. She also found it worrying that Pippa had come to Sister's defence and now Sophie had caught Sister waiting for her.

Pippa came running out of the ward. "Hello, Sophie. Sorry, I have to dash."

Sophie grabbed her arm. "Are you meeting Sister Singleton?"

"Yes. How did you know? She invited me for tea."

"Pippa, please don't go. Sister Sin is not a nice person."

"You have said that before but, honestly, she's quite kind," Pippa said with innocence.

"Pippa, please!" Sophie lowered her voice to whisper. "Listen to me. She was fired from the Bartley for …" she hesitated, trying to find the right words. "She touches girls and does *things* and bribes them with favours."

Pippa's hand went to her throat. Sophie could see the outline of pendant or locket under her uniform. "I don't believe you." The words accompanied a hurt expression and the colour drained from her cheeks.

"If you want proof, speak with Trixie. I must go. Kitty's waiting. Please, talk to Trixie and tell her I sent you. She will understand."

Pippa's head nodded hesitantly, her face pale, as she walked away. Sophie couldn't be sure she understood.

"There you are!" Kitty said, making Sophie jump out of her thoughts. "Me dogs are barkin'." She pointed to her feet. "And I need to wet my whistle." Kitty giggled at Sophie's puzzled expression. "'Dogs barking' means my feet hurt and 'wetting my whistle' means I'm parched thirsty."

"I guessed some of it. I do enjoy your rhymes."

Kitty handed Sophie the charts. "Nothing spectacular today. Bed four is unsettled and there are two new patients at the end."

"Thank you," Sophie said, chuckling at Kitty's colourful cockney slang, which lay hidden unless she was tired or upset. Sophie felt guilty for making her wait, understanding how tired she would be at the end of a shift.

It was a quiet night. The patients settled quickly. Sophie chatted with the young man about his sweetheart, Millie, and he finally slept. The new patients, one an amputee with his left leg missing, and the other a serious chest injury, had both been sedated. Sophie used her time to tidy the supply area.

At first she hardly noticed the familiar rumble. Even the red and orange hue in the sky didn't bother her. She shrugged. More fighting, more casualties. It was the sound that frightened her. An unusual and yet familiar drone she remembered hearing in London. Aeroplanes! She stood stock still, hearing it come closer and miraculously the sound diminished. She waited, her heart thumping out of her chest. BOOM! She ran outside as massive flames shot into the sky some distance away. She stared at the flames and black smoke rising into the sky. Gripped with panic, she was sixteen again, standing by the River Derwent and watching flames engulf the silk mill. Her father's screams filled her ears. "Stop it! This is not real," her internal voice yelled at her. The screams kept coming and she realized it was real. The screams were her patients. Taking deep breaths to steady her trembling body, she pushed the vision from her mind. She had patients to care for.

The white sheets that covered the young man shook as he screamed, forcing his body to curl up tight. She bent down and stroked his forehead. He calmed enough to look at her. "You are safe here, Private." He began to straighten and she glanced at the lieutenant next to him, glad she had moved them together. "Can you look after him while I tend to the others?"

"Of course. What happened? I know that sound. It's an aeroplane. Did the bloody Hun not see the red cross?"

"Whatever it was missed us and exploded some miles away."

Sophie moved around the ward in the dark. Lighting a lamp would be a beacon for enemy attack if that was happening. She could not hear anymore aeroplanes, only soldiers creeping around outside, protecting as best they could.

She calmed the patients but no one slept. An atmosphere of anxiety enveloped the ward and a low, anxious muttering could be heard between patients. The lieutenant sat at the side of the young private's bed. A patient fatherly affection soothed the distraught young man. Sophie wondered what the story was. Why did this man feel so responsible for his young charges? Had he lost a son in the war?

Sophie heard the flapping skirt before she saw Sister Potter. "Nurse Romano, is everyone all right?"

"A little shaken but, yes, we're all right. If Captain Cuthbert has a minute there is one patient who might require sedation but he's calm at the moment. Do you know what happened? Was it an attack?"

"I'll deliver the message. Orders are to keep all lights off. I see you have complied. Use the torch if necessary. We don't know what it is. Colonel Belingham doesn't think it was a raid but he can't be sure so we treat it as an enemy attack. Do you need anything?"

"I can manage, Sister."

Sophie heard "Oh good!" as Sister's skirts flapped to the next ward.

"I can manage," she repeated to herself. How well was she managing? She had ignored her patients at a critical time. It had not happened before but that night's incident had flung her into her past. Up until then, she had managed the visions, telling herself she'd be all right. She tried not to think about it, brushing them aside, but in reality she was aware the episodes were coming more frequently and intensely. It frightened her, even threatened her, as she envisaged the impact it could have on her career. Had the symptoms deteriorated? She had avoided talking to Andrew, but perhaps it was time to reach out for help.

The remainder of the night passed without incident but, as the camp awoke, there was a hushed sense of caution. Eyes watched the sky and noises made people jump. The lighthearted bantering between patients took on a serious tone as they dressed and waited for breakfast.

Kitty arrived for her shift, looking as though she hadn't

slept. Pippa brushed past Sophie without any greeting, her eyes puffy from crying. Sophie's energy spent, she made no enquiry. Handing the charts to Kitty, she related the most serious reactions to the events of last night and retreated, eager to find Andrew. Desperate for his understanding, she needed to talk.

28

Craziness of War

A ndrew was nowhere to be found. He wasn't in his office and nobody had seen him on the wards. She panicked, terrified she'd break down right there. What if she couldn't find him? She began running. Perhaps he was in the colonel's office.

"Where are you off to in such a hurry? Matron will have you scrubbing bedpans for a week if she catches you running." Sophie stopped mid-step and stared at Andrew.

"I … um … was looking for you."

"Sophie," he whispered. She wanted to fall into his out-stretched arms but his hands rested on her shoulders, holding her at bay. He bent his head, his concerned eyes peering onto hers. "You look as though you've seen a ghost."

She gave a weird laugh. "I have in a way. Andrew, I need your help. I'm going mad."

"My office." He released her shoulders and, placing a warm hand on her back, he gently guided her towards the offices. She'd never been in his office, if you called it that. It was more like a cupboard with one tiny window, a table, two straight back chairs and a cabinet. Andrew pulled his chair from behind the desk and sat next to her, deep lines of worry on his forehead.

"Start at the beginning. What happened to frighten you?"

She stared at his warm, kind face, resisting the urge to cry. She related her reaction to the aeroplane and explosion. He asked about the other times. When she finished talking, the tears came. Andrew leaned back in his chair, waiting for her sobs to subsided. He moved forward, clasping her hand. For the first time in a long time, she felt safe.

"You are not going mad. You had a normal reaction, given the situation. You handled it well. You were able to pull yourself back to the present and treat your patients. I doubt the episode lasted for more than a few seconds. It just seemed longer. Did the vision bother you as you settled the patients?"

"No. I didn't think about it until afterwards and then it terrified me. It's getting worse." Her face contorted as if in pain. "What if next time I can't pull myself out of it?"

"Sophie, it's not you that is getting worse, it's the war. You will always pull yourself back to reality."

"Are you sure?" she asked hesitantly.

"I am certain. If you were going to have a breakdown it would have happened when you first arrived here. You are coping. We need to talk about the images that trigger the episodes; the fire, the burns, and your father."

"My father?" At the mention of her father, she felt guilty as though she had frivolously discarded something important.

Andrew saw her demeanour change. "How do you see your father in the fire?"

"I don't see him. I just know he's there in the flames. I can't let go. I have to hold on so I can see him. I hear screams.

278

They're his but I can't be sure."

"Sophie, do you think it's possible that the idea of letting go of the vision will mean you let go of your father?"

She nodded, unable to speak as tears trickled down her face. He waited.

"The last time I saw him was through the flames. If I let that go, I can never save him."

"Your father was released from the flames the day of the fire and it is time for you to let go and keep him safe in your heart, not your mind. The flames are not your father. Think of the kind, loving man who worshipped his daughter."

She smiled through the tears, envisaging the man who gave her love and strength.

"You will never forget completely, but as we talk about it the emotion will lessen." He squeezed her hand. "We'll schedule some sessions. I would like you to think of the happy memories of your father. Aren't you always telling the soldiers to think of their mothers or sweethearts?"

"I need to heed my own advice," she said, a slight grin brightening her face.

"Exactly. Now I'm afraid this will have to wait until I get back."

"Get back!" She almost yelled. "From where?"

"I don't want you to worry. I have been summoned to HQ by Major General Macdonald."

Sophie gasped, her hand flying to her mouth. "Oh no, not a court martial?!"

"I honestly don't know. No reason was given, except it's urgent." His fingers traced the tears on her cheek. "The message did not come via the military police and that fact alone indicates it is something entirely different." He tried to hide the worry with an unconvincing smile. "If it was for a court martial, I would be arrested and charged."

"And Colonel Belingham?"

"The order was for me only. Pack a bag and be ready at nine o'clock this morning." He glanced at his watch. "They're coming in ten minutes so I do have to leave. Sophie listen to me, you are perfectly alright." He patted her hand reassuringly, hesitating before he gently lifted her chin. "Now, doctor's orders, get some sleep." She held her breath, waiting to be kissed. Instead he pressed her head to his shoulder. "Take care. I'll be back when I can."

Andrew picked up his heavy kitbag and she noted how full it was for a short stay.

"Goodbye, Andrew." Was she saying a permanent goodbye or would he be back? She couldn't be sure.

"I will see you in a couple of days." A horn blasted, making them both jump. "I must go."

Sophie watched him leave in an old lorry with several recovered soldiers returning to their regiments. She scolded herself for being dramatic. Of course he would be back. He always helped her make sense of the fire demons but could she ever let go of her father? She sighed, off-balance once again. How did he do that? Switch from doctor to friend. Maybe a little more than a friend?

By the time Sophie reached her quarters, she was alone. Everyone else was on duty. She flopped on her cot, glad she'd finished nights, and stared at the roof, thinking of her father. He'd loved her, teaching her to be strong. He never regretted not having a son because he had Sophie. It was ironic that his untimely death had weakened her. "Papa, help me release you from the flames?" she asked as she drifted off into that peaceful space—not awake and not quite in slumber.

She saw Alberto, her father, in the drawing room at Oak House. He took her arm as the butler announced dinner and in deep conversation about the business, they entered the dining room. She could hear her green dress swish. He smiled with admiration and pride at the young woman his sixteen-year-old daughter had become. Someone else joined them. Was it Carlos? She wasn't sure. Her attention was diverted as the happy scene darkened, suddenly bursting into flames. Alberto rose from the flames, smiling with admiration and pride. His hand gently caressed Sophie's cheek. "I'm no longer in these flames, my dear Sophie. Take your strength back. Keep me in your heart and have a wonderful life. The flames died away and her father stood before her, whole and well.

Sophie awoke, her hand on her cheek where the sensation of her father's touch lingered. A heavy burden felt lifted from her shoulders. *Dare she hope her demons had retreated or was it too soon?* The image of her father filled her with warmth although she shivered from the physical cold, having fallen asleep uncovered on top of her cot. She quickly undressed and slipped under the covers for a restful sleep.

One of the advantages of the night shift was an extra day off. Between finishing nights and starting days she had the whole day to herself. She was glad of the time to rest, write to Hillary, have a bath and wash her hair. She had the time to leave it loose to dry. Usually, her wet hair was pinned under her nurse's cap and it took days to dry. She dressed in a skirt and blouse, a rarity to be out of uniform. Smoothing her skirt, she felt like a normal person. Nurses were allowed to be out of uniform on days off but those days were rare. Most of the time they went from uniform to nightgown.

Retrieving her pen and precious writing paper, she moved her chair as close to the stove as she could to be warm and dry her hair.

Dearest Hillary,

I was so happy to receive your letter. Congratulations on passing your exams and completing the first term. Your father must be very proud of his favourite daughter. He will miss you at Christmas but I agree it is probably for the best. Christmas will be strange for all of us and I will miss you terribly. Everyone here does their best to make it happy and joyful. We have a rather bedraggled Christmas tree in the canteen with interesting ornaments, mostly handmade. The cooks have promised us a special dinner. We may even have snow. It's certainly cold enough.

I have just finished nights and have a day to catch up. You know what it's like trying to stay alert on a few hours' sleep. I will never get used to sleeping during the day.

I appreciate your assistance searching for news of Carlos' marriage, but find it strange that you could find no announcement.

Sophie heard movement outside. She stopped writing and listened before calling out. "Hello? Who's there?"

"I need to talk to you," Carlos whispered. Sophie swallowed

hard, having just written about him.

Sophie pulled the tent flap open but there was no one there. "Where are you?" she asked. Grabbing her thick shawl, she ventured outside.

"Over here." A beckoning hand appeared to the rear of the tent.

"Carlos, what on earth are you doing?" She wanted to giggle, remembering how they used to sneak off behind the shed at the silk farm.

Carlos' mouth opened and closed but not a word was spoken. He seemed rooted to the spot. "Carlos, what is wrong with you?"

"Sophie, you are beautiful. You look how I remember you in Italy. Your hair..." He took a deep breath and stammered, "you're wearing clothes." His face turned red with embarrassment as he quickly added, "I mean I'm so used to seeing you in uniform." He reached out, touching her tresses and in a low whisper said, "so beautiful."

Sophie felt her heart racing, her mouth dry and an ache in her stomach as she yearned for his touch. She was completely confused. Hadn't she felt the same yearning, saying goodbye to Andrew? Or was she confusing empathy for affection? Overwhelmed, she pushed all her feelings deep inside, snapping back to reality and aware of her surroundings.

"What is so important?" she whispered. "Someone might see us and we'd both be in trouble."

Carlos stopped staring, his colour returning to normal. "Everyone's busy. I was careful. I can't get over how lovely you look."

"Be that as it may, I don't understand why you are here."

Her voice sounded matter-of-fact, the opposite of how she felt.

"I have a message from Andrew."

"Andrew!" Confusion abounded. She was struggling to keep her voice down and process the scant news.

"Captain Andrew Cuthbert." Carlos said his full name as though Sophie was unaware of his Christian name. "He said to let you know the summons was for a psychiatric consultation and nothing more. Rather a cryptic message. I assume it means something to you?"

"It does. Captain Cuthbert was discussing a patient when he received Major General Macdonald's orders to report to HQ. He was concerned it was disciplinary."

"Ah, the Blighty ticket mix-up. It appears not. He is expected back in few days, in time for the Christmas concert."

"Is the surgical unit performing at the concert?" Sophie asked, desperate for the conversation to move away from Andrew or her youthful looks. Although she had to admit she was flattered.

"Yes, are the nurses? A contest perhaps?"

"Maybe," Sophie replied, with a competitive tone.

"I'd better go before we are discovered," he said, his eyes scanning her one last time, as though he were an artist committing her pose to a canvas.

She nodded and slipped back into her quarters. Rubbing her cold hands over the stove, she wondered why Carlos was creeping about. He could have passed the message on in a more conventional way. She shrugged and returned to Hillary's letter.

I was sorry to hear about Matron. How is she? Is she recovered? Her injury may explain why Matron Hartford is unaware of Sister Singleton's past. I believe she wrote to her after I mentioned Sister had worked at the Bartley.

Hillary, how I wish we were sitting in the common room at River House. There is so much I want to tell you. My emotions are in turmoil. I am so torn with what I think might be love but I cannot know for whom or if it is true. Romance does not belong here and I have much work to do but unexpected and untimely meetings set me off like a silly school girl. I find myself giggling at the notion, just as we would if we were together. I am in much need of your wisdom and advice. It will have to wait until I can get enough leave to cross the channel, or this wretched war is over, and neither are imminent.

You have not mentioned any love interests. I'm assuming your studies take up most of your time and the gentleman students sound dull and childish.

I will close now as I am hoping to join Trixie for lunch.

Your affectionate friend,
Sophie

Sophie missed having meals with her roommates and was eager to catch up on the news. Emily had finally admitted she was in love with Captain Evans and they had big plans after the war. He longed for his country practise in Wales and Emily thought she might enjoy living there. She wanted to return to her passion of nursing children. Marriage was never actually mentioned but the girls teased her that wedding bells were not far away. The girls often talked about things they planned to do after the war. At the same time, it seemed the war was never ending, or was it a sense of everyday normality that had crept in to daily routines. Incidents like the aeroplane explosion had unnerved the camp, bringing them back to a reality that was far from normal.

Hospitals were supposed to be neutral for obvious humanitarian reasons but all too frequently the enemy saw it as an opportunity, claiming excuses of not seeing the Red Cross or accidentally missing a railway target. It appeared that on this occasion the close call was an accident. Their boys had winged the plane and the pilot was limping back to wherever he came from before it crashed. Sophie thought the explanation was perhaps more rumour than fact.

Why did she feel uneasy about this one German aeroplane? It was silly. The sky was full of aeroplanes. They heard them on clear nights. Trixie's brother-in-law lay burned and wounded after crashing nearby, evidence of activity in the immediate vicinity. Even the fighting at the front was creeping closer to the hospital. Every day the rumours changed. One day they were days away from victory and other times new enemy tactics were defeating their troops. Andrew suggested the war was getting worse and perhaps it was. Sophie thought it was getting closer. Her acute senses were setting off alarms in her head. It might have been the unmistakable odour of decomposition or the acrid smell of explosives that were stronger or the rumble below her feet more intense, but the night horizon glowed redder from raging battles and the morning exercise calls sounded like battle cries. She had the urge to laugh at her own seriousness.

I just rationalized one set of fears and now I'm worrying about something I have no control over. She dismissed all her negative thoughts, wanting to enjoy the rest of her day.

29

Twisting Troubles

"Welcome back to the light of day," Kitty said. "We've missed you. Pippa usually works well but these past few days she's not been herself."

"I'm glad to be back. I hate nights. There seems to be nothing between boredom reducing one to converse with the night rodents and being run off your feet with unsettled patients," Sophie said, making them both laugh, and ignoring Kitty's comment about Pippa. She knew the reason for her quietness. "How's the young private?"

"No change, I'm afraid. That was a smashing idea to put the beds together. The lieutenant helps him a lot. Kind of a strange, odd couple, don't you think?"

"They are and they need each other. I'm surprised the young fellow doesn't have a Blighty ticket."

"He should have had it yesterday. Captain Cuthbert didn't come on the ward. It's not like him. Perhaps he'll come today," Kitty said. "Can I leave you to change the dressings? Pippa needs help with the bed baths."

The morning routine was uneventful, the nurses all

wrapped in their own thoughts, including Sophie. Kitty's mention of Andrew had made her wonder about his well-being. His message via Carlos had eased her mind but she wasn't totally convinced. The major general was a harsh, unsympathetic man, tasked to fight and win a war. It wasn't her place to ask questions and if she did, the only person who would know the answers was Colonel Belingham. She'd have to wait.

Taking a welcome break, she and Pippa walked in an uncomfortable silence. Sophie glanced behind her, making sure they were alone. "Pippa, did you speak with Trixie?"

"You were right. I didn't expect you to be," Pippa said with a sullen tone. "She told me about Sister's unnatural behaviour with one of the nurses at the Bartley and how she didn't understand at first. I didn't understand. I thought Sister was being kind. I miss home so much it was nice to be loved." She winced. "But not in that way. Thank you for warning me. Please believe me, I didn't encourage her. I didn't know... I'd never heard of such awful things."

"It's all right, Pippa. You did nothing wrong. You do know that, right?"

Pippa nodded, tears spilling down her face. "She was very angry and called me some terrible names." Pippa twisted her hands, shaking her head. "Horrible names I can't repeat. She said I'd been influenced by the devil and that you and Nurse King were sinful, evil people, spreading rumours."

"She doesn't like us. This is the second time we've caught her. The first time was at the Bartley when she was sent back to the convent. How she got here, I don't know. Although, it shouldn't be a surprise as Matron Hartford didn't report her violent attack on Trixie or the reason. The whole incident was covered up. Sister returned to the convent for rest and contemplation." Sophie spat out the last phrase.

"That's terrible! I can see how it would cause a lot of trouble and embarrassment to everyone concerned. I wouldn't want any such association made public. My parents would be mortified."

"It is a difficult situation and Sister knows it."

Pippa put her head to one side. "I wonder what happened to her to make her into such a horrible person. This may sound contradictory, and I'm not defending her, but underneath that nasty exterior, I saw a glimpse of kindness and a caring heart."

"You forget she had an ulterior motive."

"Even so, there was genuine kindness." Pippa gave a wry smile. "I agree it was very brief."

"Um! I do believe there is goodness in everybody." Sophie raised an eyebrow. "Sister Sin, no, I can't see it. Be careful, Pippa. She is a vengeful woman. Stay out of her way. I will be doing the same. Trixie too."

"Did I hear my name?"

"Hello, Trixie. Are you on your break too? We were talking about you-know-who," Sophie said.

"I've had enough of that woman. This morning she ripped the ward apart and reported an orderly for not doing his job. The poor man was only helping an up-patient dress. Then she came after me. 'You, my dear girl will burn in hell. Repent your sinful ways,'" the three women burst into laughter at Trixie's imitation of Sister. Catching her breath, Trixie continued. "I could hear the patients sniggering, which sent her into a rage. I think she might have hit me if Sister Potter hadn't come in at that precise moment. Hence, I'm on break and hopefully the witch will have moved on before I get back."

"I smell baking," Pippa said as they entered the canteen. "Biscuits! I'll get it."

Sophie sat on the wooden bench with Trixie beside her, whispering. "I have something to tell you before Pippa gets back. I saw Robin, my brother-in-law. It sounds so odd to say that." She grinned. "He's leaving today. They're taking him to the hospital ship and back to England to a special burn unit. He reassured me that as far as he knows, Chris is okay. He wasn't on the same mission and nobody knows our secret, not even the colonel. He's going to try and get a message to Chris."

"He sounds like a real gentleman. In fact, all three brothers are nice." Sophie tapped Trixie's arm. "Shush! Here comes Pippa."

Hot tea and fresh biscuits were consumed in a gratifying silence. The canteen looked Christmassy with the mismatched bunting and paper garlands looped over the rafters. The Christmas tree stood in the middle. Like everything else in the war, Sophie sensed the conflict of joy and sadness. Even the tree looked lonely, or was it she who felt that way? She brushed that away. What was she expecting? The extravaganza she'd experienced at the Sackville? Lavish as it was, Christmas in a hotel could be impersonal and lonely too. She grinned, thinking of Christmas at River House, surrounded by caring friends. Glancing at her companions, she realized Christmas was all about friends and caring. There was plenty of that there.

"Sophie Romano, why are you grinning? A handsome suitor perhaps?" Trixie teased.

"No, not at all," she said with a hint of guilt. Both Carlos and Andrew appeared in her mind's eye, particularly Carlos' recent visit, making her cover up her thoughts. "Christmas. I was thinking of the Christmas concert."

"Why don't we do a little play?" Pippa suggested. "I was quite good in drama class. I played Juliette in Shakespeare's 'Romeo and Juliet.'"

"I don't think this lot are the Shakespeare types," Sophie said, trying not to laugh. "What do you think, Trixie?"

"Definitely not Shakespeare. We could sing or dance."

Sophie was regretting her suggestion. None of those things appealed to her. In fact standing in front of an audience terrified her.

Sophie's frivolous remark about the Christmas concert had committed her to performing. Try as she might, her friends would not reconsider. But they did reject singing and dancing, except Pippa. She could play the piano and sing and decided she would do a solo. Sophie, Trixie, Emily and Jo decided on a funny skit. Sophie let it slip that the surgeons were also preparing one, which set their competitive juices flowing.

Christmas was a perfect boost for the girls and the whole camp came alive. The cookhouse team were being exceptionally secretive about a big surprise coming for Christmas dinner. There were rehearsals going on everywhere; skits, solos, stand-up comedy and a choir. It was going to be an interesting concert.

The festive mood dampened somewhat as rumour of a massive push filtered through the camp. A rumour the colonel confirmed with orders to prepare for heavy casualties. The bugle call came shortly after. Sophie could see a long convoy of ambulances in the distance. Stretcher bearers, orderlies and nurses gathered outside reception. Sister Potter stood next to her, stating the obvious. "It will be a long day and I suspect an even longer night." She hesitated, staring at Sophie. "Nurse Romano, I've been hearing some disturbing accusations about you from Sister Singleton. I understand you are acquainted."

"What accusations, Sister? I don't know what you mean by acquainted. Sister Singleton taught the probationers at Bartley Hospital in London. That is how we are *acquainted*." Sophie didn't like Sister Potter's accusatory tone, which was out of character. "That is, we were until Matron Hartford asked Sister Singleton to leave for unprofessional conduct." Sophie held her breath. Although that was the reason, it was not the official one. She felt threatened. "I am surprised Matron Ross is not aware of Sister's past, as I understand she is a long-time friend of Matron Hartford."

Sister Potter sounded surprised. "I was not aware that she worked at the Bartley. I don't think Matron knows either, at least she never mentioned it." Sister thought for a minute and continued, "However, Sister confided in me that she had concerns about your conduct."

"Unfounded, I can assure you. I promise you that Matron is very well aware. I mentioned the acquaintance as you call it the day Sister arrived." Sophie's voice was harsher than she intended. *What sort of accusations had Sister Sin made?*

"I merely wanted to warn you before I spoke with Matron. But maybe…" Sister Potter coughed as exhaust fumes billowed from a halting ambulance. The remainder of her sentence disappeared into the black smoke. They opened the ambulance doors and began unloading the men. Jo called for Sophie to help her as she tried to support a collapsing soldier. Sophie checked his medical card for the severity of his wounds. Seeing the T on his forehead she said, "His weakness is due to the loss of blood." She inspected the wound, looking for the tourniquet. "It's stopped bleeding." She gave a nod to a stretcher bearer, patted the soldier and smiled. "Rest, Soldier, the doctor will be here soon. You're going to be all right." Her words were soothing.

She glanced at the line of injured.

Jo whispered, "What was Sister Potter on about? Sorry. Didn't intend to eavesdrop but I was standing next to you. Sin, the bloody depraved woman, has it in for you. She is the most bad tempered person I have ever come across."

"A long story." Sophie attempted a grin, picking up on the word 'depraved.' She didn't remember ever telling Jo about how Sister Sin had coerced a young nurse into sexual favours and then attacked Trixie after she accidentally witnessed a disturbing scene. Did she know? Sophie opened her mouth to ask but whispered over her shoulder instead. "Oh heck, there she is."

Sister Sin marched determinedly towards Sophie, her tall, straight body as stiff as a post, her nose in the air and a smirk of triumph spread across her face. It initiated an involuntary shudder from Sophie. Suddenly the woman twisted around, pivoting on her feet as if she had forgotten something or changed her mind and, without uttering a word, she retreated, deliberately brushing against Trixie. She never attended the reception area and Sophie had no doubt that the intention of her visit was to intimidate. Sophie felt a rock drop to the pit of her stomach. *She's finally found her revenge. My nursing career is over.* She glanced over at Trixie who shrugged her shoulders, shaking her head with a look of 'what was that about?' Sophie shrugged back, mouthing, 'I don't know.' In truth she had her suspicions. In spite of Sister's religious acuity, she did not forgive and had obviously plotted her revenge.

The reception area filled with wounded soldiers and Sophie needed to concentrate on nursing. The men were badly wounded by gunshots, explosions, bayonets and falling debris. Teddy carried a soldier to a cot, looking at Sophie he said, "He's real bad."

"What happened today?"

"The bastard Huns attacked the trenches. Those that can talk say it were a blood bath. A whole division struck down." Teddy rubbed his brow. "Worst I've seen."

Sophie leaned over the soldier, feeling for his pulse and shook her head. "Sorry, Teddy. He's gone."

By mid-evening the ambulances had dwindled to a trickle and reception only had a few soldiers to be attended to. Most had been assessed, cleaned up and transferred to a ward or sent to surgery. Sophie imagined the queue for surgery would be long as the kind of injuries from the battle required surgical intervention. She stretched her aching back and tried to ignore her throbbing feet. Jo brought in one last casualty, an officer with multiple wounds, who collapsed. Jo caught him before he hit the floor and, with Sophie's help, they eased him on to a cot. Sophie held his wrist and felt his forehead. "He's still alive, barely. Fetch Captain Wainwright." She patted his arm. "Hang on, Sir. Help is coming." She saw horror in his face and heavy lines of worry, for his troops no doubt. He'd stayed to the end and it may have cost him his life. "You saved as many as you could. Now you need to save yourself." She felt Carlos' presence and turned, relaying the man's vitals. He gave her a warm smile and she had an urge to reach out and touch him but held back.

"Thank you, Nurse. I'll take it from here." Carlos beckoned to Teddy. "Private, see the officer is taken to the surgical unit." He hesitated, examining Sophie's face to the point that she felt awkward and shifted her gaze. "How long is it since you had a break?"

"I honestly don't remember. We just keep going, don't we, Jo?"

"I'll speak with Sister Potter. You need to rest."

"Thank you," Sophie said. "You might want to suggest Sister join us."

Carlos grinned. "I will. Good evening, ladies!"

Sophie watched Carlos' laboured steps, wanting to give him his own advice. She looked to Jo. "I doubt he's stopped since the convoy arrived. You've been here all night. Were you not needed by the veterinarians?"

"Captain sent me to help. There's only one injured dog in this battle and no horses. The only horses we have right now are not fit for battle. He's a real sport and knows my ambulance experience is needed when a convoy arrives."

The canteen, although unusually busy for the middle of the night, was devoid of chatter, the quiet broken by clinking cutlery and sighs of exhaustion. Jo filled two plates with rissoles and mash, turnips or potatoes, it was hard to tell. Sophie poured two mugs of hot, weak tea and they squeezed in at the end of a long bench. Jo tucked in as though she hadn't eaten all day, which was probably true. Sophie pushed the food around her plate, her stomach so tied in knots, even a nibble made her feel sick. She wrapped her hands around the mug, enjoying the hot liquid.

"Starving yourself won't make things better," Jo said between mouthfuls. "Don't let that bloody, ill-tempered, depraved woman get to you." She raised an eyebrow. "Or is it the handsome doctor? Perhaps I should make that plural?"

"My stomach is queasy. I can't eat. I'll have some pudding later." *What is she talking about, plural?* Sophie thought but didn't say. *And there's that word again, 'depraved.'* "Jo Griffith, you're speaking in riddles. What do you mean, plural?" Sophie said with a chuckle.

"You don't fool me, Sophie. I may be a widow, older and definitely wiser." She gave Sophie an affectionate grin. "But I haven't forgotten what it feels like to be in love. I loved Dickie from the day I set eyes on him. I know that look, except you confuse me because I see it for two men."

"Is it so obvious? Jo, I am confused. One is not available and the other... I'm not sure."

"It's bloody marvellous how you hide your feelings." She grinned. "Most of the time, anyway." Jo laughed her loud, raucous laugh, attracting attention. "Oh, sorry, not very lady-like." She laughed again quietly and added in a whisper, "I'm laughing because you have two handsome beaux pining for you and all I get is an offer from that ill-tempered woman."

"Sister Singleton?" Sophie whispered. "She ...approached you?"

Jo nodded, keeping her voice low. "A misunderstanding, that's all. You know the army's rules. I don't have an issue but the army does. Do you?"

"No I don't. Men or women should be allowed to love however they choose." Sophie hesitated. "Except when it is not love at all." The word 'rape' sat on her tongue, unspoken.

"You think too much," Jo scoffed. "No harm done so keep

297

quiet."

Angry, unspoken words lingered in Sophie's head. *That's what everyone says. Keep it quiet, no harm done. But Sister does do harm. Is Pippa all right? Exposing the woman would cause hurt and embarrassment to the victims and damage reputations.* Sophie shook her head, muttering, "Hurting young, innocent women is not right."

Jo gave her a puzzled look and shrugged her shoulders as though reluctant to say anything more. It was obvious she did not know the full story. They finished their meal in silence.

30

Christmas 1917

O nly two days before Christmas, the camp had settled back into its usual routine, allowing for rehearsal time before the Christmas concert. Buster and Teddy, with help from the able up-patients, constructed a wooden stage in the open area of the camp, that the soldiers affectionately called The Common. It was a place where up-patients gathered to smoke and everyone collected at 'Teddy's Place' for a break. None of the canteens were big enough to accommodate all the staff and patients. The concert was planned for Christmas afternoon, after they'd eaten and before darkness fell. It might be cold but if the frost and snow held off, they'd be all right.

Peals of laughter, angelic and not-so-angelic singing, along with jovial chatter could be heard everywhere. Sister Singleton did her best to quash the celebratory atmosphere but she was no match for hundreds of patients and nurses starving for fun and a festive distraction. In fact, no one took any notice of her, including Sophie, which she would soon learn was a mistake. Matron and Colonel Belingham were aware of how important the festivities were to the health and well-being of everyone, encouraging fun and overlooking minor infractions. Sister Singleton, as might be expected, was not of the same opinion. She tried to order people back to work, but her commands fell on deaf ears and being ignored infuriated her. Incensed by the disregard of her beliefs inflamed her righteous attitude and drew her dangerously close to more fantasy than was to be performed on stage.

Each performer was allowed to test out the stage. Sophie, Trixie, Jo and Emily stepped onto the wooden structure to take their turn. Several up-patients watched, whistling and cheering the girls on. Sophie glanced at her self-conscious friends giggling with embarrassment. Sensing something off, her laugh turned to a frown. Then she saw Sister Sin, watching, her lips parted in a wry grin, poised like a lioness waiting to pounce on her prey. *What is she up to?*

Sophie shrugged, continuing the mini rehearsal until a sudden, vicious verbal attack came from Sister Sin. "De-bauchery! Evil blasphemy! Sins against the Almighty!" Her outburst was almost laughable and the spectators sniggered until the accusations became personal. She jumped on the stage, turning to the patients, delighted to have an audience. First, she poked her finger at Trixie. "This one, keeps secret men, pretending she's married." Pushing her finger into Sophie's chest, she continued. "You think these nurses are your angels, well, think again. They are wicked, evil women who fornicate with the devil and with evil men." She spun around, pointing at the men. "Monsters like you!" Her voice sounded like gravel, as if she were speaking in tongues. Sophie stared at her, fear and concern tightening her throat. Had the woman gone mad? The orderlies ushered the men back to the ward.

Jo approached her, "What the bloody hell are you talking about, Sister? Someone send for Matron."

"That won't be necessary," Sister said, her voice having returned to normal. "I have informed Matron of this debauchery. Nurse Romano and Nurse King are to report to Matron's office where they will be discharged of their duties. My work is finally done. Praise the Lord!"

Sophie and Trixie stared at her, not sure what to do. The woman was their superior but she was acting mad. Should they follow instructions or wait for Matron? To their complete surprise, Sister stepped off the stage, huffed and marched away. Trixie whispered, "She's gone crazy. She knows about my marriage and that alone is grounds for dismissal. What does she have on you?"

"She has been spying on me. I suspect it will be unfounded, but difficult to disprove. Probably unseemly conduct with patients and doctors."

"I think we are about to find out. Here they come." Trixie nodded towards Sister Potter and Matron approaching them.

"Ladies! Aren't you two supposed to be on duty?" Matron asked as she walked past them. Sophie could have sworn Sister Potter winked.

Sophie looked down at her nurse's watch. "Oh heck, I'm late!" She stood watching Sister and Matron speak to Sister Singleton. "Trixie, what just happened?"

"It appears that Sister Singleton is the one being escorted to Matron's office. It's best we both get to work or we will be in trouble. More trouble? I am confused."

"That makes two of us and I doubt it's over."

Trixie and Sophie went on with their day. The up-patients

who had witnessed the outburst found it entertaining, making jokes about Sister Singleton and calling her a witch and a few other choice words. Some were ready for a fist fight if she didn't stop harassing their favourite nurses. It was gratifying to hear the protectiveness from the patients. In spite of the support, which Sophie found both amusing and affectionate, she constantly looked over her shoulder, waiting and wondering when Matron would call either of them to her office.

It didn't happen, although Sophie thought her heart would jump out of her chest when Sister Potter called her name at teatime. She relaxed when she handed her two parcels, one for her and one for Jo, and thick letters for Emily and Trixie. Receiving mail always lifted spirits but this close to Christmas, when everyone was a little bit homesick, the mail meant so much more. Eager to see what Hillary had sent her, and hoping it was something she could share, Sophie rushed to the tent they called home. She placed Jo's parcel on her bed and the letters on the desk. Kicking off her boots, she sat cross-legged on her bed and carefully unwrapped the parcel. It contained a box of biscuits from Cook, a bag of sweets, fruit drops and a copy of *The Voyage Out* by Virginia Woolf. Sophie flipped through the pages, enjoying the feel of the paper. She read Hillary's inscription.

> *To Sophie, my dearest friend.*
> *The author of this book, Virginia Woolf, is a true modern woman. A fellow female student gave it to me. As I read it, I thought of you. How I wish we were together to discuss this prose. Enjoy and much love,*
> *Hillary*

Sophie hugged the book to her chest. Reading was one of her greatest pleasures and yet she had read little since coming to Passchendaele. It was partly because of time, but mostly for the lack of books. This was a perfect Christmas present. There was another package inside, something soft, wrapped in a cloth bag and tied with a red ribbon and a note. *With Love, from Hillary.* In smaller printed letters, it read *Do not open until Christmas morning.* She felt a twinge of excitement. The presents made her think of childhood, going to mass with her parents and opening gifts. She wanted her roommates to feel the same. She spread out the brown paper from Hillary's parcel. Smoothing the wrinkles, she carefully cut it into three equal pieces and divided the string. She placed a biscuit and four colourful fruit drops on each piece of paper. She smiled, knowing that Hillary had sent the sweets, a sacrifice of sugar rations, so that Sophie could share the treat with her friends. She tied each bundle with the string and hid them in her trunk, together with her unopened present, and settled down to read Hillary's letter.

Dearest Sophie,

I am sure you have received my letter by now. At the time your Christmas parcel was not ready. I hope it arrives in time.

I shall miss you so much. It will seem odd to sit at the dining room table at River House with Cook and strangers. Cook has done her best to replace Mrs. Wilderby but it is just not the same. I shouldn't complain. She is very kind under that stern exterior. She insisted on baking ginger biscuits for you and her friend knitted your gift. I don't have a sweet tooth so I saved my sugar ration to buy you fruit drops to share with Trixie, Emily and your new friend, Jo.

I am working over Christmas. It is better to keep busy and term doesn't start until the beginning of January. As you can assume, I declined my sister's invitation on the grounds that I was working. I feel guilty making the excuse, although true and I could use the money. I did not have to work. It was my choice. Father wrote that he was disappointed but understood and sent me a train ticket as a Christmas present so I can visit him at half term. His exact words were 'we can spend time together in conversation on long walks, just the two of us.' I'm beginning to acknowledge that, perhaps, I am the favourite daughter. Neither of my sisters have questioned how I am paying for medical school. I am astounded at how ignorant they are of all things beyond their social group and family.

Thank you for inquiring about Matron. She is much better and was in the office yesterday. Her hands are badly burned and bandaged but she insists on working, although I think Beth and Sister Kay would prefer that she stay home.

I must close and run this parcel to the post office.

Much love and Merry Christmas,
  Hillary

The smell of bacon drifted into Sophie's nostrils. Was she dreaming? No, she heard Buster calling his wowter call in the distance. Opening her eyes she said, "Does anyone else smell bacon?"

"It smells like Cook's Sunday roast at River House," Trixie said, lifting herself on her elbows. "Christmas treat perhaps? The kitchen has been very secretive. Merry Christmas everyone!"

Sophie jumped out of bed and delved into her trunk. "A modest gift from me, with some help from Cook and Hillary." She handed out three little brown paper bundles and pulled the present from Hillary from her trunk. Trixie passed around small packages tied in pink ribbon and Emily produced little snowman ornaments she had made of cottonwool. Jo opened a large tin of shortbread and handed it out. A billycan of tea sat on the stove. With child-like giggles the four opened their presents, hugging their thanks. The soft package from Hillary was a warm pair of wool socks. The sweet scent of lavender filled the tent as they each unwrapped a lavender sachet from Trixie.

"We'd better get dressed if we want some of that bacon for breakfast." Sophie breathed in the very strong smell and frowned. "There must be a lot of bacon today."

Their steps were light and brisk as they headed to the canteen. The first thing they saw was the reason for the bacon aroma. A large pig was roasting over a wood fire, one of the kitchen aids assigned to keep the spit turning and the fire stoked just right. The secret Christmas dinner was revealed—a whole roasted pig.

The morning routine went fast and spirits were high for the most part, although Sophie sensed many patients were pining for home. However, the anomaly of a roasting pig over an open fire to be eaten for dinner, and the anticipation of a lively concert, filled the camp with festivity. Although temporary, it overshadowed yearning for loved ones or worry of battle.

It was a lively concert. Even the weather cooperated with sunshine. Sophie thought the cheering and whistling might be heard across the channel. With full bellies, the men wrapped in blankets and heavy coats sat, stood or kneeled in front of the stage. Orderlies wheeled bathchairs or carried those that couldn't walk. The concert started with a singsong. Everyone belted out *It's a long way to Tipperary,* followed by an off-key solo but they cheered anyway. They laughed at the comedians, even when the jokes weren't funny. Pippa mesmerized the audience with her soft angel-like voice as she sang *Let Me Call You Sweetheart.* This resulted in cat calls, even louder whistles and ear blasting cheers. The surgeon's skit of bungling an operation had the men rolling with laughter. Carlos winked at Sophie, as much as to say, your turn! She smiled back with a look of, you're on!

The girls had practiced mimicking their superiors, as they attempted to treat a soldier. Buster, a natural comic, dramatically dragged a cot onto the stage and collapsed, feigning an injured leg. This set the audience laughing before the girls even started. Sophie treated the injured leg that kept popping up and hitting her in a slap stick manner. Jo playing the part of Matron, Emily as Sister Sin and Trixie as Sister Potter pranced around giving silly orders and falling over things. By the end of the skit everyone, including Matron and Sister Potter, was laughing hysterically. Sophie glanced around, looking for Sister Singleton half expecting a barrage of abuse. She stood at the back without a glimmer of amusement, looking like a downcast, hurt child. Sophie inexplicably felt sorry for her then remembered Pippa saying that there was kindness under her facade. Sophie sensed a damaged, broken soul.

Roars of applause brought her gaze back to the clapping audience. She glanced at Carlos, who gave her a thumbs up, and acknowledged it with a grin as she noticed a man standing next to him. Could it be Andrew? The light was failing, making it hard to identify the person. To her surprise, it was him, clapping enthusiastically.

Colonel Belingham jumped on stage, reaching to assist Matron. He beckoned to the performers to join them and take a bow.

"I hope everyone enjoyed the Christmas celebration. The concert was fun and whoever it was that had the idea of roasting a pig deserves a medal." A roar of 'here, here' went up from the crowd. "Unfortunately, what I have to say next is rather more serious. I have been notified by HQ that we are to prepare to move the hospital. As many of you know, the reason we have stayed in one place so long is because of the railway. However, after that last battle, the front has moved dangerously close to our clearing station. We will begin transferring patients to other hospitals as soon as my orders are final." As if to confirm the orders, the horizon burst into colour, followed by a mild explosion. It did not seem either unusual or close and the only person who noticed was Sophie, and maybe the colonel as he hesitated before continuing. "So while we wait, celebrate and have fun. Merry Christmas!"

It took the nurses some time to settle the overexcited patients and some were anxious about being moved. Andrew appeared on the ward, looking drawn and pale. He smiled and whispered, "I survived."

She stared at him, not sure what he meant. "Survived what?"

"I'll do my rounds and speak with you later, Nurse Romano." He made a subtle gesture towards the entrance.

Sophie nodded and continued taking pulses and temperatures until the night nurse arrived. She said goodnight and found Andrew waiting for her.

"Walk with me," he said.

"You will be happy to hear that Major General Macdonald has done a complete turn-around."

Sophie looked at Andrew, wide eyed. "He has?"

Andrew glanced over his shoulder, and to Sophie's surprise, slipped his hand into hers. "I am not supposed to speak of this but I wanted to explain. It actually involves you. Remember the last time I was called away?"

"I do. You came back as though you'd been in the wilderness for days. How does that involve me?"

"I'll explain in a minute." He grinned. "Your insight amazes me. That was a close description. I was called out to a high-ranking officer who was suffering from shell shock. He'd taken off into the woods, behaving irrationally. I talked him back to reality and I was dismissed. He pleaded exhaustion and *did not need a bloody psychiatrist*. His words."

"So foolish but then we know the higher the rank, the less likely officers are to understand shell shock," Sophie said, realizing Andrew was squeezing her hand with affection and it pleased her. "What happened this time?"

"Major General Macdonald met me at the train station, very agitated. The same officer I had treated in the woods

308

had had another episode, 'Off his rocker' as he put it. We were driven to a secluded chateau, used as a hospital for officers, where I met this gentleman again. I was shocked to be honest. It was the worst shell shock I'd seen. The major general was talking to the man, telling him to snap out of it. The poor fellow retreated to the corner, weeping like a baby. The major general stared at me. He actually had tears in his eyes, pleading for answers. He had seen shell shock at its worst and I suspect that was when he changed his mind."

"What did you do? He'd already threatened you with court martial."

"Sophie, he was terrified of the situation. I suggested we go into another room to discuss the treatment and I needed some background. It turns out that the two are close friends, as close as brothers from what I could see. They went to school together, both from military families and they started their military careers at the same time. I saw the *iron man* soften with affection and worry about his friend. I explained what happens when people are confronted with atrocities that their brain cannot handle. This officer, the patient, had watched his battalion massacred. He'd followed orders, sending the men into battle, knowing they would not survive. He had not expected to either. I suspect, based on his previous episode, it was somewhat suicidal. Miraculously he lived, physically unscathed, but mentally damaged forever."

"I wondered why you were gone so long. Thank you for the message through Carlos."

"I knew you would be worried. It took this long to get the man back to reality. He is on his way home for proper treatment. Ironically, Major General Macdonald issued the Blighty ticket. He expressed his gratitude with not quite a full apology but there definitely will not be any court martial. We now have an ally, a high-ranking officer who understands the implications of shell shock."

"It is sad that it takes so much to get the message through," Sophie added.

"Once the patient was on his way home, the major general took me to the officers mess and we had a lavish dinner with wine." He laughed. "They sure live it up at HQ. I was then confronted with a list of things that had happened during his tour here. Sister Singleton had plied him with lies about Matron, Colonel Belingham and, to my surprise, *you* were mentioned. I put him straight as best I could and he was looking into it. He mentioned he had been surprised that neither Sister Potter nor Matron greeted him on the tour. Suspecting foul play, he had the military police investigate. Singleton was responsible for Matron being called away on a wild goose chase and there is a strong possibility that she used something to incapacitate Sister Potter. He will get his court martial after all."

Sophie rolled her eyes. "Wow, I didn't expect that. Did he say when?"

"No. I am assuming there is some kind of process. I had the feeling it is Matron and Colonel Belingham's call. I guess we'll find out soon."

"A lot has happened since you left." Sophie told him of Sister's ranting, omitting Trixie's marriage. "So far there have been no repercussions and a surprisingly contrite Sister Singleton."

"Colonel Belingham was at HQ for a meeting with Major General Macdonald while I was there. I assume because of the clearing station evacuation. I would guess he was made aware of the unfounded accusations. He returned with me this morning and said very little on the train, except that he too was relieved by the major general's change of heart. I believe his career was on the line."

"I am happy to hear things have resolved. I was expecting a severe reprimand or worse, based on Sister Sin's lies," Sophie said, her thoughts drifting to Trixie. *But I am worried about Trixie. They may not be able to overlook her status.*

"I'm in need of sleep but I'm glad I had chance to talk to you." He gently rubbed her forehead. "Why so worried?"

"I have learned that in times of war you never know what might happen next. Thank you, Andrew, it is a weight off my mind. I am so glad you are safe. Oh, by the way, Happy Christmas! Did you get any roast pork?"

"I did and it was delicious. Happy Christmas to you! Maybe we can celebrate just the two of us."

"I'd like that."

31

Secrets Told

The following day, Boxing Day, the camp moved in slow motion, as though everything was an effort. A let down perhaps after the previous day's celebrations, coupled with tiredness and worry about the impending evacuation.

Sophie had not slept well, dreaming of Carlos' loving face as he gave her the thumbs up. Then she had felt the warmth of Andrew's hand in hers. It was a typical dream of things being muddled, or was it she who was muddled? Her intuition prickled at the drone of aeroplanes in the distance, a reminder of London air raids. Aeroplanes were not unusual and up until then the Hun had respected the red crosses. However, so called accidental attacks from German air raids on medical facilities were becoming more common. Deep in thought, Sophie headed for the ward where Trixie was pacing outside.

"Trixie, what's wrong?"

"I've been summoned to Matron's office. I wondered if you had too," Trixie rubbed her hands together, as though the action would calm her, but it didn't.

"No. Andrew told me Sister Singleton had made accusations about several people during the major general's tour, which he thought had not been taken seriously. He didn't mention you. Do you think your secret is out?"

"If Sister Singleton found out about my marriage, she would report me. How better to get her revenge than have me dismissed and my nursing career ruined?"

"I agree, but maybe the Colonel will be lenient when he realizes you are his sister-in-law."

"I doubt it. Anyway, wish me luck. I'll let you know if I'm packing my trunk."

"Things will work out." Sophie gave Trixie a hug and waved.

"There you are!" Kitty said.

"Sorry. Am I late?" Sophie glanced at her watch.

"No, Sister Potter was looking for you. You are to report to Matron's office."

"Oh." Sophie's heart dropped into her stomach. It looked as if she was about to find out what lies Sin had told after all. "Did she say when?"

"I had the distinct sense it was urgent, so best you go now. I'll look after the patients." Kitty smiled with sympathy. Nobody liked being called to Matron's office.

Sophie ran to catch up with Trixie. It would be so much easier to go in together. Sophie called her name, "Trixie wait!" The two linked arms, took a deep breath, and knocked on Matron's door.

"Come!" Matron's voice sounded harsh, or was that what they expected?

Matron sat behind her desk. Sister Potter was searching in the filing cabinet and Colonel Belingham stood up when Trixie and Sophie walked in, closing the door behind them.

313

"Ladies," Matron bowed her head slightly. "Thank you for coming so promptly. Information has come to us that needs to be verified or denied. Nurse King, this information is personal to you. If you would prefer Nurse Romano to wait outside, I will ask her to leave."

"No Matron, I would like her to stay."

"Very well." Matron opened a file. "Beatrix Elizabeth Ashforth King. Is that your full name?"

"Yes, Matron."

"Marital status, spinster. Is that true?"

Trixie's fingernails dug into Sophie's hand. "No, Matron. I was married just before we were deployed."

"And to whom are you married?"

Trixie glanced at the Colonel. "Captain Christopher Belingham of the Royal Air Corps. I don't know his squadron or whereabouts as the information is classified."

Sophie squeezed her hand, hoping she would ease her fingers and noted that Matron's questions were curt, but her expression was warm with no sign of discipline. She turned and saw no surprise in the colonel's face. *He already knows about the marriage.*

"You do know it is against regulations for married women to serve in a war zone?"

"I do, Matron. I wanted to serve my country. I'm as capable as any nurse, married or not." Trixie almost pouted. Sophie squeezed her hand, telling her to shut up.

Colonel Belingham took a deep breath. "Nurse King, I admire your patriotism but rules are rules. I am in a difficult position." He smiled. "I discovered I have a sister-in-law, who is also a member of my camp, and has disregarded regulations."

314

Trixie stared at her feet. "Yes, sir."

"I have discussed the situation with Matron. We cannot ignore the disregard for regulations but we are aware that the complaint was made to Sister Potter with malicious intent. We hope we have found a solution. The camp is dismantling within days, patients disbursed and medical staff reassigned or given leave to be recalled when needed. Nurse King, I am assigning you two weeks' leave to return home. Once back in England, you will resign from service and nothing more will be said. Your records will remain unchanged."

Seeing Trixie's hesitation Matron said, "There is no shame in deciding to continue nursing as a civilian. Your exemplary service will not be blemished. You are an excellent nurse. Matron Hartford would welcome you back to the Bartley. However, it would be prudent to return as a married woman. I am happy to say that with the shortage of nurses, civilian hospitals are accepting married women." Matron gave a long sigh. "And it's about time."

"Do you agree with the terms, Nurse King?" Colonel Belingham's words were stern, his expression warm and a slight grin curling his mouth.

Surprised by Trixie's reluctance to reply, Sophie nudged her to answer. It was a perfect solution. The fortuitous impending evacuation covered any potential scandal, allowing Trixie to maintain her career and protected the colonel's and Matron's position. She considered it very generous. Perhaps the family tie had influenced the decision. She wondered how would they silence Sister Singleton.

Trixie cleared her throat and stood up straight. "Yes, sir! Matron, thank you. When do I leave?"

"Continue with your duties. You will be notified with

everyone else. There is much work to do, preparing the patients."

"Matron," Colonel Belingham said, turning towards the door. "We'll discuss the other matter regarding Major General Macdonald's report later."

"As you wish, sir."

"Excuse me, ladies, I have a hospital to evacuate and relocate." Colonel Belingham placed his cap firmly on his head and pulled the door closed behind him.

"Take a seat." Matron motioned towards the chairs. "During Major General Macdonald's inspections, he was apprised of several issues of misconduct, which involved senior officers and both of you. Upon investigation, the complaints or rumours were mostly unfounded. The venomous way the accusations were made have me concerned, particularly as similar accusations were reported to Sister Potter. Nurse Romano, when Sister Singleton arrived here you mentioned you had met. I believe both you and Nurse King were probationers under her tutelage at the Bartley?"

"We started our training together," Sophie said. Trixie nodded her agreement.

"Because of Sister's outburst at the concert rehearsal, I have once again written to Esther Hartford. As you know, we are acquainted. I wrote earlier but have yet to receive a reply, which is unusual. Perhaps the letter was lost. It takes time to get an answer. Is there anything you can tell me?"

"I may know the reason. Matron Ross's home was bombed and she was injured. Her hands were burned. My friend Hillary works at the Bartley and wrote to me about Matron."

"Oh dear, that is tragic. It also explains why I haven't had a reply. In the absence of Matron Hartford's account of events, is there anything either of you can add?"

"Sister Singleton physically attacked me because I innocently questioned her relationship with a fellow nurse. Sophie, Nurse Romano, witnessed my injuries. The incident was reported to Matron Hartford."

Matron frowned. "I assume she was dismissed?"

"No. According to Matron Hartford, she was to return to the convent for prayer and contemplation." Sophie hesitated, choosing not to give her personal opinion.

"I see. That might explain the complaints of harassment I have received." Matron's eyes went from one to the other. "I suspect there is more to this incident." Sophie and Trixie remained silent. "Sister Singleton has been reprimanded regarding her behaviour towards you during the concert rehearsal and she has agreed to apologize. Please inform me when that happens. No harm done."

"No harm done!" Sophie blurted out.

Matron put her hand up. "I'll wait for Esther's response. And, you would do well to accept things as they are. Amongst the accusations were implications of impropriety between you and Captain Wainwright. I believe there is some history between you?" Matron raised an eyebrow. "And there are times when I myself have wondered if there is a personal connection beyond medical interests with Captain Cuthbert. Need I say more?"

Sophie's face blushed redder than a beetroot and she wished the floor would swallow her up. Desperately wanting to reply and shield both Andrew and Carlos, for once she stayed quiet.

"I am not at liberty to say but more complaints related to Sister's conduct are pending." Matron stood up and opened the door. "Back to your duties and wait for further orders.

And for heaven's sake *be careful* and don't do anything foolish."

They both breathed a sigh a relief and grasped each other's hands. Trixie spoke first. "How in the world did Sin find out about Chris and I?"

"I'm guessing she heard you talking to Robin and told Sister Potter. I'll say this, I think the colonel already knew about your marriage and probably gave his baby brother a severe tongue-lashing."

"The colonel did not look surprised when I said Chris' name. From speaking with Robin, the elder brothers are close and protective of their baby brother. I'm disappointed that I'll have to leave here. I like nursing on the frontline. I feel closer to Chris knowing I'm contributing something."

"Look on the bright side. You could have been dismissed. At least you can contribute in the civilian world. You know as well as I do that those poor people in London need us as much as these soldiers."

"You're right as always, Sophie. It will be nice to work in a solid building with proper equipment and no secrets. Do you think Sin will apologize?" Trixie asked.

"No, I doubt it. You heard Matron's words. 'No harm done.' The same thing happened in London. Sister Sin will move on to another unit," Sophie said with a resigned tone. "Although, I wonder if Major General Macdonald's threat of court martial might be true."

"Who knows. Everything is so confusing. I'd better get back. See you later. We'll talk tonight."

Sophie didn't see or talk to Trixie that night. Instead, she found a letter on her bed.

Dear Sophie,

I have received orders to accompany a hospital train to Calais and then the hospital ship to home. Matron explained, with Sister Singleton still here, it was better all-round if I leave quietly.

I will be at home with my parents and, under the circumstances, I will tell them Chris and I eloped. My mother will not be pleased but it has to be done. I hope you get some leave and you can help me set up my new home.

See you soon.
Always your friend,
Trixie
P.S. Please say goodbye to Jo and Emily for me

The following day the feeling in the camp had evolved from the intense life-saving mode to a calmness with an edge of urgency as patients were assessed and prepared for transfer. Orderlies with voluntary aids assisting, packed equipment in crates. The doctors stood around 'Teddy's place,' drinking tea and smoking, waiting for notice of leave or orders for a new location. All this seemed in contrast to the frontline battles that could be heard and felt nearby as the night sky lit up brighter each night. Unable to determine whether the drone of aeroplanes heard in the distance was real or imagined, Sophie experienced an unease she could not explain.

C Ward was evacuating that morning. Kitty and Sophie

helped the up-patients pack their kit bags and wait for roll call. The orderlies rolled up mattresses and dismantled cots as the patients moved out. Stretcher bearers had already transported the disabled to waiting ambulances.

"Nurse, thank you for listening to me," a young private said, leaning on crutches, one trouser leg pinned to his waist where there was no leg to fill it. "I'm going home. I'm not sure what me girl will say about this." He pointed to his missing leg. "I will always remember your kindness."

"That's what I'm here for and your girl will be happy to have you home."

Sophie looked up as the clang of instruments made her jump. An anxious soldier ran into the tent, knocking into Pippa, who was packing a crate

He called out, "I can't find it!"

"Hey, Soldier!" Sophie said, grabbing his arm. "What can't you find?"

"The photo. It's all I have of them." Sophie followed him to where his cot had been. "I need to find that cot."

Buster put down the box he was carrying and fished in his pockets, revealing a photo of a pretty girl holding a baby. "Is this yours? It dropped out of the cot. I'm glad it found you." Buster handed him the photo.

"Thanks, Buster." He brushed tears away and kissed the photo.

"Come on, Private, let's get you to roll call before the sergeant has your guts for garters."

"Sophie!" A familiar voice called and Sophie froze at the Christian name and tingle from the sound of the voice.

She whispered, "No Christian names." Raising her voice she added, "Captain Wainwright, what can I do for you?"

"I wanted to say goodbye. I'm escorting these patients to the hospital ship and then I report to Base Hospital. I didn't want to go without …" He bit his lip and hesitated, "Will you write?"

Sophie stared at him. "Why would you ask me to write to you?" Angry at his suggestion, she tried to ignore the ache in her heart. She wanted to stay in touch but it was better this way.

"I don't understand. Sophie, I thought there was something between us."

"That was a long time ago. I won't be anyone's mistress." Sophie felt her throat tighten and tears sprang to her eyes. She ran off before they tumbled down her face.

Carlos called over the grinding lorry engines, "Sophie, wait ……Rosamond …." were the only words she heard as the convoy of lorries moved out of camp.

Brushing away hot, angry tears, she allowed her legs to give way and sat on the wooden verandah outside the offices. She didn't care if Matron or the colonel saw her. She had said her final goodbye to Carlos.

It was Sister Singleton who jolted her from her misery. Sophie stood up, wiped her hand across her tear-soaked face and smoothed her uniform. "My apologies, Sister, I'm just a little overwhelmed."

Sister's cold steely eyes stared at her and Sophie had an urge to back away but stayed still. "I am told it is *I* who should be apologizing."

Lost for words, Sophie returned her stare, listening for more. Instead, she heard the drone of aeroplane engines and an ear-splitting explosion. Orange flames and something heavy pinned her in a dark cavernous place.

Opening her eyes, Sophie tried to make sense of her surroundings. She felt a heavy weight on top of her. She could hear groaning and then whimpering. She was in some kind of earthy pit, light flickering through the wooden boards above her head and she could smell burning. Panic made her heart pound. She tried to remember what had happened. An explosion. An aeroplane. But where was she? She heard a dog whimpering and shook her head, wondering if it was real.

"Nanny, is that you?" Sophie remembered Nanny was trained to stay with the injured until help arrived. "Nanny, go get help." Sophie hoped the word 'go' was a command Nanny understood but she stayed put, protecting her. It was deathly quiet. The last thing she remembered was talking to Sister Sin and aeroplanes. She lifted herself on to her elbows and moved a plank that had landed on her shoulder and across her chest. Sister lay unconscious and bleeding. Sophie moved her arms and legs. Her shoulder hurt and so did her head but she seemed to be all right. She maneuvered onto her knees and crawled to Sister. "Sister, are you hurt?" A silly question, she thought, as the blood oozed from her abdomen, a piece of wood protruding.

"My back. I can't move."

"Help is on the way." Sophie smiled at her. "I think part of the office hut fell on us. I don't understand why there's no one around." She put her arm around Sister to support her head and pressed on the wound as best she could to stem the bleeding.

"It's no good. It's gone right through me. I can't feel my legs."

"Hold on. I can keep the pressure until they rescue us."

"It's no use. I'm dying and I owe ..." She gasped to get her breath. "I'm sorry, I was cruel...oh it hurts so badly. This is my penance for my sinful ways." Sophie almost rolled her eyes at the word 'sinful.'

"Shush, save your strength. I'll get you out of here. I hear voices. Someone is calling Nanny." Sophie took a deep breath and yelled as loud as her lungs would allow. "Help! We are trapped under the hut. Help!"

Colonel Belingham shouted, "Who is there? Are you injured?"

"Nurse Romano and I'm okay but Sister Singleton is here too. She is injured and needs help. I can't stop the bleeding."

"Help is coming."

Sophie smiled at Sister's pale death-like face. "You heard the colonel."

"Why are you saving me? I'm not worth saving. The devil possessed me long ago."

"Sister, don't talk like that. God forgives all sins. You of all people should know that."

"Not me. My sins are unforgivable, as are my father's ... and others ..." Tears ran down her cheeks. Sophie thought of Pippa's words about Sister having kindness hidden away.

"Sister, what is your Christian name?"

"Charlotte. My mother used to call me Charlie, because my father wanted a boy ... He was a cruel man and put my mother in an early grave ... and sent me to the nuns to be disciplined." She coughed and groaned in pain. "It was my fault my mother died. The only person in the world who loved me."

"May I call you Charlie?"

Sister nodded. "I would like that. You remind me of my

mother." She winced again as she moved.

"It was not your fault. You were a child. You have suffered enough."

"Stay with me." Sister stared at Sophie. The coldness had gone, replaced by a warmth she'd never seen before. "Don't let me die alone. I'm afraid."

"I'm here." Sophie gave a chuckle. "I don't think we're going anywhere for a while. Why don't you pray? I'm sure God will listen." Sophie felt hypocritical. Although she'd been raised in a Christian home, the carnage and heartbreak of war had led her to ask questions about a loving, forgiving God.

Sister closed her eyes and Sophie felt for a pulse. She heard voices. The rescuers were moving the debris. Sister opened her eyes and smiled. "I think He answered. Nurse Romano, thank you. You are a good person. Now I must go. God is calling me." Sister took her last breath. Sophie was taken aback at how sad she felt but was comforted that Charlotte had found peace at last.

A loud crack scared her as a hole opened above her head. She closed her eyes against the bright lantern and suddenly felt a wet nose on her face. Nanny had jumped in the hole. She patted her warm back, realizing it was cold and dusk. She'd been trapped for most of the day. Arms reached down to grab her. She tried to stand but there was no room and her body was stiff. Nanny pushed her up until someone grabbed her and gradually she felt herself pulled free from the cavern. Her head spun as her feet were placed on the ground. She felt someone's arms around her.

A frantic voice said, "Where are you hurt?"

"My head and my shoulder." She looked at her hands and skirt. She was covered in blood. "This isn't mine. It's Sister

Singleton's. It's too late, she's gone." Tears poured down her cheeks. She realized she was leaning against Andrew, whose arm was holding her upright from her waist. "I do make a habit of falling in your arms," she said, a glint in her eye.

"You do, but never without cause. Are you sure you're all right? You have a cut on your head, and your shoulder is bruised."

Sophie looked at her shoulder where her uniform was ripped, a round red swelling protruding through the torn cloth.

"What happened?"

"A careless pilot dropped a bomb. The blast caused the hut wall to collapse and pushed you and sister under the porch. We didn't know you were trapped until Jo discovered Nanny was missing. Then I heard you shouting. Why didn't you call earlier?"

"I thought I did but judging by the amount of time that has passed, I must have been unconscious for a while." Sophie rubbed her head. "I have a terrible headache."

32

A Senseless Attack

The small funeral procession followed the raw wooden casket that contained Sister Singleton's remains. It was a drizzly, cold morning, the kind of weather associated with funerals. Andrew held an umbrella above Matron; Sister Potter wore her bright yellow sou'wester, a beacon of sunshine in the dull sombre morning. It seemed an appropriate ray of hope and forgiveness to Sister Singleton. Sophie and Pippa shared a black umbrella and Jo just got wet. The dampness seeped into Sophie's aching body. The trauma of the day before was blossoming into purple bruises and her head still ached. She glanced towards Andrew, wishing she could hold his hand. She didn't feel steady on her feet but had convinced everyone she was well enough to attend. It was important to her to be there for Charlotte, Charlie, a damaged soul who knew no other way than to hurt other souls. Sophie was pleased she had seen the human side of Sister.

As they walked back to camp, Sophie hesitated, struck by the number of crosses in the cemetery. She had known the dead were buried there but it was the first time she'd either attended a funeral or walked among the crosses. She felt sad. So many lives not lived. Mothers, wives, sweethearts, brothers and sisters mourning and missing loved ones. Anger sparked her inner thoughts at the men who squabbled, yearning for power that caused such misery.

She hadn't noticed falling behind the group until she heard a voice. "How are you feeling today? You look pensive." Andrew slipped his fingers in hers, prying eyes far enough away not to notice.

"Every bone in my body hurts." She grinned at him. "I'm okay. I'm sad for all these lost souls, not just Sister's. It all seems pointless and unfair."

"War is pointless. I am looking forward to some leave. I've been assigned to HQ, under Major General Macdonald."

"Lucky you! I haven't been told yet. I would like to return to some sanity for a little while. Matron has indicated I will be needed at the new camp."

"Are you feeling edgy after the trauma of yesterday? Any flashbacks?"

"I hadn't thought about it but no, nothing. I can see the explosion, red and orange flames, but no flashback. I didn't see much because the wall fell on us almost immediately."

"Being trapped and seeing those flames should have triggered an episode, Sophie. I think you have conquered your fears."

"I felt nothing related to my father's death or the silk mill. Does this mean the nightmares and visions are gone forever?" She leaned sideways and momentarily rested her head on his shoulder.

"The mind is a strange thing. It's possible they could return but the chances are that they're gone for good." He looked at her, his eyes gentle and caring with a deep yearning. "I want to kiss you. Sophie, I'm falling in love with you."

Stunned at the confession, if that is what it was, Sophie wondered if the off balance she felt around Andrew was, in fact, love. Carlos always confused things but now he was gone and she had set him free. She did have feelings for Andrew.

"A kiss would be lovely and ill advised. I don't think either of us wants to be hustled off for inappropriate behaviour." They laughed together and Andrew squeezed her hand. She squeezed back.

The air attack, accidental or deliberate, had spurred everyone on to clear the camp. The bulk of the patients had been evacuated in the last three days and the last batch of patients were on their way to the train station that afternoon. The colonel announced they would be moving out tomorrow.

Sophie packed her trunk, grateful that she had some leave. She jotted a quick letter to Hillary to expect her at River House the following week. Matron had officially notified her of her assignment at the new facility as soon as it was ready.

It was just Sophie and Jo in the tent that night. Emily had left two days before to escort some seriously ill patients on the train and hospital ship. By chance, Captain Evans had the same assignment. There was no doubt in Sophie's mind that Emily had finally found happiness and was certain she would be receiving a wedding invitation before the end of the war.

Jo paced the tent. "It's bloody awful and terribly boring with nothing to do," she grumbled. "The animals have been moved to the veterinary unit near HQ. They wouldn't even let me go with Nanny."

"You have grown fond of Nanny. Admit it, you miss her," Sophie teased. "Don't you have dogs at home?"

"I haven't been home since Dickie's funeral. I'm afraid to walk in the house and know he's not there."

"Oh Jo, I'm sorry. What if you had a couple of dogs in the house? It wouldn't be so empty then."

"Maybe. I'm going to stay with Gwen as usual. I will have to go home when this damned war is over and see."

"Well, that's it," Sophie declared, pulling the straps tight on her trunk. "I'm all packed. Let's join the others at 'Teddy's Place.'"

The horizon glowed and the ground trembled but no one noticed. No convoys were headed to their empty casualty clearing station that night. Teddy handed out tea and smoke from cigarettes lazily twisted in the air. The jovial atmosphere of people chatting and laughing had a different ring to it. Most were looking forward to heading home. A hint of anxiety lingered under the surface for some, wondering if home was the same as when they'd left or maybe thinking of the future, although most people had stopped thinking about that.

"Quite a crowd tonight," Jo said, placing a tin of Gwen's shortbread on the table. "Enjoy, lads."

Teddy and Buster delved into the tin with appropriate moans of appreciation. "Core blimey, I ain't tasted anything like this before. Me mam's a good cook but not like this," Buster mumbled, his mouth full. "Better not let 'er 'ear me say that."

Teddy dragged over some already packed crates to sit on as the group swelled beyond the shelter. Soldiers assigned to dismantle the last of the tents needed a break. Andrew motioned towards Sophie to join him. His relaxed arm at his side touched hers. He turned and smiled and she wiggled her fingers into his only to release them, seeing Colonel Belingham walk towards them.

"Good evening, chaps and ladies! I've brought you something to warm up that tea. No point in leaving it in the mess, is there?" The colonel produced an unopened bottle of brandy. "Mind you keep your heads clear. We've got a long journey tomorrow."

"Won't you join us, sir?" Andrew stood up, offering his seat.

"No thanks, chaps. I'll let you enjoy your last night."

Most of the group threw their tea to the ground and offered their mugs for a share of the brandy. Sophie had a splash in her tea while Jo gulped hers and swigged a brandy chaser.

"Here's to the colonel!" Andrew said, raising his mug. A chorus of 'here, here' followed and then silence.

Sophie tugged at Andrew's sleeve, whispering, "Do you hear that?"

He shook his head. "No, what do you hear?"

"Aeroplane. I hear the drone of aeroplanes," Sophie said louder.

Andrew gave her a quizzical look. "There's nothing here to attack. Are you sure it's not…?"

"I hear them. Head for cover! They are coming this way!" Sophie screamed. "I'll warn the colonel!"

"Someone quash that bloody lantern!" Jo yelled. Follow me! The woods are thick near the stables." Seeing everyone hesitate, she yelled at the top of her lungs as an aeroplane dove almost on top of them. "Move! It's the only cover we have! Go ahead! I'll meet the others."

Jo ran towards the common. Sophie, Matron and Colonel Bellingham were already part way across.

"Sophie, this way!" Jo screeched as the sound of gunfire drowned out her words. Suddenly she lay prostrate on the ground.

"Jo!" Sophie screamed, attempting to run to her. A strong arm restrained her.

"Take cover, now! Follow Matron!" Colonel Belingham ordered, as Matron disappeared from view.

Buster ran from the woods to help the colonel carry Jo to safety. Sophie hesitated, wanting desperately to get to Jo and then she heard it.

The whistle!

"Bomb!" she yelled, as her eardrums burst and a blazing flash of light erupted and then... nothing but darkness.

Immersed in blackness and surrounded by utter silence, Sophie screamed but heard nothing. She felt a warm hand on her arm and sensed people around her who were strangely silent. She dared not move or even breathe and yet she was moving, bouncing. She screamed for the motion to stop as excruciating pain wracked her body. A gentle hand stoked her forehead and she felt warm breath on her cheek. She opened her eyes to more blackness and listened. Was someone going to tell her what was happening or was she in some kind of nightmare? She didn't know. She couldn't remember. She wanted to sleep.

Finally, she heard a faraway voice. "Daddy, is that you?"

Her father's face floated before her. "I'm here as always. I'll be waiting when the time comes, but not today. Dearest

Sophie, you must fight for your life."

Suddenly she felt pressure on her chest. She couldn't breathe. She coughed and the pain made her scream again. She tried to see her father's face but it had faded away. She smiled, knowing he was watching over her. She felt a kiss on her cheek and moisture, tears but not her own. Someone was cradling her head and weeping. Her hand was held firm in Andrew's. Who was Andrew? All she remembered was the feel of his hand and she wrapped her fingers around his and squeezed.

The jostling stopped and the pain eased until she was moved, carried somewhere that smelt familiar, antiseptic. Something covered her face, sliding her into a pain-free darkness. Why couldn't she remember? Why was everything quiet and unseen?

Sophie stirred, feeling the crisp sheets, smelling the persistent odour of antiseptic. She was in a hospital bed. She opened her eyes but could see nothing except shadows and shapes, recognizing a hospital ward. A shadow was sitting by her side, talking to her, but she couldn't hear him. Him. She thought it was Andrew.

She opened her mouth and the strangest sound filled her ears as she said, "Andrew is that you? I can't see properly or hear you." She started to sob and stopped. It hurt too much to cry. "What happened? I don't remember."

Andrew leaned in to her, wiping her tears. "You were hit by a bomb at the causality clearing station." He spoke slowly, waiting to see understanding on her face. "You are badly hurt." He pointed to his ribs, his head and his thigh. "You had surgery. You're going to be all right."

Sophie smiled, only understanding part of what he said. She pointed to her ears and her eyes. "Am I blind and deaf?"

Andrew shook his head. "No, it is temporary, caused by the explosion." He threw his arms in the air, imitating a blast.

Sophie laughed and stopped as pain shot through her side.

"Easy. It is good to see you laugh but it will hurt for a while." Andrew's brow creased between his eyes, his worry showing in spite of his attempt to be cheerful. He watched her fall asleep, relieved the morphine had eased her pain.

The surgeon stood beside Andrew. "How is she?"

"She was awake for a few minutes and seemed lucid. She can't see much or hear and doesn't remember. I told her she'd had surgery. I tried to reassure her the loss of sight and hearing is only temporary. I'm unsure how much she could see or understand." Andrew took a breath. "Carlos I'm not even sure what I said is the truth. At least tell me the surgery was successful."

"It was. She's lucky the shrapnel in her side broke some ribs but, by the grace of God, missed her heart. I was able to remove it intact. I set the leg as best I could. We had to be fast as we were losing her." Carlos words faltered. "I couldn't bear it if that happened. I pray there is no infection because that will kill her."

Andrew gave Carlos a sympathetic glance. "We almost lost her in the lorry coming here. She stopped breathing and all I could do was will her to breathe again. She coughed and her chest eased up and down, she was alive. It was terrifying." Andrew took her hand and sat beside the bed. "I just want to be with her all the time."

Carlos went white and stuttered, "Me too."

Andrew stared at Carlos' pale face with its pained expression, suddenly aware that Carlos loved her too. "I often wondered if there was something between…"

Carlos interrupted, "No, no, I had my chance and messed it up a long time ago. I thought she might give me another chance." He shook his head. "Too much has happened."

"Rosamond?" Andrew questioned, not quite believing Carlos.

Carlos nodded, clearing his throat. "As soon as her condition is stable, arrangements have been made for her to be transported to Calais and on to the Bartley in London. There is an excellent orthopaedic program there and she may need further surgery on her leg. The best treatment all around. Don't you agree, old chap?" Carlos slapped Andrew on the back with a smile, his eyes full of regret and sorrow, belying his expression. "We both want her well and happy." Carlos moved away and stared at the sleeping Sophie. "Goodbye, my dear Sophie." He brushed his hand across his eyes. "I must go. Another casualty clearing station is waiting for me. Andrew, take good care of her." Carlos' shoulders slumped forward as he walked away, brushing teardrops from his uniform.

"That I can promise you," Andrew called after him.

33

Bartley Hospital London

S ophie recalled little of the painful journey from Base Hospital to London. She could hear nothing except the ringing in her ears and her throbbing heart at times. Her sight was foggy as though people were floating in a mist. Close up she could see some detail and was becoming adept at focusing on lips and interpreting the words.

She missed Andrew's loving touch. He had been kind and attentive but called away before she left Base Hospital. Her patchy memory caused confusion and she couldn't figure things out. She was so sleepy.

She sensed movement, as though traveling. She'd felt the motion of waves and the shrill whistle of a train, pain as she was carried. Then she was thankful that she had been still for several hours and her surroundings felt familiar. Was she in the right place? She opened her eyes. Through the fog she saw the end of a hospital bed. Was it possible she was back in England at the Bartley? The screens were pulled around her bed. Was she dying?

A hand touched her arm. "Hey, sleepyhead. How are you

feeling?" She couldn't make out the words but the touch, the scent, was familiar. "It's me, Hillary."

"Hillary? What are you doing here?"

"Where else would I be, but at the side of my closest friend?" Hillary smiled. "You've had a long, arduous journey."

Sophie shook her head. "I'm deaf, Hillary. I can't hear you and my eyes are misty. Come closer and speak slowly. I can sometimes read your lips."

Hillary nodded, pronouncing her words carefully. "The doctor explained to me the seriousness of the injuries. I understand you are going to get better."

"I will be glad when the pain goes away and I can hear again."

"It will take time. Your hearing will come back. You need a lot of rest. I have a class this afternoon that I have to attend. I will be back later."

Sophie felt lost. She wanted Hillary to stay, explain where she was and how she'd gotten there but she was so sleepy.

Sophie panicked when she woke again. It was pitch black. Had she lost her sight completely? She slowly opened one eye then the other. *It must be night*, she thought. The ward was dark. She could see the screens around her bed and relaxed. She heard the jangle of keys and someone bent over her.

"Miss Romano, it's Sister Kay. Do you remember me?"

"Sister Kay, I recognize you from my probation days and I heard you. I heard your keys jangle!" Sophie could hardly contain her excitement.

"Shush! It's important you stay calm but that is good news. Can you hear me talking?"

"A little. Its muffled. I'm thirsty." Sister Kay held a glass so she could drink.

"Would you like a cup of tea and something to eat?"

Sister Kay helped Sophie sit up and put a pillow behind her. Taking her pulse, she made notes in her chart. "The ward is quiet tonight. I'll be back with tea."

Sophie enjoyed her tea and nibbled on a biscuit. Even the effort of drinking tea tired her out and she fell asleep again. She woke to hear people talking and things moving. It was daytime and she could see the screens around her. She wanted to see the ward.

The smell of lavender touched her nose just as Trixie's face peered around the screen. "You are awake. Can I come in?"

"Is that you, Trixie? I can smell the lavender. Are you working so soon?"

"I was hired upon my return." She held her hand up, showing her wedding ring. "Matron congratulated me on my marriage and welcomed me back as Nurse Belingham. Not a word was mentioned about my indiscretion."

"You're on the Women's Ward?"

"I am. I will boss you around and nurse you until you are well. Now, let's get you washed and comfortable. Do you think you could eat some breakfast?" Trixie chuckled. "I never thought I'd say this about hospital food but it sure tastes good after camp food. How about egg on toast?"

"Toast! Oh, that sounds wonderful."

Sophie lay back on her pillow, feeling a little better. Her side and leg were not as painful. Her sight was clearing and with the screens rolled to the side, she could see the other patients. Someone dropped a tray, making her jump at the noise. She laughed. Happy she could hear again. She tried to remember the journey to London but everything was a blur. She did remember them all laughing at 'Teddy's Place' and hearing the aeroplanes but after that, her mind went blank. Who was there and were they hurt too? She leaned into her pillow, closed her eyes and sighed with frustration. *Why can't I remember?* She remembered Andrew being with her through the pain, the terrible pain. Where was Andrew now?

Trixie returned with a soft-boiled egg, toast and tea. "Eat up. You need to get your strength back."

"Do you know where Andrew is?" Sophie asked, taking a sip of tea.

"No, I haven't seen him. Was he supposed to be here?" Trixie fiddled with the bed covers, read the chart and generally looked busy so she could talk to Sophie. "I wasn't here when you came in. Oh, I almost forgot, Chris is on leave. We haven't told his parents yet. It's been rather difficult since...." Trixie hesitated. "I told my parents as soon as I arrived home. My mother sulked for three days because we deprived her of a society wedding. Papa grunted and said he was glad I was out of his hands. Mama eventually forgave me when I reinforced the fact that I had married an earl's son and my brother-in-law would one day be the Earl of Carberly, lord of a very large estate in Sussex. Sorry, I'm sure you don't want to hear all this. You do look tired."

"Why didn't you tell Chris' parents?"

"Oh, I have to go. Here comes DrWilcox. He's early this morning." Sophie watched Trixie leave, having the distinct impression she wasn't telling her something. What difficult time was she talking about?

"Good morning, Miss Romano!"

Sophie opened her eyes and stared at a tall, robust, important looking man in a dark suit, surround by young men in white coats.

"Good morning," she responded tentatively. *Morning rounds,* she thought. *Now I know what it's like to be a patient. This is intimidating.*

"My name is Dr Wilcox." He picked up the chart from the end of her bed and began speaking to the men in white coats. "Miss Romano has suffered extensive trauma from a bomb blast at the Western Front." He lifted his eyes, a superficial smile plastered on his face as he gave Sophie a cursory glance. "A very brave lady. Nursing, I assume?" She didn't miss the belittling tone and opened her mouth to reply but he continued talking to the men as though she wasn't there. "The blast caused her to lose her hearing and sight. The trauma has left her without any memory of the event." He then yelled at her as though he'd just remembered she was deaf. "HOW ARE YOU, MISS ROMANO?"

"I am fine, thank you, Doctor. My hearing returned last night and my sight is improving."

Dr Wilcox nodded. "Good, that's very good. We'll soon have you up and about." He turned to his group and as they walked away Sophie heard him say, "The memory loss could be female hysteria or genuine trauma. Gentleman, what is your opinion?"

Sophie was seething with anger as she watched the young men who should have been fighting in the war, offer suggestions to her condition. She smiled, thinking of Hillary's description of the medical students. These men were interns or residents but just as clueless. As the discussion continued, she could remain silent no longer.

"Excuse me, Dr Wilcox!" The doctor stared at her with a look of incredulity that a patient had spoken. "I consider it rude to speak of me as though I weren't here. Not only have I served my country tending to injured soldiers on the battle front and witnessing unbelievable atrocities, but I have nursed shell-shocked soldiers. I can assure you my lack of memory has nothing to do with *female hysteria.* It has everything to do with being shot at from a German aeroplane, a bomb landing and exploding at my feet, killing my colleagues and almost killing me." As the words flew out of her mouth Sophie realized bits of her memory were returning.

Silence ensued. The patients dared not breathe. Sister McPherson, the day sister accompanying the doctors on rounds, turned scarlet with embarrassment. The young doctors stifled a laugh. Dr Wilcox looked like an oversized, stunned bunny rabbit.

Sister McPherson spoke first. "My apologies, Dr Wilcox. Miss Romano is not herself." She carefully steered the group to the next bed.

The outburst drained Sophie. Her head spun and, exhausted, she leaned on her pillow, afraid she might faint and confirm Dr Wilcox's theory of female hysteria. She felt quite unwell and her side throbbed with pain. The pain increased to the point that she was either going to scream or vomit.

"Trixie," she called, trying to get her attention.

Laughing, Trixie came over. "I've never ...." Pausing she said, "Sophie, what's wrong?"

"The pain!"

Trixie lifted the covers to see the dressing soaked in blood. She pulled the screen around Sophie and beckoned to Sister.

Sister gave Sophie a grin. "That was quite the lecture. I suggest you don't do it again, Miss Romano. You have opened the incision."

A different, kinder doctor attended to the wound. Sophie welcomed the drug-induced sleep, easing the pain and keeping her immobile.

It seemed as if she had only just closed her eyes when another authoritative male voice said, "Good afternoon, Miss Romano. Terribly sorry to disturb you."

She opened her eyes, a pained expression on her face. She felt groggy and had trouble focusing. She saw another dark suit and closed her eyes.

Trixie shook her gently. "Sophie, Mr. Forsythe is here to examine your leg."

"I do apologize for disturbing you, Miss Romano. I'm afraid it is the only time I have. Mr. Wainwright asked me to examine your injured leg. I believe he treated you after a bomb attack."

Sophie eased herself up and listened. He had a gentle, caring voice and was not accompanied by a white coated entourage. Trixie pulled the covers back to reveal Sophie's leg.

Mr. Forsythe rubbed his chin and pointed to the dressing on her side. "What happened here?"

"I got over excited and opened the wound," Sophie answered, wanting to speak for herself.

"I see." He picked up the chart and read the notes. "Nurse, make sure the wound is dressed frequently and watch for infection. May I examine your leg?" He gently moved Sophie's leg, stopping when she gave a yelp.

"My apologies, Miss Romano. It wasn't my intention to hurt you. Mr. Wainwright did a good job. I am reluctant to open up the incision. I will order an X-ray. I am of the opinion your leg will heal on its own without further intervention." He smiled at her. "It will take time and patience but we will have

341

you walking again soon." He put his head to one side and with a fatherly glance, said, "You are suffering from exhaustion. Quiet and bed rest will allow your body to heal. Can you do that for me?"

"Yes. Thank you, Doctor."

"Unless the X-ray tells me differently, I will not schedule surgery." He scribbled notes on the chart. "Rest is the best cure for you. I understand you have had quite an ordeal. I'll let you know the results of the X-ray."

Sophie was grateful for his professionalism and his respectful, caring manner. He was such a contrast to Dr Wilcox.

34

Home to River House

It was warm for early March and Sophie stared through the open window, watching the breeze bending the heads of a few early yellow daffodils. She was having her first outing that day.

Andrew arrived on the ward, wheeling a bathchair and wearing a big smile. "Hop in," he said, teasing her as he leaned over and kissed her before lifting her into the chair. Making sure her leg was supported he placed a blanket over her lap. The Bartley had a pleasant courtyard. It was not exactly the countryside but gardeners kept the lawn trimmed and seasonal flowers in neat flower beds lined the pathways with benches for patients to enjoy sunshine.

Andrew found a sunny bench surrounded by purple and yellow crocuses and pulled the bathchair to his side. "I thought I would never get here. Major General Macdonald may have taken a while to understand shell shock but now he's on a mission. I can't keep up with him. I had to plead for this leave which was promised to me weeks ago when we moved the camp."

343

"I am so glad you're here. We have two whole weeks and, with any luck, we can spend the last week at River House." Sophie reached for his hand.

He laughed. "I'm not sure Cook will approve. I will stay at my digs and visit every day." He gently slipped a stray hair from her cheek. "Don't ever scare me like that again. Promise?"

"It is not something I want to repeat. I wish I could remember more. I don't even remember how I got to the Bartley."

"You were in so much pain it was necessary to keep you sedated for most of the journey, which explains why you don't remember coming here."

"What happened before the journey? I get the feeling everyone is protecting me. Why?"

"How are you feeling?"

"Much better for the fresh air. My side has almost healed. Mr. Forsythe says I can try walking in a couple of days. As soon as I learn to walk with crutches, I can go home to River House. My eyesight is normal and I can hear, although Dr Wilcox suspects I have some permanent hearing loss. It is better than it was."

"I understand you put the pompous Dr Wilcox in his place."

"Oh! What did you hear?"

"Just that a patient had told him off and then I discovered it was you. How is he with you now?"

"Curt but he speaks directly to me now. I am sure he discusses me quite colourfully when he leaves the ward. Andrew, you are avoiding it too."

"Avoiding what?"

"Why I still can't remember things. I remember bits and

pieces. It's like a jigsaw puzzle I can't put together. Even Trixie was odd when she mentioned Chris' parents. I have a sense it has something to do with that night."

"I want to make sure you are ready. You know the brain doesn't like being pushed and you suffered a horrifying trauma."

"I want to know, Andrew. I remember the sound of the aeroplane, going to fetch Colonel Belingham and Matron, and then nothing."

"Do you remember what happened to Jo?"

"It happened before the bomb." Her forehead furrowed in deep concentration. "Jo was shot. Now I remember. The aeroplane shot her. Buster and the colonel went to rescue her. The colonel ordered me to follow Matron and I froze." She instinctively put her hands to her ears. "The sound of the bomb. I don't recall a thing after that."

"The blast rendered you unconscious. When we realized it was a bomb, things were chaotic. I wouldn't expect you to remember." Andrew stroked her cheek and lifted her hand to his lips. "Are you sure you're ready?"

"Yes, I need to know."

"I am sorry to be the bearer of bad news. Jo died instantly from the gunfire. Buster and Colonel Belingham were killed by the bomb, trying to rescue her. Several soldiers who were dismantling the last of the tents were also killed or injured." He stopped and watched for Sophie's reaction.

"That's why Chris is on leave then, for his brother's funeral. I do have a memory of screaming for Jo. I can see her falling as the bullets hit her. I knew she was dead. I didn't know Buster and the colonel were hit by the bomb."

"Are you sure this isn't upsetting you?" He kissed her face, cradling her head.

"No shell shock if that's what you're thinking. I'm just sad. Another few hours and the place would have been empty. It makes no sense. Why did the Germans attack an empty camp?"

"Goodness knows. The major general thinks it was bad intelligence. The first aeroplane might have been a reconnaissance, saw the activity, and drew the conclusion we were setting up a secret post or something. It's unlikely we'll ever know why."

"What about Matron?"

"Those of us who had reached the wood survived. Sister Potter and Matron patched you up, although we couldn't stop the bleeding. Teddy drove the lorry that rushed us to Base Hospital for surgery…" He hesitated but said no more.

"Where are they now?"

"The new casualty clearing station is already operating. Matron and Sister Potter are running it, waiting for a new colonel. Teddy may be there too."

Sophie focused on a group of bright yellow daffodils. Their nodding trumpets comforted her and lessened her sadness. "It's such a beautiful day. It's hard to believe…"

"No more talk of war. Would you like to walk, I mean a push, around the path and then we'll go inside before you get a chill? Hillary said she was bringing Cook in to see you this afternoon."

"Oh, that will be nice."

Andrew walked around the bathchair and bent on his haunches. "Sophie, I want you to promise me that if you have nightmares or bad dreams you will have the night nurse send for me."

"I promise. Talking about it and finding out the truth hasn't triggered any horror, not even my father. I do believe I've conquered the flashbacks. I am very sad because Jo was my friend and Buster was such a character. I didn't really know the colonel but Trixie will feel the loss through Chris. The brothers were close."

A week later Sophie hobbled on crutches along the corridor and knocked on Matron Hartford's office door. Beth, Matron's secretary, opened the door and immediately hugged a surprised Sophie.

"Matron wanted to see me?" Sophie asked, once free from Beth's grasp.

"She'll just be a minute. I am so happy to see you back."

"Back?" Sophie looked puzzled.

Beth giggled. "You'll find out in a minute. You can go in now."

"Nurse Romano, welcome back. I'm so pleased to see you are up and about. I understand you are being discharged today."

"I'd say it's good to be back, except I'd rather not be a patient." Sophie looked at Matron's hands, red raw from the burns and dressings wrapped around the unhealed parts. "I'm sorry to hear about your home and your hands. Hillary West is a close friend and wrote to me."

"None of us escape from this war. Thank you for your concern. I am healing, as are you." She gave Sophie a conciliatory smile. "I'll come to the point. Nurse Romano, we would like to offer you a nursing position at the Bartley. When you are fully recovered, of course."

347

"Oh. I had expected to return to my work with Matron Ross although I haven't really given it much thought."

"I'm afraid your injuries were severe. It is unlikely that you would pass the medical to return. Forgive me, I thought you were aware."

"It is remiss of me but I hadn't considered other alternatives." Sophie sat on the chair opposite Matron without being invited as her knees felt weak. *Of course, she could not return. Why had she not realized? Matron's offer was perfect. She'd always intended to continue her nursing at the Bartley.*

"If you need time to think about it, I will understand," Matron said, most likely to fill the silence as Sophie remained quiet.

"I don't need more time. I'd be honoured to work here," Sophie answered.

"I am suggesting April, as soon as the doctors declare you fit for duty." Matron stood and offered her hand. "Welcome back."

Sophie retraced her wobbly steps to the ward where Andrew was waiting to take her to River House. He gave her a knowing smile.

"You knew! And you never said a word."

"Method in my madness. I want to keep you safe because I have an ulterior motive." He kissed her cheek. "Now we have a party to attend."

"Party?"

Andrew drove to River House and helped Sophie climb the steps where Hillary opened the door. "Welcome home!" Greeting Sophie with an enormous hug, she whispered, "Sorry, I had help. My idea of a small gathering got a little out of hand."

"Aha, I'd guess Trixie?" Sophie said. Hillary nodded with a chuckle.

Sophie looked around the room, delighted to see old friends and a lot of people she either hadn't met or only vaguely remembered. Two older couples, looking uncomfortable, even awkward, as though they didn't belong, stood to one side of her.

Trixie bounced across the room with Chris in tow and hugged Sophie. "I want to introduce Chris' parents. Lord and Lady Belingham, this is my closest and very brave friend, Sophie Romano."

"I am delighted to meet you both, Lord Belingham, Milady." Sophie beamed a smile, wondering if she should add her condolences. After all, they had just lost a son.

"How do you do, Miss Romano." Lord Belingham extended his hand. Not a muscle moved in his face but his eyes twinkled with warmth. Lady Belingham gave a nod, her unseeing eyes pools of unspoken grief. Sophie wanted to comfort her. Was she grieving for her deceased son or the son who dared to marry beneath him?

Trixie turned to her parents. "You remember Sophie, Mummy, Daddy?"

"I hope you have recovered, Sophie." Lady King glowed, if a bit awkwardly. Trixie's marriage to an earl's son was a big step up in society.

"Thank you. I am recovering."

Trixie clapped her hands to get everyone's attention. Chris steadied her as she climbed onto a chair. "Ladies and gentleman, welcome to River House." She hesitated and giggled. "We are gathered here today..." Pausing, she giggled again. "A familiar phrase, most often associated with the opening line of a wedding ceremony. Obviously, this is not a wedding but it is an opportunity to celebrate my marriage to an incredibly brave pilot, my husband Captain Christopher Belingham. Chris and I were married in secret last August and this is the first opportunity we've had to celebrate. I want to thank our parents for being so understanding and for joining us today. And, a very special welcome home to my dearest friend, Sophie, who almost didn't make it. Please raise your glasses!"

Sophie leaned in to Andrew and said, "How did Trixie pull this off?"

"I don't know. It is a great idea and a perfect way to celebrate a marriage and welcome you home."

Andrew's eyes melted as he looked at Sophie. "You look beautiful." He fingered her long black hair, loose around her shoulders. She had not expected to be at a party. "Sophie, I have something to ask you. I am very nervous."

"Heavens Andrew, what is it?" She frowned, expecting bad news.

"I have to return to HQ next week and before I go, I want to ask you something."

"Andrew, no! Can't you stay a little while longer?" Sophie felt her heart wrench at the thought of Andrew not being at her side. "You want to ask me something?"

Andrew held both her hands, clearing his throat several times, and finally took a breath. "Sophie, will you marry me?" For some inexplicable reason, the room went silent at the exact moment Andrew proposed. Everyone held their breath, waiting for Sophie's reply.

"Yes, I will marry you, Andrew Cuthbert."

Andrew's arm embraced her, lifting her off the floor until

their foreheads touched. An all-consuming love melted in their smiles, finally followed by a long, passionate kiss.

Coming soon 2022
Book Three – In the Wake of Sophie's War
Updtaes: https://geni.us/NewsfromSusan
Have you read the prequel, Ruins in Silk?
https://geni.us/CYkPPZ

Epilogue

The Great War came to an end with signing of the Versailles Treaty on November 11, 1918. Sophie never returned to the front line. After convalescence at River House, Sophie continued nursing at the Bartley. She and Andrew celebrated their engagement before he returned to HQ under Major General Macdonald's command, treating shell-shocked officers at the Chateau in Belgium. By the end of the war, Carlos Wainwright was promoted to major in command of a base hospital somewhere in France. Trixie continued nursing at the Bartley and lived at River House while she waited for Chris, who had returned to his squadron. Captain Sam Evans and Emily took up their positions at the new casualty clearing station, where Sam proposed to Emily, planning to marry and live in Wales after the war.

Sophie's story continues. The Great War is over, London tries to rebuild and mend damaged souls as the Spanish flu hits hard before moving into the roaring '20s. We will once again follow these wonderful characters in their normal peacetime lives. The war may be over but battles are brewing. Poised to marry Andrew, Sophie is plagued with doubt. Book 3: *In the Wake of Sophie's War* is scheduled for release in 2022. For book launches and release updates check out - News from Susan https://geni.us/NewsfromSusan

Acknowledgements

Where to begin? Most writers are introverts and I am no exception. This book was written during the Covid 19 pandemic of 2020/2021. I relished the solitude and time to write. However, there came a time when I had to pop my bubble and appear on Zoom or FaceTime to share my writing-in-progress. My grateful thanks to the members of the Historical Writing Ladies Group. In spite of Covid lockdowns, we persevered with technology and maintained our regular meetings through Zoom. Ladies, your encouragement and critiquing has been a large part of making this manuscript into a readable and enjoyable book.

Many, many thanks to my editor Meghan Negrijn, http://ag oodideapublications.com who understands my writing, even my thoughts. She never judges, although at times I'm sure she must be frustrated, but at the end of the day our goals are the same, an excellent book.

As this story had a large military and nursing component, I invited some knowledgeable readers to assess the book for accuracy. My very humble thanks to Cathy Burton, a retired nurse, for her expertise regarding nursing procedures.

Proof readers, Susan Taylor Meehan and Margaret Southall, it never ceases to amaze me the number of mistakes that sneak through after so much scrutiny. My sincere thanks for your diligence, above and beyond what I expected.

Beta readers are invaluble and these ladies were no exeption. Many thanks to Rita Burke, Angela Sutcliffe, Debbie Stenson, Mary Rothschild and Kathleen Bigras. I am indebted to you all, for you time, diligence and incredibly useful feedback. I am convinced that typos procreate inside manuscripts.

I am blessed with so many supportive friends and family members who encouraged and helped me along the way. I appreciate you all but there is one person in particular that I owe special thanks. Nancy Morris showed me how to turn my books into a business. When I faltered, wondering if the effort was worth it, Nancy gave me a kick in the butt to continue. Thank you, Nancy.

Cover design, *always judge a book by its cover*, which makes the cover design and back cover description critical to the success of any book. Thank you to Bryan Cohen and his team at Best Page Forward http://bestpageforward.net for the description (blurb) and Book Brush with SAJ for the amazing cover design.

Resources

Historical fiction requires a considerable amount of research. I would like to mention a few of the resources I used and some of the books I can highly recommend for a great read.

A Volunteer Nurse on the Western Front by Olive Dent

This particular book was not only helpful but a very interesting read as a true story. The content was taken directly from Olive Dent's journal as a Voluntary aide Detachment Nurse who served on the Western front. This particular book was used by the BBC as they researched and filmed the T.V. series, "The Crimson Field."

All I Have to Give by Mary Wood

An excellent well-researched and engaging story of the Great War.

Some Where in France By Jennifer Robson

Jennifer Robson is an accomplished historian who is a wonderful storyteller. I really enjoyed this book and highly recommend it.

Dorothea's War – The Diaries of a First World War Nurse Edited by Richard Crewdson.

A personal account of a British Red Cross, VAD nurse, who

served on the Western Front

All I have to Give by Mary Wood
The story of a young female doctor serving on the Western Front.

Malcolm Macphail's Great War by Darrel Duthie
A novel of the Great War

Nurses of Passchendaele by Christine Hallett
An amazing account of what really happened at Ypres and the injuries treated.

Women Heros of World War 1 by Kathryn J. Atwood
A great insight into the bravery and courage of women during WW1.

Videos...

ANZAC Girls
An Australian T.V. series of the Australian and New Zealand Nurses

The Crimson Field
A BBC Television series, which supplied me with a realistic perspective of life at a casualty clearing station on the Western Front.

Passchendaele – Writer, Actor and Director Paul Gross
The Canadian forces were sent to Belgium to take part in

the final push to capture Passchendaele.

Online Searches

I used so many websites it would be boring to list them all but here are a few that I found extremely helpful:

Wikipedia - Timeline of WW 1 and numerous informative WW1 sites

The Hamilton Pen Company
Royal Flying Corps
Voices of the First World War: Shell-shock
History of the Royal Army Medical Corps
RAMC in the Great War
History of Nursing
BBC Historical Events

Also by Susan A. Jennings

The Sackville Hotel Trilogy
    Book 1 - The Blue Pendant
    Book 2 - Anna's Legacy
    Book 3 - Sarah's Choice
    Box Set - All three books
    Prequel – Ruins in Silk*

Sophie's War Series
    Book 1 - Prelude to Sophie's War
    Book 2 - Heart of Sophie's War
    Book 3 - In the Wake of Sophie's War (2022)
    Prequel - Ruins in Silk *
    *Leads into The Blue Pendant and Sophie's War

The Lavender Cottage Books
    Book 1 - When Love Ends Romance Begins
    Book 2 - Christmas at Lavender Cottage
    Book 3 - Believing Her Lies
    Book 4 - Coming late 2021

Nonfiction

Save Some for me - A Memoir
    A Book Tracking Journal for ladies who love to read.

ALSO BY SUSAN A. JENNINGS

Short Stories:
Mr. Booker's Book Shop
The Tiny Man
A Grave Secret
Gillian's Ghostly Dilemma
The Angel Card
Little Dog Lost Reiki Found

Story Collections
The Blue Heron Mysteries
Contributing author to:
The Black Lake Chronicles
Ottawa Independent Writers' Anthologies

About the Author

Susan A. Jennings was born in Britain of a Canadian mother and British father. Both her Canadian and British heritages are often featured in her stories. She lives and writes in Ottawa, Canada and is the author of The Sackville Hotel Trilogy, a combination of historical fiction, a family saga and an intriguing love story. The Sophie Series, also historical, is a collection of novels situated during The Great War. You may recognize the main character, Sophie, from the trilogy. Taking a break from the historical genre, her latest series is in contemporary women's fiction. The Lavender Cottage books feature the unusual backdrop of an English narrowboat marina. Susan writes a weekly blog, which has been taken over by her doggy assistant Miss Penny, Shih Tzu, with stories about living with an author.

Susan teaches the occasional workshop on writing and publishing. She is also available to speak at book clubs or other events. She is an avid reader of mysteries and historical fiction, especially of the Victorian and Edwardian era.

Social media links

- Susan's website: https://susanajennings.com
- Twitter: sajauthor
- Facebook: facebook.com/authorsusanajennings
- Amazon Author page: https://geni.us/SusanAmazon
- YouTube: https://geni.us/SusanonYouTube
- Updates and New from Susan: https://geni.us/NewsfromSusan

Disclaimers

Historical Accuracy:

I love history, particularly the early 1900s, the Great War and the 1920s. I am not a historian, nor am I a military person or nurse. I read copious books (many are listed in the resources section) and used the internet to search museums, historical and military sites to get an understanding of what life would be like in a casualty clearing station in 1917. I asked a million questions and I do my best to stick to historical facts. However, this is a book of fiction and for the purpose of story I have taken license in interpreting events and the social environment. If I have blundered badly, please send me a note and it will be reviewed and corrected in later editions.

A further note regarding history and current opinions and understanding, particularly towards the LBGTQ community. The views, language and attitude towards homosexuality was intolerant, at best, in 1917. These historical views are for the purpose of story and historical accuracy and do not reflect my views or anyone associated with this novel.

Canadian English:

It is important to note that English is perhaps the most dominant language worldwide. However, there are many different ways of interpreting the English language. These interpretations are not incorrect, just different. You will find familiar words with different spellings in the U.K., Canada, Australia, America and most English speaking countries. I was born in Britain but live and write in Canada. I choose to write in the Canadian style. So please, if you spot grey but think it should be gray, or colour that should be color or are tempted to replace an S instead of Z in realize, to mention but a few, these are not spelling mistakes, just the correct Canadian spelling.

I do hasten to add that as careful and thorough as my editors and proofreaders are, there are times when a pesky typo sneaks through and, for those infractions, I apologize and appreciate a note so that in future editions, the mistakes can be corrected.